Praise for

A FIRE ENDI

T0004190

"Gorgeously written . . . A lush, creepy, and deeply romantic story steeped in Scottish mythology and lore. Perfect for fans of the movie *Labyrinth* and the show *Outlander*. . . *A Fire Endless* is just as gripping and dark as [*A River Enchanted*]. . . . Ross writes like she's a lyricist playing with the chords of her character's hearts."   **—BuzzFeed**

"This novel is richer and better than the first in the series, building on and adding to the deep elemental world that Ross has constructed and supported by well-forged, believable relationships and friendships. The twists are compelling, the narrative developments are well paced, and the way everything comes together is satisfyingly neat while still feeling unexpected. Ross has skillfully brought her duology to an exciting and emotional end."   **—*Booklist* (starred review)**

"Ross creates a magical story with lyrical prose that draws the reader into the tale and its setting. Recommend this series to fans of Jeffe Kennedy, Susanna Clarke, and Terry Brooks."   **—*Library Journal***

"*A Fire Endless* is a confident, compelling conclusion to the Elements of Cadence series. . . . *A Fire Endless* has a lot to live up to—and a lot to do in order to bring the story of this duology to a satisfying ending. Thankfully, it ably does both those things with Rebecca Ross's signature thoughtful and refreshing style, crafting a conclusion that will satisfy fantasy fans, romance lovers, and those who enjoy folklore-inspired tales equally."   **—*Paste* magazine**

Praise for
A RIVER ENCHANTED

"With lush worldbuilding and lyrical prose, *A River Enchanted* feels like the echo of a folktale from a world right next to our own."
—**Hannah Whitten, New York Times bestselling**
author of For the Wolf

"*A River Enchanted* swept me away from the very first page. A memorable cast, a unique magic system, and a mystery that will keep you turning the pages long past bedtime, Rebecca Ross's adult debut is truly magical." —**Genevieve Gornichec, bestselling author of**
The Witch's Heart

"*A River Enchanted* is exquisitely written with compelling characters and romance, and a gripping story that kept me captivated. I was swept away by the enchanting and magical world Rebecca Ross crafted, and loved every moment of it." —**Sue Lynn Tan, author of**
Daughter of the Moon Goddess

"An alluring and rich tale, at once a fast-paced mystery and a love story as warm as a hearth. Like music, it will bewitch your senses, carrying you to the wind-swept hills and effervescent waters of the isle of Cadence. *A River Enchanted* made me homesick for places I've never been. This is a classic in the making." —**Ava Reid, internationally bestselling author**
of The Wolf and the Woodsman

"Riveting and richly imagined, *A River Enchanted* flows like a song you cannot forget. Rebecca Ross has crafted a tale as tricksy and elemental as the human—and inhuman—heart." —**A. G. Slatter,**
award-winning author of All the Murmuring Bones

"A gorgeous and thoughtful addition to the fantasy genre."

—**PopSugar**

"Delightfully atmospheric, this compelling first book in a new fantasy series makes for a perfect rainy day read."   —**BuzzFeed**

"A complex exploration of nature, family, and what the idea of home means, there's plenty to love here, and much to build upon in the Cadence duology's forthcoming second half."   —*Paste* **magazine**

"[Ross] has written into existence some of the most beautiful passages I've ever had the pleasure of reading in a fantasy novel. . . . *A River Enchanted* plucked just the right notes for me, holding me bound in a bewitched thrall until the final page."   —**Gatecrashers**

"The word that comes to mind when I think back on this book is 'lovely.' The characters in this novel are so well-written, you'll forget you're reading about fictional people."   —*Richmond News*

A FIRE
ENDLESS

A FIRE
ENDLESS

A NOVEL

ELEMENTS OF CADENCE-BOOK 2

REBECCA ROSS

HARPER Voyager
An Imprint of HarperCollins Publishers

A FIRE ENDLESS. Copyright © 2022 by Rebecca Ross LLC. All rights reserved. Printed in the United States of America. No part of this book may be used or reproduced in any manner whatsoever without written permission except in the case of brief quotations embodied in critical articles and reviews. For information, address HarperCollins Publishers, 195 Broadway, New York, NY 10007.

HarperCollins books may be purchased for educational, business, or sales promotional use. For information, please email the Special Markets Department at SPsales@harpercollins.com.

Harper Voyager and design are trademarks of HarperCollins Publishers LLC.

A hardcover edition of this book was published in 2022 by Harper Voyager, an imprint of HarperCollins Publishers.

FIRST HARPER VOYAGER PAPERBACK EDITION PUBLISHED 2023.

Designed by Paula Russell Szafranski
Fire illustration © Shutterstock
Map design by Nick Springer / Springer Cartographics LLC

Library of Congress Cataloging-in-Publication Data has been applied for.

ISBN 978-0-06-305604-6

23 24 25 26 27 LBC 8 7 6 5 4

FOR SUZIE TOWNSEND,
AGENT EXTRAORDINAIRE.
THANK YOU FOR ALL THE MAGIC
YOU GAVE TO THIS BOOK
(AND THE FIVE OTHERS BEFORE IT).

A FIRE ENDLESS

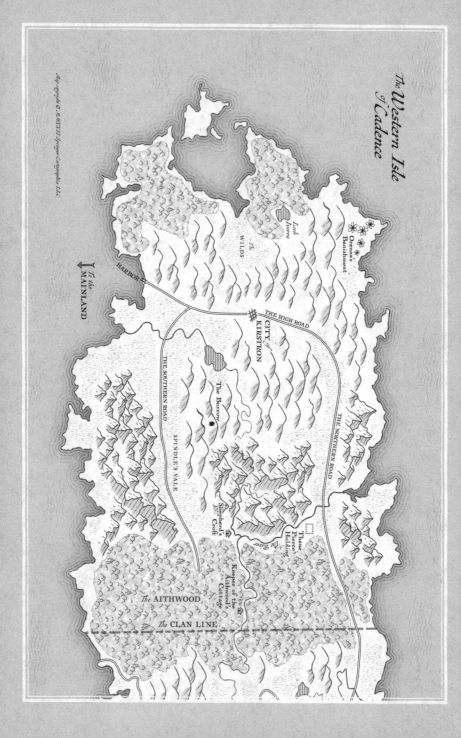

The Western Isle of Cadence

Map copyright © MMXXII Sprague Cartographics, Ltd.

To the MAINLAND

HARBOR

Loch Iaorne

The WILDS

Oceana's Banishment

THE HIGH ROAD

CITY of KIRSTRON

THE SOUTHERN ROAD

The Burrow

THE NORTHERN ROAD

SPINDLE'S VALE

Shepherd's Croft

Thane Pierce's Holding

The River

Keeper of the Aithwood's Cottage

The AITHWOOD

The CLAN LINE

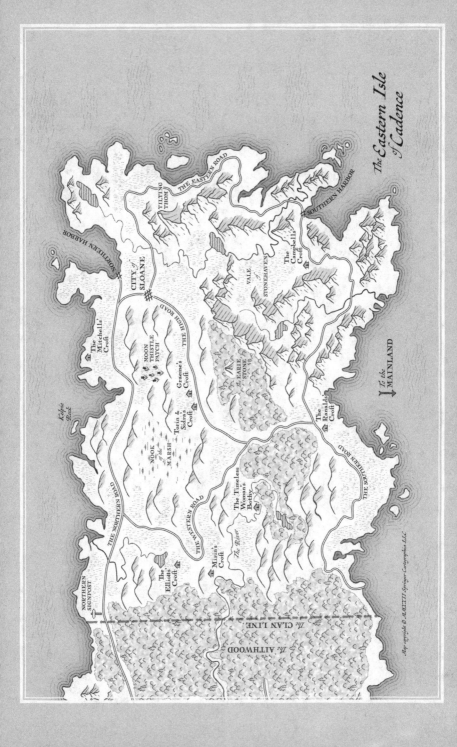

The Eastern Isle of Cadence

THE EASTERN ROAD

NORTHERN HARBOR

TILTING THOM

CITY of SLOANE

The Mitchells' Croft

MOON THISTLE PATCH

Graeme's Croft

THE HIGH ROAD

VALE

STONEHAVEN

The Campbells' Croft

SOUTHERN HARBOR

Torin & Sidra's Croft

Mt. EARIE STONE

Kelpie Rock

NOOK of the MARSH

THE NORTHERN ROAD

THE WESTERN ROAD

The River

The Timeless Woman's Bothy

The Ranalds' Croft

THE SOUTHERN ROAD

To the MAINLAND

NORTHERN SIGNPOST

The Elliotts' Croft

Mirin's Croft

The AITHWOOD

The CLAN LINE

Map copyright © MMXIII Springer Cartographics LLC

Once, Kae had carried thousands of words in her hands. As a spirit of the wind, she had reveled in the power of it—to cradle things that were both fragile and sharp—and it had always been a delight when she chose to release them. To feel the timbres and textures of those many voices, from deep to airy, from melodious to rough-hewn. Once, she had let gossip and news melt through her fingers and unspool across the hills of Cadence, watching how humankind reacted when they caught the words either like hail or like thistledown.

It had never failed to amuse her.

But that had been when she was younger, hungrier, and uncertain of herself. When the older spirits had relished biting the edges of her wings to make them tattered and weak, eager to override her routes. King Bane had not yet appointed her as his favored messenger, even with frayed wings and mortal voices as her closest companions. Kae could only fully appreciate that simpler era now as she glided over Eastern Cadence, reminiscing.

There had come a moment when things started to shift. A moment that Kae could pinpoint in retrospect, realizing it was a seam in her existence.

Lorna Tamerlaine and her music.

She had never sung for the spirits of the air, although Kae often watched from the shadows as the bard called to the sea, to the earth. Kae had at first been relieved Lorna didn't summon the winds, and yet how often the spirit still yearned for it. To know Lorna's notes were crafted just for her and to feel them thrum in her bones.

That was the moment Kae had ceased carrying words and delivering them elsewhere. Because she knew what Bane would have done to Lorna had he realized what she was doing, playing for earth and water, garnering approval and admiration from those spirits.

And Kae, who had been spun into existence by a stormy northern wind, who had once laughed at gossip and let her wings howl over the crofts of Cadence, had felt her heart splinter when Lorna had died far too young.

She flew over the eastern side of the isle now, admiring the summits and valleys, the gleaming faces of lochs and the trickling paths of rivers. Smoke rose from cottage chimneys, gardens teemed with summer fruit, and flocks of sheep grazed on hillsides. Kae was nearing the clan line when the pressure in the air drastically changed.

Her wings trembled in response, her indigo hair tangling across her face. It was an act to make her cower and cringe, and she knew the king was summoning her. She was late in returning to make her report, and he was impatient.

With a sigh, Kae flew upwards.

She left behind the tapestry of Cadence and cut through layers of clouds, watching light fade into endless darkness. She could feel time freeze around her; there was no day, no hour here in the hall of the wind. It was preserved amongst the constellations. The sensation had once been jarring to Kae: to observe time flowing so unhindered amongst the humans on the isle and then leave it behind like a moth-eaten cloak.

Remember your purpose, Kae thought sharply as the last second of mortal time cracked and fell from her wings like ice.

She needed to prepare herself for this meeting, because Bane was going to ask about Jack Tamerlaine.

She reached the gardens, suppressing a flurry of fear, a pang of resistance. The king would sense them in her, and she couldn't afford his ire. She took her time breathing and walking through rows of flowers spun from frost and snow, her wings tucked close against her back. They were reminiscent of the wings of a dragonfly, and their color was hers alone—the shade of sunset surrendering into night. A dusky mauve lined with quicksilver veins. They caught the radiance of the stars burning in the braziers as she continued to move toward the hall.

Lightning flickered through the clouds beneath her feet. Kae felt the sting of it through her soles, and she fought the urge to cower again. She hated how reflexive it was after years of feeling the light and lash of his disapproval.

He was angry, then, for having to wait on her.

Kae shivered, bracing herself as she walked amongst the pillars of the hall. The entire flaxen-haired court had already gathered, wings tucked in submission. They observed her approach—older spirits who had once taught her how to fly and who had also shredded her wings. Younger spirits who looked at her with both fear and awe, aspiring to take her place as messenger. The weight of their eyes and their silence made it difficult to breathe as Kae approached the king.

Bane watched her come, his eyes like embers, his expression so still it could have been carved from limestone. His blood-red wings were spread outward in a show of authority, and a lance was in his hand, illuminated by lightning.

Kae knelt before the northern wind because she had no other choice. But she wondered: *When will be the last time I bend a knee to you?*

"Kae," Bane said, drawing her name out with feigned patience. "Why have you kept me waiting?"

She thought of numerous answers, all of them hinged on truth. *Because I loathe you. Because I am no longer your servant. Because I am finished with your orders.*

But she said, "Forgive me, my king. I should have come sooner."

"What news of the bard?" he asked. And while he tried to sound languid, Kae heard the hitch in his voice. Jack Tamerlaine made the king incredibly paranoid.

Kae straightened. The silver web of her armor chimed as she moved.

"He is languishing," she replied, thinking of how she had left Jack, kneeling in the weaver's kail yard, staring at the loam in his hands.

"And does he play? Does he sing?"

Kae knew her kind couldn't lie. It made answering Bane a challenge, but ever since Lorna . . . Kae had become good at deflecting him.

"His sorrow seems to weigh him down," she said, which was truth. Ever since Adaira left, Jack had been a mere shadow of himself. "He doesn't want to play."

Bane was quiet.

Kae held her breath as whispers began to spin in the hall. She resisted the temptation to glance over her shoulder, to look at her kindred.

"This bard appears to be weak, just as the orchard showed us," she started to say but cut her words short when Bane stood. His long shadow rippled down the dais stairs, touching Kae with a shock of cold.

"He appears to be *weak,* you say," the king echoed. "And yet he has summoned us all. He dares to play in the open. I was merciful to him, was I not? Over and over I have given him time to amend his ways and set aside his music. But he refuses, which leaves me no choice but to punish him further."

Kae shut her mouth, her pointed teeth clinking together. Lorna had been a shrewd musician; she had learned from the Bard of the East before her, who had also been mindful of Bane and the spirit realm and had played for decades unscathed. But Jack had been given no such opportunity, Lorna having died before he returned to Cadence. Sometimes Kae watched him, as she was ordered to do of late, and she wanted nothing more than to materialize and tell him—

"I want you to carry a message to Whin of the Wildflowers," Bane said, catching Kae by surprise.

"What message, my king?"

"That she is to curse the weaver's kail yard."

Kae exhaled, but a chill traced her spine. "Mirin Tamerlaine's garden?"

"Yes. The one that *feeds* this bard. Whin is to ensure that all crops, all fruit, all sustenance withers at once and remains dormant until I say they can grow again. And that goes for any other garden that tries to feed him. If it is every eastern kail yard, then so be it. Let famine come. It would not hurt the mortals to suffer at the expense of the bard."

More whispers laced through the court. Remarks and exclamations, punctures of delight. Kae surmised that half of the wind spirits—the ones who made up the king's court—were in favor of Bane's cruelty. It would be entertaining to watch this unfold on their routes. But the ones who were quiet . . . Kae wondered if they were as weary of this as she was. Of watching Bane give the earth and the water and the fire commands that were utter nonsense. Of making humankind suffer for his entertainment.

"You hesitate, Kae?" Bane said, taking note of her silence.

"My king, I only wonder if Whin of the Wildflowers and her earth spirits will find this order inane and perhaps far-reaching."

The king smiled. Kae knew she had overstepped and yet she held her ground as Bane descended the dais stairs. He was coming to stand face-to-face with her, and she began to tremble.

"You fear me, Kae?"

She could not lie. She said, "Yes, King."

Bane halted before her. She could smell the tang of lightning in his wings and wondered if he was about to strike her.

"Whin *will* find my order inane," he agreed. "But tell her if she refuses to starve this bard off the isle, then I will see it as a challenge to my reign and I will spread my blight further. She will watch her maidens fall, one by one, and her brethren will sicken, from root to stone to branch to blossom. There will be no end to what I will do to devastate the earth, and they need to be reminded that they *serve* me."

There was no simple way forward, Kae realized. Even if Whin chose to heed Bane's order, the humans and the earth spirits would still suffer. It was evident to most of the folk that the northern wind was threatened by the earth spirits, who were the second most powerful spirits beneath him. Whin often refused to do the king's senseless bidding. She was not afraid of him; she did not cower when his lightning or his blight struck, and Kae couldn't help but marvel at her.

And so Kae said something foolish and brave.

"Do you fear Lady Whin of the Wildflowers, King?"

Bane struck her across the face so swiftly that Kae never saw his hand coming. The blow rocked her, but she managed to remain upright, eyes smarting. A roar filled her ears; she didn't know if it was her own thoughts or members of the court fleeing in a rush of wings.

"Are you refusing to carry my message, Kae?" he asked.

Kae gave herself a moment to imagine it—bearing this message to Whin. The utter disgust that would be on the lady's face, the way her eyes would burn. It was a pointless message, because Kae *knew* Whin wouldn't starve Jack off the isle. She would refuse, not just to challenge Bane but because Jack's music gave them a thread of hope, and if he left Cadence, their forbidden dreams would crumble into dust.

"Yes," Kae whispered, meeting his lambent eyes. "Find another."

She turned away from him, her defiance making her feel heady, strong.

But she should have known better.

One moment, she was upright. The next, Bane had torn a hole in the floor, a hole that was dark as night and howling with emptiness. He held Kae suspended over it—she could not move, she could not breathe. Only think and stare at the inky circle she was bound to fall through.

Even so, she did not believe he would do it.

"I banish you, Kae of the Northern Wind," Bane said. "You are no longer a favored messenger of mine. You are my shame, my disgrace. I cast you down to the earth and the mortals you love, and should you desire to ascend once more and join my court . . . you will have to be shrewd, little one. It will not be an easy task to rise after you have fallen so low."

There was a searing pain at her back. Kae cried out. She had never felt such agony before—she was burning, as if a star had been caught between her shoulder blades—and she did not realize what had caused it, not until Bane stood before her with her two right wings in his hands, shredded and limp.

Two of her wings. The shade of sunset melting into night. The shade that had been hers and hers alone. Broken, stolen. Dangling in the northern king's hands.

He laughed at the expression on her face.

She felt blood begin to flow down her back, hot and thick. It cast a sweet fragrance in the air as it continued to course down her armor and the curve of her leg, dripping from her bare toes into the void. Drops of gold.

"Away with you, earthen lover!" Bane boomed, and his court that had remained, all the sharp-toothed spirits who were hungry to see her ruin, laughed and cheered at her exile.

She had no strength to fight his hold, to respond to his jeers. Pain bloomed in her throat, a knot of tears and humiliation, and she suddenly fell through the hole in the clouds, into a frigid night sky. Even knowing her right wings were torn away, she still tried to command the air and glide with her remaining left ones.

She teetered and tumbled, head over feet, like a graceless mortal being dropped from cloud to cloud.

At last, Kae was able to get the air beneath her fingertips. She had to tuck her other pair of wings close against her back, or else they would tear. She watched as time began to shift and move again. She watched as the night began to fade into day with sunlit prisms and a deep blue sky. She could see the Isle of Cadence far below her, a long piece of verdant earth surrounded by a foamy gray sea.

Kae sought to transform herself, to render her body into air. But she discovered that she was locked into her manifested form. Her limbs, her hair, her remaining left wings, her skin and bones were all trapped in the physical world. Another punishment of Bane's, she knew. The ground would kill her, break her, when she met it.

She wondered if Whin would find her, broken amidst the bracken.

She felt the clouds melt against her face, and listened to the hiss of wind passing through her fingers. She closed her eyes and fully surrendered to the fall.

PART ONE

A Song for Ashes

CHAPTER 1

A boy had drowned in the sea.

Sidra Tamerlaine knelt next to his body on the damp sand, searching for a pulse. His skin was cold and tinged in blue, his eyes open and glazed as if he were looking into another world. Golden algae clung to his brown hair like a misshapen crown, and water trickled from the corners of his mouth, gleaming with broken shells and streams of blood.

She had tried to bring him back, leaping into the water and pulling him from the tides. She had dragged him to the coast and pumped his chest, breathing into his mouth. Again and again, as if she could draw his spirit and then his lungs and heart. But she had soon tasted the endless sea within him—brine and cold depths and iridescent foam—and Sidra had acknowledged the truth then.

It didn't matter how skilled she was at healing, how many wounds she had stitched or how many broken bones she had set, how many fevers and illnesses she had chased away. It didn't matter how many years she had dedicated to her craft, walking the line between life and death. She had been too late to save this one, and as she closed the boy's milky eyes Sidra was reminded of the danger of the sea.

"We were fishing on the shore," said one of the boy's companions. The cadence of his words was hopeful as he stood beside Sidra. Hopeful that she could bring his friend back to life. "One moment, Hamish was upright, on that rock over there. And the next thing I knew, he slipped and went under. I *told* him not to swim in his boots, but he refused to take them off!"

Sidra was quiet, listening to the ebb and flow of the tides. The foamy roar of the sea, sounding both angry and perhaps apologetic, seemed to say it was not the water spirits' fault this boy had drowned.

Her gaze shifted to Hamish's feet. His tanned-hide boots were tethered up to his knees while his friends were barefooted, as all isle children who swam in the sea were supposed to be. Her nan had once told her that most healers hold the gift of premonition, that she should always follow those feelings, no matter their oddity, and now she couldn't explain the gooseflesh that suddenly rippled over her arms. She nearly reached for the boot tethers, but then stilled her hand and turned instead to the three boys who stood around her.

"Lady Sidra?"

If I had only been here a few moments sooner, she thought.

The wind was blowing that afternoon, bearing hard from the east. Sidra had been walking on the northern road, which skirted the coast, carrying a basket of warm oatcakes and several bottles of herbal tonics, squinting into that keen wind. The boys' frantic shouts had drawn her attention, and she had rushed to aid them, but in the end she had been too late.

"He can't be dead," one of the lads said, over and over until Sidra reached out and took hold of his arm. "He can't be! You're a *healer*, Lady. You can save him!"

Sidra's throat had constricted, too narrow to allow her to speak, but her expression must have conveyed enough to the boys gathered around her, shivering in the wind. The air turned somber.

"Go and fetch Hamish's father, his mum," she finally said. Sand had gathered under her nails and between her fingers. She could feel it coating her teeth. "I'll wait here with him."

She watched as the three boys dashed along the shoreline to the path that snaked up a grassy knoll, abandoning their boots, packed lunch, and fishing nets in their haste. It was midday, and the sun was at its zenith, shortening the shadows on the coast. The sky was cloudless and scathingly bright, and Sidra closed her eyes for a moment to listen.

It was high summer on the isle. The nights were warm and star-soaked, the afternoons storm-swept, and the gardens full of soft, dark loam, their harvest imminent. Berries grew sweet on wild vines, winkles gathered in rock eddies when the tide was low, and fawns could often be seen on the hills, trailing their mothers through bracken and knee-high wildflowers. This was the season in Eastern Cadence known for its generosity and peace. A season of both labor and repose, and yet Sidra had never felt so hollow, so weary and uncertain.

This summer was different, like a new interlude had slipped between solstice and autumn's equinox. But perhaps it felt this way only because things had shifted ever so slightly to the sinister side and Sidra was still trying to adjust to how her days should be now.

She could hardly believe four weeks had come and gone since Adaira departed for the west. Some mornings it felt like yesterday that Sidra had last embraced her, and others like years had passed.

The tide surged and took hold of Sidra's ankles like a pair of cold, long-nailed hands. Tugging her back into the moment. Startled, she opened her eyes and squinted against the sun. Her black hair had come unbound from its braid and was dripping seawater down her arms as she listened to her intuition.

She began to unlace Hamish's damp boots.

The left one peeled away to reveal a pale leg and a huge foot that the boy was still growing into. Nothing out of the ordinary. Perhaps Sidra was mistaken. She almost stopped her investigation, but then the tide came again, as if urging her along. Foam and broken conchs and the hook of a shark's tooth swirled around her.

She removed the right boot, the tanned hide falling away with a splash into the shallow water.

Sidra froze.

Hamish's entire lower leg was mottled purple and blue, similar to the appearance of a fresh bruise. His veins were prominent and shimmered with gold. The discoloration seemed to be creeping up his leg and was on the cusp of claiming his knee. He had obviously hidden the ailment from his friends beneath his boot, and he must have been concealing it for a while, since it had spread so far.

Sidra had never seen an ailment so unearthly, and she thought about the magical afflictions she had healed in the past. There were two kinds: wounds made by enchanted blades, and illnesses that came as a consequence of wielding magic. Weavers who wove secrets into plaids and smiths who hammered spells into steel. Fishermen who knotted nets with charms and cobblers who made shoes from leather and dreams. In the east, casting magic through one's craft exacted a painful, physical cost, and Sidra had an array of tonics to ease the symptoms.

But Hamish's leg? She was at a loss as to what had caused it. There was no wound, so the discoloration couldn't have come from a blade. And she had never seen this symptom before in other magic wielders. Not even in Jack, when he had sung for the spirits.

Why didn't you come to me? she wanted to weep at the boy. *Why were you hiding this?*

Sidra could hear shouts in the distance. Hamish's father was coming. She wasn't sure if Hamish had told his parents about his mysterious condition, but chances were that he had not. They would have brought him to Sidra for treatment if they had known.

She quickly tethered his boots back to his feet, hiding the mottled skin. This was a conversation for later, because grief was about to grip the hearts of Hamish's parents and shatter this warm summer day.

The tide receded with a whisper. Clouds began to build in the northern sky. The winds shifted, and the air suddenly felt cooler as a raven cawed overhead.

Sidra remained at Hamish's side. She wasn't sure what had afflicted the boy. What had possibly crept beneath his skin and stained his blood, weighing him down in the water, causing him to drown.

All she knew was that she had never seen anything like this.

Kilometers inland, Torin stood beneath the same arcing sun and deep blue sky, staring at a southern orchard. The air was thick, laden with rot. He had no choice but to breathe it in—the damp soil, the weeping wood, the spoiled fruit. He didn't want to fully acknowledge what he was seeing, even as he tasted it.

"When did you first notice this?" he asked, his gaze remaining on the apple trees and the fluid oozing from their split boles. The sap was thick and violet in color; it glittered in the light, as if suspending tiny shards of gold within its viscosity.

The crofter, Rodina, was pressing eighty years. She stood at Torin's side, hardly reaching his shoulder in height, and scowled against the sunlight. By all appearances, she seemed not the least bit concerned about her sick orchard. But Torin noticed how she drew her plaid shawl closer about her shoulders, as if she wanted to hide beneath the enchanted threads.

"A fortnight ago, Laird," Rodina replied. "I thought nothing of it at first. It was just the one tree. But then it began to spread to the others in that row. I fear it will take my entire orchard soon and my crop will be lost."

Torin's gaze drifted to the ground. Small, underripe apples littered the grass. The fruit had been dropping early from the ailing trees, and he could tell the flesh was mealy. Some of the apples had started to decompose, revealing cores writhing with worms.

He almost nudged one of the apples with the toe of his boot but stopped himself. "Have you touched any of the fruit, Rodina? Or the trees?"

"Course not, Laird."

"Has anyone else visited your orchard?"

"My hired help," said Rodina. "He was the one who first saw the blight."

"And who is that?"

"Hamish Brindle."

Torin was quiet for a moment as he sorted through his memories. He had never been good at remembering names, although he could recognize faces. Truly a curse for a captain-turned-laird. He was awed by Sidra, who could conjure up names as if by spell. Recently she had saved him in quite a few instances from keen embarrassment. He blamed the stress of the past month.

"A lanky lad with brown hair and two caterpillars for eyebrows," Rodina supplied, sensing Torin's inner dilemma. "Fourteen years old and doesn't speak much but is smart as can be. A hard worker too. Never complains when I give him a task."

Torin nodded, realizing why that name had sounded familiar. Hamish Brindle was the youngest son of James and Trista, a crofter and a teacher. The boy had recently shown interest in joining the East Guard. Although Torin had been forced to relinquish his title as captain weeks earlier, passing it on to Yvaine, his second in command, he couldn't help but meddle. The long-suffering Yvaine, thankfully, let him come and go as he needed, eating breakfast in the barracks, observing the practice green during drills, and assessing new recruits, as if Torin were still one of them and not the new laird trying to learn the role that Adaira had seemed to take to so naturally.

But the truth was that it had always been difficult for him to let go of things. Of roles that had suited him. Of places he was fond of. Of the *people* he loved.

"Was Hamish here this morning?" Torin asked. He couldn't ignore the chill that touched him, soft as a shroud being drawn across his shoulders. He stifled a shudder as he stared into the orchard.

"Took the morning off to fish with his friends," Rodina said. "Why, Laird? Do you need to speak with him?"

"I think I should, yes." Torin gently guided Rodina away from the trees. The rotten scent trailed them all the way to the crofter's kail yard. "I'm going to ask him to rope off your orchard. In the meantime, don't touch the trees or the fruit. Not until I know more about this blight."

"But what about my crop, Laird?" Rodina asked, pausing at the garden's rusty gate. One of her cats—Torin didn't even want to know how many she had—leapt up onto the stone wall beside her, meowing as it rubbed against her arm.

Torin hesitated, but he held the woman's determined stare. She believed that her crop could be salvaged, but Torin sensed there was far more at play in the orchard. Ever since Jack and Adaira had played and conversed with the folk of water, earth, and wind, Torin had come to learn more about the spirits of the isle. Their hierarchy, for one thing. Their limitations and their powers. The fear they harbored toward their king, Bane of the Northern Wind. It didn't seem like all was well in the spirits' realm. He wouldn't be surprised if every tree succumbed to the blight—blight he had never seen before, he realized as he raked his hand through his hair. And he had been roaming the eastern side of the isle for nearly twenty-seven years.

"Try not to worry about your crop," he said with a smile that didn't quite reach his eyes. "I'll be back soon to ensure the ropes are securely in place."

Rodina nodded, but was frowning as she watched Torin mount his horse. Perhaps, like Torin, she sensed the hopeless fate of the trees, which were far older than both of them. Their roots ran crooked and deep beneath Cadence's surface, down to an enchanted place that Torin could only dream of.

The folk were secretive and capricious, answering only to a bard's music, and as far as Torin knew, Jack and Adaira were the only living Tamerlaines to have seen them manifest. And yet a good number of the Tamerlaines worshiped the earth and the water, the wind and the fire. Torin rarely did, in contrast to Sidra's devotion. But despite his meager praise, Torin had grown up on their lore. His father, Graeme, had fed stories of the spirits to him every night like bread, and Torin knew of the balance between human and spirit on Cadence, one side influencing the other.

He mulled over his options as he traveled by road to the Brindles' croft. The customary afternoon storm was about to break and the shadows had cooled when Torin saw a woman and a child walking along the road up ahead of him. A breath later, he realized the two were Jack's mother, Mirin, and her young daughter, Frae. Torin reined his horse to a halt.

"Cap—*Laird*," Mirin said, nodding to him.

Torin had grown used to this greeting. His old title being cut in half for his new one. He wondered if "Laird" would ever truly fit him, or if the clan would always think of him as "Captain."

"Mirin, Fraedah," he greeted them, noticing that Mirin was carrying a pie in her hands. "It looks like the two of you are heading for a celebration?"

"Not a celebration, no," the weaver said, her voice heavy. "I take it you didn't hear the news on the wind?"

Torin's stomach clenched. Usually, he always listened to the wind, in case Sidra or his father called him. But he had been distracted that day. "What happened?"

Mirin glanced at Frae. The lass's eyes were large and sad as her gaze dropped to the ground. As if she didn't want to see the news hit him.

"What happened, Mirin?" Torin demanded. His stallion sensed his nerves, sidestepping off the road and crushing a cluster of daisies beneath its large hooves.

"A boy drowned in the sea."

"Which boy?"

"Trista's youngest son," Mirin said. "Hamish."

It took a moment for the truth to sink into Torin. But when it did, it felt like a blade caught between his ribs. He could hardly speak, and he urged his horse onward, galloping the remainder of the way to the Brindles' croft.

His blond hair was snarled and his knee-high boots and plaid speckled with mud by the time he reached the Brindle farm. A crowd had already gathered. Wagons and horses and walking canes littered the path to the kail yard. The front door was wide open, leaking sounds of grief.

Torin dismounted and left his horse hobbled by an elm tree. But he hesitated beneath the boughs, riddled with uncertainty. He glanced down at his hands, at his calloused palms, marked by scars. The Tamerlaine signet ring was on his forefinger, the sigil of his clan intricately engraved in the gold. A twelve-point stag leaping through a ring of juniper. Sometimes he needed to look at it, to feel the ring cut into his flesh when he flexed his fingers, to remind himself that this wasn't a nightmare.

Within the span of five weeks, three different lairds had worn this ring.

Alastair. Adaira. And now Torin.

Alastair, who rested in his grave. Adaira, who now lived with the Breccans. And Torin, who had never wanted the burden of lairdship and its fearsome power. Nevertheless, it had found its way onto his finger like an oath.

Torin closed his hand into a fist, watching the ring flash in the storm light.

No, he wouldn't wake from this.

A few drops of rain began to fall; he closed his eyes, steadying his heart. He tried to sort through the tangle of his thoughts: the mystery of the blighted orchard, the lad who had worked that orchard now drowned, and parents whose hearts were broken. What could Torin possibly say to the family when he stepped into that cottage? What could he do to mend their anguish?

If people thought being captain would prepare him for the lairdship, they were mistaken. For Torin was coming to realize that giving orders and following structure and finding solutions had not prepared him to represent a vast people as a whole, a role that included carrying their dreams, hopes, fears, worries, and grief.

Adi, he thought, feeling a twinge in his chest.

He didn't allow himself to dwell on her often these days because his mind *always* went to the worst. He imagined Adaira bound in chains in the western holding. Imagined her sick and mistreated. Or dead and buried in western loam. Or perhaps she was happy with her blood parents and clan and had forgotten all about her other kin, her friends in the east.

Really, Torin?

He could envision her standing beside him, with her hair in braids, mud on her dress, arms crossed, and a wry lilt in her voice, ready to prod his pessimism. She was his cousin but had been more like the younger sister he had always wanted but never had. He could nearly feel her presence, for she had always been there with him through the good times as well as the bad. Ever since they were two wild-hearted children racing each other through the heather, swimming in the sea, exploring caves. And then when they were older, through heartbreaks and handfasts and births and deaths.

Adaira had always been at his side. But now Torin scoffed, chiding himself. He should have known better. All the women in his life faded away into memory, as if he were cursed to lose them. His mother. His first wife, Donella. Maisie, for a span of days around midsummer before they had recovered her from the west. And now Adaira.

I think you would know if I were dead, she said.

"Would I?" Torin countered bitterly, the words breaking his vision of her. "Then why don't you write to me?"

The wind gusted, lifting the hair from his brow. He was alone, with nothing but the rain whispering through the branches above him. Torin opened his eyes, remembering where he was. What he needed to do.

He walked through the garden and passed over the cottage threshold.

It took a moment for his eyes to adjust to the interior light, but he soon saw people gathered in the common room. He saw the food that had been brought to the family: baskets of bannocks, crocks of cheese and butter, dishes of roasted meats and potatoes, herbs and honey and berries, and a pot of steaming tea. Just beyond an open door, he saw the boy Hamish laid out on a bed, as if he were merely sleeping.

"Laird."

James Brindle greeted him, emerging from the mourning crowd. Torin held out his hand but then thought better of it and embraced James.

"Thank you for coming," James said after a moment, stepping back so he could meet Torin's gaze. The crofter's eyes were red from weeping, his skin sallow. His shoulders were stooped as if a great weight had been thrust on him.

"I'm sorry," Torin whispered. "Whatever you and Trista need in the coming days . . . please let me know."

He could hardly believe the clan had lost a child *again*. It seemed like Torin had just solved one terrible mystery of girls vanishing without a trace: Moray Breccan, the heir of Western Cadence, had admitted to the kidnapping crimes and was currently serving his time in the Tamerlaine dungeons. The girls had all been safely returned to their families, but there was no way Torin could bring Hamish back.

James nodded, gripping Torin's arm with surprising strength. "There's something you need to see, Laird. Here, come with me. Sidra . . . Sidra is here too."

The tension in Torin's body eased at the sound of her name, and he followed James into the small bedroom.

He swiftly took in the surroundings: stone walls that smelled damp, one narrow window with latched shutters that rattled as the storm broke, a host of candles burning, melting wax onto a wooden table. Hamish lying on the bed, dressed in his best garments, his hands laced over his chest. Trista sitting beside him, wiping her eyes with a plaid shawl. Sidra standing nearby with a solemn aura, sand coating the hem of her dress.

James shut the door, leaving just the four of them and the boy's body in the room. Torin stared at Sidra, his heart quickening when she said, "We need you to see something, Torin."

"Show me then."

Sidra stepped to the bedside. She murmured something to Trista, who smothered a sob into the plaid as she rose. James wrapped an arm around his wife's shoulders, and they moved back so Torin could watch as Sidra removed Hamish's right boot.

He didn't know what he was expecting, but it wasn't a leg that reminded him of the orchard's blight. The same color, the same mesmerizing flicker of gold.

"I'm not certain what this ailment is," Sidra said. Her voice was soft, but she bit her lip, and Torin knew that meant she was anxious. "James and Trista weren't aware of it, so there's no way to know how long Hamish was suffering, or what caused it. There's no wound, no break in his skin. I have no name for what this might be."

Torin had a suspicion. Panic began to bubble in his chest, climbing up his throat, rattling his teeth. But he held it down. Drew three deep breaths. Released them through his parted lips. *Calm.* He needed to be calm. And he needed to be certain of his suspicions before such news broke and wove through the wind, spreading fear and worry amongst the clan.

"I'm sorry to see this," Torin said, glancing at James and Trista. "And I'm sorry this has happened to you and your son. I don't have answers yet, but I hope to soon."

James bowed his head as Trista continued to weep into his shoulder.

Torin's eyes returned to Sidra, and it seemed she read his mind. She gave him a slight nod before she began to refasten the tethers of Hamish's boot, hiding the mottled skin.

Ever since Torin had taken up the lairdship, Sidra had come to learn that if she wanted a moment alone with her husband, it would have to be at night, in their bedroom, often whispering and maneuvering around their daughter, who was determined to sleep between them.

Sidra sat at her desk, writing down in her healing records everything she had observed that day. Her quill scratched across the parchment, filling the pages with every detail she could remember about Hamish's leg. Color, odor, texture, weight, temperature. She didn't know how helpful these details would truly be, as it was all part of a postmortem examination, and she paused, realizing that her hand was quivering.

It had been a long day, one that had drained her. She listened to Torin as he read a story to Maisie in bed.

The three of them should have been living in the castle. They should have been inhabiting the laird's quarters, with its spacious chambers and tapestry-clad walls and mullioned windows that broke light into prisms, with servants to tend to their fires and sheets and cleaning. But the truth was that this little croft on the hill was their home, and none of them wished to depart from it. Not even if the lairdship clung to them like cobwebs.

Sidra glanced up from her work, catching a reflection of Torin and Maisie in the speckled mirror hanging on the wall before her. She watched as their daughter's eyes became heavier and heavier, the girl gradually lulled into sleep by her father's deep voice.

Maisie had just turned six. It was hard to believe so much time had passed since Sidra first held her, and she sometimes thought back on what her life had been like before she met Torin and Maisie. Sidra had been young, secretly restless. A healer learning her grandmother's craft, tending to sheep and her father's kail yard, and believing her life was predictable, already written out before her, despite the fact that she was hungry for something *else*. Something that had led her here, to this moment.

Maisie began to snore, and Torin shut the storybook.

"Should I move her to her bed?" he asked, his left arm trapped beneath his daughter's sleeping form. He indicated the little cot they had placed in the corner of their room. For days now, they had been trying to coax Maisie to sleep in her own bed, to no avail. She wanted to wedge herself between them, and in the beginning that had been comforting to Sidra. To have both Maisie and Torin with her at night. But she had often caught Torin gazing at her in the moonlight, over Maisie's sprawled figure.

The two of them had to be creative these days, stealing quick moments in corners and in dusty storerooms and even on the kitchen table when Maisie was napping.

"No, let her sleep with us tonight," Sidra said.

She inevitably thought about James and Trista, and how their arms must be aching that night. Sidra had felt an echo of that pain not so long ago, and she couldn't help but gaze at Maisie for a long moment before she corked her ink and set down her quill.

A few minutes passed as Sidra reread her recordings. She suddenly noted how silent the room was; not even the wind blew beyond the walls. It felt eerie, like the quiet before a deadly storm, and Sidra turned in the chair, wondering if Torin had also fallen asleep. He was awake, staring into the shadows of the room, his brow furrowed. He seemed to be far away, lost in troubled thoughts.

"You wanted to speak to me earlier," Sidra said, pitching her voice low so Maisie wouldn't wake. "About Hamish."

Torin's attention sharpened. "Yes. I didn't want his parents to hear what I am about to tell you."

Sidra stood with a shiver. "What is it?"

"Come to bed first. You are too far away from me."

Despite the dread that weighed her down, she smiled. She began to blow out the candles, one by one, until only a rushlight remained, illuminating the way to her side of the bed.

She slipped beneath the quilts and faced Torin, their daughter dreaming between them.

Torin was quiet for a beat. He caressed Maisie's hair, as if he needed to feel something soft, something tangible. But then he began to speak of the blighted orchard. The glittering, oozing sap. The rotten, underripe fruit. Fallen from trees that Hamish had cared for.

Sidra's heart was in her throat. The words felt thick as she stated, "He caught the blight from the trees. From the spirits."

Torin met her stare. His eyes were bloodshot. There was silver in his beard, in a few strands of his hair. His soul felt ancient and sad in that moment, and Sidra reached out to trace his hand.

"Yes," Torin whispered. "I think he did as well."

"Do you think it has anything to do with Jack's music?"

Torin fell pensive. Sidra could read his mind.

When Torin had become laird, Jack had confided in both of them that Lorna Tamerlaine had once played for the spirits of the sea and earth every year. Her offering of praise had kept the east thriving, and as the clan's current bard, Jack would do the same. It was a secret only the laird and the bard held, out of respect for the folk, but it would be impossible to keep such a secret from Sidra, as she had already come to suspect that Jack was singing for the spirits. It made him ill every time.

"He sang for the earth and the sea," Torin said. "When he and Adaira were looking for the girls last month."

"But he also played for the wind, which caused it to storm for several days."

Torin grimaced. "So maybe the northern wind is displeased with something we've done?"

"Yes, maybe," Sidra said. "But I'd like to see this orchard for myself."

"Do you think you'll find answers within it, Sid?"

Sidra's lips parted, but she hesitated. She didn't want to give reassurance just yet. Not when it felt like she was treading deep waters.

"I'm not sure, Torin. But I'm beginning to believe the blight is a symptom of something far more troubling, and only the spirits of the infected trees hold the answer. Which means . . ."

Torin sighed, leaning his head back to stare at the ceiling. "We need Jack to sing for the earth again."

CHAPTER 2

S *hit."*

Jack's boot slid in a pile of manure. He nearly lost his balance and swung his arms out to catch himself, but not before he saw his little sister's wide-eyed stare. Frae had come to a halt, as if his curse had frozen her to the kail-trampled ground.

"I didn't mean that," Jack rushed to say to her. But he had never been good at spinning lies. This entire day was shit—the past *month* had been shit—and he and Frae were both trying to chase the neighbor's cow out of their yard, while preserving as much of the garden as possible.

The cow bellowed a moo, stealing Frae's attention again.

"Oh no!" she cried as the heifer began to tromp the beans.

Jack shifted to drive the cow forward, where the yard gate sat open. The animal panicked and spun around, churning up the stalks, and Jack had no choice but to step into the pile of manure again, trying to cut her off.

"Jack!"

He glanced to his right, where Mirin stood on the stone path, holding a strip of plaid in her hands. He didn't have to ask her what

she meant; he reached out and took the fabric before chasing the
cow into the backyard.

After a few more cuts and dodges, Jack finally draped the plaid
over the cow's neck, forming a loose lead. Sighing, he surveyed the
damage. Frae looked devastated.

"It'll be all right, little sister," he said, tapping her under the
chin.

Frae would soon turn nine, when winter came, and yet she had
already grown since Jack first met her, a mere month earlier. She
had gained half a hand's width in height and he wondered if she
would eventually grow to be as tall as him.

As his mother and sister began to repair the garden, Jack pulled
the cow forward. He made sure to latch the gate before he led the
beast some kilometers north, to where the Elliotts' croft lay, nearly
hidden between heather-cloaked hills.

The Elliotts had lost everything in the last Breccan raid. Their
livestock had been rounded up and driven over the clan line. Their
home and outbuildings had been burned. But slowly, their farm
was being restored. A new cottage, storehouse, and byre had just
been erected, but fences were lower on the priority list and were
still in disrepair. Their new herd of cows often drifted onto Mirin's
property, and Jack, tempted to buy a dog at this point, had dutifully
brought the animals back. But he was beginning to tire of it all. He
felt like he was living the same day, over and over.

His chest ached as he glanced to the left, where the Aithwood,
dappled in morning sunlight, grew thick and tangled. Beyond
those trees was the clan line, and beyond the clan line was the
west. It had once concerned Jack that Mirin lived so close to the
Breccans' territory. Years ago, when he was a boy, the western clan
had raided their home, stealing their winter provisions. That night
was still vibrant in his mind, a memory that was bruised by fear
and hatred.

But winter-borne worry was simply a way of life for the Tamerlaines, even with the magic of the clan line—a boundary that
couldn't be crossed without alerting the other side. The Breccans

trespassed to steal food and livestock, typically in the lean, cold months. They had to strike quickly, before the East Guard converged on them.

This was the price the Breccans had to pay for the enchantment of the clan line. While they could craft magic with ease, the Breccans' land struggled to meet their needs, and they resorted to thievery to survive. It was the opposite for the Tamerlaines: wielding magic sickened them, but they had an abundance of resources to last them through the winter with comfort. Hence the violence of the raids, and occasional bloodshed, when the clans clashed. Jack wondered if this pattern would now change, with Adaira in the west.

She had given herself in exchange for Moray. Her twin brother would remain shackled in the east as long as Adaira remained in the west. It was one prisoner for another, although Jack had seen the way Innes Breccan, the western laird, had looked at Adaira. Innes hadn't regarded Adaira as leverage, or as an enemy to be chained, but as a daughter who had been lost, as someone she wanted to know now that the truth had come to light.

I would like for there to be peace on the isle, Adaira had said to Innes when the prisoner exchange was agreed upon. *If I come with you into the west, I would like the raids on the Tamerlaine lands to cease.*

Innes had made no promises, but Jack suspected—knowing what he did about his wife—that Adaira would do everything she could to prevent the raids from unfolding again, to maintain at least a tentative peace on the isle. Such was her commitment to Cadence that she had chosen duty over her heart, leaving Jack behind when she left.

Music is forbidden in the west.

Adaira had dropped that millstone on him, mere moments before she departed. She couldn't imagine a life for him without his first love, musician that he was. But the more Jack had relived that agonizing exchange, the more he realized that Adaira must also have wanted to appear as nonthreatening as she could in the west.

And Jack was a threat in two ways: as a bard, and as the illegitimate son of the Breccan who had given her away to the Tamerlaines decades earlier.

Jack was panting now. The cow dragged its hooves behind him.

"She's written me only twice, you know," he said to the cow just as they crested the hill. He could see the Elliotts' croft in the distance. "*Two* times in almost five weeks, as if she is far too busy for me, doing whatever it is Breccans do."

It felt good to finally speak those words aloud. Words he had swallowed like stones. But Jack felt the southern wind at his back, tousling his hair. If he wasn't mindful, the breeze would carry his words in its wings for others to hear, and Jack had already suffered enough mortification.

And yet he kept talking to the cow.

"Of course, she said she missed me in the first. I didn't write her back directly."

The heifer nosed his elbow.

Jack scowled at her. "All right, I *did* write her the moment her letter arrived. But I waited to send it. Five days, actually."

They had been five long, terrible days. Jack had his wounds and his pride, and Adaira had made it evident she didn't need him with her. In the end, he realized what a mistake it had been to wait so long to send his letter. Because then Adaira had let a long stretch of days pass before she responded, as if she sensed the growing chasm between them. But perhaps they were both trying to shield themselves from what was most likely to happen—their handfast being broken after their agreement had lasted the obligatory year and a day—because Jack couldn't see how either of them could remain wed, living this way.

He laid his hand over his chest, where he could feel his half of the coin, hiding beneath his tunic. He wondered if Adaira still wore hers. The golden coin had been divided between them, and they had each been given a half at their handfasting. It was the symbol of their vows, and Jack had yet to remove it from his neck.

The heifer mooed.

Jack sighed. "I was the last one to write, actually. I wrote her nine days ago. You'll be shocked to know she has yet to reply."

The wind gusted.

Jack briefly closed his eyes, but he wondered what would happen if the wind carried those words of his over the clan line, gliding through the shadows of the west to wherever Adaira was. What would she do if she heard his voice on the breeze? Would she write to him, tell him to come to her?

That was what he wanted.

He wanted Adaira to ask him to join her in the west. To invite him to be with her again. Because he could not bear to beg her to take him, and he feared being in a place where he was unwanted. He refused to put himself in such a position, and so he had no choice but to appear utterly resilient as he waited for her to decide what was to become of them.

"It's not fair, you know," a voice called, and Jack startled, feeling as if someone had read his mind.

It's not fair to leave such a weight on her alone, when you know her life has been broken and reshaped into something unfamiliar.

Jack shaded his eyes, swallowing the knot in his throat. He could see Hendry Elliott walking up the grassy hill to meet him, a smile and a trail of dirt on the older man's face.

"After all my work trying to get the fences up, the cows still find a way to get loose," Hendry said. "I apologize, once again, if they've bothered you or your mum."

"No apologies needed," Jack said, at last handing off the troublesome cow. "I hope things are well with you and your own."

"Well enough, thanks," Hendry said, studying Jack closer. "How are you holding up, Bard?"

Jack felt his teeth click together. "Never been better."

The older man only granted him a sad smile, and Jack distracted himself by patting the cow's flank, as if he had made a new friend.

He bid Hendry and the heifer a cheerful farewell and turned away to begin the long trek back to his mother's croft. The land must have felt how his feet dragged over the grass and bracken, and the kilometers melted away, the hills folding. Sometimes the spirits of the earth were benevolent, and it became much faster to travel by moor than by road. Other times their mischief bloomed like weeds as they altered the trees, the rocks, the grass, the rise and fall of the landscape. Jack had gotten lost on the isle a few times after the spirits changed the scenery, once recently, and he was thankful when he saw Mirin's cottage come into view.

Smoke escaped the chimney, smudging the midday sunlight. The cottage was built of stones and had a thatched roof. It sat on a hill that overlooked the winding path of a treacherous river that flowed west to east. A river that had changed everything.

Jack ignored the distant gleam of the rapids, choosing to study the kail yard instead as he approached. His mother and Frae had healed the rows as best as they could, and Jack was thinking about all the things he needed to do—mend the roof before the next rain, help Frae bake another pie for the Brindles, gather more river rocks for slingshot practice—when he stepped inside the cottage.

"Do you have the berries ready for the pie, Frae?" Jack was asking as the interior shadows draped over him. The house was filled with familiar scents—the dust of wool, the gold of freshly baked bannocks, the briny smell of winkle soup. He expected to glance up and find Mirin weaving at her loom and Frae either assisting her or staying busy with her school lessons at the table. The last person he expected to find standing like a rooted tree in his mother's common room was Torin Tamerlaine.

Jack stopped abruptly, meeting Torin's gaze. The laird stood by the hearth, where the firelight caught the silver embedded in his leather jerkin, the hilt of his sheathed sword, the gold of his hair, and the gray that shone like frost in his beard, even though he was still a few years shy of thirty. A ruby brooch gleamed at his shoulder, pinning his crimson plaid.

"Laird," Jack said, his worries multiplying. Torin couldn't be here for anything good. He had never been one to pay a social call.

"Jack," Torin returned in a careful voice, and Jack knew in that instant that Torin wanted something of him, something that Jack most likely wouldn't want to give.

Jack's gaze flickered to his mother, who was stepping away from her loom. To Frae, who was rolling out pie dough.

"Is everything well?" he asked, his eyes eventually returning to Torin.

"Yes," Torin replied. "I'd like to have a word with you, Jack."

"We'll be just outside in the garden," Mirin said, reaching for Frae's hand and guiding her to the back door.

Jack watched as his little sister abandoned the pie dough, granting him a glance of concern. He gave her a smile and a nod, hoping to reassure her, even as he sought to ease his own mind.

All too soon, with the doors and shutters latched against the curiosity of the wind, the cottage fell quiet. Jack raked his hand through his snarled hair; the color of dark bronze in his fingers, it had grown longer these days. The threads of silver shining at his left temple were a reminder that he had faced Bane's wrath and lived. After coming so close to death, he'd not soon play for the spirits again.

"Can I get you anything to drink, Laird?" he asked.

Torin hadn't moved from his place by the hearth. But his mouth was pressed into a firm line, and his fingers twitched at his side. "Just Torin. And no. Your mum made me a cup of tea while I waited for you."

It was strange to think about how much Jack had wanted to be like Torin in every way when he was a lad, because Torin was brave and strong and an esteemed member of the guard. Now he was someone Jack admired—and found stubbornly irritating on occasion—and, most of all, a friend he trusted.

"Why have you come then?" Jack said.

"I need you to play for the spirits."

Jack hesitated. He could almost feel a trace of pain in his hands, in his temples, just *thinking* about singing for the folk. But this was part of his duty as Bard of the East. "I've already played for the water and the earth."

"I know," Torin said, "but there's trouble, and I need to speak with the spirits." He explained about the blighted orchard, and how the sickness had been passed to Hamish Brindle.

"The boy who drowned yesterday?" Jack asked, brows arched.

"Yes," Torin said. "Which makes me believe there is such unrest in the spirits' realm that it has bled into ours and is only going to get worse, owing to our ignorance. If you could draw forth a spirit from the sick orchard, perhaps they could tell us what has happened and what can be done to heal it. Then we'd know what we can do to protect ourselves and keep the blight from spreading."

Jack was quiet as he wondered whether he could play Lorna's ballad again to call forth the earth faeries or needed to compose his own music. He felt like he had a stone lodged in his throat when he tried to imagine inking notes of his own. He just felt so *empty*.

As Jack gazed at the blue-hearted fire in the hearth, he felt a sudden warmth at his back, as though someone stood behind him. He heard a voice, so familiar he would know it anywhere, whisper into his hair.

This is your moment, old menace. Play for the orchard.

Jack couldn't resist: he glanced over his shoulder, as if he would find Adaira standing behind him. But all he saw was a stream of sunlight, sneaking in through a slat in the shutter.

He might have been surprised that she would haunt him at such a moment, but he knew better. Because *this* was why Adaira had summoned him back to Cadence in the first place. She had asked him to sing the spirits up from the sea, to croon to the spirits of the earth, to draw forth the spirits of the wind. And Jack had done as she asked, as if he were part of the tides and the rocks and the gusts of the isle. He had done it even when he had doubted himself, because Adaira had believed in his hands and his voice and his music.

"I *would* do this," Jack said, his gaze returning to Torin. "But I don't have a harp. Mine was ruined by the northern wind, when I played for the air."

"You have Lorna's."

"Yes, her grand harp, which is for the hall. I need something smaller. To play for the spirits I have to go to where they are. To sit in their domain."

"Don't you think Lorna had one herself?" Torin countered. "She played for them all those years in secret. As you did at midsummer. Surely there is another small harp somewhere in the castle."

Jack inhaled sharply, ready to make a retort. But the words melted into breath; he knew Torin was right. Lorna must have had another harp hidden somewhere.

"Are you afraid of the pain, Jack?" Torin asked gently. "Sidra has told me that you suffer physically after singing for the spirits. She said it's something I need to be aware of. I'm to be with you when you call to them. As Adaira once was."

Jack glared at him. "It's not that."

"Then is there another reason?"

Torin's question made Jack stiffen. He let his attention drift around the room. To the strips of pie dough on the kitchen table and a jar of red berries, preserved from summer. To the loom in the corner with a plaid in its maw, a pattern emerging from countless threads. To Frae's stack of schoolbooks on the hassock, her slingshot resting on an open page.

Jack didn't know how to explain it. He didn't know how to give his grief a shape, a name, because he had been doing just *fine* the past month, letting his pain simmer beneath the surface. He slept, he ate, he worked the croft. And yet there was no joy for him in these occupations. He was simply taking up air, and he knew it and he hated it.

The truth was . . . he didn't *feel* like playing. He had let his passion wane ever since Adaira left. He didn't have the heart for it. But if Torin and the isle needed him to sing again, Jack would draw up the remnants of his music. Even if it was dangerous to do so these days, after the northern wind's warning that he should cease playing.

"All right," he said. "If we can find a harp, I'll play for the orchard."

"Good," Torin said, unable to hide his relief. "Let's go to the castle now. I have a skeleton key. No room will escape our notice."

Before Jack could blink, Torin strode past him, heading for the front door.

Well, this day is not going according to plan, Jack thought with an inward grumble, as if he had scheduled his hours with important tasks. Which he had not, of course. But there was now a good possibility that, with Torin determined to look behind every tapestry and turn over every stone in his search for a harp that might or might not exist, Jack would be stuck in the castle for hours.

Jack grabbed his plaid and began to trail Torin to the threshold, only to realize that his boots had tracked manure into the house.

He stopped short, imagining how Mirin would react when she saw it.

Jack sighed.

"Shit."

CHAPTER 3

One would think that Torin, who not only had served as Captain of the East Guard for three years but was also Alastair Tamerlaine's nephew, would know every nook and cranny of the castle. He was surprised to discover there were many hidden doors and rooms he had never known existed. Inevitably, he wondered if Adaira had been aware of them.

"No sign of it here," Jack said with a sigh, brushing the dust from his clothes.

Torin surveyed the chamber. In every corner was a stack of crates that both he and Jack had painstakingly searched through. They had uncovered tarnished candelabras, moth-eaten damask, small tapestries of harts and moon phases, bronze pots, iron griddles, plaid blankets, and silver washbasins. But after scouring for hours, they had found no trace of Lorna's second harp.

They had started in the music turret, although Jack insisted that it wasn't there. From the southern tower, they had wended their way through the corridors, leaving no door untouched. The two of them had passed through doors carven with flora and fauna, doors latticed in iron and silver, doors that were so small they both had to stoop to pass over their thresholds. Shy doors that hid in shadowed walls and proud gilded doors that gleamed in the torchlight. Torin almost felt like a lad again, caught up in the wonder that one of these doors was bound to open to another place, another realm. Like the faerie portals his father had often told him about when he was younger.

To his disappointment, the doors fed into storerooms, meeting chambers, and an extraordinary number of bedrooms, some of which were inhabited by the servants.

Now, hours later, Torin could sense that Jack was weary and anxious to return home. But Torin had never been one to give up a fight or a search easily. Leaning against one of the crates, he said, "There's a set of chambers we haven't searched yet. Alastair's wing."

Jack's dark eyes were inscrutable. But with a sweeping motion of his hand, and a hint of exasperation, he urged Torin to lead the way.

Yes, they should have searched the laird's wing first, perhaps even before the music turret, but Torin had been hesitant to enter those quarters. They were full of old memories that he both wanted to forget and yearned to relive. They were also the rooms that he and Sidra and Maisie were supposed to be living in now that he was laird, and he wasn't certain what he would find within them.

Torin walked up a flight of carpeted stairs, then down a wide, tapestry-clad corridor. This part of the castle was quiet, catching the late afternoon sun. But as Torin approached the laird's door, he paused, listening. He could hear distant voices. The servants, going about their tasks. The chamberlain, Edna, chiding someone. A peal of laughter and the clang of pots as dinnertime approached.

"Any day now," Jack said.

Torin startled. How long had they been standing here? He exhaled through his teeth, face flushing, and slipped the iron key into the door.

Not even Adaira had lived in these quarters. The last time Torin had graced them, Alastair had been on his deathbed, gasping for breath. Asking for his daughter, who was absent, somewhere on the slopes of Tilting Thom with Jack as he sang for faeries.

Torin let the doors swing open.

He stared into deep shadows, smelling a faint trace of polish, as if Edna had ordered the floors to be scrubbed clean. Slowly, he passed over the threshold, letting his memory guide him to the far wall. One by one, he threw open the curtains, exposing arched windows. Rivers of sunlight poured into the room, illuminating the large bed and its red baldachin, the paintings and tapestries that muffled echoes and lent color to an otherwise drab place, the furniture covered in white sheets.

Jack followed. Seemingly unconcerned with the main room, he headed for the door on the northern wall that led to a honeycomb of inner chambers. It was unlocked, and he slipped through it, with Torin close behind him. They came upon several wardrobes, a bathing chamber with tiled floors and stained-glass windows, two more bedrooms, a sitting chamber with a hearth, and a small library.

Torin found himself thinking, *Maisie would love it here.* But when he tried to imagine Sidra dwelling in these chambers, all he could think was how far she would have to walk to emerge into the castle kail yard. Down cold corridors and flights of stairs, passing beneath countless lintels. They were closer to the clouds than the soil in this wing. Having grown up in a valley, roaming with her father's flock and daily tending to the garden alongside her nan, Sidra would feel the distance.

"This one's locked," Jack called, his statement followed by the impatient clang of an iron handle.

Frowning, Torin walked deeper into the wing's corridor. He found Jack standing beneath a tapestry that hung from the wall, pulling on a door that Torin would have never noticed.

"How did you know a door was there?" he asked sharply.

Jack emerged from the tapestry's weight, gossamer in his hair. "Adaira and I used to have a secret door that connected our chambers. I assumed there would be something similar here."

Torin grunted, hating the doubt that snaked through him. Doubt that made him feel like an imposter. But with Jack holding up the weaving so he could find the door, he moved forward with the key.

It unlocked with a sigh.

Torin couldn't hide his shiver, the gooseflesh that rippled over him as he stepped into the hidden chamber. It was hexagonal in shape, full of bookshelves and diamond-paned windows. Long, colorful ribbons hung from the rafters above, some anchored with dried flowers and thistles, others strung with handmade stars. A threadbare rug depicting a unicorn was spread over the floor, and in the center of it was a side table, a high-backed chair, and a small harp, resting on the cushions.

"There," Torin said, his mouth suddenly dry. "Can you play this one?"

Jack brushed past him to approach the harp. It took him a minute, as though afraid to touch someone else's instrument. But it almost seemed as if the harp had been waiting for him. Finally, Jack took the harp in his hands and sat in the chair to closely examine it.

"Yes," he said. "It's been gently looked after since Lorna's death."

"By whom? Alastair?" Torin mused aloud, noting the silver pot and the cup of murky, half-drunk tea on the side table. Envisioning his uncle sitting in that chair, sipping tea and holding Lorna's instrument, as if it had been yesterday, Torin shuddered again.

"No," Jack replied, plucking one of the strings. The note resounded in the chamber, a sweet yet lonely sound. "Adaira, I would guess. She told me Lorna once tried to teach her how to play, but the music never took to her hands. But she learned how to care for the instruments. I think she must have been maintaining them until I could return."

It was well known that music was fickle on the isle. A small number of people could handle instruments at all, and even then, only a bard and a harp could draw the spirits. For as long as Torin could remember, the east had always had a bard to sing lore and historic ballads, save for those few years between Lorna's death and Jack's return. But music had been woven into their isle life, long before the clan line was ever formed.

Torin met Jack's stare.

The bard's eyes glistened as his jaw clenched. He was first to break their gaze, casting his attention to examine the harp. Torin took that moment to look over the bookshelves, then withdrew a few tomes while giving Jack the privacy he needed.

What other secrets did you hold, Adi? Torin wondered as he surveyed the shelves. His gaze eventually was caught by a book with loose parchment between the leaves. He pulled the volume from the shelf and was surprised to find that the paper tucked within was a child's sketch. He knew instantly that this was one of Adaira's old drawings.

She had depicted three sticklike humans, but Torin recognized them. Adaira had drawn herself, standing between Alastair and Lorna and holding their hands. A horse hovered in the sky above them, as only a child could imagine happening. Thistles claimed one corner of the paper, and stars another. Beneath the illustration was her name, written with the R backwards, and Torin smiled until it felt like his chest had cracked open.

It all happened so quickly, he thought. When the truth about Adaira's origins had come to light, Torin had scarcely had time to think about how that news affected her, so absorbed had he been in trying to sort through his own emotions. And then it had simply been easier to wallow in the denial. It was easier to suffocate the memory of her last days in the east.

But now he imagined it.

He wondered what Adaira had felt when she realized that she had grown up under a lie: that she wasn't the blood-born daughter of the parents she had loved, as Alastair and Lorna had led everyone to believe, but the offspring of the western laird, their greatest enemy. That she had been stolen over the clan line and secretly laid in Lorna Tamerlaine's arms as a bairn. What had she felt when the clan that had once adored her turned on her, relieved when she exchanged herself for Moray?

Torin shut the book, unable to look at her drawing a moment longer. Before he could stop himself, he said, "Do you think she'll return to the east, Jack?"

"I don't see it happening." Jack plucked another sad note from the harp. "Not until she believes Moray has paid his penance in our holding."

That would be a decade. Adaira's twin brother had committed a terrible crime against the Tamerlaines, stealing their daughters away in a cruel act of vengeance. That the east had withheld Adaira from her blood family justified Moray's actions—in his mind—as he kidnapped Tamerlaine daughters, again and again. All in the hope that the kidnappings would spur Alastair to reveal the truth about his daughter—a revelation that would give Adaira the chance to return to the west on her own.

"Has Adaira ever said anything to you in her letters that gives you a sense of alarm?" Torin asked next.

"No," Jack replied, but his eyes narrowed. "Why? Has she written something to you that makes you think she's in trouble?"

Torin traced the gilded spines of the books on the shelf. "She's hardly written to me at all. Just one letter, shortly after she departed, to let me know she had settled in and was doing well. Same to Sidra." He paused, wiping the dust from his fingertips. "But she hasn't responded to any of the letters I've sent to her since. Sidra believes it's only because Adi is trying to bond with her parents and needs the distance from us to do so. But I wonder if they're intercepting her letters and my words are never reaching her to begin with."

"I'm currently waiting for her next reply," Jack said, rising with the harp tucked beneath his arm. "But she's given me no reason to believe she's in danger. I think Sidra is right, and Adaira is choosing to put distance between us. I have a hard time imagining Innes Breccan wanting to harm her, not when her heir is shackled in our dungeons. But neither would I be surprised if Innes still regards us as threats—to both Moray and Adaira—and so maybe the western laird finds your letters unsettling. Maybe she feels she has no choice but to interfere, as you say. And yet what can we do about it?"

Nothing.

They could do absolutely nothing, short of starting a war with the Breccans, which Torin did not want to do.

"Will you write to her again, Jack?" Torin asked. "And let me know when she replies?"

Jack was silent for a moment, but his countenance had gone pale, and his cheeks had a strange, hollow look, as though he were holding his breath. Jack was worried about Adaira too then. He was trying to maintain a sense of calm for Torin's sake.

"Yes, I'll let you know," the bard said. "I should be going now, to prepare the orchard's song."

Torin nodded his gratitude, but he lingered in the room a few minutes after Jack had quit the wing. Eventually, Torin returned to the main bedroom. He stared at the shrouded furniture, the bed his uncle had died in.

There was a vast difference between someone dying and someone leaving. Alastair was dead, but Adaira had chosen to leave. And while Torin knew she had done so to keep peace on the isle, to prevent winter raids, to enable the Tamerlaines to imprison Moray without conflict, her decision still roused a medley of feelings in him. He couldn't help but dredge up the familiar, icy resentment toward his mother. His own flesh and blood who had abandoned him without a backward glance when he was a boy.

But the truth was . . . he was angry at *himself*, for letting Adaira strike such a terrible bargain with Innes Breccan and exchange herself for Moray. For letting Adaira surrender her right to rule and become a prisoner of the west. He was angry at the Tamerlaine clan for turning on her so quickly when she had done nothing but sacrifice for them. He was angry that he had no idea what was happening to her on the other side of the isle.

What sort of laird was he?

He dragged the coverlet off the bed, then the sheets and pillows. He ripped away the blankets that covered the furniture until he exposed a desk with stacked parchment, quills, and a tall bottle of whiskey that threatened to overturn. Torin caught the glass bottle in his hand, knowing it was Alastair's favorite. He stared at it, tempted to hurl it against the wall and watch it shatter into hundreds of iridescent pieces. But he sighed instead, and the blistering ice within him melted into melancholy.

Surrendering, Torin sat on the floor. Dust motes spun in the air around him. He listened to his breaths heave, filling the lonely room with uneven sound.

He knew what a laird *should* be.

A voice for the clan. Someone who listened to individual needs and problems in order to help meet and solve them. A leader who strove to improve all aspects of life, from education to healing measures to croft acreage to building repairs to laws to resources to justice. Someone who knew their people by *name* and who could readily greet them by such if they passed on the road. Who ensured that the east remained in balance with the spirits, and who likewise was a shield against the Breccans and their raids.

Adaira had carried out all of these responsibilities, effortlessly, and Torin wished he had paid closer attention to how she and her father had done it. Even now, kilometers away, Adaira was the shield for the east while he sat on a floor, trying to wrap his mind around all that had gone wrong.

There was a firm knock on the iron-latticed door.

Torin winced. But he was too weary to speak, too weary to drag himself up to his feet. He watched as the wood creaked open and Edna appeared.

"Laird? I heard a noise," she said. This wizened woman had seen it all in her many years of caring for the fortress, yet her eyes went wide as new moons when she saw Torin sitting on the floor. "Is everything all right?"

"Perfectly fine," he said, holding up his hand to stop her from approaching. "I was simply getting the room ready for Sidra. We'll be moving in soon."

"*Oh.*" To her credit, Edna sounded more pleased than shocked. "That is wonderful news, Laird. We've been hoping the two of you and your sweet lass would be joining us here. Is there a date when I should have things ready?"

Torin imagined Sidra stepping into this chamber. This was the room where he was destined to sleep beside her, a chamber where he would draw sighs from her mouth and hold her against his skin, night after night. These were the walls that would watch and shelter them for the remainder of their days on the isle.

"Next week," Torin said, clearing his throat. "And don't worry about this . . . mess. I'll tend to it."

"As you want, Laird." Edna bowed her head and slipped away, latching the door behind her.

Torin groaned, leaning his head back. He stared up at the timber beams of the ceiling. It was both a salve and a misery to be alone, but he eventually remembered the bottle of whiskey beside him.

The glass caught the fading sunlight, casting Torin's hand in amber.

He opened the bottle and breathed in the scent of charred wood and smoked honey. He drank one sip. Then another.

He drank until the fire dulled the ache of his wounds.

Sidra knocked on Rodina Grime's door, a basket hanging from the crook of her arm. She knew the blighted orchard was behind the cottage, out of sight, though Sidra could smell its rot on the breeze. A fermented sweetness, laced with a sour tang.

She stifled a shiver as Rodina opened the door.

"Come in, Sidra," Rodina said, beckoning her inside with a gnarled hand. "I have a cup of tea waiting on you."

Sidra smiled and followed the crofter into a spotless kitchen. She had brought a pie in her basket, knowing that while Rodina often appeared unemotional and aloof, the old woman had been shaken by Hamish's death. She had lived here alone with her cats and sheep and orchard ever since her spouse passed years earlier. She most likely needed someone to talk to about what had happened.

As Sidra cut them each a slice of berry pie and shooed one of the cats off the table, Rodina settled into a straw-backed chair. She was a gruff, reserved woman who didn't like to talk much. But there was something about sudden death that shook a heart down to its roots. Especially when death had stolen someone so young.

"A good, honest lad," said Rodina, shifting her plaid shawl to drape it across her front, as though she was chilled. She accepted the pie from Sidra but made no effort to pour the tea, so Sidra did so. "He never complained. Was always here on time, right at sunrise, every day. I was thinking to leave him my croft, since I never had children. He would've taken good care of it, he would have."

Sidra set down the kettle. She stirred a spoonful of honey and cream into her tea, doing the same for Rodina when she nodded. A second cat jumped up on the table, and Sidra gathered the tabby into her lap as she took the chair opposite the elderly woman.

She listened to Rodina praise Hamish for a while longer, eating her pie and sipping her tea, the cat purring on her lap. All the while, Sidra's mind was whirling. She didn't know how to tell Rodina that Hamish had drowned from the blight, which he had caught from her orchard. She didn't know if she *should* impart such news, but Sidra also needed as many answers as she could glean.

"I can't keep this from you a moment longer," Rodina suddenly murmured with a grimace, revealing crooked front teeth. "I lied to your husband yesterday when he came to look at my orchard."

"And what did you lie about?" Sidra asked quietly. The cat on her lap ceased purring and cracked open one slitted eye, sensing the tension in the air.

"Torin asked me if I had touched any of my sick trees, or the fruit," Rodina began. She hesitated, shifting her plaid shawl again. This time Sidra noticed why. The crofter had been hiding her right hand. That was why she hadn't poured the tea, and why she had been eating her pie so slowly.

Sidra stood. The cat flailed but landed on his feet, but she could scarcely hear his disgruntled meow.

"May I please examine your hand, Rodina?"

"I suppose I have no choice," Rodina said sadly. "But please be careful, Sidra. If you catch this from me, your husband will have my head."

"He will do nothing of the sort," Sidra said, walking around the table. "Besides, I have good reason to believe we cannot catch the blight from each other. Only from the infected trees and fruit."

Rodina frowned. "How do you know that?"

Sidra laid a gentle touch on the crofter's shoulder. "Because Hamish also had it, on his leg. He and one of his brothers occasionally shared the same pair of boots, as well as slept in the same bed. And his brother hasn't caught the blight, even as I have reason to believe Hamish was sick with it for some time."

Rodina's eyes filled with tears. She glanced away before Sidra could see them fall. "I was worried he might have caught it. I should have *said* something."

"There is no time for regrets, Rodina. You didn't know, nor did Hamish. But now that we are aware of this trouble, I need to find answers as quickly as I can. And you can help me with that."

Sidra waited. Finally, Rodina nodded and held out her hand.

She had picked up one of the apples four days earlier. Sidra could see where the blight had started on the heel of her palm as a small, harmless-looking bruise. Every morning Rodina had noticed it growing. Her entire palm was now mottled violet and blue. In contrast, the lines of her palm shone, brilliant with golden filigree. She was perhaps one more sleep from the blight's spread to the inner curl of her fingers.

Sidra refrained from touching Rodina's hand, just to be careful, but she studied it closely and wrote down all the symptoms Rodina could provide her. Her hand ached often; her fingers felt stiff. Mobility was hindered, but Rodina's swollen joints might be responsible for that. She had more headaches lately, and a few days of an upset stomach.

"Do you think you can heal me, Sidra?" the crofter asked. Her voice was gruff, but her tone didn't fool Sidra. She was wary of false hope.

Sidra set down her quill. "To be honest? I'm not sure, Rodina. But I'm going to do everything I can to help you, to stop its spread and to ease your discomfort." She reached into her basket, withdrawing a few vials of her home-brewed tonics and salves. They were earmarked for another patient, but Sidra wanted Rodina to begin taking something immediately.

She wrote down instructions and tore the page loose from her book.

Rodina sighed, hiding her infected hand beneath the plaid again. "Thank you."

"I'll come to visit you tomorrow morning," Sidra said. "But if you need me before then, call for me on the wind."

The crofter nodded and then arched her brow. "I suppose you want to see the orchard for yourself?"

"Yes."

"As I thought." Rodina pointed to the back door. "Just beyond the kail yard. But please . . . be careful, Sidra."

Sidra stood before the blighted orchard with nothing more than a mewling cat and the northern wind for company. She studied the trees, feeling as if they were watching her in return as she took in the burls in the applewood, the shuddering of branches in the breeze, the spattered fruit, the slow drip of tainted sap.

One of her first thoughts was that the blight might be connected to Adaira's departure. As soon as the east had given her up, it had begun to suffer. Sidra wondered whether Adaira's presence among the Tamerlaines had kept the isle in a tentative balance. Had it become skewed ever since she crossed the clan line? Or perhaps the Tamerlaines were finally being punished for stealing from the other side of the isle. They had taken Adaira and raised her as their own without guilt, almost as easily as the Breccans plundered the east in the winter.

But now as she beheld it, Sidra realized that she had seen this blight before, in another copse. There had been a suffering tree— Sidra had felt the spirit's agony as it bled violet and gold—and she had reached out her hand to touch and comfort it, only to be ordered by the very ground not to do that.

This blight, then, was not a new development. It had been on the isle since midsummer—before Adaira's departure—but something had just recently made it worse. There could be other places that were suffering, other trees in the east that could pass the sickness along to the clan.

Torin needed to make an official announcement.

Sidra took a step back, preparing to leave. The wind gusted, a shocking burst of cold as it dragged hair into her eyes and tugged on her shawl. The heel of her boot slid over something soft, but she regained her balance. Frowning at the long grass, she lifted her foot and drew up her hem to look at it.

One of the rotten apples glistened in the morning light. It was now smudged on her left boot heel, a streak of violet and gold and a writhing worm. She stared at her foot numbly, as though she had been charmed into stone. Sidra was hardly able to comprehend how the rotten apple came to be there; she had been very careful in her approach. There had been nothing but grass and the cat around her, who had scampered back to the kail yard.

She carefully wiped the heel of her boot and used the rake that Rodina had set aside to push rotten fruit back beneath the trees, careful to avoid stepping beneath the boughs.

Only a small trace of gold remained on her boot. She realized she needed to walk home barefoot and immediately burn her shoes in the outdoor firepit. That course of action felt a bit extreme at first, and she tried to steady her thoughts.

She hadn't touched the fruit with her bare skin, as Rodina had. Only the heel of her shoe had come in contact with it, but she wondered if the same had happened to Hamish. If the blight had seeped through the leather hide of his boot.

"Don't worry," Sidra whispered as she removed her boots, careful not to touch the heel. She walked along the road, her bare feet warmed by the sun-baked dirt. The basket swung from her arm as she quickened her pace, boots dangling from her fingertips.

You'll be fine.

~~~~~~

CHAPTER 4

Adaira stood in a wind-battered cottage, staring at the dead body crumpled on the floor.

A chair had been overturned, along with a small bowl of parritch. The oats on the ground, now stained with blood, drew flies through cracks in the wattle-and-daub walls. Herbs hung from the low rafters overhead, trailing dusty wisps into Adaira's braided hair, and for a long moment the fire was the only sound in the room, crackling as it burned through the peat in the hearth. The shutters were closed to ward off the breeze, and the house was full of shadows, even at midday. But the sun rarely burned through the clouds in the west.

A chill settled into her marrow, and Adaira shivered.

Despite the interior's dimness, she could see that the deceased was a thin man with white-streaked hair and threadbare garments. His arms had been caught at crooked angles, and the enchanted blue plaid knotted at his shoulder had protected his heart but not his neck. The blood that had spilled from his sliced throat had long since dried into a circle beneath him, the shade of wine in midwinter light.

Adaira longed to look away. *Look away,* her heart whispered, and yet her gaze remained fixed on the man. She had seen dire wounds as well as death before, but she had never stood in a room where murder had been committed.

Innes Breccan was saying something at Adaira's side, her voice deep and raspy, like a blade trying to saw through damp wood. The western laird was never one to let her emotions melt through her guard—she was a cold, calculating enigma—but after four weeks of living with her, Adaira could hear two things in her mother's voice: Innes was exhausted, as if she hadn't slept in a long time, and she wasn't at all surprised to find a man slain on her lands.

"Was it an enchanted weapon, Rab?" Innes asked. "And if so, can you tell me what kind?"

That was *not* the first question Adaira expected her mother to voice. But Adaira had grown up in a place where enchanted weapons were scarce. Only a few Tamerlaine smiths were willing to take on the cost of forging them. In the west, nearly every Breccan of age carried one.

Rab Pierce crouched down to examine the body more closely. His leather armor creaked with his movement, the blue plaid wrinkling over his chest as he stretched out his hand. He had just turned five-and-twenty, and while he had a muscular frame, his face was still round with youth. His straw-colored hair was cropped short, and he always looked sunburnt. Adaira surmised that was from all the hours Rab spent riding against the wind and rain, since the clouds hung thick and low in the west.

She watched as Rab examined the man's neck. Eventually he shook his head.

"It looks to have been done with an ordinary blade," Rab said, glancing up at Innes. "A dirk most likely, Laird. I also noticed the cottage and the storehouse are both empty, as are the paddocks. This man was one of my mother's most reliable shepherds."

"Are you saying someone killed him to steal his food and livestock?" Adaira asked. She didn't want to sound shocked, but neither could she ignore the cold trickle of suspicion at the nape of her neck.

This dead man's croft wasn't far from the clan line, and she wondered if his sheep had originally been stolen from the Tamerlaines. Had he profited off Breccan raids of the past, taking Tamerlaine goods and livestock as his own?

Adaira's compassion for the murdered man began to wane. She remembered the winter nights laced with worry and terror when she was a child. She remembered being woken by the sound of feet rushing down corridors and voices slipping through cracked doors. She remembered Alastair and Lorna giving orders and mustering the guard to defend and aid the Tamerlaines who suffered from the Breccans' pilfering.

In those days, Adaira hadn't fully understood *why* the raids happened. All she knew came from the opinions that had been passed down to her: The Breccans were their enemies. Their clan was bloodthirsty and callous, greedy and coldhearted. They preyed upon the innocent people of the east.

As Adaira had gotten older, though, she had learned the power of biases, and she had longed for truth. For facts that weren't relayed with a certain slant that made one clan look better than the other. She had delved into the lore of the isle and discovered that the Breccans had raided even before Cadence was divided by magic. Descendants of a fierce and proud people, Breccans were born with swords in their hands and hot tempers and possessive bonds.

But when the clan line had been created by the doomed marriage and deaths of Joan Tamerlaine and Fingal Breccan, the western side of Cadence had truly started to falter. What good was magic in your hands if your kail yard couldn't feed you through the winter? What good was an endless supply of enchanted swords and plaids if your sheep had no grass to graze upon? If your water was murky and the wind blew so harshly from the north that you had to rebuild your homes and outbuildings with south-facing doors?

Adaira still hadn't grasped how it was for the Breccans until she had lived in the west and seen for herself the haggardness of their land, the lack of sunshine, the constant threat of the northern wind. She saw that they rationed their food in the summer, hoping it would last through the winter, but it inevitably didn't. She saw how much easier it was for them to steal from the Tamerlaines than from their own clan.

She had passed so many graves in the vale. Graves of children and young people.

It made her heart ache to wonder if they had starved when the snow came.

Rab's hooded eyes slid to Adaira, as if he heard her thoughts. She held his stare, unflinchingly.

Of Rab Pierce, she knew three things.

The first—he was a favored son of one of the west's thirteen thanes. As such, he was to inherit a large swath of land and was considered a powerful noble.

The second—he seemed to appear at the most convenient as well as the most *inconvenient* of moments, as if he often planned to cross paths with Adaira.

The third—his gaze often strayed to the half coin she wore at her neck.

"Yes, someone stole from him," Rab finally said, rising. "But only because this summer has proven to be scarce, and the stores ran low." His attention returned to Innes, his eyes softening, imploring. "Laird, I would ask for your wisdom."

Adaira wasn't entirely sure what his statement meant—there seemed to be a further implication to it—but her mother did. Innes said, "I'll consider your request. If this man's sheep were stolen, you should be able to follow a trail to where they were herded and find the culprit. In the meantime, please see to his burial."

Rab bowed his head.

Adaira followed Innes from the cottage into a dismal kail yard where the crops grew thin and sparse, the fruit small from strong winds and too little sunshine. She mounted the horse she had left waiting by her mother's steed at the gate.

The clouds hung low, swallowing hilltops and all sense of time as the two women rode along a muddy road. When it began to mist, Adaira breathed in the wet air, feeling the moisture bead on her

face, along her arms, but the enchanted blue plaid she wore kept
her warm and dry. In the east, she had possessed *one* enchanted
plaid shawl, which she had worn nearly everywhere, knowing how
much it had cost Mirin Tamerlaine to weave it. In the west, however, Adaira had been given *five*, as well as an enchanted blanket to
sleep beneath at night. The prevalence of magical raiment among
the Breccans continued to be a shock to her.

Adaira's attention was suddenly drawn to her left, where she
knew the Aithwood grew thick and tangled. If it had been a clear
day, she would have been able to see the forest, and perhaps envision the cottage on the barrow just beyond it.

The place where Jack had been raised. The place she had last
seen him.

"Let's stop here," Innes said abruptly, turning her horse from
the road.

Adaira didn't know *where* they were stopping—she could see
no structures or crofts through the haze—but she followed her
mother. It looked like Innes had taken a cow trail, worn down to
mud, and Adaira was further surprised when she dismounted.

Innes left her horse beneath a crooked rowan tree and stepped
over a stream, fading into the mist without a word or a backward
glance. Realizing the laird wasn't going to wait on her, Adaira hastily slid from her sheepskin saddle. She left her horse beside Innes's
and hurried after her, stepping over the stream and following a
footpath worn down in copper-tinged bracken.

She tried to make sense of what was happening, but this was
only the fourth time she had ridden with Innes beyond the castle
walls. Adaira strained her eyes against the gray air, but she couldn't
see any trace of her mother. She quickened her pace, the bracken
brushing against her knees, but didn't know if she was walking
in the right direction. She didn't know if the laird was testing her,
to see if she would obey and follow without hesitation, or maybe
to assess how the land would take to her. If the hills would shift,
stranding her for days like a mainlander. Like someone who didn't
belong.

Adaira hadn't ventured through the west on her own yet to see if the spirits would try to beguile her. The few times she had left the castle she was with Innes, and the folk seemed to know better than to trick such a laird. But Adaira also wouldn't have been surprised if the spirits in the west were too weak and tired to make mischief.

She parted her lips, but then bit back the urge to call after her mother.

She sharpened her vision, paying attention to the path she was following. A rock appeared every nine strides, like a marker. Her hands were cold, in defiance of summer, and she could taste the clouds as she drew in deep breaths, but she was steadier now as she wended her way through the ferns.

And then she felt *it*.

She was approaching something massive. A structure, or a hill most likely, because the air suddenly tasted like loam. Adaira noticed how the wind in her face eased and the way sound changed. She slowed her pace as the hill materialized, a shadow in the mist. Innes stood at the foot of it, waiting for her.

"I wanted to show you this place," the laird said. "In case you ever need to shelter here."

"What is it?" Adaira asked, studying the hill with narrowed eyes.

"Come closer so you can watch how I find the door."

Adaira moved forward as Innes touched a large stone protruding from the hillside. A blue light flared in the rock, winking like an eye, and the stones on the ground began to vibrate in response. Adaira stepped back, alarmed as the stones rose and gathered into a lintel on the hillside. A door appeared next, made of smooth pale wood, and Adaira almost laughed, disbelieving.

"Is this a spirit portal?"

"It's a burrow," Innes replied. "A wind shelter made with tools forged over magical fire. There are ten spread out across the west. Most are easy to spot, with their south-facing doors, but some are meant to be difficult to locate. This one is such a burrow. My grandmother personally built it in her time as laird, and if you're ever stranded by a northern storm, or perhaps need a place to hide, you should come here."

Adaira was quiet. They didn't need wind shelters in the east, and the idea was strange but intriguing to her. She nodded, sensing Innes wanted some physical reaction from her.

The laird turned and opened the door. She stepped into the burrow, but Adaira hesitated, stiff with reservation. How did she know Innes wasn't fooling her? How did she know that Innes hadn't brought her to an underground lair to be imprisoned?

Adaira couldn't deny that she had been expecting imprisonment as soon as she arrived in the west. Her twin brother was shackled in the Tamerlaines' fortress, so it was natural to assume Innes would do something similar to her. Adaira had, after all, agreed to be the Breccans' prisoner, and they could do with her whatever they saw fit as long as peace was upheld.

But her time in the west hadn't gone quite in the way she expected.

Innes had given her a comfortable bedroom in the castle that overlooked the "wilds," a term for land that was under protection and that no one could claim. No hunting and no building and no harvesting whatever grew there. Breccans who wanted to travel across the wilds had to remain on deer trails and approved pathways. It seemed a strange list of requirements to Adaira, but for a land that struggled to thrive, it made sense that the laird would need to enforce laws to protect it.

In her first week, Adaira had scarcely left her room. She had stood before her windows, watching the mist descend over the wilds and listening to the bell that chimed in the castle turret every hour, keeping time. She had thought the west beautiful in a strange, sad way. Its lines were harsher, its colors muted, and its overall feeling was one of desperation. The landscape reminded Adaira of a dream, or a lament. It was both familiar and new, and she found it difficult to draw her eyes away from it. She wondered if that was part of the land's few but compelling charms—its brutal honesty, as well as its untamed aura.

When she realized that Innes wasn't going to lock her in her chamber, Adaira had begun to test her new boundaries.

She learned that she could move through the Breccans' castle without a guard. Some places, however, were off-limits to her. She could bathe in the underground cistern so long as she told Innes when she planned to go, and Adaira had come to love the dark, warm waters of the large cavern. But the cistern, though a communal place, was always deserted when she went, making it apparent that Innes didn't want her meeting other clanspeople. Adaira swam alone, save for a female guard who watched over her. As if Adaira might attempt to drown herself.

She could also read in the library. She could visit the gardens and the stables, but she couldn't leave the castle grounds without Innes or David, Adaira's father and the laird's consort. She couldn't wander to the southern or eastern wings of the fortress, or down to the hold, where prisoners were kept. She was permitted to take her meals in the privacy of her chamber or with her parents in theirs. She could write letters, but she always had to deliver them to David first, and he also brought the letters that arrived for her.

It hadn't taken Adaira long to notice that the wax seals on Torin's, Jack's, and Sidra's letters had been tampered with. Her father was reading her post before he gave it to her, which meant he was also most likely reading the words she sent east. She wanted to be angry at this revelation and knew that her fury would have been justified.

But she was no fool.

Of course they would read her letters to ensure that she wasn't plotting their demise with her eastern family. Of course they didn't trust her yet. It was best for her to pretend that she didn't know about the interference with her mail, and also to keep her correspondence as nonthreatening as possible.

Every week had been full of small tests, quiet assessments to challenge her ties to the east and her future in the west. Innes and David were measuring how pliant she was as they tried to determine if it was possible for her to fully adjust to their way of life.

So far, Adaira had been extremely pliant. But she couldn't deny the constant ache in her body, as if she had aged a century in one night. She felt cold and hollow every morning when she woke alone to the gray light of the west.

"Follow me," Innes said. She had melted into the burrow's darkness and was waiting. "And shut the door behind you."

Adaira exhaled, her thoughts breaking into fragments. She sought to calm her heart because this burrow was merely another test. She didn't need to be afraid, even though she couldn't deny the tension that was gathering in her body. Limning her choice to flee, or to fight.

And yet where will you go if you run? her heart asked. *The east cannot take you back. And what would you fight with? Your hands? Your teeth? Your words?*

"Cora." Innes spoke again, sensing her hesitation.

It was the name Adaira had been given at birth. A name bequeathed to a small, sickly child who Innes had thought belonged with the spirits more than with the west. Years later, the name still refused to fit her. It rolled off her like rain.

Adaira stood in the meager light of the burrow's threshold, staring into the darkness. She couldn't see Innes, but it sounded like she stood to the right. There was no way to discern how vast the enclosed space was, or what hid within it.

She took her first step into the burrow. Her hand shook as she latched the door, fully closing herself into the shadows with Innes.

"Why do you think I've brought you here?" Innes asked softly.

Adaira was silent. Perspiration began to bead her palms as she weighed her answer.

"You want me to trust you," she replied at last.

"And do you trust me, Cora? Or do you still fear me?"

It was strange how easy it was to speak the truth with darkness as a shield. Adaira didn't think she would have had the courage to say the words if she had been holding Innes's gaze.

"I want to trust you, Laird. But I still don't know you."

Innes was quiet, but Adaira could hear her breathe. Long, steady draws of air. There was a sudden shuffle of boots, betraying Innes's movement as she said, "Stretch out your left hand. When you find the wall, walk alongside it. You'll know when to stop."

Adaira held out her hand, grasping at the darkness until her fingertips grazed the cool, earthen wall. She did as Innes had instructed, walking beneath veins of roots until her toe hit something solid.

"Good," Innes said. "Now reach down. There is a flint and an enchanted blade before you. Use both to make a flame."

Adaira's hands fumbled, feeling the edges of a crate. But it was just as Innes had said: a large, angular piece of flint and an antler-hilt dirk rested on the wood. Within one strike, the tip of the steel ignited like a candle.

The wavering flame cast a ring of light around her. Adaira took in what she could now make of the burrow. It wasn't as big as she had initially believed; she could see the far end of the structure where two cots were erected, side by side, their straw mattresses covered with piles of folded blue plaids. More crates were stacked along the wall, full of earthenware jugs and flasks. Candles rested on every horizontal surface, strung with cobwebs. In the heart of the room were two chairs. Innes was sitting in one of them, legs crossed and fingers laced over her lap, as she watched Adaira's observations.

"Come join me," Innes said when their gazes met. "We need to talk."

Adaira walked to the center of the burrow and lit the candles that rested on an overturned crate between the chairs. She sat, facing Innes, although her attention was stolen by the enchanted dirk she still held. In the east, they didn't have blades with such magical abilities as fire-making, although it wouldn't be beyond the skills of Tamerlaine smiths to forge one. The cost to their health for crafting such enchantment would be steep, though, and not many Tamerlaines wanted to pay it.

Adaira blew out the blade's flame, then set it beside the candles on the crate. Looking at Innes, she watched the firelight dance over her mother's lean face. The woad tattoos on her neck looked stark against her pale skin.

"You say you have yet to wholly trust me because you do not know me," Innes said. "But you are my daughter, and you have nothing to fear from me." She paused, glancing down at her hands. At the blue ink printed across the backs of her fingers. "You have this moment to ask me anything. I will answer you if I can."

Adaira was stunned by the offer. There were a few questions that had been smoldering in her thoughts since she had arrived, but she needed a moment to think.

She wanted to know why music was forbidden in the west; if she could understand it, perhaps she could safely invite Jack to visit. But before she could invite Jack, she needed to know where his father was—the man who had secretly given her to the Tamerlaines after Innes ordered her to be abandoned in the Aithwood.

Had they executed him? Did he still live? Adaira had no idea, and she couldn't face Jack without having an answer. It was another reason why she had slowed her correspondence with him; she lived in daily dread that he would ask about his father in a letter and David, reading it, would realize whose son Jack truly was.

Adaira could only hope that Jack was shrewd enough to read between the lines she was writing to him, that he realized their letters were not private. That he wasn't taking offense at the distance she was keeping.

But dwelling on it always made her feel ill, as though she had swallowed mouthfuls of seawater.

Tucking a tendril of damp hair behind her ear, she pushed Jack and their stilted correspondence far from her thoughts. Then she delayed a moment more, removing a burr from her plaid. The query burned on her tongue—*Where is the man who carried me eastward?*—but when Adaira glanced up and found Innes regarding her with a tenderness she had not yet seen in the laird's face, the words melted away.

She couldn't ask that question yet. It would put a wedge between them, and who knew when Innes would grant another opportunity like this. Adaira would have to wait a while longer.

"Did you ever think of me?" she whispered. "All the years I was gone . . . did I ever cross your mind, even when you thought I was dead?"

Did you ever regret your decision to give me up?

"Yes," Innes said. "Although I never thought you dead. I believed you had been taken by the spirits of the air. There were some seasons of my life when I could not pass a day without thinking of you. I would walk the Aithwood and I would listen to the wind, and I would imagine you as a spirit, blowing across the wilds. It was a small comfort, though, and one I did not deserve."

Adaira cast her eyes down to the dirt floor. She didn't know how to respond, or what to feel, but she felt speared by her mother's response.

"I had another daughter, after you," Innes continued. "Three years after you and Moray were born. She emerged into the world weak and small. Just as you had been, only this time I knew better than to believe her a changeling and give her up to the folk."

"What is her name?" Adaira's heart began to pound. She didn't know what expression was on her face, but it must have been drawn with longing, because the laird glanced away, into the shadows.

"Her name was Skye."

Was.

"What happened to her?" Adaira asked.

"She was poisoned by one of my thanes," Innes replied.

"I . . . I'm sorry."

"So was he, after I was through with him."

"The thane?"

Innes nodded as she reached into the inner pocket of her jerkin. She retrieved a small glass vial and held it up to the candlelight, studying the clear liquid that moved within it.

"Why do you think I brought you with me today to see the shepherd's body?" the laird asked.

Adaira shivered. Her mist-dampened clothes were beginning

to feel heavy and chafed her skin. The turn of their conversation made her anxious, and she resisted the urge to crack her knuckles. "You wanted me to see that your people are desperate and hungry enough to kill each other for resources."

"Something you've never encountered before in the east, I take it? Since the Tamerlaines have never known true hunger or want," said Innes. "You've never seen how both can drive you to do things you'd never consider before."

It was true; even if a neighbor's crop didn't do well, or the Breccans stole from them, others in the Tamerlaine clan would rally and help provide what had been lost. The laird could even distribute provisions from the castle stores. There was never a need to hoard or steal, although it still happened on rare occasions.

"In some ways, I'm glad for it," Innes continued. "I'm relieved that you've never gone days without eating, or drunk water that made you sick, or had to fight someone you once loved to take what they have. But it has made you too soft, Cora. And if you are going to thrive here, you must wear those places down to bone."

"I understand," Adaira replied, perhaps too quickly. But she was keen to find acceptance among her blood clan, to reach that point where she was no longer regarded with mistrust, or watched everywhere she went, or doubted when she spoke.

And in some small, hidden place in her chest that she was almost afraid to acknowledge, Adaira wanted to earn her mother's respect.

Innes's blue eyes narrowed, her fingers closing over the vial to conceal it in her fist. She brought her knuckles to her lips for a moment, and Adaira felt perspiration trickle down the curve of her spine. She wondered if she was about to face her first challenge to slough off the softness.

"When Rab Pierce requested my 'wisdom,' he was asking me to consider blessing a raid on the east," Innes explained. "Doing so staves off crime and desperation among my people, and my dungeons are already full of criminals. When Rab finds the culprit who murdered the shepherd, there will be one more hungry person locked into the darkness."

Adaira was silent. A protest was rising in her throat, but she curled her tongue and kept the words between her teeth.

"With your brother in the Tamerlaines' holding," Innes said, "I cannot bless a raid on the east. But there is another way I can quell the growing hunger of the clan, one that I will announce tomorrow night when I summon my thanes and their heirs to a feast in my hall."

She tossed the vial across the space. Adaira's hands were clumsy with surprise, but she caught it before the glass could tumble to the ground.

"What is this?" she asked hoarsely, watching the liquid settle.

"It's called Aethyn," Innes answered. "It's what killed your sister. The only poison in the west that we don't have an antidote to counter. Because it has no odor or taste, someone's drink can be poisoned with no fear of detection."

Adaira's body turned leaden. If Innes had commanded her to rise, she wouldn't have been able to. But her blood was coursing, hot and swift in her veins. "Are you asking me to poison one of your thanes tomorrow night?"

Innes was quiet, a beat too long for Adaira's liking. "No. I am asking you to attend this dinner, so I can formally introduce you to the Breccan nobility as my daughter. But you cannot come and sit at a table among them without being prepared."

"So you are asking me to poison *myself* with it first?"

"Yes. It's a small dose."

"But it could kill me?"

"Not in that amount. It will act as a buffer, a protection, should your cup be poisoned with a deadlier dose. You *will* feel side effects, however, and you'll need to continue taking the doses in order to build up a tolerance to it."

Adaira laughed, wondering if she were dreaming. But she bit the inside of her cheek when she saw Innes's countenance turn cold.

"And what if I don't want to poison myself?" she asked. "What then?"

"You stay in your room tomorrow night. You don't come to the feast, and you don't officially meet my nobles," Innes replied, rising. She began to extinguish the candle flames with her fingertips. The burrow slowly succumbed to darkness once more. "But the choice is yours, Cora."

CHAPTER 5

F rae was sprawled on the rug before the hearth, reading one of her books, when the fire suddenly died. There was a flash of heat and a *pop* before the wood crumbled into ash, and Frae lurched back with a gasp, watching as the flames were extinguished into smoke.

She was so surprised by the odd behavior of the fire—she had just added a fresh log to the blaze—that it took her a moment to know what to do. The cottage felt off balance without a lit hearth. Frae closed her book and cautiously rose to her feet. Mirin had given her the task of making tea for supper, and the kettle on the iron hook still needed to boil. She decided to start a new fire with the kindling in the basket and the flint, but as the sparks flew and refused to light, Frae knew something was wrong.

Mirin was in the kail yard, gathering greens for dinner, and Jack was in his bedroom. Frae had seen the new harp he had carried home yesterday, and it had taken everything within her to swallow the questions she wanted to pepper him with.

Where did you get the harp? Does this mean you're going to play again?

She worried that it would irritate him to ask him too many

things, or somehow dissuade him from strumming the new harp, even though Jack had always been gentle and kind to her. And she knew he must be busy with something important since he had been cloistered in his bedroom since yesterday.

Frae still decided to go to him first with her troubles.

She approached his door and knocked. "Jack?"

"Come in, Frae."

The door creaked open, and Frae politely peered inside. She saw her older brother sitting at his desk before the window. The shutters were open, welcoming in the cool summer dusk and the song of an owl, and on his desk was a strange array of moss, bracken, wilted wildflowers, small branches, and braided grass.

"What are you doing?" she asked, drawn to the strangeness until she stepped closer and saw that he had been writing musical notes on parchment.

"I'm working on a new composition," he said, setting down his quill to smile at her. Ink stained his fingers and his hair looked messy, but Frae didn't say anything. She had noticed Jack was not the neatest of people and often left his plaid and clothes crumpled on the floor.

"Will I get to hear it?" she asked.

"Maybe. This song is for an important task, but I can play another one just for you."

"Tonight?"

"I'm not sure," he replied honestly. "I'm afraid I need to get this ballad done as quickly as possible."

"Oh."

"Did you need help with something, Frae?"

That reminded her. She blurted out, "The fire died."

Jack frowned. "Do you need me to build a new one?"

"I mean, I *tried* to," she said. "It won't light, and I don't know what to do."

Her brother rose from his chair and walked into the dim common room. Frae followed, biting a hangnail. She watched as Jack reached for kindling in the basket, as he stacked fresh wood in the hearth. The flint sparked in his hand, but the fire refused to take. Eventually he leaned back on his heels, starting at the ashes.

"Do you think it's because of the harp?" Frae whispered.

Jack glanced at her sharply. "The harp?"

"The new one you brought home yesterday. Perhaps the fire wants you to play it."

He didn't have time to respond. The front door swung open as Mirin returned from the garden. Their mother draped her shawl by the door and then glanced at them.

"What happened to the fire?" she asked, setting her harvest basket on the table.

"I think the kindling and wood might be bad," Jack said, straightening.

Mirin arched a dark brow, noticing the pile of wood stacked beside the hearth. She and Frae had just gathered it two days earlier from the Aithwood. And it had never refused to burn before.

"I'll go gather some fresh wood from the forest," Jack offered.

Frae's heart stuttered in her chest. She reached out to snag Jack's sleeve. "But it's almost night! You shouldn't go into the Aithwood when it's dark."

"I'll be careful," he promised.

Frae almost rolled her eyes at him. Sometimes Jack didn't listen very well, especially when he was wrapped up in his music and seemed to forget which realm he lived in.

"Your sister's right," Mirin said. "Save it for tomorrow, Jack. We can eat cold soup by candlelight tonight."

Frae watched as Mirin attempted to light the tapers. The sun had fully set now, and darkness was blooming in the cottage. But Frae could see how her mother struggled with the flint. Her fingers were stiff from all the magical weaving she had been doing lately. Not even Sidra's salves could help with the inflammation, and Frae shivered when Mirin handed the flint to Jack in defeat.

But when Jack tried to light the candles, the fire wouldn't take to the wicks. In the dimness, Frae could see her brother's deep scowl and the gleam of worry in his eyes.

"What are we going to do?" Frae asked.

"Come, both of you sit at the table!" Jack said in an unusually sprightly voice, setting the flint aside.

When Mirin and Frae continued to stand, shocked by his bright tone, he took their arms and guided them. He sat Mirin down first, then Frae, before he turned to the kitchen cupboard and rummaged through it.

"What are you doing, Jack?" Frae asked, rising from her seat. He was acting like nothing was wrong, and it puzzled her.

"I'm bringing you dinner. Please sit down, Frae."

"But the fire!"

"We don't need it tonight," Jack said over his shoulder. Again, the blithe tone of his voice didn't quite match his personality. But Frae couldn't deny that his cheerfulness made her feel better about their situation.

If Jack wasn't worried, then she shouldn't be either.

Frae resumed her seat, glancing at Mirin. Her mother was watching her, and she seemed sad until their gazes met. Then Mirin smiled, reassuringly, but Frae felt a twinge of worry again. Her mother had been weaving too much lately, and that made her sick from the magic she spun. Frae needed to help her more. But if the fire refused to light in the hearth, they wouldn't be able to work in the evenings. . . .

Frae was distracted by Jack, who finally delivered dinner to the table.

He brought them a sliced bannock, fresh-churned butter, a pot of honey, smoked herring, and a wheel of cheese. Frae could hardly see it spread along the table, but her stomach growled when she smelled it.

"Who needs warm soup anyways?" Jack said, pouring each of them a small cup of milk, since the tea had never been brewed. "This here is true tavern fare, where stories and ballads are born."

"Tavern fare?" Frae echoed.

"Yes. Fill your plate and begin to eat, and I'll tell you a story,"

Jack said, sitting in his chair. "A story that has never been spoken on this isle before tonight."

Frae was intrigued. She quickly filled her plate and began to eat, listening as Jack regaled them with a story from the mainland. Or, he *claimed* it was from there, but Frae wondered if he was making it up as he went.

Either way, it was a good story, and she didn't notice how dark it was until she had eaten her fill.

"Come, Frae," Mirin said, rising from the table. "I think we should retire for bed early tonight. The fire has told us that we need rest. Thank your brother for dinner and come with me."

Frae stood with her empty plate. She was going to set it in the wash barrel, but Jack took it from her hands.

"I'll take care of it," he said. "Go with Mum, little sister."

Frae hugged him and thanked him for the story. When Mirin took her hand and guided her through the darkness to their bedroom, she followed.

Frae couldn't see anything as she removed her boots. She found her oaken chest, though, and reached into it for her nightgown. By the time she had managed to dress herself in the dark, Mirin was waiting in bed.

"Why didn't the fire light, Mum?" Frae asked, settling close to Mirin's side.

Her mother drew the blankets up to their shoulders. "I'm not sure, Frae. But it's something we'll tend to tomorrow. Go to sleep, darling."

Frae didn't think she would ever be able to sleep that night. She lay awake for a long while, eyes open to the darkness, full of thoughts and questions. Eventually, though, she drifted off. And she dreamt of the Breccan again. The one she had seen dragged into their cottage weeks ago. A prisoner who had wept Mirin's name.

The man with red hair. The same color as Frae's.

She was never afraid when she saw him, even though he was her enemy. She sensed he was in trouble, and that was why he was reaching out to her in her dreams. He would say her name and then fade away before she could reply, every single time.

But she didn't know who he was or how to help him, not in the real world and not in her dream world either.

She didn't know how to save him.

Jack quietly cleaned the kitchen in the dark. With Frae and Mirin retired to bed, he could finally let down his guard. He sighed as he sat at the kitchen table, buried his face in his hands, and wondered what he was supposed to do about the fire.

Without it, they would slowly die. They would have no choice but to leave this cottage and croft, and he knew Mirin would refuse because of the loom. It was her livelihood and she wouldn't abandon it, but Jack also knew it wasn't the wood or the kindling or even the flint that was causing problems. It was fire itself, and it angered him. To know whatever fire spirit guarded his mother's hearth had turned malevolent, refusing to ignite.

He stood up from the table and felt his way to his bedroom.

The shutters were still open, and he could see the night sky beyond the hills. The stars had gathered like crystals spilled across dark wool, and the moon was rising behind a wisp of clouds. Jack stood at his desk, wondering if he could continue his composition by celestial light, but he could hardly see the notes he had inked earlier.

He should go to sleep then. What else was there to do in the dark?

He started to unfasten his boots and reached out for the bed, then felt Lorna's harp, resting on the quilt. He inadvertently touched one of the strings. It hummed in response, eager to sing, and Jack felt something rouse in him, like cold embers flaring beneath breath.

He froze, his mind racing. The desire to play and sing had fallen dormant over the past few weeks. Adaira had called music his first love, and now it was stirring again inside him, like a flower blooming beneath frost. He had known it would return to him eventually, but he had predicted that he would have to reach the point where not making music had become unbearable before he surrendered. Then he would have no choice but to crack open his own stubborn bones to find the music there, gleaming in his marrow.

Jack hesitated only for a moment before giving in to the music. He wrapped his fingers around the harp's wood frame and carried it out the back door.

He found the place where he had last sung and played. A gentle piece of ground with a view of the river and the Aithwood. He sat in the starlit grass with his face toward the west.

It was here that Jack had played his harp until his nails tore and bled. He had played until his voice was frayed and his heart felt molten as gold over fire. He had summoned the river and the woods and the Orenna flower to bring Moray back to him, Frae bound in his arms. And the spirits had answered and done as Jack bid. It was a heady power, and one that he had privately reveled in.

But it wasn't power that he wanted that night.

He stared into the Aithwood's shadows as he brought Lorna's harp to his chest, slipping its leather strap over his shoulder. He felt like he was embracing a stranger, but he knew that the instrument would soon warm to him, as he would warm to it in return. They would find a rhythm and a balance as they learned each other's quirks and secrets and tendencies.

He just needed to *play* it.

Jack placed his fingers on the strings, but he didn't pluck notes from them. Not yet.

He had written to her again, as Torin had requested. He had sent his letter with a raven the day before, but Adaira had yet to reply. Jack was irritated, worried, annoyed, overwhelmed by her silence. He wanted to believe that he would know if something had harmed her, even with the distance between them. He was her other half, and he was bound to her as she was to him. But perhaps Jack had sung too many ballads of everlasting love and fated partners.

Perhaps love made one foolish and weak.

He let himself sink into that weakness as he remembered swimming with her in the sea. Singing for the spirits at her side. He remembered the drawl of her voice as she dubbed him her "old menace." How moon thistles, braided into her hair, had complemented her sharp beauty. How she had bent a knee to him once, her proposal succinct and yet endearing. The way she had smiled at him during their handfasting.

He remembered the taste of her mouth, the softness of her skin, the rhythm of her breaths. The way their bodies had met and aligned as they came together in her bed. The words he had spoken to her, vulnerable and bare and limned with light.

He plucked a string; it rang out bright as the stars above him. He felt the note echo in his chest. He coaxed another forward and listened as it took to the open air. Sweet and warm now, sunlight spun during night.

"If I am weak for wanting you, then let me embrace that weakness and make it my strength," he said, his gaze fixed on the west. "And if you must haunt me, then let me haunt you in return."

Jack began to play. The eastern wind blew at his back, tangling his hair, and he closed his eyes. The music began to unfold in his hands, intrinsic and spontaneous. It was a song he discovered as he went, and he allowed himself the freedom to relinquish the fears, the worries, the uncertainties he had been carrying. To let go and simply *breathe* the notes. To melt into the fire of his music.

He didn't sing for the isle or for himself. He sang for what had been and what could still be.

He sang for Adaira.

daira stepped into the Breccans' hall with jewels woven into her hair and what felt like ice gleaming at her fingertips. It was the poison in her blood, making her feel cold. She curled her hands into fists until she felt the nails bite crescent moons into her palms, reassuring herself that she wasn't made of frost.

She had swallowed the poison because she wanted to attend this dinner and meet the nobility. She wanted to listen to their conversations and show that she had a place at their table. But Adaira also couldn't ignore the twinge of apprehension she felt when she thought about Innes and a potential raid.

If the Breccans were already growing hungry in high summer, resorting to stealing and murdering each other, their desperation would only grow worse come autumn and winter. Eventually, Innes might bend and bless a raid. If she did that, Adaira's place in the west would feel precarious. A raid would put Torin in a dangerous position as well, forcing him to choose whether to kill the Breccans who trespassed or not, whether to demand restitution or let it be. Adaira worried that a raid would plunge the isle into war.

But if she was at the table, staring Innes in the eye, Adaira thought the laird might not be so inclined to approve of raiding.

Her heartbeat was slow, far too slow. She could feel the pulse in her throat, like salt crackling in her veins, and she wondered if the vessel in her chest would cease pumping altogether the moment she sat at the table. If she would breathe her last at this treacherous dinner. The faltering rhythm of her pulse made her feel both heady and languid. Strangely, there was no fear lurking within her, even though she knew she should be feeling the sharp edge of it.

This was her first time in the hall, which she had expected to be a dingy, wood-smoked room with narrow windows and hay strewn over its muddy floors. She had expected an untamed place, whittled down by the elements and stained with old blood.

What met her, then, nearly stole the shallow breath in her lungs.

The pillars were hewn from wood and carved to resemble mighty rowan trees. Their branches formed an intricate arbor over the highest point of the ceiling, and chains of red gemstones and iron chandeliers dripped from them. Hundreds of candles burned from above, their wax melting into stalactites. The stone floor was polished so fine that Adaira could see her reflection in it. The windows, arched along the walls, were made of mullioned glass patterned to mimic the Orenna flower—four red petals dusted with gold. Adaira could only wonder how the sunlight would look burning brightly through such glass.

She slowed her pace, letting her attention drift to the center of the room, where the long table was set for the feast. The thanes and their heirs were already present and sat in their appointed chairs. The hall hummed like a hive with their conversations, punctured by clinks of silverware and goblets.

Adaira stopped between two of the rowan pillars.

She was late.

The feast had already begun, even though Adaira had arrived exactly when Innes had told her to. She knew her heart should be racing now. It should be pounding, but instead it was barely beating. The ice branched through her veins as the Aethyn continued to eat its way through her. Adaira stayed in the shadows, observing the Breccans.

No one had noticed her entrance, except for the guards stationed at the doors, but they had been as unmoving as statues and only silently watched her. Adaira took a moment to let her eyes rush over the nobles, some of whom she recognized and some of whom she had never seen. At last, she found her mother sitting at the head of the table.

Adaira almost didn't recognize her.

Innes wore a black dress shot through with gold-threaded moons. The neckline was cut square, displaying the interlocking woad tattoos that danced across her chest. A net of blue jewels was draped over her white-blond hair, which hung loose and long, brushed into a waterfall down her back.

Adaira took two full breaths before Innes felt the draw of her stare.

The laird's gaze flickered to the threshold, her eyes shining with firelight and boredom as if all her thanes were full of predictable stories. But they narrowed when she saw Adaira waiting in the shadows.

You deceived me, Adaira wanted to hiss at her. *You have made me look a fool, arriving late to a dinner I poisoned myself for.*

She was sick of the tests and the challenges and the meddling. She was sick of doing everything Innes and David asked of her. She had made it nearly *five* weeks in their holding unscathed, but she was *exhausted.*

Adaira took hold of the thick blue fabric of her dress, sewn with tiny silver stars, and was about to turn her back on Innes and leave when the laird rose. The high-backed chair scraped loudly on the floor with her abrupt motion, capturing the nobles' attention. Conversations died in midsentence as the thanes gaped at Innes, wholly unaware of what had interrupted their dinner until the laird held out her hand.

"My daughter, Cora," she said. Her voice was deep and smoky, as if she had spoken such a name a hundred times. And perhaps she had. Perhaps she had breathed it into the wind, year after year, hoping Adaira would hear and answer her.

The hall suddenly become a cacophony of sound as the thanes rushed to rise. One by one, they stood for Adaira, turning to watch her approach.

She walked across the hall, taking her time. She didn't look at the men and women gathered at the table, wearing their finest raiment and glittering jewelry. She didn't even look at David, who was standing to the left of the laird.

Adaira kept her eyes on Innes. Her mother with the jewels that burned in her hair and the moons on her dress and the hand she held out to her daughter. She could read Innes's mind and the hint of feral expression on her face: *This is my flesh and blood, cut from my cloth, and she is mine.*

Adaira tried to remember if Lorna or Alastair had ever looked at her in such a protective way, as if they would carve out the heart of anyone who dared harm her. She tried to remember, but her memories of them were soft, woven with warmth and laughter and comfort.

Never had Adaira feared her parents in the east.

She could vividly remember sitting on Alastair's lap when she was young, listening to him tell her clan stories in the evening. He had trained her to wield a sword when she had finally pestered him enough about it, and they spent countless sun-drenched hours on the training green, sparring until she had learned all the guards and could protect herself. She remembered how, as she had grown older, he would invite her into his council chamber and ask for her advice on matters, always ready to listen to her.

She could recall riding the hills with Lorna until their horses were lathered and the wind had carried their laughter south. They would often sit in the grass and look out at the sea, eating lunch from their saddle packs and talking about their dreams. She remembered lying on the floor of the music turret, reading and listening as Lorna practiced on her harp, plucking notes and singing ballads that filled Adaira with courage and nostalgia.

The love Innes was extending was nothing like Alastair's and Lorna's.

It was sharp and angular, like the blue jewels in her hair. It was fierce and possessive, built from bloodlines and traditions and a wound that still ached after twenty-three years. And yet Adaira was relieved to finally behold and understand it—to know that affection gleamed within Innes. It was as though the harshness of the wind had carved her down into a spear that could strike but also defend unto death. To be loved by Innes was to dwell behind her shield in a land where thanes poisoned daughters.

Adaira suddenly realized she held far more power here than she had dared to believe. The coldhearted Laird of the West might be desperate to earn her love in return, uncertain if it were even a possibility after so much time and distance.

She also realized that Innes had asked her to arrive late for no other reason than to give her an entrance that would unsettle the thanes, who now had food in their teeth and wine swimming in their blood. A sly but brilliant move.

Adaira reached the chair that awaited her at Innes's right-hand side.

She sat, and then her father and the nobles followed suit. Innes was the last to resume her seat.

A servant stepped forward and filled Adaira's goblet with wine. She glanced at the platters that ran along the tabletop like a spine, now holding broken loaves of dark bread, roasted mutton, potatoes and carrots sprinkled with herbs, truffles and speckled mushrooms, wheels of soft cheese, and jars of pickled fruit.

"Help yourself, Cora," Innes murmured.

Adaira wasn't hungry—another side effect of the Aethyn—but she filled her plate, feeling the weight of the nobles' gazes on her. They were watching her every move, and it wasn't until she had taken her first tentative bite that she understood why some of them were regarding her so shrewdly.

She was sitting in the chair that had been Moray's.

"Always a pleasure to see you, Cora," Rab Pierce said, lifting his goblet to her.

Adaira found him across the table, three seats down. She knew full well why he was making a point to speak to her. Most of the nobles gathered that evening had yet to see or meet her, and Rab wanted to show his advantage by calling her by name and addressing her with such familiarity.

His mother, Thane Griselda, sat beside him. She wore jewels in her auburn hair and on every knuckle of her fingers, which cradled a goblet to her chest. Her expression was pinched and her skin pale as cream, betraying how often she spent time indoors. She watched Adaira eat, her hooded eyes glittering like a cat observing a mouse.

Adaira flexed a hand beneath the table, feeling the ice crack beneath her skin.

"Indeed, Rab," she said. "I hope you've settled the trouble that was on your land yesterday?"

Rab was quick and replied, "You'll be pleased that I have. Perhaps we can speak more of it later?" His gaze dropped to the low neckline of her dress, where her golden half coin rested against her skin.

Adaira knew the Breccans wore rings to represent marriage vows. She knew they didn't wear half coins around their necks, as some of the Tamerlaines did, but she had also made it clear to Rab that she was married and spoken for. And yet his eyes still lingered, as if he saw a challenge in the broken gold she displayed.

She didn't have a chance to respond to him. Innes shifted the conversation to other matters, and Adaira chose to sit and listen, trying to pick up on the dynamic of the nobles. Some spoke often, while others were silent and pensive. One of the quiet ones was David, and Adaira caught his eye across the table a few times.

Her father was watching her closely, his brow furrowed.

Maybe he disliked her sitting in Moray's chair.

She didn't have the energy to care what he thought as she sipped the wine. Her stomach was beginning to ache. Her hands were going from icy to clammy, and she wondered if the Aethyn was about to finish burning through her.

She almost spilled her goblet when she set it on the table. It clanked against her plate, drawing Innes's attention.

"I've gathered all of you here tonight to make an announcement," the laird said suddenly, her voice rising above the others until the table froze with silence. "It has come to my attention that crime is growing again as resources become scarce. That the people under your watch are hungry, and autumn's frost is still weeks from arriving."

"Are you blessing a raid, Laird?" one of the thanes asked. "If so, I will lead it."

Adaira stiffened. She could feel the heat of Rab's stare, and of his mother's. The eyes of the nobles bore into her, curious to see how she would react if her mother called a raid.

"There will be no raids," Innes said. "But I am lifting the restriction on hunting. For two days only, you may hunt the wilds and the forests of the west. Each of your houses has the chance to kill up to five beasts, whether they be boars or deer, and up to twenty fowl, yet no more than that number. You will have to be shrewd and careful in deciding how the spoils are divided and should conflict arise, you will settle it swiftly."

Whispers sprouted along the tables. Adaira could tell that the thanes and heirs were surprised by Innes's announcement.

"You would risk the conservation of our lands rather than let us freely take from the east?" another thane asked. "I'm not certain how wise this is, Laird."

"The land has rested for months now," Innes said. "As long as you adhere to the regulations I'm enforcing, the wilds should recover in time for the autumnal hunting season." She stood, bringing the feast to an end. "Go now and make your preparations. The hunt begins tomorrow at dawn."

Adaira rose with the others. As she made brief eye contact with Innes, she remembered the laird's instructions—*as soon as I make my announcement, return to your room.* Adaira began to wend her way through the hall.

She was walking beneath the carved arbor of rowan branches when Rab appeared at her side, close enough to brush her arm.

"Are you joining your mother on the hunt tomorrow?" he asked.

Adaira shifted away from him but had no choice but to slow her pace to reply. "No. I won't be riding with her."

"And why is that?"

"I have no interest in the hunt."

"Shouldn't you, though?"

Adaira sighed, reluctantly meeting Rab's gaze. "Why do you say that?"

"She blames it on Moray being imprisoned by the Tamerlaines, but *you* are the true reason why Innes won't bless a raid," Rab said, lowering his voice. "I think many of us are beginning to wonder if you aren't part spirit after all, setting a charm on her to do what you want."

Adaira clenched her jaw, uncertain how to respond.

"Ride with me tomorrow," Rab whispered, stepping closer. Adaira refused to lean away, to give up her ground. Even when she could feel his wine-stained breath coast over her face. "Prove that you are one of us after all, and not a spirit of the wind. Prove that your blood is of the west and you have no intention to harm our clan."

"I don't need to prove *anything*," Adaira replied through her teeth. "And I don't know why you continue to chase after me when I have no interest in you."

"Because you're lonely," he said softly, holding her gaze. "I can see it in your eyes. I can see it in the way you walk. You need a friend."

A knot welled in Adaira's heart. She hated that he was right. She hated that his perceptiveness only deepened her loneliness.

"And you'll soon learn, Cora," he continued, "that this is a land full of long, cold, treacherous nights. Perhaps you won't be surprised to hear that I am lonely, just as you are."

"I'm married," she said, finally giving herself the freedom to step away and let the distance swell between them. "As I have said to you before, I'm not interested in you or in what you can offer me."

She began to stride away from him.

"You say that now," Rab called after her. "But I promise, when the seasons begin to pass and your husband refuses to join you here, you'll change your mind."

Adaira turned to pin him with a cold stare. "I won't be changing my mind about you."

"*Rab!*" Griselda called sharply, embarrassed by how her son was panting after Adaira. "It's time to go."

Rab sketched a polished bow before he melted into the crowd.

Adaira released a deep exhale, hoping her face was composed. She noticed that some of the milling nobles had observed her tense exchange with Rab, and she didn't know what to make of it. If she now appeared vulnerable and weak. There had been no scheming, deadly court to dance with in the east, and she told herself, *You've lasted five weeks. You can endure many more as long as you don't lose your temper.*

But just before Adaira departed the hall she saw Innes, still standing at the table, watching it all with dark, inscrutable eyes.

It hit her half an hour later, when she was in her bedroom unwinding the cold blue jewels from her hair. The last ice of the Aethyn dose melted, and Adaira began to shake. She reached out to the desk to steady herself. Her vision was blurring at the edges. Perspiration dripped down her neck as her stomach roiled, again and again, like a storm-churned tide.

Innes had warned her of how unpleasant it would be when the first dose of the poison wore off. It would get a little easier the more she imbibed it, but only if she could hold the contents down.

"*Spirits,*" Adaira whispered, gripping her abdomen.

She closed her eyes and trembled, her skin shining with sweat. The fire burning in the hearth was making everything far too warm, and she made her way to the nearest window. Her hands were so damp that it took three attempts to unlock the leaded glass, but it finally swung open and cool air began to waft into the chamber.

She closed her eyes, trying to distract herself from the pain that tore through her like a claw.

It soon took her to the floor.

Adaira bared her teeth and strangled a scream as she writhed on the rug.

You will think you are dying, Innes had said to her earlier. *You will think that I fooled you into taking a lethal dose. But the pain will pass quickly if you can hold it down and withstand the brunt of it.*

"I can't," Adaira wept as she began to crawl to her chamber pot. "I can't *do* this."

Her arms gave out before she could reach the bureau, where the pot was stored. She lay facedown on the floor, fighting the pain until every fiber of her body was strung so tight that she felt like her muscles and veins would snap within her. She dug her fingernails into the rug, into her hair. She tried to distract herself from the agony that burned through her body, but Adaira had never felt so weak and helpless before.

She touched her neck and found the half coin. It was like an anchor, and she closed her fingers around the coin's golden edge, feeling it cut into her palm. She thought of Jack until thinking about him was nearly as unbearable as the pain and started to drag herself forward. But through the roar of her pulse and the din of her memories, she heard it—a very faint thread of music.

Adaira stilled. Bowed over on the floor, she fixed her attention on the sound. It was a harp, playing faintly in the distance. The music grew stronger, louder, carried on the wind that sighed into her bedroom.

Who would dare to play in the west? She wondered if she was hallucinating.

She wondered if she was dying.

And then he began to sing.

"*Jack*," Adaira whispered, at first so overwhelmed by the sound of his voice that she couldn't discern the words he sang. But her blood stirred to his music. She drank in his voice, the notes he gave to her, and soon the overwhelming tension in her body began to ease.

She closed her eyes, lay on her back, and listened to Jack sing of what had been, of what could still be. She breathed when he did. Her chest rose and fell, rose and fell, with his notes until they felt knitted into her lungs, holding her steady. She envisioned him sitting on a hill in the dark, illumined by constellations, his face to the west.

And when it ended, when his voice and his music faded into silence, Adaira opened her eyes.

The last cramps in her body were subsiding.

She stared up at the ceiling, watching the shadows dance as she continued to breathe slowly and deeply. She was about to drift off to sleep when a peal of thunder shook the castle. The stones rumbled beneath her, and the pitcher and washbasin rattled on the side table. The wardrobe doors swung open. Books and candlesticks vibrated on the mantel.

The fire nearly died in the hearth.

Lightning flashed erratically as the wind began to howl. The temperature plummeted, as though summer had crumbled into winter, and Adaira shivered on the floor as rain began to pelt the window. The storm that broke was perhaps one of the most vicious she had ever experienced. It was fear that dragged her up to her unsteady feet and made her hurry to latch the window before the wind tore it from its hinges. She saw that the gale had cracked the glass.

Thunder boomed again, shaking the fortress to its roots.

Adaira backed away from the window, her heart in her throat as the lightning split the darkness like tree roots, claiming every corner of the sky. The backs of her knees found the bed, and she sat. She watched, blinking the blurriness from her eyes, as the storm continued to rage.

Her memories drew her back in time.

She had been this afraid once before, on the ledge of Tilting Thom. Bane had materialized, furious at Jack for singing. The storm he had wrought as punishment had been a terrifying experience . . . but she hadn't been alone.

Jack had been with her. His fingers had been laced through her own.

You're lonely . . . I can see it in your eyes. I can see it in the way you walk.

Rab's voice was the last one Adaira wanted to hear, but his words reverberated through her, striking her weak points. She drew her knees to her chest, wondering who she was becoming. She tried to see herself in a month, in a year. Through springs and summers, autumns and winters. Through rain, drought, famine, plenty. Would she grow old here, living out her days as a hollow shell of who she had been? What was her true place among the Breccans?

As hard as she tried, she couldn't see the path she wanted to forge.

But perhaps that was because she still didn't know where she belonged.

"Cora?"

She gingerly rose to answer the knock on the door and found Innes waiting in the corridor.

Adaira must have looked worse than she realized, because her mother stepped inside and shut the door, concern shining in her eyes.

"Don't worry," Adaira said in a strange tone. A voice that sounded old and defeated. One she didn't recognize. "I held it down."

Innes was silent for a moment, but then she reached out her hand, caressing the damp waves of Adaira's hair.

"Come sit," the laird said.

Wearily, Adaira sat in a plush chair by the hearth. She was astonished when Innes began to gently remove the remaining jewels from her hair, setting them in the wooden box they had been delivered in earlier that day. They weren't sapphires, but they were beautiful all the same. Small yet fierce stones, glittering like ice. Adaira was wondering where they came from—if the jewels hid in western mines—when the laird began to brush the tangles from her hair.

It made her think of Lorna and all the evenings she had done the very same.

Adaira clenched her eyes shut, forcing the tears to dissolve beneath her lashes. She hoped Innes didn't notice.

"You said the other doses will get easier?" she whispered as a distraction.

"Yes. Do you want to keep taking them?"

Adaira was quiet as Innes continued to brush her hair into silk. She thought it very possible that Innes would have blessed a raid if Adaira hadn't been present at dinner. There were many facets of her blood mother that she didn't fully understand, and Adaira sighed.

"Yes." She fell quiet, listening to the storm. Then she asked, "How old was my sister when she died?"

Innes paused. When she spoke, her voice was raspy. "Skye was twelve."

Adaira envisioned her sister—long blond hair and bright blue eyes, a girl who was on the verge of becoming a woman—writhing on the floor as she succumbed to a slow, painful death. Innes on her knees, helplessly watching and holding her until the end came.

Another peal of thunder shook the walls.

"Will the nobles be able to hunt tomorrow if it's storming?" Adaira asked.

"It will make things very difficult." Innes set down the brush. "And it cannot happen again, Cora."

Adaira stiffened. "You heard him play?"

"Yes. His music has provoked this storm, and there is no telling how long it will now last." Innes walked across the room, opening the wardrobe to find a clean chemise. She laid it over the foot of the bed.

"I don't understand why the west is suffering if Jack was playing in the east," Adaira said. "It was a mere play of the wind that brought the notes here."

"I'll tell you what my grandmother once told me," Innes replied. "Music in the west upsets the northern wind. The spirits are drawn to a harp when it's in the right hands, and the songs can make them stronger or weaker, depending on the intent behind the bard's ballad. A bard could sing them to sleep or compel them to war against themselves. Given the curse of the clan line, I imagine there is a steep cost to a bard when they sing for the spirits in the east, but in the west it makes a bard incredibly powerful. There are no checks upon the bard, and so the northern wind has become that boundary, driven by the fear that the spirits could be controlled by a mortal."

Adaira was quiet, but she thought about all the times Jack had suffered when he sang for the folk. The aches and pains he felt. The blood that often flowed from his nose, the way his fingernails would split and his voice would turn hoarse. He could play for only so long before the magic debilitated him.

But after listening to Innes's explanation, Adaira couldn't resist imagining Jack singing in the west. Hearing him play to the spirits at no cost to his body.

She shivered, unable to hide the warmth that coursed through her.

"The Breccan clan has survived this long under the northern wind's constant watch," Innes continued, "but only because we fear and heed it and have locked away our music and our instruments. And I have not reigned this long only to turn foolish and challenge Bane when my winter stores are running low and my people are hungry. *That* is why your bard must not sing for you again even if he is in the east, nor must he come here with any intent to play. Do you understand, Cora?"

Adaira thought of the last time she had seen Jack. The last time she had spoken to him.

Sometimes she relived that blistered moment in her dreams, only to wake curled up on her side, weeping into the darkness.

She had loved him enough to let him go. And yet she did not feel stronger for it. Not when she realized her decision had been fueled by fear.

She had often imagined what her life would be like if she had let Jack accompany her into the west. He would be stripped of his music, forbidden to play. He would be in a land teeming with enemies, first because of what he was, and then because of whose blood ran through his veins. He would be separated from his mother and sister, who he had just reunited with in the east.

And Adaira, who had been crushed by her first love and still carried deep wounds from it, hadn't been able to see Jack being happy with her. Not if the price was giving up the essence of who he was. Eventually, he would want to leave. He would leave her, as all the people she loved inevitably did.

But the words he had sung to her earlier that night, words that had drifted over a dark expanse of kilometers . . . he longed for her, even after she had put such a distance between them. Even with all her fears and mistakes and scars.

He still wanted her.

"I'll write to him," Adaira said quietly.

CHAPTER 7

Jack didn't see Adaira's letter until sunrise, when he was walking through the kail yard. The fire still refused to burn in the hearth that morning, and he was weary from a night laden with strange dreams when he saw the raven perched outside his window, patiently waiting at the shutters. Wondering how long the raven had been there, Jack approached the bird. As soon as he retrieved the pouch fastened to its breast, the bird took off with a caw and a flap of iridescent wings.

Jack opened the leather flap, which was beaded with rain, and withdrew a crinkled letter. He recognized Adaira's handwriting on the front, where she had spelled his name in big, flourishing letters. He was about to break the seal but paused when he noticed something strange. There was a slight red stain beneath the circle of wax. Almost as if a previous seal on the letter had been removed and replaced with this one.

Chills swept through him.

Surely not, he thought as he carefully opened the letter. Yes, he could tell there was a scratch on the parchment. Someone had removed the first seal and tried to replicate it with a second.

His heart was pounding as he read:

My Old Menace,
I hate to be the bearer of wonderfully bad news, but I fear to
tell you that the song you played for me last night was carried
on the wind, making its way into the west. Can I even begin
to tell you how much I savored the sound of your voice? I
don't think I can, so read between the lines of this letter and
imagine it.
  Regretfully, due to the storm your music roused, I must
now ask you to please refrain from singing for me or doing
so in a way that would cross the clan line. I realize this
letter might be alarming, but please don't let it distress you.
I am doing well, finding my place here more and more with
each passing day. I've been busy, as I mentioned to you in
past letters, and I apologize again if my correspondence is
lacking.
  Of course, I miss you, and am (yes, quite selfishly) pleased to
know at the very least, storms aside, that you are singing and
playing again.
  Give my love to Mirin and Frae.
—A.

Jack could hardly breathe.

She had heard his music. The eastern wind had carried his
voice, his notes, over the clan line. He glanced upwards and fixed
his gaze on the western sky, which looked darkened by storm.

The Breccan territory was known to be a gray land, heavily sheltered by clouds. But Jack was worried now—worried that he might
have caused trouble for Adaira.

He reread her letter and studied the strange seal again. A suspicion was creeping over him, and he couldn't shake it off. It drew
him back into the dim, fireless cottage, where Mirin was weaving
in the shadows, patiently waiting for sunlight to spill in through

the windows to fully light her loom, and Frae was still sleeping. Jack merely nodded to his mother and slipped into his bedroom, where he found Adaira's two other letters tucked into the leaves of a book.

He studied them closely and saw similarities between all three wax seals. It wasn't as noticeable on her first letter, but it was on the second.

Bastards.

The Breccans were reading her letters, which meant they were most likely also reading the ones Jack wrote to her. And perhaps he shouldn't have been surprised by this notion, but he was. As her husband, he had expected—at the very least—the courtesy of privacy when it came to their correspondence.

He skimmed all three of her letters again, this time seeing things he hadn't before. By instructing him to "read between the lines of this letter," she had made them obvious.

"Quite subtle of you, Adaira," he murmured, but his face flushed. He hated that it had taken him so long to realize it. As he sat at his desk, Jack wondered if the two of them could communicate in code.

He pushed aside his composition for the orchard and found a blank piece of parchment. He opened his inkwell, found his quill, its nib almost worn down, and wrote:

Dear Adaira,
Duly noted.
And you're correct (not surprisingly) to say that your letter caught me off guard. But let me add this: the last thing I ever wanted was to cause trouble for you and the west. My sincerest apologies that I didn't consider this a possibility. But I see it as well as know it now. I will do what I can from here to rectify my mistake.
Also am glad to hear that all is well with you, and I hope to hear from you soon.
—Your one and only O.M.

P.S.—I did imagine your reaction between the lines. You can imagine mine now.

P.P.S.—Forgot to add that Mirin and Frae send their love.

Jack reached for his wax pourer, only to remember there was no fire to heat it. He leaned back, raking his hands through his hair with a huff of annoyance. Who were their closest neighbors? The Elliotts, if the hill spirits didn't play mischief and tack on a few more kilometers.

Jack imagined asking to "borrow a flame" from them and thought how ridiculous that sounded. But then he wondered if maybe other eastern hearths had gone dark last night.

He gathered up his letter, struck by an idea.

There was someone besides the Elliotts he needed to visit.

Sidra was crushing a medley of herbs with her pestle and mortar, a pot of oats bubbling over the fire, when she heard the dog bark. She had learned the different sounds Yirr made, and this one meant someone was at the gate.

She set down the pestle and quietly strode to the door, cracking it open to find Jack standing on the kail yard path, his gaze cautiously set on Yirr.

"Hush, Yirr," Sidra said to her dog. "It's all right. He's a friend."

The black-and-white collie whined but sat, allowing Jack to step closer.

"You're here early," Sidra remarked.

Jack smiled, but he seemed flustered. "Sorry. I should've thought about that. I hope I didn't wake you or Torin, but I needed a flame and to show you something important."

"A flame?" Sidra was intrigued, welcoming Jack inside. "And no, Torin is already at the castle for the day. Maisie is asleep, though, so if you could keep your voice low?"

Jack nodded and stepped over the threshold. Sidra latched the

door and offered him a seat at the kitchen table, pushing bundles
of herbs aside.

"Can I get you anything to eat or drink, Jack? I've got parritch
on the fire, as well as a kettle for tea."

"No, but thank you, Sidra. Just a flame and your wax seal."

When she gaped at him, he held up a letter.

"For Adaira," he clarified.

Sidra shut her mouth and quietly stole into the bedroom to
fetch the wax and seal from her desk. Maisie was still sprawled in
the middle of the bed, sleeping in a tangle of blankets, and Sidra
glanced at her daughter before returning to the common room.

"Dare I ask what has happened?" she said, watching as Jack
began to warm wax over a candle flame.

"Yes," he said. "The fire has died in Mirin's hearth, to begin
with."

Sidra's heart stuttered. "What?"

She listened as Jack recounted the previous night, as well as
that morning. How nothing would light, not kindling or wood or
peat. Not even the candles.

"This is troubling news," Sidra said, but her attention was
quickly caught by Jack's disastrous letter-sealing skills. "And that is
quite a bit of wax you're using."

"Aye," he said vibrantly. "And good luck to the bastard who
opens this first."

Sidra lowered herself to a chair, watching as Jack pressed the
Tamerlaine seal into the huge mound of wax.

"They're reading Adaira's post?" she drawled in disbelief.

"Yes," Jack replied. "And I should have realized it sooner. All
of us should have. Tell Torin not to write anything sensitive in his
letters, because the Breccans are reading it."

"How do you know this, Jack?"

Jack explained, showing the wax stain on Adaira's recent letter,
which he had brought with him. "They remove her seal, or ours,
read the letter, and reseal it."

"That's . . . I can't even think of a word to say!"

"Despicable?" Jack offered.

"*Yes*," Sidra hissed. "Poor Adi. Do you think . . . ?"

"She's all right, but now it makes sense why her letters have been few and far between."

The kettle began to hiss on the hearth. Sidra made to rise, but felt a sharp twinge in her left foot. It was so unexpected that she almost lost her balance, and Jack quickly stood, hand outstretched to catch her.

"I'm fine," she said, waving away his concern. "Here, do you want a cup of tea before you go?"

"No, but thank you for the wax and the flame," Jack said. "I also came here to ask you for a tonic or two."

"What for?" Sidra asked, removing the kettle from the iron hook.

Jack was quiet for a beat, drawing her attention. He was gazing down at the letter in his hand, with its blob of a seal, but when he glanced up once more, a faint smile was on his lips.

"I'm going to sing for the spirits again."

Sidra waited until Jack had departed and the cottage was quiet once more.

Exhausted, she sat down in the chair that Donella had once haunted when the ghost had paid her seasonal visits. She poured herself a cup of tea and watched the steam rise in the morning light.

You're procrastinating.

She sighed and unlaced her boot, letting it slip from her foot. She reached for her stocking, drawing it down her leg. There were any number of reasons why her foot had emitted that sharp ache, and she wanted to reassure herself, to brush away her worries. There had been nothing to see that morning when she dressed. She knew, because she had been keeping a close eye on it.

With the stocking peeled away, Sidra stared down at the curve of her foot, then blinked, shock tangling like briars in her chest. There was a small spot that could nearly pass for a bruise but wasn't. A mottled touch of purple and gold on her heel. Blight was seeping beneath her olive-toned skin.

Sidra drew the stocking back onto her foot.

CHAPTER 8

Adaira had never seen such a sad, dismal library. She stood before the bare shelves, sifting through the scant collection of tattered books. Pages were torn and stained, ink was smudged, and the spines were cracked, barely holding on by their threads. She paused, gently leafing through one of the books, but she didn't feel like reading. Her temples still throbbed faintly from the Aethyn dosage, and her vision remained blurred around the edges.

"I thought I would find you here."

She turned, not at all surprised to see her father standing before one of the rain-streaked windows, a tall silhouette against the storm light. With Innes away for the next two days, hunting with the nobility, Adaira had expected David to keep an eye on her.

"How are you feeling today?" he asked.

"I'm fine," she replied. She set the book back on the shelf. "Do Breccans borrow books from this library only to keep them?"

"You are disappointed with our collection?"

Adaira chewed on her lip, glancing around at the bareness. "I can't seem to find what I'm looking for."

"That's because you are in the old library."

"There's another?"

He only inclined his head, a quiet invitation, before he walked away. Adaira followed him through the stone-carved aisles, staring at his fawn-brown hair, brushed long and loose beneath the silver circlet on his brow. He was dressed in a blue tunic and armor—a leather breastplate with fine stitching, vambraces on his forearms, boots that gleamed with enchanted stealth threads, the gloves he never took off his hands. A sword was sheathed at his side, as if he had been heading to the armory before taking a detour to the library.

He stopped in the shadow of a door made of pale, radiant wood.

Adaira said, "This door is locked. I've already tried it."

"Of course it's locked," David replied in a wry tone, as if he were amused that she had attempted to pass through it. "Give me your hand."

She hesitated at first. But she was curious.

Adaira stretched out her hand.

She didn't flinch when David withdrew his dirk. She bit her tongue when he nicked her fingertip, her blood welling bright as a ruby.

"Now touch the door," he said.

She shivered but laid her hand upon the wood, letting it taste her blood. It unlocked, swinging open with a creak. Adaira stared at the chamber within, a room full of books and scrolls and candles.

Before that moment, she hadn't given much thought to the mortal-forged enchantments that might hide within the Breccan fortress, because such things had been nonexistent in the east. Now it felt like her father had just shared a secret with her, much as Innes had done with the burrow. Another measure of trust and freedom, and one that she yearned for. To move through the castle and open doors that she had once believed locked to her.

"The new library," David said, seeming to sense the deep eddy of her thoughts.

Adaira glanced up at him. He wasn't smiling, but she was startled for a moment to see that his hazel eyes were alight with mirth, as if she had caught a reflection of herself within him. She passed over the threshold.

She was greeted by the scent of old parchment and leather. Iron candelabras and beeswax candles. Wine-dark ink and cedarwood. This room was not as big as the other library, but it didn't feel as ancient either. Adaira walked the aisles, noticing that the shelves were hewn from wood that held a faint gleam.

"An enchanted library?" she asked.

"In some ways," David replied. "This castle was built long before the clan line was formed, when magic began to flow freely from our hands and craft. But the shelves are much younger, cut by an enchanted axe. Lay your hand upon one and tell it what you are looking for. If the library holds such a book, it will show you."

Adaira stopped before one shelf, wondering if she dared utter what she wanted. It was dangerous to expose such things. But ever since her conversation with Innes the night before, it was all Adaira could mull over. *We have locked away our music and our instruments.* Which meant they hadn't been destroyed but were still somewhere in the west. And that made Adaira believe that the Breccans still harbored a shred of hope. That they longed for those days in the past when music had filled their halls, when they hadn't bowed in fear to the wind.

There also was more to what Innes had shared with her, whether the laird knew the truth or not.

Adaira traced the wooden shelf, letting her fingers linger upon it.

"I'm looking for a book of music," she whispered. "I'm looking for records of the last Bard of the West."

Only silence answered her. She let her hand fall away, then turned when David approached her.

"You won't find any books like that here," he said. He didn't sound angry or annoyed, as Adaira half expected him to be. He sounded weary and sad.

"Why? Surely the Breccans once had a bard. Someone to hold the history and stories of your people."

"We did, and he caused a terrible amount of trouble for the clan," David replied. "Instead of playing to strengthen the people, he played to gain more power for himself. Instead of playing to make harmony among the spirits, he played to command them. It didn't take long for the fire to grow weak, the crops to fail, the tides to flood, and the wind to become far harsher than it should."

"How long ago was this?" Adaira asked.

"When Joan Tamerlaine crossed into the west to marry Fingal Breccan," David said. "That is when all the problems began. A legend I'm sure you know well."

Adaira did, although the tale she had been told was most likely different from the one David had heard. She had been fed the eastern version, which painted Joan as a selfless woman who bound herself to the Breccan laird to secure peace for the isle. But Fingal had wanted her only for her beauty and never had any intention to cease his violent raids on the east. Joan and Fingal had quarreled and killed each other in the thick of Cadence, spilling each other's blood as they died entwined, both full of hatred and spite. Their enmity had created the clan line, a magical boundary that separated the west from the east, and the spirits of the isle and their magic had been greatly affected by it.

"Yes, I know the legend," Adaira said.

Dwelling on Joan reminded her of the broken book Maisie had given her. It was missing its second half but was full of handwritten legends and stories. The book had once belonged to Joan, and Adaira suddenly wondered: *Is the missing half here in the Breccans' library?* Perhaps Joan had left it behind when she attempted to flee to the east.

Adaira laid her hand upon the shelf. "I would like the second half of Joan's journal."

Again, the shelves remained quiet. No rustle of movement or flicker of magic.

She sighed. "Some enchantment. I'm not entirely sure you've been forthright with me."

"You merely ask for things we don't have," David said. And then he shocked her by abruptly saying, "Did the eastern laird teach you how to handle a sword?"

"Yes, of course he did," Adaira answered, inevitably thinking of Alastair. "Why do you ask me that?"

"I would like to measure your skills," he said, turning to the doorway. "To see for myself how well they taught you."

"In the rain?"

David paused on the threshold, hands laced behind his back. "You'll soon learn that if we halted our lives every time it storms, there would be little life remaining to live. We make the most of what we have here."

Half an hour later, Adaira had chosen a long sword from the armory and followed David into a training ring. Or she had assumed it was a training ring. Once she stood in the center of it, she realized it was an open-air arena. Wooden stands for a vast audience surrounded them. The sand beneath her boots was riddled with ankle-deep puddles; she could feel the water begin to seep through the leather as she tripped over a mound.

"What is this place?" she asked, raising her voice so David could hear her over the downpour.

"A place for me to test your skills," he replied, walking to the center of the arena.

Adaira followed, struggling to see him in the rain. Her hair was drenched and her clothes felt heavy and rough against her skin. She couldn't explain the disquiet she felt or what had sparked it. The eerie, empty arena. The uneven ground she was about to spar over. The difficulty of seeing in the storm. The lingering effects of the Aethyn in her blood.

"Have you changed your mind, Cora?" David asked, sensing her reluctance.

Adaira came to a stop, three paces away from him. "No."

"Then draw your sword."

Her hand found the hilt. As she drew the sword from its scabbard, wielding a weapon for the first time since arriving in the west, Adaira wondered if this was another test. She didn't know much about David. She had conversed with him only when she had dinner with him and Innes in their quarters and when he delivered her letters. Letters that he read, as if he trusted neither her nor Jack, Sidra, and Torin. As if she had come to live with them for no other reason than to plot the Breccans' demise. Adaira felt her anger stir as she held her sword in middle guard.

"Does Innes know you've armed me?" she asked, a touch wryly.

"I never do anything without Innes knowing," David said, deeply serious. "Now . . . take a strike at me."

Adaira lunged forward, teeth clenched. She took a hard cut at David, but he moved effortlessly, as if he were part of the rain. He blocked her with his sword, and Adaira stumbled back, her hands stinging from the clash.

"Again," he said.

Adaira blinked against the water streaming down her face. Stars danced at the corners of her eyes and her head continued to throb, but she didn't want to look weak in front of him. She soon fell into stride with the storm and the uneven ground, drawing from her memories. The lessons Alastair had once given her. Torin observing and calling out tips. Warm, sun-drenched days on the training green at Castle Sloane.

David blocked her cuts with ease. Again and again, as if he were reading her mind, knowing her actions before she took them.

It became infuriating. Adaira couldn't even make him flinch. She couldn't provoke him to strike back—their sparring was simply her cutting and him blocking—and she began to strike at him with harder cuts, her feet digging a trench around him in the sand.

"You're striking me in anger," David finally said. "Why?"

Adaira stepped back. Her lungs were burning, her arms trembling. She stared at David through the wash of rain and tried to read his expression, but his face was like stone.

She sought to measure her anger, but its roots ran deep within her. Anger at David for letting Innes give her up. For holding a small, weakly child spun from his own blood and breath and believing she was better off in another realm. For not fighting for her.

And yet, if he hadn't given her up, Adaira would have never known the Tamerlaines. Lorna and Alastair, who had loved her as their own, but lied to her. Torin and Sidra and Maisie. Jack, who would have never been born had the Breccans not handed her over to the Keeper of the Aithwood.

Her emotions suddenly felt tangled, her chest small and cracked.

But the only words she could find to say to him were, "You're reading my letters."

David was quiet. Adaira could tell she had caught him off guard.

"You think it wrong of me," he finally stated.

"As a laird's consort? No," Adaira replied. "But as a father? Yes."

This time when she cut her sword at him, he moved. He blocked and lunged, forcing her into a short guard to protect herself. They fell into a stilted dance of a spar, kicking up clumps of sand and splashing through small streams. If this had happened a week earlier, Adaira might have felt a thread of fear. Fear that David had brought her to the arena with the intention to test more than her skills. But she realized now that he was giving her a way to channel her fury and the hurt that lurked beneath it. He was letting her unleash her anger on him, as if he knew the two of them couldn't move forward without this altercation.

She bared her teeth, catching him by surprise with a feint to the left. His block was slow. He winced as if in pain, and Adaira reacted without thinking. Her sword grazed his side. If she had pushed any harder, the sword would have pierced him.

David grunted and swung around with such speed that Adaira couldn't parry his blade. It struck her upper arm, slicing through her drenched sleeve.

She stumbled away, dropping her sword. The fiery pain was disorienting, and the world felt like it was tilting. She grasped her arm, the blood welling between her fingers.

"Dammit," David said, sheathing his sword. "Cora? *Cora!*"

She fell to her knees. She felt like she was sinking in a bog, and she gasped for breath, tasting the brine of the rain. Her blood felt cold, crackling with frost. Had his sword been enchanted? She hadn't noticed radiance in the steel, but perhaps she had missed it in the storm. When she drew her hand away from her wound, she saw that the blood had beaded on her skin. It looked like tiny red jewels, slowly deepening to a dusky blue color as they hardened. They glittered in her palm like chips of ice.

"What is this?" she whispered, letting the gemstones tumble from her hand.

"Cora, look at me."

A man stood before her, in sharp relief against the gray rain. It was Alastair, reaching down to steady her.

"*Father?*" she breathed.

Hope crushed the last air from her lungs as she plunged into darkness.

She was lying on a bench when she came to, staring up at a shadowed ceiling. The air smelled like crushed herbs, stringent salves, honey, and black tea. For a moment, Adaira thought she might be in Sidra's house, and her heart twisted in her chest when her memories flooded back.

She was in the west. She had been sparring with David in the rain. Her blood had spilled like gemstones through her fingers.

Adaira turned her head, blinking into the candlelight.

David was sitting on a stool before a battered worktable. Shelves lined the stone wall before him, crowded with glass jars and earthenware vessels, pestles and mortars, clusters of dried herbs. He must have felt her gaze because he turned to look at her.

"Did I faint?" she asked, mortified.

"Yes. Do you want to sit up?"

She nodded, allowing him to help ease her forward. Her vision swam for a moment, but she blinked until she felt steady.

"I don't understand what happened," she said. "I've never fainted at the sight of blood."

"You should have told me you were still feeling the effects of the Aethyn," he gently chided.

Adaira licked her dry lips. When David handed her a cup of water, she saw the small blue jewels, gleaming on the tabletop.

"I thought your sword was enchanted," she said.

"No. The poison was still in your blood." He took one of the jewels between his gloved fingertips, holding it up to the light before setting it on her palm. Adaira studied it, realizing the jewel was similar to the gemstones she had worn in her hair at the thanes' dinner. The same jewels Innes had been wearing in hers.

"Whose blood was in my hair last night?" she asked in a wavering tone.

"It belonged to the thane who murdered your sister," David answered.

"I still don't understand."

"Aethyn is a flower that grows here," he said, refilling her cup with water after she drained it. "It blooms only in the most perilous of places, which makes it deadly to harvest. But if one *does* survive in obtaining it, then the true strength of the flower comes forth, and it creates a poison that settles in the blood like ice. It slows the heart, the mind, the soul. In heavy doses, it is lethal, and there is no antidote to counter it. In lighter doses, one builds up a tolerance to it, or it can be used to punish one's enemies. Either way, it turns shed blood into blue jewels, and many of the nobles wear these stones as jewelry to display their ruthlessness."

Adaira continued to gaze at the jewel in her hand. It was tiny, not nearly the size of the ones she had worn in her hair. The blood of the man who had killed Skye.

"I take it the higher the dose, the larger the jewels?" she said.

David paused for a moment before saying, "Yes. As your blood foretold in the arena, you have only a trace left in your body."

"When you pricked my finger earlier, to unlock the door," Adaira began, meeting David's gaze, "why didn't it turn into a jewel then?"

"Because the door accepted your blood before it could," he answered simply.

She stifled a shiver. Her clothes were still damp from the rain, and she could feel the gritty sand that had worked its way into her boots. She wanted to bathe in the warm cistern, to wash away the past hour. But when she set the cup aside, a sharp pain flickered through her arm.

Adaira pushed up her sleeve.

A long, thin wound wrapped around her upper arm, but tightly woven stitches had brought her skin back together. She traced them, feeling the ridges and the dull ache they inspired.

"I'm sorry," David said hoarsely. "I never meant to hurt you."

Adaira let her sleeve fall. She was almost afraid to look at him because she could hear the layers of his apology.

I'm sorry for breaking your skin. I'm sorry for reading your post. I'm sorry for abandoning you to the spirits. I'm sorry I let you go without a fight.

She could feel the raw edges of her heart. She could still see Alastair, reaching down to draw her up from the ground. From her pain and her confusion. Only it had never been him. It had been nothing more than a poison-addled mirage—she had seen what she *wanted* in that moment.

She cleared her throat and drawled, "Are you afraid of what Innes will do when she finds out you scratched me?"

David laughed, a sound so rich and warm it startled Adaira, but she soon smiled, unable to resist.

"Yes, Innes will be very displeased with me," he said, reaching for a swath of linen on the table. "I will be paying my penance for a while. Here, let me see your arm."

Adaira drew up the sleeve again and watched as David carefully dabbed a honey salve over the stitches.

"You're a healer," she stated.

"Yes. That surprises you?"

Adaira bit her lip, gazing at the leather gloves he wore, as if he didn't want to touch others. "A little, yes."

He began to wind her upper arm with the linen. "It's how I fell in love with Innes."

"That sounds like the making of a ballad," Adaira said.

A corner of David's mouth lifted, but he suppressed the smile. "Innes was the third child of the laird. The youngest. She felt as if she had much to prove to be chosen as the next ruler of the west, so she was constantly training, pushing her body to be faster and stronger than her brothers. She was constantly sparring, until whatever weapon she chose to wield became a part of her."

He paused as he finished bandaging Adaira's arm. "As you might imagine, she garnered quite a few wounds over the years. She would always come to me, asking me to heal her. And so I did, though I was angry with her for how frequently she knocked upon my door, bleeding and broken, sometimes so battered that she had to sleep in my bed so I could watch over her through the night. I was angry not because she was inconveniencing me, but because I was afraid she would one day push herself too hard and fail to show up at my door."

Adaira was silent, imagining this younger version of Innes. The vision roused tender and sad feelings that made her shoulders curl inward.

"She would always say that her wounds made her resilient, that her scars prepared her for the lairdship more than fine quarters and richly spun clothes and abundant feasts," David said, rising from the stool. "But that's enough for one day. You'll want to visit the cistern, I take it?"

His abrupt change of topic was jarring, but Adaira sensed he was closing whatever door had just cracked open. His face looked flushed, as though he regretted speaking so openly.

"Yes, that would be nice," she said.

"Then I'll make arrangements for you to visit," David offered. "In the meantime, this sword is now yours." He indicated the sheathed blade propped by the door. The one Adaira had chosen for their spar. It wasn't an enchanted sword, but it was still a weapon in her hands.

She arched a brow. "You're officially arming me?"

"Is it a mistake for us to do so?"

"No. But you seem to fear that I have ill intentions toward the west."

David leaned against the edge of the table, arms crossed. "You speak of your post."

She nodded.

"If I wrote a letter to Moray," he began, "would the eastern laird read it? And likewise, if Moray wrote to me—which he hasn't— would the eastern laird read it too before sending it?"

Adaira felt the heat rising in her skin. "I don't think that's a fair comparison, given what I haven't done versus what Moray has."

"That much is true, Cora. But even in the face of such truths, you cannot deny that the Breccans and the Tamerlaines have a long, bloody history, and unfortunately you are caught between the two clans."

"By no choice of my own," she said.

David was silent, but Adaira knew he felt the sting of her words.

She stood with a sigh, thankful she felt steady. She reached for her new sword, belting it to her waist. She liked the weight of it, and how reassuring it felt.

It felt like power.

"Whatever happened to him?" she dared to ask.

"To whom?" David said.

"To the man who carried me eastward."

David turned away and began to clean up his worktable. But a chill had fallen between them. When he finally spoke, his voice was clipped, as if the rapport they had been building had crumbled. "I'm afraid I can't answer that, Cora."

Dismissed, Adaira left the chamber, which fed into the armory. She eventually found her way back to the winding corridors.

Adaira walked slowly, lost in her thoughts and pondering what she had just learned. Her heart was heavy until she reconsidered David's parting words to her. If he was refusing to answer her question, then chances were that Jack's father wasn't dead.

He was still alive.

CHAPTER 9

"You're certain about this, Jack?" Torin asked for the third time, pacing through the long grass.

Jack glanced sidelong at him, thinking *now* was not the best time for doubt. Not with his new harp in hand and the sick orchard spread before them, dappled in shade. But neither could he fully fault Torin for being skeptical. Jack vividly remembered the night he had first sung for the spirits. He had struggled to believe Adaira's wild claim that his music was powerful and binding enough to entice the folk to manifest.

"I'm certain," he said.

Blue evening shadows draped the orchard, half of which was now consumed by the blight. Rodina had been sent away from the croft, and only Torin and Jack stood in the twilit yard. Even all the cats had been rounded up, which had been no simple feat.

Jack eased closer to the trees to study the glittering sap. The month before, when he sang to the earth, the alder trees around him had become maidens. The pennywort had transformed into lads. Wildflowers had woven together to form a ruling lady. Stones had found their faces.

So while Jack's eyes saw blighted apple trees, he also sensed that it was the maidens in the parallel realm, the spirits who dwelt in these trees, who were ill. If he could summon and draw one of the maidens from a healthy tree, then perhaps she could provide answers.

"When can you begin playing?" Torin asked.

"I'm ready now," Jack replied. He settled in the grass, the harp in his lap, and began to warm his fingers with a scale. "Whatever manifests, don't draw your weapon, Torin."

Torin was silent, but from the corner of his eye, Jack saw the laird's hand twitch toward the hilt of his sheathed sword.

Jack began to play the ballad he had penned for the plight of the orchard. He sang an invitation to the trees, sang his worship of their existence. His notes resounded in the air, settling like snow on the branches, gleaming like frost on the bark. He sensed the trees falling solemn, their shadows running long and crooked over the grass as they answered his call.

A maiden with white apple blossoms in her emerald hair began to spin herself from the boughs and leaves. Her face, still forming from a burl, wrinkled as if she were in pain.

Jack was so intent upon her transformation that he didn't see the storm blow in. He didn't feel the shift of temperature until it was too late. The northern wind blasted through the grove, slashing the last light of eventide. Jack lifted his eyes to study the dark clouds boiling overhead. A stinging rain began to fall.

He knew this wind.

"Should you stop?" Torin asked, sensing the danger that lurked just beyond the clouds.

Jack considered stopping, but for just a breath. He had to ask himself: What sort of bard did he want to be? Would he be one who sang in defiance of the northern wind? Or would he fall prey to fear and submit to what Bane wanted, which was his eternal silence?

Angry, Jack continued to play, his nails plucking music from the strings faster and faster, as if he could outplay the storm. But a strange tingling rippled over his skin. He could feel it in his teeth. A hum of warning.

He had experienced this before. On a mountaintop with Adaira. When he had summoned the four winds without knowing the cost of such foolish bravery. When he had held Bane captive for one mesmerizing, desperate moment.

Playing his music had nearly killed him that day.

"Stand down, Jack!" Torin's shout was hardly discernible as the storm howled. "*Stand down!*"

Jack pressed on, his voice rising and weaving into the wind. The clouds darkened, and the gusts grew so strong they nearly lifted him off the ground. The rain pelted his face and his hands, and yet Jack didn't stop, didn't sway, didn't bend to the northern wind.

He had a moment of unexpected relief, even as the raging storm came terrifyingly close. If Bane was here, then he was no longer wreaking his havoc in the west. Adaira might be standing under a blue sky, enjoying a break in the clouds.

The thought fueled Jack onward as he continued to sing for the orchard, but his voice was small and weak compared to the northern wind. He drew a deep breath, filling his chest with air so cold it made him think of winter. He strummed onward, even as his nails began to weaken.

The magic was eclipsing his strength. He could feel the pain surging through him.

I'm pushing myself too hard, he thought. But he had Sidra's tonics ready in his satchel, and he knew he had more to give.

"Jack! *Enough!* Cease this!" Torin's order melted in the storm as the laird was blown off his feet and forced to scramble in the grass.

Jack watched the dark clouds split above him, pulsing with lightning. He felt the rustle of invisible wings encircle him, taunting him. And then they withdrew, leaving him vulnerable and alone. He was one lyric away from being struck. He sensed it, felt the white-heat crackle and gather around him. The hair on his arms rose.

I will not bend I will not bend I will not—

He surrendered.

He bent.

He dropped the harp and knelt.

His final note died in the storm. He closed his mouth and swallowed the last of his ballad.

Bane's lightning struck the closest apple tree. It was the spirit who had been transforming to answer Jack's call. The beam sliced the maiden in half, clean through her heart. The sound rent the air, and the earth shook and wept.

The tang of scorched applewood permeated the grove. Smoke rose from the orchard, dancing on the wind.

Jack felt the edge of his mortality. Terrified, he fell to the grass, face first.

A throb of emotions knotted in his chest. He was relieved that Bane hadn't struck him. He was terrified that he had been *one* lyric away from being divided himself. One lyric away from being cut through his own heart. He was ashamed that he had not outlasted the northern wind, and that a tree had taken the punishment for his defiance.

Jack knew then what sort of bard he was as he lay there, dazed, in the mud.

A weak and foolish one.

Adaira was in the castle stables, brushing one of the horses and listening to the rain drip from the eaves. She liked to come here, to hide herself in the comforting scent of horses, tanned leather, and sweet summer grains. It was a place that felt comfortable, a place that felt like home. The grooms had finally become accustomed to her daily visits and allowed her to curry a few of the gentler steeds on her own.

A bird flew into the stall and found a perch in the corner. Adaira watched as it shook the rain from its wings. She continued to curry the horse, but she imagined what it must feel like to be a bird, to have the freedom to fly from place to place.

A moment later, the storm abated.

Adaira paused, then stepped around the horse to slide open the stall window. The dark clouds were breaking, the northern wind retreating.

Shouts echoed through the barn. Horses whinnied, stomping their hooves. The bird darted out the window with a chirp.

Adaira slipped from the stall and followed the grooms into the castle courtyard. She gazed toward the western horizon, squinting against the brightness. Unfamiliar in a land of clouds and winds, light had arrived, fragile yet radiant, transforming the gray west into a world of glittering windows and steaming cobblestones.

Adaira smiled as she watched the sun set.

Torin, sore and exhausted, his eyes still haunted by lightning, stumbled home in the rain. The song for the orchard had failed, and now he needed another plan.

He had no idea what to do.

He stepped into the cottage, tore off his drenched plaid, his muddy boots, his anger, and his indecision, leaving them all in a heap by the door. It was only then that he noticed how quiet and serene the house was.

The fire in the hearth was burning low, casting rosy hues on the walls, making monstrous shadows out of Sidra's drying herbs, which hung in clusters from the ceiling beams. Yirr was curled up on the rug, one eye open. The fragrance of supper still lingered in the air: warm bread and roasted quail and potatoes, rosemary and apple cider. The floor was swept clean, and the rain tapped against the shutters.

Sidra appeared in the doorway to their bedroom, illumined by candlelight, her dark hair brushed into loose waves. She was wearing her chemise and stockings, and her eyes were swollen. He had woken her. How late was it? He seemed to have lost track of time.

"Is Maisie . . . ?"

"She's with your father tonight," Sidra replied. She stared at Torin a moment, and he feared she would ask him what had happened. But she didn't. She only whispered, "Have you eaten? I can warm you up some supper."

"I'm ravenous," he said, but he caught her before she could move to the kitchen. He had felt scattered in a hundred different directions until he took her in his arms and her softness, her warmth, met his body and sharpened him, brought him into focus. He heard the catch of her breath when he pressed his mouth to her neck, his fingers unlacing the ribbons of her chemise.

"Torin," she gasped. He felt her stiffen as her raiment began to loosen. This response from her was unfamiliar, unexpected.

At once, he stopped.

"Sid? What is it?" He tucked her hair behind her ear, anxious to see her face. When her eyes remained downcast, he gently lifted her chin, so her gaze would find his. "Is something troubling you?"

He thought perhaps it was the news of the fire dying in Mirin's hearth. Or the fear of the blight spreading further. Every passing hour seemed to bring something heavy and strange.

Sidra drew in a deep breath, and he swore he saw a flash of sorrow in her eyes. But then it was gone like a storm breaking. She smiled at him, the smile that made him forget everything apart from her, and she took his hands and guided him into their room.

He marveled yet again that he had won her love, that the isle had made their paths cross. Her fingers slid free from his and he stopped, intently watching as she backed away from him. She blew out the candles, one by one. Darkness unfurled, and the room felt far too vast, the distance between them almost painful.

Torin's heart quickened as he listened to her clothes hit the floor somewhere to his left. Her bare feet drew close to him again; her hands reached out and found him, unfastened his belt, lifted his sodden tunic away.

Somehow, they made it to the bed. Torin's skin was gooseflesh beneath her confidence, his hair still dripping from the storm. But Sidra's mouth was hot, crushing against his. He had her memorized; he did not need light, nor did she.

His fingertips traced the curve of her back. He could hear her breathe in the darkness, shallow and quick, in contrast to his own breathing. She moved like there was nothing in this world but the two of them and he surged forward to bury his face in her neck. There was a faint scent of earth on her skin—loam and herbs and crushed flowers—and he kissed her mouth, her collarbones, the crook of her elbow, tasting her sweat. He was both lost and found within her, and when she cried out, he swiftly followed her over the edge.

Afterwards, it took Torin a few moments to remember the fleeting sadness he had seen in Sidra's eyes. She lay against him, her hair streaming across his chest, her skin damp against his.

He traced the flare of her hip, waiting for his heart to calm. "What did you need to tell me, Sid?"

"Hmm?"

"Before. When I came home. You started to say something . . ."

She shifted away from him. Torin tightened his hold on her, and she chuckled at his insistence and kissed his shoulder. "I wanted to ask how the orchard song went. Was Jack successful? Did you speak to one of the spirits about the blight?"

Torin groaned, the memory flooding back into him. "No."

He told her of the debacle, how Jack had defied his orders to halt the ballad. How the lightning struck a few paces away from the bard, and how everything seemed to shatter in that moment— earth, sky, rain, light. Shatter and then come back together in alarming clarity.

"I don't know what to do, Sid," he whispered, his fingers sliding into her hair. "I don't know what to do, and all I can think is how unfit I am to be laird. This must be a punishment for something. The isle must find me lacking."

"Enough." Sidra's voice was sharp. "You're a good laird to our clan."

His hand wandered, finding her face in the dark. His thumb traced her lips. "With you at my side."

"Yes," Sidra whispered but pulled his hand away, kissing his palm, his mouth. "Now sleep, Torin."

He didn't have the strength to disobey her. He drew the quilt up around them, and she settled against him.

He was almost asleep, the rain lulling him into the beginnings of a dream. But then he startled, and his thoughts were spinning. Descending.

"Are you still awake, Sid?"

"Yes."

He couldn't breathe for a moment, and she shifted, turning to face him in the darkness, as if she sensed his worry.

"If I should become cold . . . a stone-hearted man," he whispered. "If I ever do something you don't agree with, I want you to tell me."

"Always," she promised.

Her voice was calm, a smoky reassurance. He had never felt safer than he did in that moment, lying in her arms in the dark as the rain eased up beyond the windows.

And he dreamt of simpler days, when he was a boy running through the heather.

Sidra lay awake, her eyes open to the night. She had been awake for hours, with Torin's steady breaths stirring her hair, his arm a pleasant weight upon her.

She was supposed to tell him that night. She had wanted to tell him, but when the moment had come, she had found the words nearly impossible to speak.

Even so, she had been prepared for that. For the words to fail her. She had planned to then show him. She would bring him into the room and sit on the edge of their mattress. Pull away her stocking and show him the place on her heel. The blight was spreading, faster than she had hoped. It was reaching for her toes, and she had yet to find a cure, despite the countless hours she had labored over it, the prayers she had uttered to the spirits.

What can heal this blight?

She feared the spirits wouldn't be able to answer her. And she didn't want to tell Torin she was infected until she had a plan, a cure.

She could let him live in ignorance another day.

CHAPTER 10

J ack didn't go to the castle after the orchard failure. He knew Mirin and Frae were there, tucked away in one of the guest suites for the night, and he pictured them for a moment: Mirin would be restless without her loom, and Frae would be doing her school lessons, most likely reading aloud to keep their mother distracted. But they would be warm and safe, sitting beside a crackling fire in the hearth.

Jack was deeply thankful to Sidra for making the arrangements for his mother and sister to sleep in the castle until the flames returned to Mirin's hearth. It was both a relief and a mystery that no other cottage had lost its fire. Only Mirin's.

Jack mulled over those thoughts as he walked through the rain-soaked hills, all the way to his darkened home, carrying his hunger, his defeat, and Lorna's harp.

The cottage felt hollow without firelight, without his mother and sister. Jack stood in the darkness, dripping rain onto the floor. He listened to the sounds of the house as if he might find inspiration within its deep shadows—the beginning of a song he had yet to hear on the isle—but there was only the tap on the shutters, and the creak of the latched door, and the storm gradually abating beyond the damp walls.

With a sigh, Jack removed his drenched garments and then fumbled in the darkness to find the oaken chest in his bedroom. After dressing in dry clothes, he felt his way back into the common room. He tripped over one of Frae's scarves, stumbled into Mirin's hassock. But at last Jack reached the hearth, full of cold ashes.

He had been waiting for this moment. A moment when he could be alone with the mischievous fire spirit.

Jack sat on the floor directly before the hearth with his harp, then reached into his satchel to find the remedies Sidra had made for him. He had already taken one in the orchard, and now he drank another to dull the pain beating behind his eyes. He opened a tin of salve, which he rubbed onto his hands. His knuckles ached and his fingernails felt jagged in the dark, but soon the magic of Sidra's herbs began to trickle through him and his pain ebbed.

He stared into the darkness, his mind full of luminous worries.

The fire spirits were the only ones he had not encountered face-to-face yet. Last month he had called to the sea, to the earth, to the air. But not the spirits of fire. Jack had discovered by talking with the other spirits that fire was the lowest in their hierarchy. Fire resided beneath the great power of air, beneath the solid weight of earth, beneath the strength of the sea. The fire spirits were considered the least of the folk, and Jack didn't know why something so vital had so lowly a standing.

He exhaled a deep breath and began to think about the notes he would play for the fire spirits and the words he would sing for them. A ballad began to take shape in his mind, and Jack decided to lean into it, improvising as he had done with Adaira's song. He was learning that there was great power in such music, in letting himself go.

He brought the harp to his shoulder, closed his eyes, and began to find notes. A scale rose to meet him and Jack hummed, seeking words to accompany his music.

All he knew was the cold dark. All he wanted was fire and fire alone.

He sang to the spirits, to the dead ashes in his hearth. He played for fire and the memory of flames.

His eyes remained closed, but he felt the warmth on his knees, on his face. He could see the light growing, and he opened his eyes to watch the kindling crackle, bright and eager. The fire spread to the wood, igniting with a sigh, and suddenly it was blazing, wild and unhindered. The fire danced high and wide. Jack had no choice but to shift backwards, its unbearable heat almost scorching his skin.

What have I done? he wondered, but he continued to play and sing, encouraging the fire to rise higher, wider. Soon, it was escaping the hearth. *I will burn the house down.*

When he thought he could play no more—his harp was smoldering in his hands, the strings sparking beneath his fingertips—the fire gathered itself together into the shape of a tall man. It was difficult to look upon his face at first. Jack squinted and ended his ballad, his voice fading. But the heat and light finally calmed, and he studied the fire spirit, awestruck.

The spirit was translucent but his manifested body seemed solid as it radiated with the shades of fire. Blue and gold, red and ocher. His face was like a mortal man's: narrow, with a heavy brow, a long nose, a cleft in his chin, and a mouth pressed into a thin line. But his eyes glimmered like embers coming back to life. His hair was long, constantly changing color. His arms were thin, malnourished, but his hands were strong, his fingertips like candle flames. Yes, there was a hungry look about him, as if he knew he was burning down his resources and there was not enough fuel to keep him alive.

"At last, Bard," said the fire spirit. His voice, like one long hiss, the words twisting in his mouth, sent a shiver through Jack. "At last you summon me."

Jack's face felt blistered, but he didn't dare move away. "Or perhaps you have summoned me?"

The spirit cackled, amused. "You speak of the cold ashes. Yes, it was the only way I could think to gain your attention."

"Why do you need my attention? How can I ensure my mother and sister have fire in this hearth? You are life to us. Surely you know that." As soon as Jack spoke the words, he regretted them. It was *foolish* to make bargains with spirits.

"There is indeed something I want of you," the fire spirit said.

"And what is that?"

The spirit opened his mouth. Flames danced on his tongue, but only ashes fell from his lips. Jack knew that the spirit's voice had been hindered by Bane.

"The northern wind has bound you," Jack whispered. He could still taste the tang of lightning in his own mouth. He could still feel the prickling of his skin.

How had a spirit of the northern wind grown so powerful? Who or what had crowned Bane, making him king of all others?

The fire spirit slumped, weary. "'Tis so, Bard. I am shackled by the northern wind. My king. I can only speak so much, and my time grows short with you."

"Should I continue to play for you? Would that strengthen you?"

"No, no. That harp is . . . he might hear you and arrive to interfere, as he did in the orchard." The spirit paused, measuring his words. "I have come to warn you, Jack of the Tamerlaines, Jack of the Breccans. My king is afraid of . . . I cannot say it, but he will soon strike the isle. Your clan cannot stand alone against him, nor can the spirits of earth and water. You will need to unite with them and join your rival clan. The isle is stronger as one, and perhaps you will be able to . . . to defeat . . . dethrone . . . *him.*"

Jack sat forward, wide-eyed. "You speak of Tamerlaines and Breccans uniting?" He almost laughed but caught the sound just before it slipped from his mouth. "And you cannot mean me. I'm not the one capable of accomplishing such a task."

Because it is impossible, he wanted to say. Unfathomable. And yet this fire spirit stared into Jack, saw the slant of his preconceptions and beliefs and lineage.

Jack was both Tamerlaine and Breccan.

His face flushed. He felt stricken by the insurmountable odds of this request.

"You are the one to bring unity, Jack. The Tamerlaines will need the Breccans, and the Breccans will need the Tamerlaines. Do not forget the earth, the sea. They are experiencing the pangs of rebellion; they are resisting his call to turn against mortals."

"Is this why the orchard has been sick?"

"Yes . . ." the fire spirit's voice was fading, his body turning diaphanous.

Jack sensed he had only a few moments left with the spirit. His mind whirled with questions he needed answers to. He struggled to decide which ones to voice, which were most important to ask before the fire died.

"Tell me how I can dethrone Bane."

The spirit hissed, pained. "I cannot . . . my mouth is barred from speaking that knowledge. You will have to travel west, Bard. You will find the answer among the Breccans."

Jack's heart became thunder. Travel west. To Adaira.

"How can we stop the blight?"

"That is not my knowledge to give. You must seek that among the earth spirits."

"Will you promise to keep this hearth alight?"

The spirit bowed. Smoke began to rise from his shoulders. "I swear it, Bard. So long as you strive to do what I ask."

Unite the clans. Discover the way to dethrone tyrannical Bane. *All simple tasks,* Jack thought, becoming almost hysterical as their implausibility sunk in.

"Take care with that harp you wield. Now I must go. Do not summon me again, or he will know."

Yet the spirit shifted closer. Jack resisted the temptation to wince, to flee from the sudden wash of heat he felt. Wide-eyed, he watched as the spirit reached out his hand, pressing his flame-riddled thumb against Jack's lips.

This time Jack flinched. The pain was sharp, like a blister suddenly rising, but after a breath it abated, leaving a remnant of numbness in his lips.

Jack watched the spirit shrink himself back into the hearth, his body giving way to flames. But his face was still there, observing Jack. It occurred to him that this spirit had been watching him from the hearth since he was a boy.

"Who are you?" Jack said.

"I am Ash. Laird of Fire. Be valiant; do not bend until the peace comes. I will be waiting for you, Jack."

The spirit vanished, but the fire in the hearth remained, burning heartily, casting light and warmth upon Jack as he continued to sit on the floor. He had never felt more chilled, more anxious, and more ill prepared.

But strangest of all . . . he could taste ashes in his mouth.

CHAPTER 11

The full moon arrived on a clear, warm night in the east. A stream of its silver light found Torin sitting in the castle library with a glass of whiskey in hand. He was at Alastair's desk, papers and ledgers and a map of the Eastern Cadence spread before him. Candles burned along the tabletop, casting rings of light on the stacks of parchment, but the darkness felt thick in the room, gathering in corners and in the rafters.

"Laird?"

He glanced up to see Yvaine stepping into the library. She was a few years older than him, with curly black hair and a scar on her jaw that she had earned during a Breccan raid. A brown-and-red plaid was fastened at her shoulder, a sword sheathed at her side. Her palm was still healing from the enchanted wound Torin had given it weeks ago, so she would be bound to the eastern territory.

"Captain," he said. "I surmise you bring an update on the new recruits?"

"No." She came to a stop on the other side of the desk, noticing the whiskey in his hand. "The blight has spread to the Ranalds' orchard."

Torin's heart sank, but he was sadly not surprised. "Has anyone caught it?"

"Yes. Their youngest son. I've roped off the orchard and given the family strict orders to stay away from the trees, even the healthy ones. But I wanted you to know."

"Thank you, Yvaine." He glanced at the map and the places he had marked upon it. Places where the blight had appeared. So far there were three, and he feared only more would crop up. "I'll let Sidra know."

Yvaine was quiet for a long moment. Her silence drew Torin's bloodshot eyes to her.

"What is it?" he asked gruffly.

"Have the two of you discussed your move to the castle yet?"

"No."

"I'm beginning to feel like I need to set a watch over your croft, Torin."

"You'll do no such thing, Yvaine."

"But you understand why I feel this way?"

Torin didn't want to have this conversation. But yes, he knew. He was the laird, and he was living in a cottage on a windswept hill. He was traveling to and from the castle every morning and night, alone, sometimes before the sun rose or after it set.

"What if something happens to you?" Yvaine murmured. "Who is next in line for succession? Who am I to go to if something befalls you because you stubbornly refuse to have a guard?"

"Sidra," Torin said. "If something happens to me, speak with her. The lairdship passes to her first, and then to Maisie."

"Not your father?"

Torin thought of Graeme. His father lived on the croft next to theirs, but he had become a recluse, ever since his wife had abandoned them.

"My father declined his right to rule long ago," he replied.

"And Sidra knows she's next in line?"

Torin rubbed his brow. No, Sidra didn't know. They hadn't talked about this yet, and it was just one more thing on his list of heavy topics to broach with her.

Yvaine sighed. "Go home, Torin. Go home to Sidra and *speak* to her. The two of you are carrying enough as it is, but I think living in the castle will make things easier and safer for you both."

"Easier?" Torin scoffed. "Do you understand that my wife is fond of her croft and her kail yard? That she grew up in the vale and needs her space?"

"As many of us understand and also feel," Yvaine said gently. "But sometimes we have to make do with the hand fate deals us."

Torin was too tired to argue. He merely nodded to the captain before she left to return to the barracks for the night.

He took up his quill and marked the Ranalds' croft with an X on the map. Another pocket of blight. Another person sick.

The east was changing, molting into something Torin didn't recognize.

It felt like the beginning of the end.

He poured himself another glass of whiskey, which gleamed in the slant of moonlight. Soon he poured another, and then another. Before long, he felt nothing at all. He would not remember falling asleep with his face pressed to the map.

The full moon arrived on a cool, cloudy night in the west. Adaira opened her bedroom windows, the air sweet with petrichor as she read Jack's letter by the hearth fire.

> *I did imagine your reaction between the lines. You can imagine mine, now.*

She smiled. He knew then. He *finally* knew their correspondence was being read, and she couldn't express how relieved and thrilled that made her. She bent over the parchment to reread his every word, wondering if he had hidden a message for her to decode, when a rap sounded on her door.

Adaira quickly folded the letter and tucked it into Joan Tamerlaine's half-bound journal. She rose to answer the knock, but she knew who had come to see her. She had been waiting for this visit, ever since the hunt had ended.

Innes stood in the corridor, dressed in her customary tunic, leather armor, and enchanted blue plaid. A sword was sheathed at her side, as if she had just come from the wilds, but her silver hair was bound in damp braids and her skin scrubbed clean of dirt and sweat, confirming that she had visited the cistern. A golden circlet gracing her brow winked in the torchlight.

"How was the hunt?" Adaira asked.

"It was fine," Innes replied tersely. "David told me he wounded your arm."

"It's nothing—"

"Let me see it."

Adaira stifled a sigh and drew up her sleeve. Innes gently unwound the bandage to survey the sutures, which had started to itch as they healed. She pressed her thumb to them, and Adaira was uncertain what she was doing until the laird nodded and rebandaged the wound.

"No fever, but you'll tell me if it begins to fester?"

Adaira nodded, noticing the crosshatching of scars on Innes's hands and fingers, on her forearms. Some of them were nearly hidden in her interlocking blue tattoos, but others seemed to be framed by the woad, as if to commemorate them.

Adaira wondered if there were scars hiding beneath her raiment. Scars that could testify to near-mortal wounds she had received. Deep cuts and punctures that had endured for moon phases and taken patience and wrung prayers to see heal.

"Did that happen to you once?" Adaira asked. "Did you have a wound that almost killed you?"

"What makes you think so?" Innes countered, but her voice was wry.

"David told me how the two of you met," Adaira began quietly. "About that one night you slept in his bed so he could watch over you, because he was worried you might stop breathing and he couldn't bear the thought of it."

Creases gathered at the corners of Innes's eyes. The beginnings of a smile. Adaira had never seen such an expression on the laird's stoic face, and she waited to see it transform her.

That didn't happen. The smile turned into a grimace, and Innes said, "I've had my share of wounds, and David knows them all. But that isn't why I'm here. There's something I want you to witness tonight, so grab your plaid and come with me."

Adaira was curious and did as Innes asked. She took up her plaid and pinned it to her shoulder, then followed her mother into the intricate sprawl of corridors.

She was still learning her way around the castle, but ever since David had showed her how to open enchanted doors and given her a sword—which she was nearly certain he had done so she could protect herself from the likes of Rab Pierce—Adaira had been eager to explore on her own. To learn the quirks and secrets of the Breccan holding.

She recognized where Innes was guiding her. It was the same route David had led her along to the armory, but instead of heading downstairs, Innes guided her up a flight. On the next floor, they approached a set of doors carved with wolves and fruit-laden vines. They creaked when Innes pushed on their iron handles, opening to a balcony that overlooked an arena.

Adaira stopped short and gazed down. This was the same ring where she had sparred with David in the storm.

The sand was freshly raked, waiting for new boot prints. Adaira couldn't help but shiver when she remembered falling to her knees and watching her blood harden into gemstones. She wondered if those gleaming pieces of her had been raked deep beneath the sand.

She let her eyes drift, taking in more of her surroundings. Without rain, the arena felt almost like a place Adaira had never seen before. It was well lit by iron-bracketed torches, and the wooden stands that surrounded the ring were overflowing with spectators. Breccans sat shoulder to shoulder, nursing cups of ale and wine and eating cold dinners from their satchels. Their hair was wind-snarled, their shoulders wrapped in plaids and shawls to ward off the slight chill of the night. Some were talking while others looked weary, like they might fall asleep where they sat. Even children were present, whining and crying and sleeping in their parents' arms. The older youths entertained themselves by chasing each other up and down the stands.

The Breccans quickly took note of her presence on the balcony. Their murmurs grew like a wave building up, their attention like pricks upon her skin.

She looked at them as they looked at her.

But Adaira soon sensed that the Breccans were *required* to be present. As she stepped closer to the edge of the balcony, she was struck by the same feelings she'd had the day before, when she had followed David out onto the sand. Eerie, unsettled feelings. She didn't like this place. Even with the firelight and the countless people around her, something about it felt sinister.

"Join me, Cora."

Innes's voice was calm and deep. As if she sensed Adaira's aversion.

Adaira turned her attention away from the arena to study the balcony. Lit by standing candelabras and framed with blue curtains, it was not a large space. Two high-backed chairs were set close to the stone balustrade, where the laird could sit and watch whatever unfolded in the arena, and a small table was within reach. A bottle of chilled wine and two gold-chased goblets rested on it.

Innes had already sat down in one of the chairs and was pouring each of them a glass of wine. Adaira stepped closer, her left knee popping as she lowered herself to sit.

"Is something happening tonight?" she asked, accepting the goblet that Innes handed to her.

"Yes."

Adaira waited for Innes to expound on that, though she was learning that her mother was not a woman of many words. All these one-worded answers were going to drive Adaira mad, and she almost spoke curtly but caught her tongue when Innes pointed upwards.

"Any time I call for a culling," the laird began softly, "the clouds break, as if the northern king wants to witness from above. It is the only reason why I believe the spirits enjoy watching our lives unfold on the isle."

Adaira gazed up at the sky. The clouds broke like long, pale ribs, exposing a luminous full moon and a smattering of stars.

She stared at the night sky, captivated by its beauty, which she had so often seen and taken for granted in the east. The sight softened her, and the tension that had been building since she beheld the arena eased. She thought of Torin, Sidra, Jack, vivid images of them coming to mind: Torin riding the hills. Sidra harvesting night blooms in her garden. Jack walking along the coast, harp in hand. All of them lifting their eyes to the same moon, the same stars. How close to them she was, and yet how far away.

The thought made her chest ache, as though a dirk had pierced her, hilt deep.

The moon-drenched visions broke when the arena door swung open with a bang.

A tall, armored man stepped forward. His boots crushed the sand, and the light gleamed on his steel breastplate. Woad was imprinted on the backs of his hands, on the cords of his neck and the shaved portions of his head. His face was stern until he smiled. And when he raised his arms, the clan cheered.

Adaira could feel the roar reverberate through the wood under her feet. She exhaled, watching as the man lowered his arms. The clan fell quiet again in response, and he swiftly forgot about the crowd when he looked to the balcony. Adaira felt his eyes trace her face as he stepped closer, then stopped in the center of the arena.

"Laird Innes," the man said, his voice raspy, as if he had spent years shouting. "Lady Cora." He bowed to them both, holding the stance until Innes spoke.

"Begin the culling, Godfrey."

He straightened, the corners of his lips tilting in a crooked smile. He turned to address the crowd next as he walked around the perimeter of the ring. "The dungeons have overflowed this past moon. Every cell has been filled, awaiting this night. Every sword has struck a whetstone, every axe has been sharpened until it shines. Tonight, however, is one that is wholly devoted to Lady Cora, who has returned home to us after many long years away."

Adaira stiffened. "Who is this man?" she asked Innes in a whisper.

"The Keeper of the Dungeons," Innes replied.

"And why is this night devoted to me?"

The laird made no response, keeping her gaze on Godfrey as he came to a stop in the arena. Adaira was about to ask again, more sharply, when the dungeon keeper continued.

"On this full moon, I bring you one you've seen fight before. You know him well, although both his name and honor have been stripped from him. I bring you Oathbreaker!"

Sounds of dissent sprouted in the crowd. Adaira frowned, leaning forward as a tall man was escorted into the arena. He wore a ratty tunic and boots, and his pale knees and forearms were stained with grime. A leather breastplate freckled with old blood was buckled over his chest. A full helm shielded his face, and his wrists were shackled behind his back until he was brought to a halt, standing to the left of Godfrey. One of the guards unfettered the prisoner, freeing him from the irons, and what looked to be a dull, mundane sword was set into his hands.

Adaira stared at the one called Oathbreaker, surprised by how still and quiet he stood, like a mountain in the sand. There was no way to tell his age, or even to catch a glimpse of his expression. But he seemed hewn from stone, and she had the prickling sensation that he was staring at her through the slits in his helm.

"Next," Godfrey continued in a booming voice, "I bring you one who has never stepped foot in this arena before. A young man who had days of great purpose before him until he committed an irrevocable sin."

Adaira was frozen in her chair as the second prisoner was brought forward. He also wore a tattered tunic, soft hide boots, and a leather breastplate that looked as if someone had died wearing it. But his head was free of a helm, to show his face to the crowd.

He was young. Younger than her by a few years. His grimy face was creased in fear, and he seemed to be frantically looking for someone in the crowd.

"I bring you William Dun," Godfrey announced. "Who murdered a shepherd to steal his resources as well as his flock. And we know what we do to those who kill and take what doesn't belong to them!"

The crowd hissed and booed.

"Please, Laird," William begged, falling to his knees. "Have mercy! It wasn't my—"

Godfrey nodded to one of the guards, who swiftly gagged William with a strip of dirty plaid. Adaira winced as she watched. The young man's voice melted away; she couldn't hear his agony over the roar of the spectators and the wool of the gag, and one of the guards slid a dented helm over his head.

"He's not permitted to speak?" Adaira asked Innes, alarmed.

Innes took a sip of her wine. Her eyes were on the arena, but she said, "Do you remember the other day? When you and I stood in the shepherd's croft, beholding a murdered man? I asked Rab to follow the trail the flock had left, to find the culprit."

"Yes, I remember," Adaira said, but she went cold at the sound of Rab's name.

"All evidence led to this boy's croft. His mother claimed that he came home with blood on his boots, and that she saw him hide the stolen sheep with their own flock."

"And so you decided to hold no trial for him?" Adaira murmured, unable to hide her disgust. "Because of information *Rab* gathered?"

"I don't know what your trials look like in the east, Cora," Innes said, glancing at her. "But we let the sword speak for us here. As we live by it, we die by it. There is no greater honor. And the culling gives criminals the chance to either redeem themselves with a courageous death or prove that they deserve to be pardoned and granted an opportunity to return to the clan."

"Is that all?" Adaira challenged.

But Innes was silent, refusing to argue. Her attention was fixed on the arena again.

Adaira's mind reeled. In the east, the Tamerlaines conducted spars to mimic true combat, but hearings were held when crimes were committed. Those who were guilty were allowed to argue in defense of themselves, and only then did the laird pass a fair judgment.

Adaira set down her wine, unable to drink it. She watched as Godfrey stepped back. The sound of a ram's horn signaled the commencement of the fight.

The crowd roared. Adaira felt the sound vibrate through her. She sat, stiff and white-knuckled, as Oathbreaker took a cut at William Dun. The sword almost grazed the younger man as he stumbled back, awkwardly moving his sword in a sad attempt to parry.

Oathbreaker held the advantage in this fight, in strength and size and skill. He didn't slow. He pursued a scampering William around the arena. The crowd began to grow weary of watching the one-sided fight until Oathbreaker at last knocked the sword from William's hands. Weaponless, William began to run, his swiftness his only defense.

"Innes," Adaira breathed. "Innes, *please—*"

"*Cora.*"

Her name was a stinging lash against her soul, but also a warning. Some Breccans were watching the fight, but some were watching the balcony, measuring her reaction.

Adaira held in her pleadings, but her blood turned to ice as she made herself witness the culling. She felt as though she had taken another dose of Aethyn. Her stomach knotted, and perspiration gleamed along the lines of her palms like rain-limned webs. She wiped it away on her plaid, only to feel sweat begin to dampen her tunic and boots, as if she burned with fever.

She watched as William finally stumbled and fell, sprawled on the sand. The same sand she had bled and fainted on. The place where her father had drawn her up to her feet in the rain.

Oathbreaker stood above the boy, but something about his posture and stance looked weary. As if he had lived a hundred years and had seen far too much. As if he didn't want to bring this spar to an end.

He hesitated only for a moment before he plunged his sword into William's throat.

There was a crack of bone and an eager spray of blood.

Adaira closed her eyes.

She focused on her breaths, the way they whistled through her teeth.

Let it end, let me wake in the east.

But there was no waking from this nightmare. There was no waking to her chambers in Sloane, with the painted wall panels and the shelves full of books and the sunlight streaming in through the windows. There was no Jack, no Torin, no Sidra.

Adaira opened her eyes to a dead boy on the sand, his blood a crimson shadow beneath him.

Her gaze drifted to Innes.

Her mother sat straight-backed in the chair, hands resting on her knees. Her expression was so poised and neutral that she could have been limestone. She didn't seem callous, but neither did she seem thrilled, and her profile was sharp, firelit. She watched the arena without blinking, her blue eyes like a frozen loch in midwinter.

Adaira didn't know if Innes had turned the lairdship into this figure, or if the lairdship had molded Innes into what she was. But *this* was the woman Adaira had come from. Bone and breath and blood. A woman who blessed raids and called for cullings to clear out the criminals in her dungeons. A woman who hid scars and never appeared weak before those she didn't trust. A woman who had given up her heir and only son in order to bring Adaira home.

Adaira began to rise. She didn't want to be a part of this another moment, but Innes's low voice stopped her.

"If you leave now, you won't get the answer to your question."

Adaira slowly resumed her seat. "What question?"

Innes only indicated the arena.

Adaira returned her attention to the ring. Oathbreaker had come to stand before the balcony, solemn and bloodstained.

Adaira wondered if, having been victorious in this encounter, he would be given his freedom. Were his past crimes absolved, since the sword had proven him worthy to live?

"Down to the keep," said Innes.

Oathbreaker simply stood for a moment more, and Adaira wondered if he had heard her mother's verdict. But then he bowed his head and removed his helm, revealing his face.

She saw that he was older, a man in his middle years. His hair and beard were bedraggled, threaded with silver, and yet not even the conditions of the dungeons had hidden the fierce auburn sheen of it. A copper hue that drew the eye and held it, and Adaira's pulse skipped. He looked familiar, and she wondered . . . had she seen him before?

What oath had he broken?

But seeing the sadness in the downturned corners of his mouth, in the gleam of his eyes as he continued to gaze up at her, Adaira knew.

The sword fell from his hand in defeat.

"You asked David what happened to him," Innes said, watching Adaira's reaction. "The man who carried you east."

Adaira's breath caught as Oathbreaker turned away, his bloodstained armor dripping red constellations onto the sand. Her heart rose in her throat, and for a moment she couldn't breathe. She could only watch him through the tears that stung her eyes. Tears she refused to let fall. Not here in this place. Not with hundreds of gazes upon her.

She watched as Jack's father disappeared through the doors, returning to the dark maw of the dungeons.

CHAPTER 12

I 'm leaving," Jack said the moment he stepped into the castle library. He was so eager to make the announcement that it took him half a moment to realize that Torin was wincing, slumped over the desk, and shielding his eyes from the sunlight that streamed in through the window.

"You what now?" Torin growled as he painstakingly dipped a quill into an inkwell. It looked like he was trying to write in the ledger and was doing a poor job of it. The lines were crooked, and blots marred every other word.

Jack closed the door behind him, taking a closer look at Torin and the amount of whiskey left in the bottle by his elbow.

"Long night?"

"Something of the sort." Torin sighed, flicking the quill away. "You say you're leaving. Where to?"

Jack hesitated. The words still tasted strange in his mouth. He thought he knew the proper way to break this news to Torin—who possessed the power to deny him permission to leave—and yet his carefully laid argument crumbled in that moment.

Torin's brow lowered. "Don't tell me you're returning to the mainland."

"No," Jack nearly laughed. " Of course not."

"Then where? The suspense is killing me, Jack."

"I'm going west," he said. "To be with Adaira."

Torin stared at him for what felt like a solid hour. A dark, angry gaze that made Jack bristle.

"Has she invited you to be with her then?"

Jack drew a sharp breath. "No."

Torin chuckled and leaned back in his chair. Jack frowned, wondering if Torin was still drunk. Was this conversation doomed from the beginning?

"I need you here, Jack."

"What for? I have proven myself to be quite useless. Ask the orchard if you need further proof."

"On the contrary. You are the clan's hope."

Jack grimaced, but he was prepared for this statement. Perhaps he was selfish for thinking of himself and Adaira first, the isle second, the clan third. But he would never forget how quickly the clan had turned on Adaira. He would never forget their doubt, their scathing judgment, their sharp comments when they realized she was Breccan by blood. How deep their betrayal had cut her, even as she strove to hide her pain.

No, Jack would never forget. He remembered names and faces, and who had said what. It would be a long while before he'd want to sing and play for such people. At least, not until they apologized to Adaira.

And to lose her now would be worse than drowning, worse than burning. If he was the one to play for unity—if he had been asked to bring down the tyrannical king of the spirits—then he needed Adaira at his side in order to accomplish those impossible tasks.

"I spoke to a fire spirit," Jack said. He hadn't planned to fully confess to Torin about dragging himself home in defeat to a darkened cottage and singing to the ashes. But Jack saw no other way to convince the laird. Torin listened with a narrowed gaze, but he seemed to grasp every word Jack was uttering, and even the ones he didn't. The implications of what Jack was saying.

Torin leaned forward, propping his elbows on the desk. The signet ring gleamed on his forefinger as he covered his face for a moment, as though he wanted to wake from a dream. But when his hands dropped, Jack saw the resignation in his bleary eyes.

"Who am I to hold you back then?" Torin said, in a heavy voice carved by sadness. "If you have been appointed by a spirit to go, then you should go, Jack. Go and be with Adaira once more. Sing the isle to unity. We shall be here, waiting for you to return if fate wills it."

Jack stood silent for a moment, overcome.

A smile teased Torin's mouth. "You expected me to oppose you?"

"Yes," Jack confessed. "I know it seems that I'm abandoning the clan and my duties."

"Don't worry about what others are going to think. But I suppose I should ask you how and when you plan to depart."

"I'll go by river," Jack replied. "As soon as I can."

"Meaning today?"

"Most likely."

"Eager, are we?" Torin countered.

"I've been away from her long enough, I think," Jack said.

Torin held his gaze for a beat, but nodded. "I sense there's nothing I can say to hold you back. Not even how foolish this is, to cross over without alerting Adaira."

"My correspondence with her has been closely monitored. Nothing I write to her is private."

"Yes, Sidra told me," Torin said. "And you still think it wise to take Adi by surprise with your arrival?"

"I've written her a letter in code," Jack said. "I think she'll be able to read between the lines and know I'm coming to her."

"You'll leave it all to that chance then?" Torin crossed his arms. "What if Adaira doesn't get your letter, or your 'code' is so subtle she doesn't realize it means you are *physically* coming to her? What then?"

"Then she'll be surprised to see me," Jack said. Before Torin could retort, he added, "And I'd like for you to write a letter of my intent. I'll carry it with me in case I do run into trouble."

Torin frowned, but he reached for a piece of parchment on the desk and began to write a—lamentably—crooked message. He let Jack read it. The letter was succinct yet practical, stating that Jack had arrived in the west to reunite with his wife, Adaira, and bore no ill will toward the Breccan clan.

"Good," Jack said. "Can you seal it for me?"

Torin seemed a bit annoyed, but he heeded Jack's request, sealing the letter in wax with his signet ring.

"Anything else I can do for you, Bard?" Torin drawled.

Jack shook his head, but then caught himself. "Will you keep an eye on my mum and sister while I'm away? They've managed just fine without me the past eight years or so, but I'll be worried about them regardless. I don't know how long I'll be away."

Torin's mood turned somber. "Don't worry. Mirin and Frae will be looked after. And I want you to write to me, as soon as you reach Adaira in the west, so none of us worry about you." He paused, as if he wanted to say more.

"I'll send word."

Torin remained quiet, pensive.

"What is it?" Jack prompted, his patience beginning to wane.

"You know that you don't just need *my* permission to leave," said Torin.

Yes, Jack knew. He sighed.

He still needed to speak with Mirin.

He found his mother at home, the croft habitable once more now that the fire had returned to the hearth. Mirin stood at her loom, weaving. The cottage was quiet, the air full of spinning dust motes and the golden scents of parritch and warm honey. Frae was gone for the day at the school in Sloane.

"Don't tell me another cow has gotten into the garden," Mirin said, her attention focused on her work.

"No," Jack said. "I've come to ask you about my father."

Mirin's fingers froze, but her eyes darted across the chamber to meet his. He thought she might brush away his questions; she had done so for years when he was a boy, when he had been desperate to know who his father was and why he was absent. But Mirin must have seen the determination in his stance and his distant gaze, as if he were halfway to the west.

She rarely stepped away from her work, but now she left the loom. "Sit down, Jack," she said, busying her hands with preparing a pot of tea.

Jack sat at the table, patiently watching her. She poured them each a cup before taking the chair across from his, and he noticed she looked pale and exhausted. It was all those enchanted plaids she wove, and he resisted the temptation to glance at the loom.

"What do you want to know?" Mirin asked.

"What his name is to begin with."

She hesitated, but her voice was clear when she spoke. "Niall. Niall Breccan. He took the clan name when he was appointed Keeper of the Aithwood, as a measure of his fealty."

Jack thought about that for a moment, mulling over his father's name. *Niall Breccan.* "And you said he lives upstream, not far from you?"

"Yes. A cottage in the woods, by the riverbank." Mirin's fingertips traced the rim of her teacup.

"Does he live alone there?"

"As far as I know, he does. Why? Why are you asking me this, Jack?"

"Because I'm going west to be with Adaira, and I would like to find him."

Mirin hardly reacted. It was then that Jack realized she had been waiting for this moment. She had been expecting him to pack up his bags and cross to the other side of the isle ever since the truth had been revealed and Adaira had departed. The entire month he had waited before leaving was apparently a longer period of delay than Mirin had expected.

"I need to tell you something, Jack," she whispered, and his heart lurched with dread. "I saw your father, weeks ago. On the night when the Breccans came here, demanding to speak with Adaira. The night everything changed." Mirin paused. She laid her palm over the base of her throat, as though it ached. Jack could only hold his breath and wait. "As you know, your father gave up the secret of the river to Moray Breccan. I suppose Niall must have then struck a deal, one that enabled him to see me one last time before he was punished for his crime of giving Adaira to the east. So they brought him to me. Frae and I . . . we were there, in that corner, preparing for a raid, and the Breccans dragged your father into the house, bound as a prisoner."

Wondering why Mirin had never mentioned this encounter before, Jack wanted to be angry with her. But then he watched her wipe her tears away.

"They called him 'Oathbreaker' and stripped him of his title and name," she continued. "I hardly had time to draw breath, I was so shocked to see him again. And I said *nothing* as they dragged him away."

Jack moved around the table, so he could sit at Mirin's side. He took her hand, felt how cold and lean it was. Her hand that had woven countless secrets into plaids. He held it now as she wept. She had been suppressing these tears for weeks, for *years*, and they came fast and furious now, the sound of a heart that had broken. Jack quietly bore witness to his mother's pain, to the sacrifices she had made, to the weight she carried, alone, as a woman who loved a man she could never claim.

"I'm sorry, Mum," Jack whispered, squeezing her hand.

Mirin blotted away the last of her tears. "I tell you this, Jack, because I don't know if your father is living. They may have executed him for his crimes."

The thought had passed Jack's mind, but hearing that possibility shaped by Mirin's voice suddenly made it feel far more real. His heart was heavy as he continued to hold her hand.

"And I knew this day was coming," Mirin continued, turning

her dark eyes to him. Eyes dark as the ocean at night. "I knew that you would cross the clan line to be with Adaira and to find the answers you've always hungered for. I know that you want to go now, to not lose another minute. But if I may ask this of you, Jack, stay one more day with us. Spend one last night here with Frae and me. Partake in one last morning meal with us."

He nearly winced at the request, because his determination was keen. He had sent his letter to Adaira and wanted to follow it immediately. He wanted to stand in the west before the sun set.

Mirin continued, "I have this feeling, Jack. That once you cross over to the west, you'll never come back here. You'll never return to the east."

Her revelation quelled his impatience. His mind went quiet, and his heart seemed to go hollow. There were only his breaths, rushing in and out, and his pulse, echoing in his ears.

He nodded, because he couldn't argue with the validity of her request. He told himself that he could gladly spend another evening here with her and Frae. For one more night, he could eat at this table, sit by the hearth, and bask in his mother's stories. He could sing a ballad for his little sister, who was still eager to hear the Tamerlaine songs. He could wake one more morning to watch the sun rise in the east.

"All right," he whispered. "I'll leave tomorrow morning."

Mirin sagged with relief. "Thank you, Jack."

He granted her a slender smile. But deep within he was sad. And beneath that sorrow, he was furious. He hated how his life and the people he loved were divided and separated from each other. He was chilled by the thought that he might never see Mirin and Frae again, and yet he couldn't bear to be estranged from Adaira and unknown by his father.

I will bring the two halves together, he thought, even though it seemed so impossible he could have laughed. *I will play for peace in the west, and I will see my family made whole.*

"Promise me one thing, Jack," Mirin said, breaking into his reveries by taking hold of his face with her hands.

"Anything," he said, waiting.

"Don't tell them you're Niall's son."

He nodded, but his hope began to wither. His excitement dimmed. He would have to go unclaimed once more. He would have to act as if the west held no roots for him. His mother's request made him feel old and weary.

"Keep your blood ties a secret," Mirin whispered, urgently.

"Don't worry, Mum," Jack said. "They'll never know."

CHAPTER 13

~~~~~~~~~~~~~~~~~~~~~~~~~

E at your kail, Maisie," Sidra said, watching her daughter from across the table.

"Daddie doesn't make me eat it," Maisie stated, glaring at the greens on her plate.

Sidra resisted the temptation to look at Torin's empty chair, his plate filled with a now-cold dinner. "Your father would if he were here. Eat your kail, please."

"But they taste like dirt."

"They taste like the *earth*," Sidra said in a gentle tone. Spirits below, she was so tired. Her head was throbbing, her foot was aching. . . . "They taste of life and bright sunshine and the secrets that hide deep down in the soil. Secrets that make you strong and smart once you eat them."

Maisie's pout eased. She poked at her kail with careful interest, but as soon as she put it in her mouth, she spat it out onto the table.

"*Yuck!*"

"Maisie Tamerlaine," Sidra said sharply. "That is enough. You have always eaten your kail."

Maisie frowned and shook her head. "I don't wanna eat it."

Sidra closed her eyes and rubbed the pain in her temples. Her patience was fraying, and she couldn't remember the last time she had felt so exhausted, so worn out.

She tried to tell herself this weariness arose from how hard she had worked that day to find a remedy. She had ground her herbs and mixed blends she had never tried before. She had steeped them into stout teas and turned them into salves. She had rested her foot on a cushioned stool. She had also exercised the foot, walking across the hills to visit her patients. She had wrapped her foot in warm linen and then held it beneath cold river water until it went numb.

Sidra was attempting everything she could think of, hoping to halt and reverse the blight that was spreading on her heel. But she feared that only time could reveal if any of her methods were successful, and time was not on her side. Judging from how swiftly Rodina's hand had been overtaken, she predicted that she might have another week before the blight claimed her entire foot.

Rodina had also said that recently she had more headaches and stomach troubles, which Sidra was now experiencing. Her entire body felt exhausted, and she had no appetite. All she wanted to do was lie down and sleep.

You're tired because you worked so much today. You slept poorly the night before. The weather is changing . . .

She tried to convince herself that there was some other reason for her fatigue. That her gnawing exhaustion and headache and short temper were not due to the blight gradually creeping along the arch of her foot.

"What's wrong?"

Maisie's voice brought Sidra back to the evening. How long had she been sitting there, eyes closed, leaning into her hand? Long enough for a stubborn six-year-old to grow concerned. Sidra tried to smile at her daughter, to reassure her, even though she felt as if she might crumble into tears.

"I think I'm just tired, Maisie."

"Then eat your kail, Mummy."

Sidra blinked, realizing she had not eaten much of her dinner. Her stomach was churning.

She had to tell Torin tonight. She had to tell him she was infected. If he ever came home, that is. He had failed to come home the night before, and his absence had worried her, more than she liked. She had remembered all the nights she slept alone, when he worked the night shift.

Sidra suddenly felt divided. She wanted to see him and was waiting for him intently, listening for the sound of his boots on the front stoop. She was waiting for the door to swing open. To feel his gaze touch her, his hands not far behind. Until she imagined his face when he learned the truth.

How do I tell him?

"Are you sick, Mummy?" Maisie persisted, her brow furrowed in concern.

"I just have a little headache, sweet lass."

Sidra had been very careful that day. When Maisie was at the house with her, she had kept her stockings and boots on, to hide all trace of her infection. It was only when Maisie visited Torin's father, Graeme Tamerlaine, at his croft next door that Sidra worked herself into a sweat trying to uncover an antidote.

But children have a keen way of things. Sidra made herself lower her hands from her brow and eat her kail.

It seemed as if Torin would not be joining them for dinner.

Sidra rose and scraped everything off his plate, feeding it to the dog. Why did she even cook for him? Why couldn't he send her a note with a raven if he was so intent on remaining at the castle?

When she decided to put Maisie to bed early, the child's whining intensified. The lass wanted one of the cats to sleep with her, which Torin allowed only on certain days. Sidra decided to let two cats in. Then Maisie wanted a story, but none of the ones in Sidra's lore book. Only a new one would do. Sidra's eyes were so tired she could hardly see the words on a page, let alone create a story spontaneously. But she scrounged up a legend about Lady Whin of the

Wildflowers, adding that she grew the finest kail yard and diligently ate her greens every night.

"I want a different story," Maisie said.

"Tomorrow, if you are a good lass," Sidra said, blowing out the candles. "I will tell you another story. Now. Go to bed, Maisie."

Sidra shut the bedroom door and leaned on it, staring at the table. All the food and dirty plates were still set out. She contemplated leaving everything where it was. Perhaps Torin would clean it up whenever he decided to come home?

Sidra snorted. Knowing better, she carried a few dishes to the wash barrel. One of the teacups broke when she began to scrub it. She stopped, surprised when she realized she had cut her finger. She watched as her blood left a small trail in the water.

Sidra was still staring absently into the wash barrel when Torin finally arrived.

He removed his boots and hung his plaid. His face was haggard, his eyes bloodshot when he looked at Sidra. And then his gaze dropped to the table, which was still a mess.

Sidra's heart softened toward him as she sensed how weary he was.

But then he briskly said, "Where's my dinner?"

It took everything within her not to slam and break all the dishes in the wash barrel.

"I fed it to the dog." She returned to her scrubbing, the cut in her finger throbbing with her pulse.

"Of course you did," Torin muttered, and Sidra, again, thought she might lose her mind. But she held her tongue, her temper simmering just beneath the flush of her skin. She watched as Torin heaved a sigh and sat down in Maisie's chair. He began to eat his daughter's cold dinner until he noticed the half-chewed kail sitting on the table beside the fork. "Never mind this. I should have remained at the castle."

Sidra whirled, intentionally breaking a plate against the cupboard this time. Torin had always known her to be a gentle spirit, and whatever he saw in her eyes gave him a moment's pause as pottery shards cascaded to the floor.

"If I knew when you were coming home, I could have dinner ready for you," she said.

"If *I* knew when I was coming home, then I would tell you." He rose from the table, rattling the dishes. "But most of the time I don't, Sidra. It would make my life much simpler if we moved into the castle."

She froze, knowing this had been coming. The sudden panic that tightened her ribs made her feel like a bird trapped in an iron cage. She thought about all the castle stairs she would have to walk up and down. Her foot responded with a twinge of pain.

"It would simplify your life, but not mine, Torin."

"In what way, Sidra?"

"Because this is where I work," she spoke through her teeth. "All of my herbs grow in this kail yard. I need to be near them to find the blight's remedy."

"Grow them in the castle kail yard!" he said with a toss of his hand.

"If it's easier for you to live in the castle," she began, "then live there. You have before. Maisie and I will be fine here."

It was a low blow.

She saw it in Torin's expression as if she had struck him.

The distance swelled between them. It felt like the floor had cracked at their feet.

Her anger began to cool, replaced by misery as she watched Torin stride to the door. His face was guarded, blanched. He appeared to feel nothing at all as he donned his boots, gathered his plaid.

Stop him. Don't let him go.

But Sidra was frozen, pride and fear holding her captive. She watched Torin walk out, slamming the door in his wake. The shutters clattered, and the fire guttered in the hearth. She listened to his footsteps fade as he walked deeper into the night.

She heard Yirr let out a few barks in the yard, sharp notes of warning. Or perhaps he was pleading with Torin to return.

Then it fell quiet.

Sidra slid to the floor amid the shattered pieces of the plate she had broken. She drew her knees to her chest and numbly stared into the shadows.

Torin didn't go to the castle, and he didn't remain on the roads. He strayed onto the moonlit moors and wandered until he was weary, his boots rubbing blisters on his heels. He craved a drink. He wanted something to plunge him into oblivion, and his hands shook. Only then did he choose to stop. The stars watched as he wrapped himself in his plaid and lay down in the grass, hoping that slumber would distract him from his thirst.

But sleep was elusive, and his thoughts descended into dark places.

Sidra had thrown him out.

He couldn't believe it, and he bristled until he thought about the night before. He had drunk so much whiskey that he fell asleep in the castle library. He had never come home, and he didn't even send word to her. She must have been worried, lying in the dark, wondering where he was.

Inevitably, he thought about the laird's quarters, now redecorated and ready for them to inhabit. Torin had known the move would be difficult for Sidra. He had *known* it, and yet he had still managed to butcher the conversation, approaching it with such impatience and insensitivity that he couldn't fault her for telling him to leave.

He groaned, his anger melting into starlight. He shivered as he remembered the other recent night, when Sidra had joined with him in the dark, impassioned. And what of the flash of sadness he had seen in her? Something was bothering her, and the realization that she must not feel comfortable enough to tell him made him feel like he had a stone lodged in his stomach.

And why should she tell you? You are short-tempered and short-sighted and never come home on time. You drink too much and are stuck in the past.

He sat in the grass a while longer, reminiscing. Only weeks ago, an enchanted blade had struck him and stolen his voice. The words he had been unable to utter had burned in him like coals. How he had longed to tell Sidra all that he had been withholding from her.

He didn't want to waste time anymore, time that he could never regain. Had he not learned this lesson in the harshest of ways by now? *Wake up!* the isle seemed to say to him. *Open your eyes, Torin. Look at who you are becoming.*

Torin rose, brushing the dew from his plaid. He didn't want to be away from Sidra a moment longer. He didn't want to let anything come between them.

As he began walking briskly toward home, a light flickered at the corner his eye, stealing his attention. It looked like firelight from an open door in the distance.

Torin halted. There had been no houses in sight when he entered this valley. But he couldn't deny that he now saw a bewitching door piercing the darkness of the hills. It was beckoning him to come closer.

He approached it carefully, his hand finding the hilt of his dirk.

An arched door was carved into the side of a hill, with long tangles of grass hanging over its lintel. Torin stood before it, transfixed. He squinted at the passage beyond the door, attempting to discern where it led to, but the path turned, leading deeper into the earth. To a place Torin couldn't see.

This was a spirit portal.

He had dreamt of uncovering one when he was a boy. After he had devoured the tales his father told him, he had begun searching for portals on the isle, though they were concealed from mortal eyes. They hid within rocks and waterfalls and trees. Within grass and tides and gardens. The doors presented themselves only to those the spirits highly regarded.

Torin now stood before an open door that would lead him into the unknown, and he was struck with fear.

Where do you lead? Why have you opened to me?

The light began to dim. The door was about to close, and Torin had to swiftly weigh the risks against the advantages of entering.

If he passed through the door, he would be granted the chance to speak to the spirits face-to-face. He knew this invitation was extended because of the blight, for which he was desperate to find answers. If he declined and let the door close, he might never have this chance again to learn the truth about what they were facing in the orchards. The blight would continue to spread from tree to human, perhaps eventually claiming them all.

But if he entered . . . there was no telling how long he would be gone. It would most likely be only a day or two, but Sidra wouldn't know where he was. The thought of how she would worry pierced Torin like a spear. He imagined what his absence might do to her.

And yet there was one truth that he knew without doubt: she was strong enough to live without him. She would move forward, even with him gone. She would ensure that things ran smoothly with the clan until he returned.

"*Sidra,*" he breathed into the wind.

He knew the choice she would make if she were the one to stumble upon the door.

Torin hesitated only a moment longer, then passed over the threshold.

CHAPTER 14

J ack stood in the river, staring upstream.

It was midmorning, and he had delayed as long as he could, eating breakfast with Mirin and Frae, tending to last-minute tasks around the croft. Now it was time for him to leave.

He had packed light—a few spare tunics in his satchel, Torin's letter, and his harp.

You will find the answer among the Breccans.

Ash's voice echoed through him as Jack took a step forward.

The water rushed around his ankles, seeping through his boots, and meadowsweet grew in frothy white clusters along the riverbank. The Aithwood, dense with pine, spruce, hemlock, and rowan, became gnarled the farther upstream he walked. Blooming bedstraw and violets peppered the forest floor, and shadows cast by the tree canopy trickled over Jack's shoulders, shielding him from the sun. A few leaves drifted down to the water as he slowly withdrew his dirk from its sheath at his belt.

He waited until he was standing on the clan line, the edge of two realms. He thought about his father carrying Adaira through this river twenty-three years earlier, when she was a small, sickly infant. Niall Breccan's blood in the water had hidden his passing back and forth over the clan line, time and time again, to visit Mirin's cottage on the hill. Moray had also taken advantage of this secret flaw in the magical boundary, as well as the power of the Orenna flower, to kidnap the girls and roam the east without fear.

Jack was not the first to use the river, to let his blood drip down into the rapids before crossing from one side of the line to the other. He wasn't the first, but he hoped to be the last. Perhaps his music would be strong enough to mend this wound in the isle.

He drew the blade across his palm.

The pain was vibrant, but only for a moment. As soon as his blood began to well and drip from his fingers, melting into the water, he stepped forward.

He crossed the border into the west.

Adaira stood before the enchanted door of the new library, sword belted at her waist and a satchel full of parchment hanging from her shoulder. She didn't know what she would find beyond the radiant wood, but she hoped it was a quiet room full of nothing more than books and scrolls. She had avoided both Innes and David since the culling, refusing to sup in their rooms or join them for rides across the wilds. She knew she couldn't avoid them for much longer, but when she did stand before them again, she wanted to have all the knowledge she could gather.

She wanted to make her case.

Adaira pricked her finger and laid her hand upon the wood. The wood accepted her blood, then unbolted its enchanted lock.

She crossed the threshold meekly, her eyes scanning the chamber. But it was as she had hoped: she was the only visitor. She set down her satchel on a scribing table that stood before a trio of mullioned windows. It was early morning, and the gray light was still too dim to properly write and read by, so she took her time lighting the candles around the room.

Adaira drew in a deep breath, tasting years of paper and ink.

She reached out to the nearest shelf and touched it.

"Please show me all the books and records you have on the culling," she whispered. She didn't dare to hope for a response—not until she heard a rustling and saw that two scrolls had pushed themselves forward and were nearly dangling from the shelf.

She took both with gentle hands and carried them to the table, where she sat and began to read.

One thing quickly became apparent: the culling had been happening since the clan line was created, nearly two centuries ago. When the folk's magic had become divided and unbalanced by Joan and Fingal. The west suddenly had a surge of enchantment-made craft in their hands, yet they also had failing gardens and waning resources as a consequence. People were soon hungry and desperate, and so crime had started to crop up among the crofts and the city like weeds.

Adaira was strangely relieved to know that Innes hadn't started the culling but rather had inherited the practice when she became laird.

She read on and eventually gleaned the information she had most wanted to find: there was no way to free a prisoner from the dungeons without having them fight in a culling. Fighting not only gave criminals the chance to die honorably, as Innes had mentioned, but also redeemed the guilty by proving they deserved another chance. Another important purpose of the culling was to help deter future crime by making the clan stand witness to it.

Adaira began to write down what she learned, filling page after page with notes and thoughts and questions she still had. She had skipped breakfast, though, and when her stomach began to growl, her recording was interrupted. She leaned back in her chair, staring at what she had gathered.

"How do I free you?" she whispered, envisioning Jack's father again.

By all culling rules, he should have walked free after he killed William. But Innes had refused to pardon him, and all Adaira could think was that her mother wanted to make him suffer for what he had done. How many times had he fought in the arena? How many more of his fellow prisoners would he have to kill before he was redeemed in Innes's eyes?

There had to be another way for him to be absolved, Adaira thought as she rose with the scrolls in her arms. She returned them to the shelves and thought for a moment about what she should ask for next.

She laid her hand on the shelf and said, "Please show me all the books and scrolls that depict Breccan traditions and law."

It seemed like half of the books and scrolls in the library pushed their way forward to be noticed, and Adaira sighed, suddenly overwhelmed. She should have tailored her search better, but she selected the ones closest to her and brought them to the table.

She began to read, recording elements she thought either were fascinating or could be helpful in her appeal for her father-in-law's freedom. But it seemed that even with legal loopholes and strange past traditions, one law couldn't be avoided.

The laird of the clan always had the last word and could disregard laws in special circumstances. Lairds had most often used this power when a personal offense had been committed against them—such as when a once-trusted man of the clan gave the laird's daughter away to the enemy.

Why don't you tell Innes the truth?

Adaira chewed on her lip, wondering if it would make the situation better or worse to tell Innes that the man who had given her to the east was Jack's father. Initially, when Adaira wasn't yet certain how angry and vengeful Innes and David were over what had happened in the past, it had seemed safer to keep that fact hidden to protect Jack, Mirin, and Frae. She had worried that Innes might impose a harsh judgment on Jack's father—wiping out his entire family, for instance, or punishing him even further for having children with the enemy.

She wondered if just the fact that he was Adaira's relation by marriage would be compelling enough to convince Innes to let him go. But Adaira remembered that merely *asking* about where Oath-breaker was had turned David cold, breaking the rapport they had built. And then Innes had invited Adaira to watch him fight in a duel to the death, as if his life were meaningless.

Adaira felt that she needed something *more*. Not a way to catch Innes off guard necessarily, but a way to get her attention. She needed to figure out how to look shrewd rather than soft when it came to freeing Jack's father.

She retraced her notes.

There was one small tidbit of tradition that she had found fascinating. It was the "draping of the plaid," or giving someone protection under your name and prowess. In the past, such protection had been extended by thanes or the laird, those who held power and sway in the west and, as such, could serve as a formidable shield for others who had little influence. But even then, there were stipulations to be met.

The life of the one being protected had to be in danger. The thane or the laird had to remove their own plaid and drape it over the individual they were protecting, while speaking a specific set of words. Most of all, the draping of the plaid had to be performed publicly, so that the entire clan would become aware of the ramifications of harming the one being shielded.

Adaira wondered if she could embrace this tradition without offending the clan. Without offending *Innes*. Could she drape her father-in-law with her plaid on the basis of this old tradition? If she did, no one would be able to harm him without essentially harming her.

She was mulling over this possibility, trying to predict all the ways it could spin and turn and how Innes might oppose it, when an unexpected burst of sunlight warmed the table.

Adaira glanced up at the window.

The clouds had broken for a reason: something had cut through them.

At first, she thought she saw a large bird, falling through the air. A wounded creature. But then she saw a flash of silver, like the light of a star. Arms and legs trying to harness the wind. An iridescent sheen rippled behind the person like a torn sail.

Electrified, Adaira stood, leaning toward the glass. She watched as a spirit with indigo hair and tattered wings fell to the earth.

PART TWO

A Song for Embers

CHAPTER 15

Sidra didn't realize Torin was missing. Not until the newly appointed Captain of the East Guard came knocking on her door around midday.

"Yvaine?" Sidra said as she stood on the threshold, assuming the captain had come for an ailment. "How can I help you?"

"Hello, Sidra." Yvaine's voice was unusually grave. "Is Torin at home?"

It was the last question Sidra expected. For a moment she could only blink, because the question sounded ridiculous. Torin was *never* at home during the day. Yvaine, of all people, would know this.

It also brought back the night before in stark relief. She could still see the expression on Torin's face when she dismissed him, the pain and shock reflected there. She could still taste the warm air that had billowed around him as he opened the door to the night and left.

Her regret that morning was like a bruise, tender on her arm.

"No, he's not," she said, but her stomach clenched. "Why?"

"I was hoping to find him here."

"He's not at the castle? I assumed he would be with the guard for midday drills."

"I haven't seen him today," Yvaine said. "We were scheduled to have a meeting with the council this morning, to discuss the blight. He never showed, and as you and I both know, that's not like him."

"He and I argued last night," Sidra confessed hoarsely. "He left here angry. I assumed he went to the castle to sleep."

"If he did, no one saw him."

"Then something must have happened to him after he left. I . . ." Sidra couldn't even speak of what might have happened. The words felt as sharp as fractured glass in her mouth, threatening to cut her into ribbons if she said anything. But she saw the possibilities unfold in her imagination. Torin, storming away in the dark. Walking through the hills. Falling into a bog. Breaking his leg on treacherous ground. Beguiled by shifting hills and lochs and valleys.

"Mummy!" Maisie was tugging on her skirt. "Can I have an oatcake?"

Sidra roused herself from these thoughts, but the dread continued to weigh her down. She inhaled sharply and glanced at her daughter, rosy-cheeked and smiling in hope.

"Yes, just one," Sidra said.

Maisie scampered away to the kitchen table, and Sidra refocused her attention on Yvaine. The captain's face was guarded, but her dark eyes were gleaming with fear. The same fear Sidra felt, as if they stood in a sinking boat, losing precious time as cold water crept ever higher.

"Where would he go?" Yvaine murmured. "I can begin to canvass the hills, but the search will go faster if you can tell me of a place that is significant to him. Or perhaps to you?"

Sidra thought for a moment. Her frantic memories flashed like sun on a loch, difficult to grasp, but one came to the forefront. She thought of her old home, where she and Torin had first crossed paths. A place where the two of them had decided to become one, even as the world seemed to be crumbling around them.

"The Vale of Stonehaven perhaps," Sidra answered. It was a peaceful place on the isle, full of lush grass and wandering sheep, where time seemed to slow down. Picturing it in her mind, Sidra suddenly found it difficult to imagine Torin being harmed there. "I honestly can't think of anywhere else," she said, "but let me take Maisie to Graeme. Give me a moment, and I'll ride with you."

Yvaine nodded and returned to where her horse was tethered by the gate.

Sidra left the door open and backed away. Her feet turned leaden as her worries began to multiply at an alarming rate. As she stared at the last place she had seen Torin, a thunderstorm brewed beyond the threshold. Soon the rain began to fall, and the wind stirred up dead leaves. Her garden bowed to the storm, the herbs drooping, the kail getting splattered with mud.

Only then, when she felt the summer mist fan across her face, did Sidra's mind begin to lay out clear instructions. She would find Torin, but she first needed to take Maisie to Graeme.

She pinned her green plaid to her shoulder and braided her hair, preparing for a long slog in the rain. Then she slipped on Maisie's leather shoes and wrapped her in a heavy shawl, and together they dashed up the hill to where Torin's father lived.

Graeme was surprised but delighted to see them on his front stoop, speckled from the rain.

"Ah, Sidra, Maisie, come in, come in!"

Maisie trotted inside, becoming instantly distracted by the bowl of mainland trinkets Graeme kept on a stool. His house was messy, disorganized, and full of treasure. Sidra didn't mind the clutter, although Torin could hardly abide it. She tried to calm her pulse as she shut the door behind her.

"May I have a word with you, Da?" she said quietly.

"Of course," Graeme said. "Come sit at the table. Let me pour you a cup of tea."

Sidra remained where she was, her heart pounding so hard she could feel it in her wrists, in her neck. Her stomach began to churn, and she fought the temptation to cover her nose. She couldn't tell if it was her anxiety or the strange rank smell in the cottage, but she was struggling to hold down her breakfast.

"I can't stay," she managed to say, and her terse tone finally caught Graeme's attention.

"Oh." Her father-in-law set down the teapot, brows raised. "Can you sit for a moment at least? Give the storm a moment to die down?"

"Yvaine is waiting for me by the road," Sidra said, but she began to shake. She couldn't hide it, and Graeme quickly moved forward, taking a gentle hold of her arm.

"Come, sit a moment, lass," he whispered. "You look pale as a wraith."

"I . . ." Sidra sighed, and it felt like her chest had cracked beneath the pressure of her fear. She let Graeme guide her to the table.

"Tell me what's on your mind, Sidra," Graeme said as he poured her a cup of tea.

Sidra sat on the bench and accepted the cup, even as she felt time tug at her. She needed to rejoin Yvaine. She needed to be combing the hills for Torin. She was wasting precious moments, sitting here with a cup of warm tea in her hands.

But Graeme knew Torin nearly as well as Sidra did, and he might have insight that she didn't as to where his son might have gone.

She ensured that Maisie was distracted—she was, having found the cat curled up by the fire—and she whispered, "Torin is missing."

Graeme lowered himself to the chair across the table from her, listening as Sidra recounted the night before. Her voice was hoarse by the time she finished, asking, "Do you have an idea of where he might have gone? We can search there first."

Graeme let out a puff of air, as if Sidra's revelation had just socked him in the stomach. He scratched his gray beard—an action that made Sidra instantly think of Torin. She blinked away her tears, waiting.

"Your guess is as good as mine, Sidra," he finally said in a sad voice. "But I heard him calling for you last night."

"*What?*" she exclaimed, rising from the bench. "Did he say anything else? Was he in distress?"

"He didn't sound distressed, no," Graeme rushed to add, also standing. He tilted his head toward Maisie, who was now regarding them with wide, worried eyes. "He spoke your name fondly, but he seemed to be sighing in resignation. Like a farewell."

Sidra didn't know what to make of this news, which felt like a dagger in her belly when she imagined it being his dying breath. Torin had called for her and she hadn't heard him.

"I need to go," she said, stepping away from the table. She could scarcely feel the floor beneath her boots. Her stomach was clenching again. "If you can watch Maisie . . . I'll return soon."

"Sidra? Sidra, *wait*," Graeme was saying, but she was already out the door.

Yvaine and six guards were waiting for her at the road, mounted on mud-splattered horses. It was still raining, but summer storms were fickle on the isle and it was always best to carry on as usual rather than wait for clear skies.

Sidra approached the spare horse the captain had ready for her and drew herself up into the saddle.

Her foot twinged in pain, and she gritted her teeth. She had forgotten all about her woes with the blight, and she hated how those worries now simmered at the back of her mind when she was hell-bent on finding Torin. She couldn't hold everything at once, all these misgivings and fears and dreads.

Breathe, she told herself, drawing in air that tasted like clouds. *You're going to find Torin. And then you'll handle the blight.*

Yvaine waited to ensure that Sidra was settled, reins in hand, before she gave orders to her guards to split up into pairs. They would each take a section of the east to search and report back to the castle at sundown. But most importantly, they were to search discreetly. Neither Yvaine nor Sidra wanted the clan to know Torin was missing.

The guards cantered through the rain to their appointed destinations. Sidra watched them melt away before glancing sidelong at Yvaine.

"Where are we searching?" she asked.

"The vale, as you suggested," the captain replied. "But there is only one thing I ask of you, Sidra." The mare sidestepped beneath her, sensing the tension in the air. "Stay within my sight at all times. Can you agree to that?"

"Of course," Sidra said, surprised. But she shivered at the way Yvaine was gazing at her, as though Sidra was in danger of vanishing next.

They rode through the last of the storm to the vale, which was bright and sunny and sweltering. The bracken sparkled with leftover rain and the small creeks were swollen, cutting serpentine paths through the valley floor.

There was no sign of Torin.

From there, Yvaine and Sidra pressed northward, checking caves, thickets, the coast.

"I don't think he would have wandered this far," Sidra said, fighting the nausea that was rolling through her again. She had taken a few sips from Yvaine's flask and eaten a portion of food from her saddlebags when the two of them rested in very brief moments for the horses' sake. But the truth was that they had been riding hard for four hours now, and the sun was beginning to sink toward the west.

"Where do you want to go next then?" Yvaine asked.

Sidra guided them back toward the nook of the marsh. She was worried that Torin might have wandered into it, though it was a farfetched possibility because Torin knew the east like the lines on his palm. He never got lost, even when hills shifted. Even in the dark, the nook wouldn't have taken him by surprise.

But Sidra still wanted to see it with her own eyes. When they arrived there, she beheld the marsh's calm presence. Birds swooped overhead and damselflies dusted the surface of the shallow water. Clusters of bog myrtle and stalks of golden-starred asphodel danced in the breeze.

Sidra thought back on how Graeme had described Torin's call as *a sigh of resignation,* which Sidra had a difficult time envisioning. Torin wasn't a man who was quick to surrender, and for the first time since Yvaine had knocked on her door and broken the news, Sidra began to consider that maybe Torin had gone somewhere. Maybe he wasn't wounded and lying in a gully. Maybe he was hale and alive and had simply . . . left.

The thought struck her like a splinter. Sidra tried to uproot it. Cast it aside. But her resistance only made the realization nestle even deeper.

There was another realm that ran parallel to theirs, and it was beginning to bleed into their world through the blight. Sidra needed to be realistic. There was a good chance that the spirits had ushered Torin elsewhere, whether it be a shifting glen or a hill that she couldn't see. If so, Sidra was powerless to find him.

"Sidra," Yvaine said, interrupting her thoughts. "I think it's time I take you back to Graeme's. The sun is setting, and it looks like another storm is blowing in for the night."

"I can keep searching," Sidra protested, but her voice was faint. Her head was splitting again, her back aching.

"No," the captain said firmly. "I need you to eat a good meal and rest tonight, safe at Graeme's. I'll come for you at first light tomorrow morning, and we'll discuss this further."

"Discuss *what*?" Sidra snapped, but her anger was a short-lived spark. She met Yvaine's gaze, saw the same truths lurking in the captain's face.

Torin wasn't dead or missing. He had gone *somewhere*— somewhere they couldn't locate.

Sidra sighed.

She rode with Yvaine back to Graeme's croft, just as eventide's storm billowed like ink across the sky. She thanked Yvaine and the horse that had carried her all afternoon, then watched the captain ride away toward Sloane.

Sidra trudged through the garden to Graeme's front door. Her legs were sore from hours of riding, and she couldn't tell if she was starving or nauseous again, not until she stepped into the cottage.

Maisie was sitting at the table, about to eat supper. Graeme had something sizzling in the skillet, and he glanced up, relieved to see her.

"There you are," he greeted Sidra. "Just in time for dinner. Here, I've got you a plate ready . . ."

The aroma of the food hit her like a fist, instantly making her gag.

Sidra covered her mouth and turned. She stumbled back into the kail yard, trying to make it to the gate, but she couldn't. She knelt and heaved between the rows of vegetables, her fingers sinking into the wet soil. Again and again she vomited, until she was scraped empty and the rain was falling like whispers on the leaves around her.

Shaking, with tears dripping from her lashes, she wiped her mouth and closed her eyes. *Breathe,* she told herself, as the thunder rumbled above her and the wind stilled.

She felt a warm, steady hand on her shoulder. She knew it was Graeme, and she sat back on her heels.

"I'm sorry," she began to say, but he tightened his hold on her, wordlessly halting her apology.

"I take it you didn't find him," Graeme said sadly.

Sidra stared into the distance, watching night deepen. "No. There's no sign of him."

"Do you think the folk have ushered him away?"

She nodded.

"Then you must know that he wouldn't have left if it hadn't been the only path he saw to take," Graeme said. "Especially knowing of your condition."

Sidra froze. How did Graeme know she was sick with the blight? There was no possible way he could know, and she looked at him with dark, glittering eyes.

"How do you know about me?" she rasped. "I haven't told anyone. Not even Torin."

"Well, quite simply. You see, my wife did the same thing," Graeme said, and his voice had grown so wistful that Sidra found herself gaping at him. "When she was carrying Torin. Once, blood pudding had been her favorite. And then she suddenly couldn't stand to have anything to do with it. I couldn't eat pudding for years, even after Torin was born. Because Emma couldn't bear the smell of it."

"I . . ." Sidra's voice broke. She began to sift through her symptoms.

Her exhaustion. Her headaches. Her irritation. Her waves of nausea.

She had been so preoccupied with trying to solve the blight—which she had blamed for all of her symptoms—that she hadn't kept proper track of her moon flow. Now, she realized, she was late.

Sidra laid her hand on her belly. She thought of how often she and Torin had come together lately. Ever since he had been home in the evenings, sleeping beside her. They had talked about growing their family. Both she and Torin wanted another child, a child they would have together, and they had decided to stop taking their contraceptives and begin trying. And yet Sidra hadn't thought it would happen so soon. She certainly hadn't anticipated reveling in this news without Torin, but now that it had bloomed in her thoughts, Sidra knew it was true.

She let the wonder wash over her until she moved and felt the uncomfortable stiffness in her left foot, a keen reminder that the blight beneath her skin was expanding, climbing up her bones. Soon it would completely devour her, and what then? Could she even survive it, let alone her child?

"Sidra," Graeme said, "if Torin has truly been spirit-taken, then you must prepare for him to be gone for a while."

"What?" she panted, her mind far away.

"He might be gone for weeks. Months. I don't want to say this, but it could even be years."

Sidra blinked at Graeme. She struggled to fathom what he was saying, but then it cleft her heart like an axe.

"No, surely they wouldn't hold him that long," she said. "The earth . . . the spirits wouldn't do that to me."

Graeme was silent for a moment. But then he said, "There was a poem I read in Joan's journal. She mentioned a ballad about time moving much more slowly in the spirits' realm. One day in their world might be one hundred in ours."

Sidra opened her mouth to protest, but the words faded. She knew Graeme was right.

She envisioned Torin in her mind's eye, returning to the mortal world and looking just as he had the night he left. Young and handsome and corded with strength. Walking into their house only to find it empty, cobwebbed. Discovering her headstone in the graveyard, beside Donella's. Realizing that Maisie was grown and gray-haired and that this other child—this son or daughter that he had never known about—had also lived a full life. Realizing he had missed it all.

"What are you saying to me, Graeme?" Sidra whispered, her fingers curling into the loam. She took a fistful of earth and held it, trying to steady herself.

"I gave up my right to rule long ago," he said, squeezing her shoulder again. "You know that ever since Emma departed, I have been unable to leave my croft. But even before that, I never had a desire to rule, and Alastair knew it. So did Adaira. When she passed the lairdship to Torin, she was following the correct line of succession. And with Torin now incapable of being present, the east falls to you, Sidra."

"I don't want to rule," she said, reflexively. The same fear she had felt when Torin had told her they needed to move into the castle—the fear of irrevocable change and the unknown—began to beat against her ribs again. "I can't do it."

"You must, Sidra. You need to keep the east together. You must rise and lead this clan."

"I *can't*."

"Why do you say that?"

She bit the corner of her lip until the pain shot through her mouth. "Because I'm carrying enough as it is! I can't bear anything else. It will *crush* me, Graeme."

"Then tell us how to help you. Give your burdens to us, the tasks that weigh you down. You shouldn't be carrying it all alone to begin with."

She didn't know what to say. It was too much to think about, this notion of dividing all her responsibilities into slices and giving them away.

"The other day," Graeme said, "I was thinking about all the different paths our lives take, how little choices here and there suddenly guide us to places we never expected. How sometimes even the worst of experiences turn us into what we need to be, even though we would rather avoid the pain. But we grow stronger—we grow sharper—and before we truly even know it, we are looking back on it all. We see who we were and we see who we have become, and it is why the spirits watch us and marvel."

Sidra remained silent, still clutching the garden soil in her fist.

"Mummy!" Maisie's voice broke through the night. "Why are you on the ground?"

"I was just coming in to get your dinner," Graeme replied brightly before Sidra could scrounge up a false smile. "Go back inside before your feet get muddy, lass. I'm right behind you."

Sidra could hear Maisie patter away. She sighed, feeling so tired she didn't know how she would drag herself up.

Graeme's hand slipped from her shoulder as he rose. "Take a moment more," he said gently. "Then come inside and sit by the fire. I'll toss the blood pudding and air out the cottage and find something else you'd like. Perhaps something simple, like parritch and cream?"

"That'll be fine," Sidra whispered. "Thank you."

Graeme returned to the house, leaving the door open. He unbolted the shutters, as promised, to let the odors escape, and

Sidra closed her eyes, listening to the thunder and the rain. To the pounding of her heart.

She wrestled with her fear until she let go of the soil and stared at her dirt-streaked hand. She could almost hear Torin's voice, whispering into her hair.

Rise, my love. Rise.

CHAPTER 16

J ack found the cottage on the riverbank, just as Mirin had described it. He stood in the cold rapids, the cut in his palm clotting, and he stared at the house that belonged to his father.

Hedged by the tall ancient trees of the Aithwood, the cottage was quaint. Stone and mortar walls, shuttered windows, a thatched roof mottled with lichen. A steady trickle of smoke rose from the chimney, and a path led from the bank to the kail yard gate. A wordless invitation, it seemed, to those who arrived by river.

Only the garden betrayed the idyllic view. The vegetables were thin and bent to the south, as if the north wind had zealously raked over them. And though it did not storm, the light was bleak.

Jack emerged from the river and moved along the stone wall toward the cottage. He had yet to see a flicker of life, aside from the fowl in the coop, as he stood against the northern side of the house, waiting to see if he was spotted. But no sound came from within. He carefully walked the path around to the front, then knocked on the door.

He didn't know quite what he was expecting—Mirin had implied that his father might be dead—and so when an elderly woman answered the door, Jack merely gaped at her.

The woman's eyes widened, just as shocked to see him. Her gaze flickered beyond him, as if she expected to find a company of men in his shadow.

"I'm alone," he said gently. "I'm—"

"Don't speak yet," she warned. He felt a slight breeze touch his hair. It was the west wind, the one Jack trusted the most, though he still felt a lingering trace of fear when he remembered the manifested forms of these spirits. "Come inside, lad."

As Jack entered the cottage, his gaze roamed about the chamber. His father's house was a simple abode with a hearth anchoring the common room, its stacked stones darkened from soot. A collection of animal skulls and candlesticks sat crookedly on a mantel of woven branches. A desk aligned with one wall was crowded with a haphazard stack of leather books and parchment and inkwells. A large basket held a family of walking sticks by the back door. Cast-iron pots and herbs hung from the kitchen rafters.

Jack tried to envision his father living in such a place, but failed to conjure an image.

He at last met the woman's gaze and said, "Where is the Keeper of the Aithwood?"

"My son isn't here," she answered.

Somehow Jack maintained his composure. But his heart resounded with shock and amazement to realize he was beholding his grandmother. Someone he never even imagined meeting. Here was another thread, another root to bind him to the west.

Helplessly, he studied his nan.

Her hair was silver, bound in a braided crown. Her face was freckled and grooved from years facing the brunt of the wind. She was petite and wiry, her Breccan plaid apron fastened over a simple homespun dress. Her shoulders were stooped, as if she had carried a heavy weight all her life, and her eyes were blue as the eastern sky after a storm.

"Have I grown a second nose then?" she asked, but her voice was light, teasing him.

Jack blinked and flushed. "Forgive me. I—"

"Are you hungry? Sit by the hearth, and I'll bring you something."

He continued to stand, dazed by her trust and hospitality. But then he noticed that she was taking in his details as well. His long, brown hair with its quicksilver streak, his tall, slight frame, his elegant hands and his new moon eyes. And he thought, *Perhaps she sees a trace of her son in me. Perhaps she knows who I am to her.*

"Go on now," she prodded, and he sensed it would be foolish to cross this woman.

Jack couldn't help but smile as he slid his leather satchel from his back. He sat in the chair by the hearth, where a low fire was burning, and watched his grandmother shuffle to the kitchen table, where some sort of cake rested beside a bundle of herbs.

He wasn't the least bit hungry, but when his grandmother brought him a slice, he accepted it.

"You're Niall's son," she said.

Jack froze, the cake halfway to his mouth. Here he was, already breaking his promise to Mirin with the first Breccan he'd met.

His fear must have been evident, because his grandmother said, "Don't worry. I'll hold this secret as I've held many others over the years. Your smile gave you away."

"My smile?"

His nan nodded. "Aye. You must favor your mother in quite a few ways, but you have my son's smile. I would know it anywhere."

Her statement nearly brought tears to Jack's eyes. He had never realized how starved for connection, for family, he was until that moment. He forced himself to eat the cake by way of distraction, hoping it would fill the hollow spaces he felt. She made them two cups of tea and sat across from him at the hearth. The silence grew awkward, as if neither of them knew how to break it.

"Do you have a name?" she finally asked, gently.

"My name is John, but I've always gone by Jack."

His grandmother's brow creased. She was frowning, and at first Jack thought she was displeased, but then she spoke, her voice warbling with emotion. "John was my husband's name."

All this time Jack had hated the birth name Mirin gave him. He had refused to answer to it. Now he saw his name as another thread weaving him into the family he had longed for.

"I'm Elspeth," she said, clearing her throat. "But you can call me whatever you like."

Did she mean he could call her Nan?

Jack took a sip of tea. It was weak, as if she had steeped the herbs multiple times before, but it was sweeter than Mirin's brews, and he savored it.

"And why have you come to the west, Jack?" Elspeth asked.

He smiled again, because the answers felt impossible and strange, as though he were in a dream. But here he was, sitting across from his grandmother in his father's house on western land, a situation he would have never thought he'd experience. "I've come to be with my wife."

"You're wed to a Breccan?"

He nodded, almost saying the name Adaira before catching himself. "Lady Cora."

Elspeth's eyes widened. She took a sip of tea, as if to wash down what she truly wanted to say. The gesture made Jack nervous, and his mind began to race.

"Have things been good here for her?" he dared to ask. "I had hoped the clan would be welcoming."

"Yes, yes. Lady Cora seems to have found her place among us, although I've been banished to this cottage since the truth emerged. And sometimes the wind refuses to carry news this deep into the woods."

"You've taken my father's place in the Aithwood then?"

"Not quite," Elspeth said, tilting her head to the side as she continued to regard Jack. "What all do you know, lad?"

"About my father? Not much," Jack confessed. "I hoped to find him here."

"I'm sorry to say that he won't ever return to these woods."

Jack's heart quickened as he waited for her to continue. When the silence stretched long between them, he whispered, "Has my father been executed?"

Elspeth sighed. "No. He lives, but he's imprisoned in the castle keep, shamed and stripped of his name, and there he will most likely remain until his last day."

A prisoner with no hope of a pardon. It was a terrible thought, and yet Jack's hope rekindled, just knowing his father was still alive.

"Tell me more about yourself, Jack," Elspeth said, drawing his attention back to the moment. "What was your life like in the east?"

He hesitated, wondering how much he should tell her. But then, realizing this moment might never come again, he said, "I'm a bard. I attended the mainland university for ten years before returning home to play for the Tamerlaines."

Elspeth froze, her teacup halfway to her mouth. "A *bard*?"

He nodded, perspiration beginning to bead on his palms. He hoped he hadn't erred, telling her who he truly was, although he couldn't deny that he instinctively trusted her. All the same, he noticed her gaze darting to the satchel at his feet before flickering to her windows, which were shuttered, to keep the wind's curious tendrils at bay.

"I know music is forbidden in the west," he said. "But I—"

"That it is," his grandmother said firmly. "And for good reason."

"Can you tell me why?"

Elspeth set aside her teacup, then laced her gnarled fingers together on her lap. "The legend states that music's troubled history in the west began not long after the clan line was created. I'm sure you know the story of Joan and Fingal, and how their doomed marriage and deaths divided the isle?"

Jack nodded. "I know it all too well."

"As I thought you would, being a bard," Elspeth said. "But in the days before the isle was divided, the west was known for its music. It wasn't uncommon for there to be multiple bards across the land, spinning air into ballads with every season. The hall brimmed with it, night after night.

"There was one particular bard named Iagan who was greater than all the others, whose music was revered and beloved amongst the families in the west. He soon disliked the thought of there being competition among his kind and thought that it would be best for the clan to only have one appointed bard. This mindset soon took root, and musicians in the west began to lay aside their instruments, until there was only one—Iagan—and he played for the Breccans wholeheartedly.

"Not long after that, however, came the breaking. The isle changed; the west began to decline under the curse. Our spirits were weakened by the disunity, and soon Iagan's music caused more trouble than good."

"How so?" Jack asked, bent toward her tale.

"There was no end to it," Elspeth said. "There were no boundaries, no way to contain his music. When Iagan played, immense power flowed through him, and the land suffered even more for it, because he drove the spirits to serve him, directing their magic to himself rather than to the land and the sea and the air and the fire. Soon the clan became angry and afraid. The music they had once danced to in the hall was now causing the crops to wither in their kail yards, their creeks to dry up in the pastures, their fires to burn cold in their hearths, and the wind to blow strong and relentless against their cottages. They begged Iagan to cease his playing, to lay down his harp and find another way to serve the clan. But Iagan, who had been devoted to music since he was a lad, couldn't imagine giving up that which he loved more than his own life.

"He was banished from the castle, sent to live alone in the wilds. But still he played, disrupting the precarious balance of the spirits. For you see, all that those in the west had was their ability to churn magic into their craft, weaving plaids like steel, forging enchanted weapons. But when Iagan played, he momentarily stole even that magic for himself until all the Breccans had were empty hands and hungry bellies.

"In the end, his music cost him. A group of Breccans decided they had no choice but to slay him. They gathered around his cottage, teeth bared and swords drawn, ready to spill his blood on the soil. But when it comes to endings . . . well, they can take many shapes, can't they?

"Some legends claim that the mob cut off Iagan's hands and sliced out his tongue, leaving him to die a slow, soundless death. Other legends say that Iagan surrendered to his fellow clansmen, swearing to never play another note again if they would let him live. Some legends boast that a body was never found, that Iagan must have been drowned with his harp in the loch that surrounded his home.

"Any of these endings could be true, but what we know is that a great storm blew in that day, cold and dark and merciless, full of lightning and thunder. Speculation says that the mob caused it or Iagan, but the darkness hasn't faded since that day, and the west became a gray, quiet land."

Jack was quiet for a beat, soaking in the story. He had suspected that playing for the spirits in the west would be very different from playing for them in the east. He briefly imagined what Iagan must have felt: the intoxication of creating such magic without cost, of drawing all the enchantment of the isle unto himself. The praise, the worship. The power.

Jack had to break up the image in his mind before it enticed him any further.

"So now I must ask you, Jack," Elspeth said, glancing down at his satchel again. "Do you carry an instrument with you, and what do you intend to do with it?"

"I do have my harp," he answered, watching her face groove with displeasure. "I've been instructed to bring it. But I will be very mindful and careful."

"You should leave behind your harp," his grandmother said sharply. "Bury it somewhere deep or give it to the river and tell no one that you are a bard. Or else I fear it will see you slain, Jack. The Breccans still fear the power of a song, and if they knew you had dared to bring an instrument with you . . ." She shook her head, as if she couldn't bear to imagine what might come next.

Her words chilled him, making him doubt his conversation with Ash a few nights ago. Jack wondered, *Did I imagine it all? Am I losing my mind?*

Thinking back on that encounter now made it suddenly seem like a feverish dream. Perhaps Jack had been missing Adaira so deeply that he had only heard what he *wanted* to hear, to be given an excuse to cross the clan line. After taking in Elspeth's story, Jack felt he had made a foolish and dangerous mistake to be in the west with a harp.

The fire in the hearth gave a loud pop, and a spark arced across the dim space, landing on Jack's boot. Elspeth didn't notice, but Jack sensed that Ash was speaking to him again, perhaps reaching out his hand and tapping Jack's foot to reassure him. Jack relaxed in the chair and sipped his tea.

"Thank you for telling me the story," he said. "I'd never heard it, and I will keep it at the forefront of my mind."

Elspeth still seemed unsettled, but she nodded, wearily. She seemed to know there was no persuading him to give up the harp. Then she said, "I see there's a gleam in your eye, lad. As if a question is burning you up from within."

Jack drained his tea to the dregs and then met Elspeth's gaze, his breath feeling thin and shallow. His heart was pounding, as if he had been running for hours.

"Indeed. Can you tell me where I might find Cora?"

CHAPTER 17

T orin walked the earthen corridor, his posture bent as vines dragged like fingers over his hair. The passage curved, lit by strange clumps of bramble ensconced on the walls. *It isn't true fire*, Torin thought, frowning every time he passed a torch. The light was pale, with a blue heart. It held no heat, only secrets it seemed. He feared the flames would make him forget who he was if he stared at them too long.

Eventually, he came to a door.

He was fairly certain this was the same threshold over which he had entered, and he hesitated. When he had stepped through this door a few minutes earlier, he had been awestruck. He had believed the passage would lead him somewhere else. To a different door.

Why would it bring him back to where he started?

He sighed, realizing this earthen passage was nothing more than a giant circle burrowed in the ground like a rabbit warren. What was the point of such a thing?

Disappointed, Torin opened the door and emerged back into the world.

He was initially surprised by how quiet, how reverent, the land was. He felt like he was in a painting, fixed in time. Then he noticed it was twilight, the moment when day and night are equal. The hills were now covered in gleams and shadows, and Torin's pulse quickened.

It had been early night when he passed over that bewitched threshold. Now it was dusk?

Torin gazed at the sky, looking for the trail of the setting sun so he could determine in which direction south lay. But there was no sunset. The entire sky was a rippled medley of lavender, cerulean, and gold, as if the sun had set on every horizon. He felt dizzy, trying to make sense of it. A few stars glistened, scattered around the moon.

"Hail, mortal laird."

The voice was deep and mirthful, startling Torin. He turned and was shocked to see a man standing nearby.

No, not a man. One of the spirits.

He was tall and broad chested, and his skin shimmered with a green hue. His square-jawed face was perfectly shaped and cut by a dimpled smile, and his eyes were dark like summer soil, boasting long lashes. His ears were pointed, and his hair, flowing wild and free, almost looked like fine grass; small yellow blossoms and heart-leafed vines grew within the tangles. He was barefoot—flowers bloomed from the tips of his toes and fingers—and he wore only a pair of trousers that appeared to be spun from bark and moss.

At last, Torin thought, but he couldn't move as he marveled at the hill spirit. He had never seen one manifested. He had never heard one speak so clearly.

"You are surprised that we have welcomed you here, Torin of Tamerlaine?" the spirit remarked.

Yes. The word beat in Torin's mind, but it failed to find its way to his mouth. So he continued to stand there, dumbfounded.

"You should not be," the spirit continued, and when he moved his hands, petals fell from his fingertips, drifting like snow. "Come, we are assembled and waiting for you to join us." He turned to lead the way over the moors, and Torin finally roused his voice.

"I must go to my wife first. She'll be concerned about me. I've been away longer than I thought."

The spirit paused and regarded Torin with a strange, almost dangerous light in his eyes.

"Sidra is indeed wondering where you are," said the hill spirit, and Torin's heart lurched to hear how her name rolled in the spirit's deep-timbred voice. As if he were very familiar with her. "You will see her soon, but for now, I must ask you to make haste and join the assembly. Our time grows short."

Torin relented and followed the spirit, but he took care where he stepped. He could suddenly see the lads in the pennywort patches, the hungry maws in the mud puddles, the sleeping faces in the rocks, and small creatures made of woven grass.

He nearly stepped on one, and it let out a rustling hiss.

"Ah, take care, mortal laird," the hill spirit said, but he was amused. "The ferlies can sting if they are angered. Follow in my steps."

Torin heeded him, mimicking the long strides of the spirit. It felt like kilometers passed by with every breath. "I've never noticed these things before."

"Things?"

"Spirits," Torin corrected himself, with a grimace.

"You didn't notice because your eyes were closed to us. You walk in our realm now. Come, just ahead."

The pace quickened. Again, Torin had that sense that acres were rippling beneath every step he took, and he felt dizzy. The light never changed either. He was trapped in dusk, and he thought of Sidra. *Sidra, I am coming, I am coming . . .*

The hill spirit led him to a place he recognized. The sacred hill of the Earie Stone.

A great company had gathered here. Willowy maidens with leaves in their long tresses, young men with arms and legs like kindling. Old men shaped from wood, with reddened burls for noses, and old women woven from silver-leafed vines. In the center of them stood Lady Whin of the Wildflowers, the ruler of the eastern earth spirits, with her long dark hair, golden eyes, and crown of yellow gorse. Her skin was the shade of heather—a soft purple—and like the hill spirit, she had flowers blooming from her fingertips. She extended her hand to him, and the hill approached her, wove his long fingers with hers. Whispered something in her hair as the blossoms drifted around them.

Torin halted, transfixed by Whin as she stared at him.

He began to sweat as he felt the prickle of countless eyes on him. All the congregated spirits were watching him, and he didn't know what to say or where to look. Was it rude to meet their gaze? Was it folly to speak first?

He waited, and finally the hill spirit stepped away from Whin.

"I bring you Torin of the Tamerlaines," he said in his soothing deep voice. A lilt of summits and valleys. "Mortal Laird of the East."

The spirits were silent, but they bent their heads to him in respect.

"Welcome, Laird," said Whin. "It has been a long time, by mortal reckoning, since one of your kind has been invited to our realm."

Torin bowed, uncertain. "I'm honored to be here, Lady Whin." *Now tell me why you have summoned me. Tell me what you want.*

Whin smiled, as if she had read his thoughts. "You wonder why we have invited you?"

"Indeed. Although I have a suspicion that the invitation has something to do with the blight."

At once the air became colder and the shadows crept longer. The spirits were visibly disheartened, afraid. Torin could feel their worry faintly beating beneath the ground.

"Our sisters of the orchard have been stricken," Whin said, and her words began to thicken, like honey on her tongue. As if she were facing resistance as she spoke. "We . . . we have not obeyed our . . . king's command, and so we have suffered his ire. He struck the orchard first, but he will soon strike again."

Questions swarmed in Torin's mind. He wanted to demand answers, but he drew a deep breath instead. "I'm sorry to hear of this. The blight has also spread to a few mortals of my clan. I'm at a loss, and I hope that you can guide me. Tell me how to fix this terrible dilemma."

Whin looked at her hill spirit, who stood beside her, watching Torin with inscrutable eyes. "Ah, but that is why we have invited you here, Torin Tamerlaine," Whin said. "Because we need your help."

"Mine? What can I do?"

"You are the one who can solve the riddle of the blight," she explained. "We are powerless against it, but you . . . you are capable of healing us."

Torin gaped. He felt the blood drain from his face, his stomach knot. "Forgive me, Lady, but I have no knowledge, no insight. I have no idea how to help you."

"You will have to pay close attention then," the hill spirit said. "The king left a riddle, and should you solve it, the blight will end."

Spirits below, Torin thought, *I must be having a nightmare.*

He brushed his hand over his beard, shifted his weight from foot to foot. He didn't have the time, the energy to do this. But then an idea sparked, and he said, "Let me return to the mortal world. I will bring you a bard who can solve this riddle for you."

Whispers spun among the spirits. His mention of Jack had visibly stirred their emotions; some sounded hopeful, others doubtful.

Whin's pleasant face hardened. "Your bard must not come here."

"But he is very shrewd, very capable with riddles," Torin said, even though he knew Jack was in the west by now.

"No, mortal laird. We almost welcomed him into our domain when he sang to ensnare us," Whin said, but then she paused, unable to further explain. A tremor moved through her as she remembered.

"We should have claimed him then," said one of the ancient, burl-nosed men.

The hill spirit gave him a sharp glance. "But the bard would not have entered our hold willingly. He must come on his own volition. We would have paid a steep price if we had claimed him without his agreement."

"And we cannot claim him now. Ash," Whin said, with a curled lip as she uttered his name, "has seen to that."

"If Ash could move faster," someone muttered, "then it would end."

"Ash has been all but extinguished. How can we trust him?"

"We must not trust fire," one of the vine women said. "Never, never trust fire!"

"I don't understand," Torin said, beseeching Whin. "Why not invite the bard? Why not bring one more capable than me to help?"

The spirits merely stared at him.

"Please," Torin murmured, holding his palms up. "Please, my people are not well. They need me. I cannot be away from them any longer. You will need to choose someone else to help you in this realm, and I will do my best from mine."

More silence. And long, piercing stares.

Torin flushed. He felt oddly vulnerable for a reason he couldn't understand. One of the alder maidens said, "Tell him, Lady Whin. He will strive to help us if he knows. Tell him about his—"

"Quiet," Whin ordered, and the maiden wilted.

Torin studied the alder girl, seeing that her eyes were like dew. He looked back at Whin and said, "What does she speak of?"

Whin could no longer hold his gaze. She glanced away, and Torin felt stung with dread.

"Tell me *what*?"

"It is not our place to say. You can find the riddle in the orchard," she said. "The sooner you can solve it, the sooner we are healed and the sooner you can return to your realm. But not before then, mortal laird."

Astounded, he watched as the spirits began to depart. They were leaving him here, standing on the sacred hill.

Torin spun and dared to take the arm of the hill spirit. "*Please*," he begged. "I need to return home. You said that I could see Sidra after the assembly."

The hill spirit sighed. He suddenly appeared old and weary, as if he were withering. "Yes. Go and see her, mortal laird."

Torin waited, but nothing happened. The hill spirit unhinged himself and began to leave with Whin, flowers drifting in their wake.

Very well then. Torin would find his own portal home.

He knew where he was now, and he strode over the fells, trampling hissing clumps of ferlies and kicking frowning stones out of his path. Soon the road rose to meet him, and Torin ran along its winding path, the light and darkness still suspended in equal measure. It was not day or night, but he had a terrible sensation that time had been flowing quickly in the mortal realm.

He saw his and Sidra's croft in the distance, and his heart lifted. He didn't know what he would say to her, but an apology was waiting, ripe in his mouth as he reached to open the kail yard gate. His hand passed through it.

Torin stopped, bewildered.

He tried again, but his hand—which looked every bit as solid as he knew it to be—passed through the iron brackets once more, as if he were ethereal.

He cautiously moved forward, passing through the gate. He felt no pain. Nothing but his growing dismay.

"Sidra?" he called, his voice ringing in the ever-present dusk. "Sid?"

He reached for the door, but his hand passed through the wood. He stared at it, then saw that his hand was whole and visible again when he brought it back to himself.

He felt the solid constraint of his flesh and the cadence of his heart. He felt the air swell in his lungs. And yet he couldn't feel the gate, the wood.

Unsettled, he melted through the front door and found himself standing in a shadowed common room. No fire burned in the hearth. No candles were lit. No dinner was on the table.

"Sidra! Maisie?" he called for them, walking through the table, through the walls. He searched the cottage, his terror mounting, but his wife and his daughter were not there.

Torin stood in the common room again, his breaths ragged,

telling himself to be calm. He must calm his mind, solve this mystery.

He began to notice other things. Sidra's herbs were missing. Her clothes were gone, as were Maisie's. Their possessions were no longer here. They had moved. Moved . . .

He remembered one of the last things he had said to her.

It would make my life much simpler if we moved into the castle.

Swallowing the lump in his throat, Torin passed through the front door again. He ran down the road to the city of Sloane. The thoroughfare was bustling, as it often was at midday. It hummed with life, and Torin called out to one of his guards, stationed at the gate.

"Andrew? Andrew, have you seen Sidra?"

Andrew didn't hear Torin, and didn't see him. Not even when Torin came to stand before him, almost nose to nose.

"Can you hear me? *Andrew!*"

The guard was completely unaware of him.

Torin had no choice but to step around Andrew. He began to jog down the street. He waited to make eye contact with someone. He waited for one of his people to call out a greeting to him, as they always did when they saw him.

No one noticed him.

When a lad ran right through him, Torin came to a halt and watched the child continue on his way, completely oblivious that he had just scampered *through* someone else.

Torin held his panic at bay and entered the castle, following the trail of excited conversation up the stairs to the laird's wing. He heard Sidra's voice. The beloved sound sent a pang through him, as if he hadn't heard her speak in years. The doors were open, and Torin came to a stop on the threshold, his eyes seeking her.

Sidra stood in the center of the room, facing him. Light must have been streaming through the window behind her because she was golden. Illuminated.

"We are very thrilled to have you here, Lady Sidra," said a servant woman. "Shall I have another small bed brought up? For the wee lass?"

Sidra smiled. "No, but thank you, Lilith. Maisie will sleep with me for now."

"Until his lairdship returns?"

"Yes."

"Very good, my lady. Ah, here is your afternoon tea."

Torin was vaguely aware of the air stirring around him. Of another servant walking through him. He was staring at Sidra, desperate for her eyes to shift, to see him standing on the threshold.

Sidra.

But she glanced down as the servant brought a tray and set it on a round table by the window. There was a silver pot of tea, spouting fragrant steam into the air, and a mince pie, warm from the oven.

"Thank you, Rosie," Sidra said to the girl who had delivered the refreshment, but her voice was strained.

Rosie curtsied and left, passing back through Torin. Lilith remained to serve Sidra. The attendant was talking about something as she sliced into the pie, when Sidra suddenly covered her mouth.

"W-where is the chamber pot?"

Lilith set down her knife with a clatter, eyes wide as Sidra began to fumble at the bureau's twin doors, where the pot was stored. The servant rushed to help her, but Sidra was already on the floor, retching into the bowl.

"Shh, my lady. It's all right," Lilith said in a motherly tone, holding Sidra's hair as she continued to vomit. "It's all right."

Torin remained standing in the arch of the lintel, frozen. *What is this?* he wondered with a frantic heart. *Why is she ill?*

"Was it the pie, Lady?" Lilith asked, taking the pot when Sidra had finally finished.

"I think so," Sidra said faintly, still kneeling on the floor. "I also can't stand the smell of blood pudding."

Since when have you hated blood pudding, Sid? Torin thought, concerned.

"Ah. Well, we will take great care to avoid those foods for now. Here, let me help you up." Lilith eased Sidra to her feet. "I was the same with my first bairn. I couldn't stand the smell of kail boiling in the pot. Which was rather unfortunate. I was sick for months."

Bairn?

Sidra wiped her mouth, forlorn.

"But that's not to say it won't pass quickly for you, Lady," Lilith hurried to amend. "The first three months are difficult, but I am sure you will feel back to normal very soon."

Sidra was quiet, lost in her thoughts.

Torin had ceased breathing.

"How far along are you?" Lilith asked gently.

"Seven weeks as of yesterday." Sidra drew her fingers through her hair, her face pale. "And I would ask you to hold this confidence for now, Lilith. I don't want the clan to know yet."

"I won't speak a word of it, Lady," the attendant reassured. "But I'm glad to know, so I may be of help to you. Such as telling the cook to cease making you mince pies." She began to gather the tray. "Does anything else sound good to you at the moment? Perhaps an oatcake?"

"No," Sidra said, with a watery smile. "I think I should rest for now."

Lilith nodded and moved to the door. But she paused, glancing back at Sidra with a sheen of pride. "Does his lairdship know, Lady?"

Sidra closed her eyes, briefly. "No, not yet. I . . . plan to tell him when he returns from his trip to the mainland."

"Very good, Lady Sidra. Ring if you need anything."

Lilith walked through Torin. The doors shut, wood and iron aligning with his lungs. Slowly, he stepped forward, fully entering Sidra's new bedchamber.

He didn't realize how desperate he was for her to see him, hear him. Not until he was halfway to her, his heart wildly beating, and found he couldn't take another step.

She stood in the light, breathing slow and deep, a palm pressed to her chest.

Torin's joy flooded him, blurred his vision. He was overcome by it; he wanted to drown in this delight with her. He and Sidra had made a child together. He forgot he was a spirit. He forgot he was made of shadows and air, and he closed the distance between them.

"Sidra," he whispered ardently. He reached out to caress her hair, but he couldn't feel it. His fingers passed through her as if she were a dream.

She didn't hear him. She covered her face with her hands, smothering the break of a sob.

Torin's joy dissolved the moment her hands fell away, the moment her reddened eyes met his.

Her face was blank. No flicker of recognition stirred within her. She didn't see him as she gazed absently at the wall.

"Sid," he said. "Can you see me? Hear me?"

She sighed and walked into him. A shudder rippled in his spirit. Frost crackled along his bones. He had never felt so cold in all his life.

Torin turned and watched as Sidra went to the window, struggled with it for a moment, then managed to open it. She rested in the waft of brisk, fresh air.

He thought on what he had heard her say to Lilith. That he was on a mainland trip. Already, Sidra had covered his absence with deceit, to maintain order and normalcy. He thought it wise of her, even as he hated that she had to lie for him. And she had moved into the castle, giving the appearance that all was well.

"I'm here with you, Sidra," Torin whispered, aching.

She raised her head. The breeze lifted the hair from her shoulders.

He waited, hopeful. Had she heard him? Some small thread of him believed that she had. That her soul sensed that his was near.

Sidra reached for the curtains and drew them closed with a snap. The golden light that had limned her faded, but Torin's vision remained the same. He could see her clearly as she walked to the bed and sat on the edge. Her hands hesitated as she reached for her boots, her brow creased with worry. But then the moment passed, eclipsed by her exhaustion, and she shucked off her shoes, crawled into the bed, still wearing her dress and stockings, and pulled the quilts up to her shoulders.

Sidra rested, quiet, unmoving.

Torin waited until he heard her breaths deepen and knew she was sleeping.

He felt unmoored, lost, until he remembered the riddle in the orchard. He was trapped in the spirit realm until he solved the blight.

He let his anger rise, ignite.

He walked through doors, walls, mortals. Across the rise and fall of the land, to where the orchard lay.

CHAPTER 18

J ack would face a potentially life-altering choice when he emerged from the Aithwood. Adaira resided in the Breccans' city, deep in the heart of western territory, and he could reach her in one of two ways: by the northern road or the southern road.

"Both will lead you around the mountains and into Kirstron," Elspeth said as she packed provisions for him for the long walk. "And both present you with different dangers. If you take the northern road, you'll have to pass by Thane Pierce's holding and lands, which you should avoid at all costs. If you take the southern road, you'll have to pass through Spindle's Vale, a highly traveled route known for trickery. Either way, you'll need to be very careful."

"Thane Pierce?" Jack echoed.

"A noble family who like trouble," his nan muttered in disdain. "Even if you take the southern road to avoid passing their holding, you should still be prepared to run into Rab Pierce. He and his men are known for their roaming ways and have been patrolling the roads lately as a self-proclaimed 'watch of the west.' There's been more crime this summer than usual, and a thane's son like Rab likes to feel important by enacting 'justice.'"

Jack didn't like the sound of Rab. In the end, he decided to take the southern road through the valley to avoid the Pierce holding altogether. It would take him two days to reach the city by foot if he set a hard pace. Those two days were bound to feel like two years, knowing Adaira was on the horizon, and Jack was tempted to veer into the hills, to see if the land would fold and shorten the distance for him.

"Don't stray too far from the road," Elspeth said, reading his mind. "As I said, the vale is known for mischief. The mist gathers thick, and it's easy to get turned around without the sun or moon for guidance. But if you must depart from the road, follow the deer trails. The animals here are wise when it comes to knowing places to go and places to avoid."

Jack nodded and accepted the provisions with gratitude. "And what of the city and the castle? Anything I should know about them?"

"Aye," Elspeth said. "Entering the city will be no trouble. It's sprawled around the castle, so you'll have to pass through its streets whether you arrive from the north or the south. The castle itself is nearly impenetrable. It's surrounded by a moat and built on a hill. There is only one way to access the fortress, and that's by bridge. It's heavily guarded, so you'll have to think of a reason to get across. Perhaps pass yourself off as a merchant or trader."

"I'll do that," Jack said. "Thank you, Elspeth."

His nan, hands on her hips, tilted her head and stared at him. "Are you not afraid, Jack? I've just told you the path you plan to take is going to be riddled with impossibilities and danger, and you look as thrilled as a lad who's been let out of class early."

He almost laughed. "I know I should be afraid. But I'm where I'm supposed to be. And I'd soon become miserable if I forfeited my fate in order to remain 'safe.'"

Elspeth only snorted, but he could sense she was moved by his words. She laid her hand on his cheek and said, "Then go, Jack."

He bid his nan farewell, leaving her in the garden. She stood at her gate and watched him follow the river's path upstream. He wondered if he would have the chance to visit her again, or if this had been the one and only time he would ever spend with her.

Soon the Aithwood began to thin around him. Gray light shone through the canopy like bars of tempered steel as Jack wove his way closer to the forest's edge. He slowed when he saw a glimmer of gold in the shadows. When he smelled a sweet familiar rot.

Jack carefully approached a sick rowan tree. He didn't know if he was shocked that the blight was also present in the west, or if he should have expected it. He took a moment to examine the surrounding trees and saw that another one looked recently stricken as well. Jack wondered if the Breccans had done anything to contain the blight, or if they had yet to learn that such destruction was creeping across their territory.

He would talk to Adaira about it, to see if she had any insight that he didn't. But then Jack thought of Innes Breccan. Would he want her to know the east was struggling with the blight? Should he keep that information concealed from the west?

Jack grimaced, uncertain. He would deal with it later, after he had reunited with Adaira.

He carefully wended his way through the rest of the forest and reached the boundary, the place where the trees ended and the land unfurled.

He took his first full view of the west.

The hills, speckled with copper bracken and yellow-tipped woad, rolled into a steep mountain range whose peaks were crowned by low-hanging clouds. The river flowed from a place hidden between two summits, clear and babbling over large, smooth stones. The air smelled like burning peat, damp moss, and brine from the distant sea.

Jack turned to the left and set off at a brisk pace. Determined to stay focused on the journey and to never let his mind wander, he noticed every twisted tree he walked beneath, every bird that fluttered past. He listened to the wind, to the sounds it carried. He passed through thin patches of heather and climbed over rocks softened with moss.

Jack soon came upon the first croft—a sprawling farm of stone fences, a muddy yard, and a cottage that looked crooked in the wind. It felt dark and abandoned. Disquieted, Jack pressed onward to find the southern road.

He passed a few other crofts and at last found pockets of life. Sheep bleated and children called to one another as they went about their afternoon chores. Smoke rose from hearth fires, and women tended to their gardens. Jack's anxiety spiked when he started to pass people on the road.

He kept his head down and his pace steady, fighting the urge to stray from his route. The swirling mist was both an advantage and a challenge: it cloaked him and yet made it difficult to discern what lay ahead.

By twilight, Jack had no idea how many kilometers he had covered and his feet were riddled with blisters. He decided to find a place to make camp for the night. Elspeth had packed him a simple but hearty meal, along with a flask of ale, and he thought of the story she had shared with him about Iagan as he followed a deer trail leading away from the road. Eventually, he found a cluster of bracken to bed down in.

An eastern wind was blowing, whistling through the valley. It felt cold for a summer night, and Jack shivered, longing for his plaid as he ate a cheese pie. He didn't hear the riders, not until the party was nearly upon him, and by then it was too late to dash behind a cover of rocks.

He froze in the bracken, watching as six riders drew closer in the dusky light. Young men, mounted on lathered horses, dressed in leather and hunting plaids. They were heavily armed with swords, long bows, arrows, axes. Blood was splattered across a few of their chests.

Pass me by, Jack prayed. *Take no note of me. I'm insignificant, beneath your attention—*

"And who might you be?" asked one of the riders, a man with straw-blond hair and a ruddy complexion, as he walked his stallion in a circle around Jack.

Jack rose, hoping his satchel would remain hidden in the bracken fronds. He was quiet for a moment, suffering their scrutiny with as much dignity as he could muster. They took in everything about him: the lack of tattoos on his skin, the absent plaid, his simple but durable clothes, the way his boot leathers crosshatched up to his knees. The braids in his hair.

"My name is John," he said.

"John who?" a second man asked, his narrow-set eyes suspicious.

"I've no surname," Jack answered. "I claim what my laird gave me."

"Where are you traveling to, John Breccan?" the blond rider inquired, his stallion finally coming to a halt. His five companions mirrored his actions, forming a ring around Jack.

"Castle Kirstron."

"What awaits you there?"

"My wife."

"Ah. She must be anxious to see you then. Come join our party. It's unwise to travel the valley alone at night. You can share our fire."

Jack's mind raced, seeking a polite excuse. But he couldn't find a way out of this, and so he nodded and allowed the hunting party to herd him to a small glen. When he noticed one of the riders lifting his satchel from the ferns, Jack's fear ignited, burning his lungs, his heart, his stomach.

A camp was swiftly made. A fire was kindled in a ring of stones, and skewers of rabbit and potatoes were set over the flames. The horses were hobbled and tended to, and bedrolls were laid out on the grass. Flasks of ale were passed around, and Jack pretended to drink, hoping to ease their mistrust of him.

"No plaid?" the blond commented.

Jack, who had certainly taken note of the plaids draped across the six men, shook his head. No doubt the weavings were enchanted, although Jack wouldn't be able to know without touching one. "It's with a weaver at the moment." He dared to study their features. The firelight spilling across their noses and lips made them appear haggard. "You have yet to tell me your own names."

The blond—the apparent leader—took a swig from his flask. "I'm Rab Pierce, and these are my men."

Wonderful, Jack thought drolly. *I choose the southern road to avoid the Pierce holding and I still manage to have Rab stumble upon me.*

"I've never seen you before," Rab said. "Where do you live?"

"On a small croft not far from here."

"Hmm." Rab didn't seem convinced, but he didn't press Jack for further answers. "You often enjoy nightly walks?"

Jack nodded, but sweat was beginning to seep through his tunic. The man with the narrow, beady eyes and a chain of tattoos around his neck began to hand him a bannock, and that's when it happened: one moment Jack's hand was outstretched in acceptance, and the next it was twisted behind his back and he was harshly thrown facedown in the grass. He resisted the desperate urge to flail, to fight.

He lay quietly and breathed through his teeth as one of the riders took the dirk sheathed at his belt. Jack's only weapon.

"Bind his wrists and ankles," said Rab.

"Why are you binding me?" Jack raised his head from the loam. "I'm no threat to you." He felt Narrow Eyes begin to fasten his wrists together, painfully tight, and then his ankles. Eventually, Jack was set back up like a puppet, and he watched as Rab sifted through his provision pack, dividing the meager spoils among his men. And then came the harp.

Jack could hear Elspeth's warnings echo through him—*you should leave your harp behind, bury it somewhere deep or give it to the river, and tell no one that you are a bard.* He watched as Rab yanked the harp from its sheath. The instrument gleamed in the firelight, the simple carvings in its frame seeming to move and breathe.

"Why are you carrying a harp?" Rab asked, meeting Jack's gaze.

"It was given to me."

"And who gave it to you, John Breccan?"

Jack didn't answer. He could scarcely breathe, feeling the wind tousle his hair like cold fingers.

"Do you recognize this, Malcolm?" Rab asked Narrow Eyes.

"Aye. Looks like one of Iagan's harps."

"As I thought." Rab's smile was a sharp crescent. "You stole this from Loch Ivorra."

Jack frowned. "I've never been to Loch Ivorra. And I didn't steal this harp."

Rab carefully slid the instrument back into its sheath, but he kept it beside him on the grass. "I know what you are, John."

"If that is so," Jack said, his cadence rising, betraying his agitation, "then you would understand why I carry a harp that was given to me."

Rab leaned forward. "You are a liar and a thief. I don't believe anything you've told me, and you aren't going anywhere until you give us the truth. All of it."

Jack held Rab's stare. His heart was drumming against his ribs, and his hands were going numb. This was not how he had envisioned his time in the west unfolding. This was not how his journey was to progress, and his hope began to wane.

"I'm a messenger of peace," he said, which provoked a chorus of chuckles from the Pierce men.

"Of course you are," Rab said with a chuckle.

"I carry a truth blade, which you've taken, and wear no plaid," Jack continued. "I'm a bard, and this harp was given to me by Laird Torin Tamerlaine, who wrote that letter that rests by your foot, supporting my claims. Read it for yourself."

The bold statements killed the men's amusement. The camp fell deathly quiet. There was only the crackle and pop of the fire and the distant howl of the wind as it passed over the glen.

"You carry no weapons but a truth blade," Rab finally echoed, ignoring the taunt of Torin's letter. "But that also is a lie. Your harp is perhaps more dangerous than any enchanted steel."

"It holds no danger unless I play it," Jack said. "And you should let me go before my wife hears of this."

"I take it your wife is Lady Cora?" Rab teased, and his comrades laughed.

"Yes," Jack said.

The men froze.

"My wife is Lady Cora," Jack repeated, calmly. "Her name was Adaira when she was in the east, when we were married. I'm traveling to her now, and I would appreciate it if you let me go without any more trouble—"

Rab was fast. He delivered a sharp blow to Jack's face to silence him. Jack was momentarily dazed by the impact. He tasted blood in his mouth and spat it in the grass, his eyes watering as he looked at Rab and his barely contained fury.

"You are not a bard," Rab said. "You only pretend to be."

"If you doubt me," Jack rasped, "then set my harp in my hands and I will prove myself to you."

"I will cut off your hands before I set a harp in them." Rab slid the sharp tip of his dirk beneath the neckline of Jack's tunic. At first, Jack thought Rab was about to slit his throat, but Rab found the golden chain that hid beneath Jack's clothes. His half coin.

In one swift movement, the necklace broke with a metallic snap.

Jack hadn't removed the coin since Alastair had draped it over him. The day he handfasted himself to Adaira. A terrible ache bloomed in Jack's chest. He stared at Rab as he tucked the golden half coin into his pocket.

"What you are is a thief and a charlatan," Rab said with a sneer. "And we don't take kindly to either one in the west."

"Are you afraid of me then?" Jack said, his voice full of ire. He pulled at his bindings. "Are you—"

Rab grasped Jack's hair, shoving him forward and down. He held Jack's throbbing face over the fire, dangerously close. The heat was suddenly becoming more and more unbearable.

"Tell us the truth, thief," Rab taunted, forcing Jack even lower. "Tell us who you are and why you stole the harp from Loch Ivorra, and perhaps we will let you go and water your fantasies of being married to a laird's daughter."

Jack closed his eyes, feeling the fire's heat begin to scorch his face. "I have told you . . . the truth. If you doubt me, use my truth blade."

Rab inched his face lower. Jack kept his eyes shut, expecting to feel the lick of the flames any moment. But it never came, and the heat and light suddenly vanished.

A slew of curses ensued.

Rab's fingers tightened in Jack's hair.

Trembling, Jack opened his eyes.

The fire was gone, burned into ashes. Only a trail of smoke remained behind to dance, elusively.

"The wind must have blown it out," said one of the men, but he sounded wary.

Jack panted in relief, the sweat dripping from his nose. He knew it hadn't been the wind, and he searched the ashes for a sign, a word, a face. But his vision blurred as Rab yanked him back and threw him down on the grass.

"You should let me go," Jack said. "You should let me go before you interfere with something you have no knowledge of and probably want nothing to do with."

"Oh, I will let you go," Rab said, looming over him. "But not yet, *thief*."

Jack tried to brace himself for the blow. But he was defenseless. Rab's boot caught him in the temple. Jack saw a smattering of stars, heard a trickle of laughter.

He was looking at his harp, at Torin's unopened letter, when Rab's foot struck him again.

Jack folded into the darkness.

CHAPTER 19

Adaira had mastered the art of sneaking out of Castle Sloane in the east. She told herself it should be no different here in the west at Castle Kirstron, even though the Breccans' holding was designed to keep people *out* and there were still many passages she had yet to be given permission to roam. But three things gave her confidence:

She could now unlock enchanted doors with her blood.

She had a sword she could carry anywhere.

She had ridden through the wilds enough times with Innes to have gained a good sense of the land.

Adaira dressed in a long-sleeved tunic and leather jerkin. Her hair was a similar shade to Innes's and would swiftly give her away, so she covered it with the drape of her blue plaid. She then belted the sword to her waist and packed her leather satchel with all the supplies David had left with her to tend to her stitches—fresh linen bandages and a small jar of healing salve. She also packed a flask of wine and a bannock left over from breakfast.

Taking the corridors, she eventually emerged into the courtyard.

No one paid her any attention.

Adaira stood on the flagstones, deliberating. She had tried to estimate how far away the spirit had fallen. It was well beyond the city walls, in a part of the wilds, kilometers away. She imagined the spirit was now lying broken and exposed on a hillside. Adaira's heart quickened as she glanced sidelong at the bustling stables.

She had to reach the spirit first, before anyone else did. And she would find them sooner if she rode, but requesting a horse from a groom would alert her parents.

Adaira hesitated. She hadn't been granted permission to venture out on her own and knew she risked Innes's anger by doing so.

The wind gusted, ringing the hour's bell.

She would have to go by foot then. Adaira turned to the portcullis and warily approached the bridge.

It took her past another heavily guarded entrance, and since she looked like any other Breccan woman moving from fortress to city, Adaira was able to weave her way to the westernmost gate. She expected to hear talk of the fallen spirit, but the markets and streets were preoccupied with nothing more than their daily routines.

Was I the only one to witness her fall? Adaira wondered as she at last emerged from the city. The wilds undulated before her, and she began to chart her course. But it was far more difficult than she had anticipated. The western hills were a bewitching, deceptive place, swarming with valleys and mist and veined with rocks. Adaira would crest one rise, believing she had come upon the place where the spirit fell, only to discover another hill in the distance.

She passed through a glen and a small forest, startling a company of red deer and a pair of doves. Where the trees thinned, Adaira saw a loch—a small circle of dark water, hedged by the foothills. In the center of the loch was a tiny island that held a cottage, its dilapidated stone walls nearly conquered by vines and lichens and impossibly tall thistles. A narrow footpath bravely ran from the island to the land, providing a way to reach the cottage.

Adaira stared at it, shivering. The cottage was abandoned, and she wondered who had once lived there as she continued onward.

She soon saw a promising sign. A few branches on a lone elm were splintered, as if the tree had attempted to catch a falling spirit.

Adaira strode directly to it. She traced the tree's trunk, looked up into the path of brokenness. Something had indeed fallen through these boughs. A raven was perched amid the damage, peering down at her at with curious, beady eyes. And then she noticed something sticky and wet beneath her fingers.

Slowly, she drew her hand away.

She studied the honeyed substance that glistened on her fingertips. It was golden and boasted a sweet aroma, like nectar.

She wiped the spirit's blood on her plaid and studied the ground until she saw a minuscule path, bending the grass. Her eyes traced it carefully. The path was made by narrow feet that had dragged every other stride, obviously because of a wound. Beads of that sweet-smelling blood glittered on the grass every few paces, catching the dim sunlight like dew. The traces of blood brought Adaira down into a valley and then up to a daunting outcrop of jagged rocks, their many facets mimicking a host of frowning faces.

Seeing the path she needed to take to reach the ledge at the top, Adaira breathed into her hands to warm them. It had been so long since she had walked the hills alone. Since she had climbed into caves and swum in the sea. Adaira felt a spasm of nostalgia, but she shook it away before it set its claws into her. She began to climb.

She reached the small ledge, where the blood pooled in thick drops. The trail seemed to end here, and Adaira searched the rocks around her, eager to find another lead. But she soon realized this was it. The path went cold. She crouched by the beads of golden blood, confused until she felt the wind sigh through her hair.

"Of course," Adaira said, unable to hide her disappointment.

Why did I presume that I could find you? That you would need my help?

She stood and tried to convince herself to begin her descent down the rocks. That was when she felt a slight tremble beneath her. A faint vibration, like laughter in one's chest. And then there was the damp smell of a cave, a breathy welcome.

Adaira pivoted, astonished to see a slender opening in the rock. She was certain it hadn't been there before, but she sensed that the rock was inviting her to step within its mouth, should she be brave enough. She reverently entered, worried that she needed a torch, but she soon realized that mysterious fire burned along the cave walls. The fire looked like tangles of brambles, and the flames were white. Fire but not fire. Frowning, Adaira leaned in closer to study it. . . .

She heard a shuffle of feet. The soft clink of wind chimes, followed by a hiss.

Adaira glanced to her right.

The fallen spirit stood two paces away, and her hands were up, wordlessly commanding Adaira to come no closer.

Adaira merely studied her at first. The spirit in her manifested form was slightly taller than her, slender, composed of elegant lines and curves. Her hair was long, a rich indigo in the magical light. Her ears were tapered, and her face was heavily scratched, as were her forearms. The nails on her fingers and toes were sharpened into points and her skin was a pale blue, save in a few places: her right shoulder, her left collarbone, and a portion of her legs were blotched with brilliant gold, as if she had been illumined with a paintbrush. She wore silver-linked armor that sounded like chimes every time she moved, and one of her thighs was carved with a deep gash. Amber-hued blood continued to drip slowly down her leg.

She had only her two left wings, one larger than the other, both stained mauve. They were iridescent in the strange cave light, strung with intricate filaments like the wings of a dragonfly. Both hung limp and tattered behind her, resting on the cave floor.

"I've come here to help you," Adaira said. "I saw you fall from the clouds," she added as she began to step forward.

Again, the spirit motioned her to stay back, a warning flash in her eyes.

"I don't want to harm you," Adaira whispered, stung by the spirit's coldness. "Please, let me help you."

The spirit's face softened.

She recognizes me, Adaira thought. She continued to study the spirit and realized that she must have been present the day Jack summoned the four winds. The day when Adaira had stood face-to-face with Bane and he had taunted her.

The spirit parted her lips to speak, but no sound emerged. Devastation stole across her lacerated face. She laid her hand to her throat, as if a hook hid within it, anchoring her voice.

"You can't speak?" Adaira surmised, sadly.

The spirit nodded. The loss of her voice seemed as fresh to her as the wound in her thigh.

"Will you let me tend to you?" Adaira brought her provision pack forward. But she patiently waited and was surprised when the spirit nodded and came to her. There was no fear in the spirit's limping gait, no hesitation. Why, then, had she held Adaira at bay at first?

The spirit must have read her thoughts. She pointed to the strange fire, then back at Adaira. She made other urgent motions.

Don't look directly at this light.

"I understand," Adaira said. They were standing in between realms. A dangerous, uncertain place, neither mortal nor spirit.

The spirit eased herself down, away from the enchanted light, and Adaira knelt beside her. She opened her satchel and brought out her supplies, wishing that she had learned more from Sidra when she had had the chance.

She gently reached out and touched the spirit's knee. The moment their skin met—warm and cold—Adaira's mind was flooded with a dizzying array of images.

There was a hall in the clouds, tall pillars that melted into a night sky. Stars burning in braziers. The rustling of hundreds of wings. And Bane, sitting on a throne with his lance of lightning.

Kae . . . why have you kept me waiting?

Adaira flinched at the sound of the northern king's voice. She jerked her hand away, and as soon as the contact was broken, the images melted from her mind. Her breath hitched when she met the spirit's eyes, beholding the same shock within her.

"I was seeing your memories, wasn't I?" Adaira whispered. "Your name is Kae."

The spirit nodded. She seemed both troubled and relieved. The king had torn off her wings and stolen her voice, but he hadn't thought to restrict her memories.

Kae held out her lean, sharp-nailed hand.

Adaira took it, their palms aligning. She closed her eyes and sank into the memory again, feeling threads of emotion. Defiance, regret, longing, anger, sadness. Kae's emotions, she realized. By the time Kae's wings had been severed and she was falling, Adaira's heart was pounding so hard that she had to break the contact between them.

She took a moment to steady herself, then met Kae's gaze again.

"Bane was asking about Jack," Adaira said, swallowing the fear that was rising within her. "Is my . . . is he in trouble?"

Kae moved her hands, but Adaira couldn't draw meaning from her elegant motions.

"Can you show me the last time you saw him?" Adaira rasped, hoping it wasn't too much to ask.

Kae turned pensive, as if she were thinking, sorting through her memories. But she held out her hand again, and Adaira took it.

She tumbled into a flashing, disorienting string of memories. They were limned in gold, and Adaira realized she was flying, soaring over the isle.

She saw Jack kneeling in Mirin's kail yard, staring into the distance. His face was downcast with despair—an expression Adaira had never seen on him before—and her heart wrenched. *I've hurt him, far more than I realized,* she thought with a flare of guilt. He knelt there for a while, unmoving, until he heard Mirin call for him, and he began to uproot carrots from the soil.

He was walking Frae to school, holding her hand, listening to her talk.

He was sitting on the hillside in the dark, playing his song for Adaira. The harp strings glinted in the starlight as he coaxed sweetened notes from them.

She wanted to linger with him there for a hundred years. She soaked in the sight of him, her blood coursing, but the vision suddenly shifted. Adaira's consciousness reeled in response, but she clung to Kae's hand, remembering this was the spirit's memory. Kae had left Jack on the hillside to chase after an eastern spirit. A golden-haired faerie with clawed wings who was carrying Jack's notes in her taloned hands.

Don't cross the clan line with those notes, Kae hissed at her.

The eastern spirit only laughed, soaring faster on her route.

Kae briefly caught the spirit, shredding the edges of her right wing with her teeth. The spirit was slowed down for a moment, but then she tore free and pressed onward. The Aithwood groaned beneath the gale the two of them spun—one pursuing, one dodging—but soon they had spilled into the west. Kae let the eastern faerie go, with her tattered wings and her cruel amusement.

Frantic, Kae wheeled to blow north, but Bane had already heard the music and felt the stirrings of old magic.

Jack then sat before an orchard, strumming and singing for the trees. Adaira tried to make sense of his intentions. Was he singing for the earth? For the orchard? But then Kae's perceptions narrowed, directing Adaira's attention.

The spirit's emotions felt snarled, a medley of fear and worry and annoyance. Kae's wings were churning up cold air, blowing in Jack's face.

Stop playing! He's heard you. He's coming!

Jack was completely unaware of Kae as he sang. The spirit cowered as the storm blew in. She retreated but kept watching from a distance. She saw the moment when Bane's lightning nearly struck Jack.

Kae lingered long enough for the storm to pass. Long enough to ensure that Jack was able to rise and survey the steaming orchard. Rise and gather his harp. When she passed by him, the air from her wings gently brushed the hair from his brow.

A warning, a chide, a reassurance, a comfort.

Kae released Adaira's hand.

It took a moment for Adaira to reorient herself, chilled as she was by Kae's memories. She blinked until the image of Jack had fully faded. Only then did she look at Kae with canny eyes, studying her elegant stature, the sharpness of her features, the golden blotches on her shoulder, collar, and shins.

"You were protecting him," Adaira said, shivering in awe and gratitude. "Why? Why would you risk yourself like that?"

Kae extended her hand again.

Adaira slowly accepted it, a pulse of apprehension in her throat. She didn't know what else Kae could show her, and she braced herself to see Jack again. She braced herself to see Bane and his flash of merciless lightning.

Neither of them appeared.

It was a quiet stretch of the eastern coast at night. The tide was suspended, and the foam was churning up the spirits of the ocean. Lady Ream, the ruler of the seafolk, was present, sitting beside a woman with a harp. A woman Adaira recognized with a pang. She inhaled sharply, as if her heart had been pierced.

It was Lorna.

She was young. Her face was pale and smooth, her eyes bright in the moonlight. Her long dark hair was loose, teased by a soft western wind. *It's strange to see your mother at your own age,* Adaira thought, both delighted and saddened by the sight.

Lorna was speaking to Ream as if they were old friends, and Adaira wanted to know what they were saying. She attempted to move closer, belatedly remembering she was fastened to Kae's body and memory. Kae was standing far enough away that Lorna and Ream and the host of other sea spirits wouldn't notice her, but close enough to direct the winds and ward off the eastern, southern, and northern faeries.

But Kae trusted the western wind. Adaira could feel it in Kae's chest, like a flame had been lit, and she watched as they blew gently across the sand with their midnight hair and soft, mothlike wings.

Kae seemed lulled for a moment. Her guard dropped as she continued to gaze at Lorna.

A northern spirit arrived. One of her own kind, with needled teeth, a vicious smile, waves of flaxen hair, and crimson wings. Kae caught him before he could steal Lorna's words. She bit his arm, shredded the edges of his wings.

He fought her, dragging his sharp nails over her collarbone, drawing her rich, golden blood. But he was no match for her, and he knew it.

He submitted, wings tucked low, and faded away to the star-streaked north.

Kae remained where she was on the fringes, watching until Lorna, nose bleeding and wincing in pain, had reunited with Alastair on the moonlit hills.

Why did you play without me, Lorna? he was saying, concerned as he wrapped his plaid around her shoulders. *I'm supposed to be with you always.*

Tears welled in Adaira's eyes as she watched her parents. She didn't know how much of the emotions she felt were hers and how much were Kae's. They seemed tangled together as the memory faded.

Their hands drifted apart.

Adaira wiped her tears, her heart aching. It took her a moment to tamp down the sob that wanted to rack her chest and flatten her on the cave floor. But she held herself up, determined to process what she was feeling.

She hadn't realized how tender her grief was until she saw her parents, hale and alive, in a memory. How much she longed for their company and mourned their absence. She hadn't realized how much she missed them, but neither had she realized how *angry* she was at them for raising her as a Tamerlaine and never telling her she was truly Breccan.

But such anger would only rot her from within, reducing her to smoldering ashes, because the truth was that Lorna and Alastair were both gone, buried beneath eastern loam. Being furious at their deceit did nothing to them but everything to her, and anger would wear her down into dust. Adaira wanted to avoid that fate. She didn't want to let something that had been good in her life turn sour.

She soon felt Kae watching her, as if she were trying to read the emotions passing over Adaira's face. Adaira met the spirit's gaze. Kae looked weary and shone with perspiration, as if sharing her memories had been taxing. But Adaira heard the words Kae wanted to speak in that moment.

All those times Lorna had played for the folk, Kae had been there, whether the bard was aware of her presence or not. Kae watched over her to ensure that Lorna had enough space and safety to sing. She had chased down other spirits, both inflicting and taking wounds.

All those times Jack had played for the folk, Kae had also been present, doing her best to shield him from Bane and other spirits who would harm or taunt him.

I wish I had known, Adaira thought, her eyes resting on Kae's tattered wings. The deadly points of her nails. The pale blue sheen of her skin, splotched with gold. The wounds and lacerations that were bleeding onto the cave floor.

Adaira had always respected the spirits and had faith in them when it was due. She often thought of them as capricious in nature, fickle as a summer storm on the isle, as neither good nor bad but somewhere in between. Blowing whichever way pleased them most. She had never imagined that something so fierce and clawed and cold and infinite as the northern wind could come to love something soft and gentle and mortal.

Adaira realized it then. Those golden blotches on Kae's legs, shoulders, and collarbone weren't natural to her skin, as Adaira had first believed.

They were testaments to conflict and battles. To wounds she had endured.

They were scars.

Adaira climbed down the rock face. Once she was steady on the ground, she turned to watch Kae descend, staring at the spirit's torn back and remaining wings.

Kae's wounds were already beginning to knit themselves together, the new beginnings of gold-feathered scars. Adaira had cleaned them with her salve, uncertain how helpful such earthly remedies would be for a spirit of the air, but the ministrations had seemed to comfort Kae.

Adaira had drawn a few leaves from her indigo hair and wiped the debris from her cuts.

"You can't stay here," Adaira had said to her, glancing around at the cold, bewitching cave. "But there's a place nearby. A cottage where you can rest and heal, and where I can come and visit you."

Kae had seemed hesitant, as if she feared walking beneath the wide expanse of cloudy sky, but she followed without resistance. She couldn't remain in this cave, not if Adaira wanted to easily find her again. And there was no way to know how long Kae would be banished from her home.

Adaira waited until Kae's long, bare feet had found the ground. Together, they walked up a hill, down another, until Adaira found the trees that hid the loch and the abandoned cottage.

"I don't think anyone lives here, but let me check first," Adaira said. "Wait here for me, in the cover of the trees. I'll wave to you when it's safe to join me."

Kae nodded, but her eyes were wide, her face lined with wariness. Adaira wondered if she knew what this place was, or who had once lived here. As an immortal and a powerful spirit of the northern wind, Adaira imagined Kae knew most of the secrets that Cadence held.

That realization made gooseflesh ripple over her skin as Adaira moved forward alone, taking the narrow bridge of earth to the small island. She had to forge through thistle patches and wiry shrubs, which had overcome a very small kail yard, to get to the cottage. She tore layers of red vines from the door, only to discover a faint radiance in the wood. The door was locked by enchantment.

She paused, studying it. Whatever rested beyond this threshold was either valuable or dangerous. And a drop of Adaira's blood would most likely grant her access to it.

She unsheathed the sword at her side, just enough to catch a glimpse of the blade and a flash of her own reflection. She touched her finger to its edge until she felt the sting of her skin breaking.

Adaira laid her hand on the door. It unlocked as soon as the wood absorbed her blood, and she carefully eased the door open. She took a tentative step inside, her eyes sweeping her surroundings.

The one chamber of the cottage had packed dirt floors and timber beams overhead. Furniture from a time long past was coated in dust and strung with gossamer. There was a hearth, a kitchen nook with rusted iron pots, a small bed in one corner covered with moth-eaten blankets, and a table scattered with ancient books. A bowl sat at the head of the table, surrounded by scattered parchment, as if the last person who lived here had been interrupted at breakfast.

There was a strange silence to the place, almost like the sound of water, of being held beneath the surface. Or maybe it was the silence of the wind beyond the walls, as if this little island on the loch had frozen in time. The air was heavy and far too still.

Adaira stopped at the table and looked at the sheets of parchment scattered across it. They held a musical composition. For a moment, she could only stare down at the inked notes in disbelief, her heart quickening.

Innes had said the west locked away its music and instruments. Adaira had just found part of it.

She walked deeper into the shadows. Through the dusky light, she saw the far wall. It glistened, as if it breathed.

Adaira's hand found her sword hilt. She dared to take a step closer, frowning. And then the sight of what hung on the wall struck her like a fist and she halted, wide-eyed as she stared at an array of harps.

A few of them still had their strings and hung on the wall. Most of them had cracked from the weight of being untouched for years and lay in scattered pieces on the floor. But there was something else on the wall, gleaming in the light.

As Adaira stared at the slender segments, her blood turned to ice. Bones.

A skeleton was hanging on the wall.

~~~~~~~~~~~~~~~~~~~~~~~~~~~~~~~~~~~

CHAPTER 20

S idra sat in a chair before Moray Breccan's cell. The dungeons were cold and dimly lit. Water dripped from the ceiling, and the air was laced with every scent imaginable—wet stone, burning pitch, stale hay mattresses, and human refuse.

She almost vomited, but by sheer will held everything down.

Moray sat on the edge of his cot, watching her intently through the iron bars. In the beginning, he had been shackled to the wall. Eventually, Torin had ordered Moray's wrists and ankles set free, but he was still confined to his small cell. It had taken a while longer, but Torin had then agreed to let Moray request a few books from the library and given him a proper blanket to keep warm with and a plaid, void of all enchantments, to wrap around his shoulders.

Of course, the plaid was red and green, colors the Tamerlaines favored. It took a few days in the frigid bowels of the castle for Moray to finally relent and start wearing it.

"Have you heard from Cora?" Moray rasped.

Sidra continued to stare at him. She would never forget that he had kicked her in the chest and beaten her into the heather. That he had taken her daughter, provoking the worst anguish Sidra had ever known.

"Have you heard from my sister?" Moray persisted.

"Adaira is well," Sidra said in a clipped tone. "Why have you asked to speak with me?"

"May I write a letter to her?"

"No."

"If I dictate a letter, would you transcribe it for me?"

"No," Sidra said again.

Moray's eyes seemed to grow darker, like night descending on a loch. But Sidra held his stare, unflinching.

"Where is the laird?" he finally asked, and his tone was smug. "It's been a while since I've seen your husband. How does he fare?"

"I'll tell him you asked after him," Sidra said, beginning to rise.

Moray panicked and stood, holding out a grimy hand. "Wait, Lady! There's something I'd like to ask you."

Sidra resumed her seat, but only because her foot was throbbing. "If it's more books you want, you've had plenty. If it's another blanket, I'll consider it. If it's to write your parents, my answer is no."

"How much longer?" Moray asked, slowly sitting back down on his mattress. He pulled the Tamerlaine plaid tighter around his shoulders. "How much longer will I be here, and is there a way I can prove my honor? Perhaps you could choose your finest, strongest warrior and let us fight to the death, see which of us prevails?"

Sidra was shocked, and he must have seen it in her expression.

"Let the sword decide if I deserve to live or die," he said.

"No."

She didn't tell him this, but the council had decided to keep him imprisoned for a decade. Ten full years. By then, the anger the Tamerlaines felt toward Moray's sins would be diminished, and they would return him to the west with a long list of conditions. But most important, Adaira would be able to finally come home if she wanted.

Ten years.

Adaira would be thirty-three.

Moray shifted. His irritation was beginning to show, but he surprised her further by saying, "Do you have siblings, Lady Sidra?"

She didn't want to answer personal questions. She didn't want to give this man any knowledge about her or her past.

She was silent, but he smiled.

"I take that as a yes," Moray said. "I have a twin, as you already know. But I also had a younger sister. Her name was Skye."

Sidra was quiet. She hated how her interest was piqued.

"Skye wasn't like most of us," he continued. "She wasn't drawn to swords or spars or challenges. She preferred books and art and was so tender toward animals that she refused to eat their meat. My parents adored her, even as she seemed to be such an odd creature amongst our kind. And when the rumors spread, rumors that she was destined to be a greater ruler than me, I couldn't find it in my heart to be jealous of her. She was such a light in our darkness. A constellation that burned through the clouds."

Sidra listened, shivering beneath the warmth of her plaid. "And what happened to Skye?"

Moray glanced down at the floor. "Every month my parents call their thanes and their heirs into the castle hall for a feast. It's a dangerous, unpredictable night, because there's always a thane or two who is scheming to take the rulership. Because I'm their heir, my parents had been dosing me with poison and dressing me only in enchanted garments with orders to always have a blade in my possession. They were paranoid, you see. They had lost Cora to the 'wind,' and they couldn't bear to lose another child. I will always wonder why they didn't take the same measures with Skye, but perhaps they thought the clan as a whole loved her.

"A fortnight after Skye turned twelve, a feast was held. She and I were present, as was customary, and she was sitting at my right. She had flowers in her hair, I remember. She was radiant, laughing at something one of the thanes' daughters had said. And then it happened, so quickly." He fell quiet, lost in his remembrance.

"What happened?" Sidra prompted.

Moray's gaze returned to her. "Skye began to cough, so she drank her wine. And then I noticed she kept flexing her hands, and she seemed sluggish. Soon her breaths were labored and shallow, as if her heart was beating slower and slower. I reached out to touch her—she was chilled, as if ice had crept beneath her skin. I knew it then. I had felt such things before in my own body, long ago when I first started taking the Aethyn in safe doses. But there is only one way to be sure. I took the dirk from my belt, and I sliced her palm."

"Why?" Sidra asked. "Did you think it would let the poison escape?"

"There's no countermeasure, no antidote for Aethyn," Moray said. "But it turns spilled blood into jewels. And I watched my sister's blood drip from her palm. I watched it transform into cold gemstones, so brilliant it looked like fire was within them, and I knew by their size alone that she would die within the hour. I will never forget the fear in her eyes when she looked at me, nor the sound my mother made when she saw Skye's blood, glittering as jewels on the table."

Sidra was silent for a long moment. "I'm sorry."

"I don't want your apology or pity," Moray said in a low voice. "What I want is to know how long I'm to be imprisoned here. I want to know how long you plan to keep me away from my only remaining sister. My *twin*."

Sidra stood, ignoring the twinge of pain in her foot. She held his gaze for a long, disquieting moment.

Once, such a story would have softened her, even if it came from an enemy's mouth. It would have roused her empathy so much that she would have felt compelled to take action, to be of service. But ever since Torin had left . . . ever since she had felt the blight creeping under her skin, turning her veins to gold . . . she had been faced with no other choice but to harden herself. To turn her soul into something strong and unyielding as stone.

"Days can feel like years, can't they?" she said. "I remember that very feeling when my daughter was stolen from me. How every day felt like a decade as I wondered where she was and worried about her. Missing those hours with her that I will never regain. And for my daughter, knowing the fear of that moment will be imprinted in her memory."

The confidence in Moray's expression faded. His posture drooped, and his breaths hissed through his teeth. He was silver-tongued, Sidra knew. She had heard him tell a story before and knew that he could string words together like spells. Maybe in another life he could have been a bard, putting his skills to good use instead of wielding them for his own selfish purposes.

"Perhaps you should have thought of that consequence, Moray," Sidra said as she turned away. Her voice echoed through the prison, cutting through both shadows and torchlight. "Your sentence is ten years."

Torin arrived at the blighted orchard angry, hungry, and not at all amused by the thought of solving the spirits' riddle. The world around him continued to thrive in this dusky landscape—sun setting, moon rising, stars gleaming like crushed diamonds. There was one snippet of blue sky, streaked by clouds, but the northern horizon, Torin noticed, looked stormy, darkened. He could see lightning dancing in the faraway clouds.

"He comes at last," drawled a familiar voice, and Torin turned to behold the hill spirit again, standing a safe distance from the orchard.

"Where is this riddle?" Torin asked.

The hill spirit, vines and flowers tangled in his long hair, smiled at his curtness.

"Do you remember the apple tree that was struck by lightning when the bard played for the orchard?" the spirit said.

"How could I forget that night?"

"The king's riddle is written in the split wood. Come, I will read it for you. But take care in the orchard; if you touch the blight here, you will also fall prey to it."

Torin nodded and carefully followed the hill spirit as they approached Rodina's orchard.

Torin had already scrutinized the trees from his side of the realm, and now he could see the spirits who were ailing. The sight made him pause, stricken. Maidens of the orchard sat at the foot of their appointed trees, their long hair dry and snarled like burnt summer grass, their faces wan and beaded with amber sap. The apple blossoms that graced their hair and drifted from their fingertips were wilted, and their skin was dappled from the blight, in purple hues with veins of gold. One maiden sitting against a very sick tree looked to be the most severely affected.

He came to a halt near her, and while he knew he shouldn't approach any closer, he felt a terrible weight of sadness in his heart.

"That is Mottie," the hill spirit said. "She is the lady of this orchard. She was first to fall ill."

"What did she do?" Torin asked in a low voice, but then instantly regretted his question when the hill spirit gave him a sharp look.

"She refused to obey an order of the king, an order that would have plunged your realm into famine."

"Your king . . ." Torin hesitated.

"You can speak his name here, only do it carefully," the hill spirit advised.

"Bane."

"The very one."

Torin drew his hand through his hair, conflicted. "He doesn't sound like a worthy king."

"I must refrain from adding my own comment to that, mortal laird."

"How long has he reigned? Can he ever be . . . defeated? Can you not rule yourselves?"

The hill spirit's mouth bent with a tragic smile. "There must always be a ruler in our realm. The same with yours. Bane has reigned for nearly two centuries now. A long time by mortal reckoning. The price of defeating him would be very steep, and most are not willing to pay it."

Wanting to ask more, Torin drew breath and was sifting through his store of questions. But the hill spirit, who seemed tired, was quickly leading the way to the cloven apple tree, the very ground where Jack had once played in the storm. "Come, mortal laird. Here is the riddle."

Torin remembered Mottie and nodded to her, but the lady of the orchard hardly responded. Her eyes were glazed as she watched him approach the split tree, its trunk lying in pieces in the grass.

"This tree was once Starna, but she is now lost to us. When the king lashed out and broke her in response to the bard's music, he left behind these words, scorched in Starna's heart. Can you read them, mortal laird?"

Torin stood before the tree, squinting. He saw nothing but whorls of wood, red and chestnut brown, and the vein where lightning had blasted. A white, merciless streak.

"I don't see anything."

"Look closer."

Torin stifled a sigh and squatted to study the lines of the wood. It took him a moment, but he finally saw the words. "It's not in my tongue. I can't read it."

"As I suspected," the hill spirit said. "That is why I am here with you."

"Read it to me then," Torin said, and when the silence stretched long between them, he added, "Please."

"The riddle goes as follows: Ice and fire, brought together as one. Sisters divided, united once more. Washed with salt and laden with blood—all united will satisfy the debt you owe."

Torin continued to squat, listening. But that was the end, and he found he was more confused and frustrated than before.

"What does this mean, hill spirit?"

"Even if I knew, I could not tell you."

"Read it again."

The spirit did so, in a steady and calm voice, and Torin ruminated on the words. But they made no sense to him, and he stood up with a groan.

"This is impossible," he said, throwing up his hands. "How am I to solve something like this?"

"If you were unworthy of this challenge, we would not have chosen you," the hill spirit replied. "Were we wrong, Torin of the Tamerlaines?"

Torin stared at the wood, the smooth edges of a language he couldn't read. A mystery he had no idea how to solve. *Ice and fire, sisters divided, salt and blood.*

"My wife would know," he said, meeting the hill spirit's steady gaze. "If you'd allow me to speak to her, allow her to see me. She could assist me in this."

"I'm afraid it cannot be done," the spirit said, but he didn't sound at all remorseful. "Once you leave our realm, you cannot return here as you once were."

"I want to speak with her," Torin insisted. He was haunted by the memory of Sidra vomiting into a pot, standing forlorn in a castle room in which she had never wanted to live. Alone and burdened and thinking he had deserted her, with his child growing within her. "I won't progress in solving this riddle until you grant me that small mercy."

"You can see her all you desire, mortal laird."

"But *she* cannot see *me*. She doesn't know where I am."

"She knows where you are," the hill spirit said, and Torin stiffened. "She knows, and she understands why and what you must do."

"You act as if you have spoken with her," Torin said through his teeth.

The spirit only smiled.

Torin's anger began to simmer. His fingers flexed at his side before curling into a fist.

"We cannot tell you how to solve this riddle," the spirit said. "But if you pay close attention, we can help guide you."

"Then guide me," Torin said, exasperated.

The hill spirit cocked his head, as if he were regretting his choice of human helper. But then he became ethereal. One moment he was standing before Torin, the next he was an array of grass and hills and flowers, all the wild beauty that flourished beneath his care.

Torin was caught in a web of annoyance. He looked to the road he had come from, the road that would lead him to the castle, to Sidra and his daughter. He was homesick, and he ached for them.

He failed to see the trail of wildflowers blooming in the grass.

Frae walked home from school with a group of children now, since Jack was no longer there to escort her to and from the city. The boys and girls she walked with lived in crofts scattered throughout the spine of Eastern Cadence. Frae lived the farthest from Sloane, and so she traveled the last portion of her route alone. But by then, she had only two kilometers to go, and Mirin's cottage was almost within view. Her mother had promised to be waiting for her at the gate to greet her that afternoon.

All the schoolchildren had new rules to follow. Frae liked to repeat them in her mind, because she didn't want to accidentally break one.

Rule number one was that they had to walk home together and not leave the younger ones behind.

Rule number two was that they had to stay on the roads to avoid being fooled by enchantments.

And if they happened to break rule number two, above all else they had to avoid any tree that showed symptoms of blight or was roped off by the guard. Three children had already fallen sick from the blight, not including Hamish, and Frae was very anxious about catching it too. She was relieved that there weren't many trees on her mother's lands, save for the Aithwood. And Frae rarely went very deep into that forest.

She squinted against the late afternoon sunshine as she walked along the road. She was still considered one of the younger children, and as such, she trailed behind the older ones. But she kept up a good pace, even with her satchel of books slung over her shoulder. Her wooden sparring sword was looped into her belt, and she cradled the bowl she had made for her pottery class in her hands because she didn't want to put it in her bag, worried it would crack. She was thinking about how she could make a bigger and even *better* bowl next time when something struck her in the chest.

It hit her right above her heart, and even though her enchanted plaid was draped across her body, the impact made her stumble. Her arms flailed, and she watched as her bowl fell to the road and broke into pieces at her feet.

For a moment, Frae was so stunned she could only gape at the shards. The bowl she had worked so hard to shape and stain, the bowl she had waited so patiently to set in the kiln, had just *broken*. And so easily, as if those hours had meant *nothing*. But then something else was thrown at her. She flinched as it sailed past her, narrowly missing her face.

Someone was throwing mud balls at her. The one that had struck her chest was still stuck to her plaid, smelling like stinky marsh water.

She glanced up. She wasn't sure who had thrown it at her, or why. Maybe it was an accident?

"My mum says her father's a Breccan," one of the older boys said to the others up ahead on the road. He glanced back to sneer at her, then chuckled at the sight of the mud on her plaid.

"Breccan spawn," another lad hissed.

"She shouldn't be wearing that plaid."

"Disgusting."

A third mud clot was hurling toward her, and Frae was so upset she froze, unable to move. She waited for it to hit her, to knock her down and break her into pieces, just like the bowl, but it never came. She watched, astounded, as one of the older girls intercepted it, raising her book to stop the mud ball in midair.

It squelched against the book cover. The girl slung it off to the side of the road, as if she did this every day, and then wiped the book on her tunic to clear off the residue. She turned and fixed a cold stare on the boys, who had stopped in their tracks and were watching her, their mouths ajar.

The girl never said a word. She didn't have to, because the boys turned and rushed onward.

"I'm sorry about that, Frae," said the girl, and Frae wasn't sure what surprised her more—the fact that this older student knew her name or that she had taken a mud clot for her. "Are you all right?" The girl knelt and began to gather up the pottery pieces.

"I . . ." Frae's voice quivered. She drank the words, afraid she would cry.

I wish Jack were here, she thought, wiping away a tear that slipped free. *If he was, this wouldn't have happened!*

"This is a very pretty bowl," the girl said, admiring the etchings Frae had decorated it with. "Yours came out much better than mine." She glanced up and smiled. She had two dimples and freckles across her nose, and her brown hair was in one long, thick braid.

Frae blinked, still shocked this girl was speaking her.

"My name is Ella, by the way. Here, let's walk together."

Before Frae could scrounge up a reply, Ella had removed the mud clot that still clung to her plaid and eased her forward.

"You don't have to walk with me," Frae finally whispered.

"I'd like to, though," Ella replied. "If you don't mind my company."

Frae shook her head, but she was too nervous to look at Ella, or to think of something to say.

They walked together, watching as the children ahead of them began to turn from the road one by one as they reached their crofts. Frae knew Ella must have already passed her home, because soon it was just the two of them left and Mirin's hill was coming into view.

"My mum's just there, waiting on me," Frae said, pointing.

"Oh, tell her I said hello," Ella said, carefully handing the pottery shards to Frae. "Perhaps we could walk with each other again tomorrow?"

Frae was embarrassed that she had let Ella carry her broken bowl the entire time. *You should have asked for it, so you didn't bother her!* But she had been too meek to raise her voice. Now her mind still reeled, and so she merely nodded.

"Good. I'll see you then, Frae." Ella smiled and began to back-track along the road, her long braid swaying as she walked.

Frae turned to take the path that would lead her home.

She paused, staring down at the pieces again. She didn't want her mother to see the broken bowl, so she hid the shards in the tall grass. Then Frae panicked, because she also didn't want Mirin to know those boys had thrown mud at her—she didn't want Mirin to know what those boys had *said*—but her plaid was stained. She quickly removed the green-and-red-checkered wool, turned it inside out, and draped it back over her head. *There*. Mirin would never know.

Frae sighed and continued along the path, her heart lifting when she saw Mirin waiting for her at the garden gate.

"Frae? What is this?"

Frae was reading by the fire later that evening, but she stiffened at the sound of Mirin's voice. Without even looking up from the page, she knew what her mother was asking about.

Slowly, Frae lifted her eyes.

Mirin was holding up her mud-stained plaid, which Frae had tried to hide, crumpled up behind her oaken chest.

"Why is your plaid dirty, darling?"

"I slipped on the walk home," Frae murmured, glancing away. Her face felt hot, and she hated lying. She *hated* it, but she couldn't bear to tell Mirin the truth.

Her father's a Breccan.

Frae felt ashamed of those words. She didn't know what to do, but it felt far more terrifying to speak the words aloud to her mother. Because what if they were true?

"You should have told me earlier, Frae," Mirin chided gently. "Then I could have washed it for you before the sun went down. You'll have to wear the older plaid tomorrow."

Frae nodded, relieved when Mirin set her mud-stained plaid aside.

While her mother wove on the loom, Frae continued to read.

Or she tried to. The words swam on the page, and Frae's heart felt heavy and sad. She missed Jack, and he had only been gone for a day. The cottage felt vastly different without him, like a wall had crumbled and cold air was creeping in.

"Mum?" Frae asked, hopeful. "Have you heard from Jack?"

Mirin lowered her shuttle. "No, but remember what he said before he left? It will take him a few days to reach Adaira. And then he will send word to us."

"You'll tell me when the letter arrives?" Frae asked, worried she might miss it.

Mirin smiled. "Yes. We'll read it together. How does that sound?"

"That sounds good," Frae said, returning her attention to her book. But the words still seemed to blur together. She couldn't focus on them, and she sighed. "Mum?"

"Yes, Frae?"

"What do you think Jack is doing right now?"

Mirin was quiet for a breath. "I imagine he is sleeping beneath the western stars in a valley."

"Sleeping?"

"Yes. If he's traveling and it's dark, the best thing to do is make camp and rest."

"He's not with Adaira?"

"No, not yet. The west is very big, I hear. There are many hills cloaked in bracken and woad and wildflowers and mist."

Frae perked up. "How do you know that, Mum?"

"Someone once told me, darling."

"Who?"

Mirin stilled for a moment, and Frae thought she saw her mother's mouth press into a thin line. But she must have imagined it because Mirin continued to weave, seamlessly.

"A friend told me. Now why don't you read aloud to me, Frae? I would love to hear another story in one of your books."

Frae glanced down at the open page. She thought for a moment, chewing on one of her nails. She wondered: *If my father is a Breccan, does that mean Jack's is too?*

For some reason she couldn't explain, the idea gave her comfort.

It reassured her that Jack would be safe in the west.

Frae began to read aloud to Mirin.

CHAPTER 21

J ack woke with a splitting headache, his cheek pressed against cold stone. He didn't know where he was, and his heart began to pound.

Don't move yet. Don't panic.

From his place sprawled on the floor, he took in his surroundings.

Rough-hewn walls of rock, a constant dripping sound, moldy hay for a bed, a bucket of refuse in one corner, overwhelming darkness with only one source of light to pierce it—a torch burning in a sconce beyond an iron-barred door.

He was in a prison.

He tried to swallow his fear, but it caught in his throat. His mouth was parched, as if he hadn't had anything to drink for hours. He felt frozen to the floor as he continued to lie there, unmoving.

But his mind was burning, racing, *reeling.* For a moment he couldn't remember anything, his memories spilling through his fingers like water. Like wind.

Don't panic, he told himself again. *Relax and remember what happened. What brought you here, and how will you get out of it?*

His tongue stuck to his teeth as he controlled his breaths—slow, deep drafts of air. The tension began to ease its iron grip on his lungs and heart, and Jack coaxed his mind to remember what had happened.

There had been a hill, a bracken patch. Rab Pierce and his men on horses. A firepit, a pretense of friendliness. Jack remembered that they had taken his harp and his golden half coin. He remembered thinking that Rab would slit his throat. That when they had held his face over the fire to burn him, the flames had spontaneously died into smoke.

Jack shuddered, wondering how long he had been lying on this floor. Then his thoughts turned to how he was going to free himself.

He began to move, testing his arms. They felt weak as he pushed himself up.

"Ah, the Mad Thief wakes at last," said a voice with a strange lilt. A voice so close that Jack could have reached out and touched its owner.

Someone was in the cell with him.

Dread pierced his chest like an arrow as he slowly angled his head to the left.

A fellow male prisoner sat against the wall, legs extended before him and crossed at the ankles. He was young and pale with a hollow aura about him. A scar marked his cheek, drawing up one corner of his mouth into a permanent grimace. His hooded eyes caught the sheen of torchlight as he regarded Jack.

"Where am I?" Jack said, his voice croaking. He tried to swallow again.

"A curious thing, to not know where you are. Although they did say you possessed only a shred of your wits."

Jack merely stared at his cellmate.

"You're in the dungeons of Castle Kirstron, Mad Thief," the man said with a sigh.

"Why do you keep calling me that?"

"It's what we do here. We call each other by our crimes. Think of it as a whetstone, sharpening you every time you hear it."

Jack rolled his lips together. He was full of countless retorts and questions and emotions, all of which he wished could escape from him, like steam. But he was caught in a web, and panicking would only draw the spider toward him sooner.

"Then what do I call you by?" he asked.

His cellmate tilted his head to the side, a fringe of dirty blond hair shifting over one of his eyes. "I'm Thief too. Most of us are here."

"Not mad, like me?"

"No. You should be honored that you garnered such a title. Whatever did you steal?"

Jack glanced away, settling as comfortably as he could on the ground in a sitting position. His right ribs smarted in pain, and he gingerly touched them, wincing. He must have been thrown over Rab's horse, then bruised by the gallop to Kirstron.

"I stole nothing," Jack finally said.

"Ah. You're one of *those* kinds," mused his cellmate.

"What kind is that?"

"The ones who are in denial when they come. It may take a few days or weeks, depending on how stubborn you are. But you'll soon admit to your crime, if only to see the moon and stars one last time. To look upon the face you love in the crowd, even from a distance."

Jack's attention sharpened as he tried to make sense of the man's words. "Is there a way for an innocent person to get out of here? A trial, or a proceeding?"

His cellmate snickered. "Oh, there's a way. I'm surprised you haven't heard of it."

"I'm not from these parts. Do enlighten me, Thief."

The man smiled, his scar puckering his cheek. "There are many ways to enter these prisons, Mad Thief. But there are only two ways out. The first? You die of the cold and the damp. The second? You face the culling."

If there was one thing Jack was truly bad at, it was hand-to-hand combat with swords. He could make rocks sail with alarming accuracy with his slingshot, and he was good at sneaking from one place to another. He could even shoot and handle a bow decently. But he had never been strong at spars when he was a student in Sloane, taking classes with the other isle children. Those hours of practice on the castle green had been difficult and often humiliating for him. Which was rather hilarious to think about, considering how much Jack had once aspired to become one of the East Guard.

He sat against the wall of his prison cell and mulled over all the details of the culling Thief had given him. It didn't sound real, and Jack had initially wondered if his cellmate was trying to have fun at his expense and was teasing him for his lack of knowledge. But Jack had to remind himself that he was in the west and in the thick of the Breccan clan. It shouldn't surprise him that they died by their swords as they lived with them, and that an honorable death was still important to them, even to criminals.

According to Thief, the culling was held in an arena, and most of the clan attended as witnesses. Fighting for your life before hundreds of eyes was terrifying to imagine, but it was also the only ray of hope Jack had at the moment. If the clan attended the event, there was a very good chance that Adaira would be present. At the very least, the laird would be there and Innes would recognize him.

So Jack needed to be chosen for the next culling. It was the only way he could see himself escaping this place if the damp cold didn't kill him first. He was so desperate to get free that the thought of being slain in the arena didn't rattle him. *Yet.*

"How does one get selected for this culling?" he asked.

"It depends," Thief replied. "Sometimes they go by how long a prisoner has been here. Sometimes they do a random selection. But it's why they put you in the cell with me. I've been selected to fight tomorrow."

Jack had to bite his tongue to hold back his eagerness. He breathed once, twice, before saying calmly, "Would you be willing to let me go in your stead?"

"You want to die tomorrow then?" Thief countered.

"I can hold my own with a sword," Jack lied.

"It's not you. It's the one you'd be facing tomorrow, should I let you take my spot."

"I thought you said prisoners who won the spars were pardoned and welcomed back into the clan."

"Not Oathbreaker."

The hair rose on Jack's arms. He shivered, clenching his jaw to keep his teeth from rattling. But that name was familiar, roused in a memory shaped by Mirin's voice. *They called him "Oathbreaker" and stripped him of his title and name.*

His father was here, somewhere in the dungeons. Sitting alone in the cold dark, breathing the same dank air as Jack. He was *here*, and he had fought time and time again in the culling. He should have been pardoned many times over, but something or someone was holding him back, waiting for him to finally be slain.

"I take it you've heard of the old tragic Oathbreaker," Thief drawled. "Since you're not pestering me with questions."

"How many times has he fought in the culling? Why hasn't he been freed?"

"More than I can count. And the laird doesn't wish it. Simple as that."

"How just of her."

"Careful, Mad Thief. Don't forget where you are. Don't speak ill of the laird."

Jack fell silent, grinding his molars as he imagined his father fighting, killing, shackled, unforgiven. Over and over and over. Jack didn't even know what he looked like—he had never seen Niall Breccan—but would his father know it was him should they meet in the arena? Would Niall see all the traces of Mirin in Jack's features?

Jack raked his fingers through his hair, distressed. It was a dangerous risk to take, and he could taste it in his mouth like blood. It would be foolish for Jack to face his own father. A man who was so strong and angry that he was undefeated in the culling. A man who had seen and held him only once when Jack was a small bairn.

"Will you trade places with me?" he asked again.

"Perhaps," Thief replied around a yawn. "But perhaps I'm tired of being in this cell. Perhaps I want to try my luck tomorrow in the arena." He moved to bed down on the hay. "All I know is this: don't wake me while I sleep, Mad Thief. Or I'll kill you myself."

Time seemed to melt in the dungeons.

Jack didn't know if it was morning, noontide, or night. He paced the cell to keep warm. He thought about the letter he had sent Adaira. It should have reached her by now, and he wondered if she would read between the lines. If she would realize he was here in the west, and if she would look for him.

She would never think to check the dungeons. Or would she?

A clang echoed down the stone corridor.

Jack paused, glancing at the iron door.

"Mealtime," Thief explained. He had scarcely moved from his place on the hay, but he sat forward on his haunches.

Jack approached the door, trying to see as much of the corridor as he could. A guard was pushing a rickety cart full of dinner trays, stopping at every cell to slide it under the door. When the man reached Jack's cell, he paused.

"Get back," he barked impatiently.

Jack startled at the gruffness but eased away from the door. "May I speak to Lady Cora?"

"Pierce said you would ask that. No. You can't speak to her." He roughly slid the dinner tray beneath the door.

It looked like a slice of bread with a burnt crust, a bowl of watery soup, a mealy apple, and a wedge of cheese. Thief leapt to hoard the tray, taking it back to his corner. He began to shove the bread into his mouth, but he watched Jack with glittering amusement.

"*Please*," Jack said to the guard, unable to temper his desperation. "Cora will want to see me. I promise you."

The guard ignored him and moved on to the next cell.

Jack sagged against the wall, exhausted. He slowly slid down to the floor and stared absently ahead of him. He was so far away in that moment that he nearly forgot about Thief, even as his cellmate slurped the entire bowl of soup.

"Who is Lady Cora to you?" Thief asked eventually.

Jack wanted to ignore him. But he needed to stay in Thief's good graces if there was any chance of them swapping places.

"She's my wife."

Complete and utter silence.

When Jack glanced sidelong at Thief, he saw that his cellmate was gaping. And then the laughter came, as Jack knew it would. He suffered through it without a word, stoic and brooding, and Thief finally wiped the tears from his eyes.

"Married to Cora. I haven't heard that one yet." He chuckled as he tossed the mealy apple to Jack. The only part of dinner he was going to share.

Jack sighed. He took a bite of the fruit, felt its juice drip down his chin.

Thief said, "Now I see why they call you mad."

Jack was dozing when the guards finally came for Thief.

The door unlocked and swung open with a bang, and Jack jerked awake.

"Up with you, Thief!" one of the guards said. "Time to prove your honor in the arena."

Jack watched as Thief slowly rose to his feet, brushing stalks of hay from his tunic. He took one step forward but then paused to look at Jack.

"Mad Thief would like to take my place in tonight's fight," he said. "I've agreed to it."

Jack's heart became electric. It began to pump so hard and fast that he saw stars dance at the edges of his vision. He pushed himself up to his feet.

"This true?" the guard asked brusquely. "You want to fight tonight?"

"Yes," Jack whispered. He hated how small and weak he sounded.

"This is the thief Pierce brought in," said one of the guards toward the back of the group. "He wants to be present when this one dies."

"Well, go ask him if tonight will work. He's already here, in the arena."

One guard hurried away with a torch while the others stepped outside the cell and locked the door, waiting for Rab's approval. Of course it came, as Jack knew it would. He knew Rab Pierce was eager to see his blood spilled.

As Jack stepped forward, allowing the guards to shackle his hands behind his back, he looked one last time at Thief, who was sitting on the floor and leaning against the wall, in the same spot Jack had first seen him.

"Good luck to you, Mad Thief," he said, tipping his head as Jack was hauled forward. "I'm afraid you're going to need every bit of it, facing Oathbreaker."

CHAPTER 22

Dear Adaira,

*You'll be surprised by this letter. You'll be surprised that I'm
writing to you so soon after my previous letter, especially given
my past record of letter-writing responses. I know I let a shame-
worthy number of days pass between my replies to you, and for
that I can only blame my stubbornness and pride.*

*I hope to serve my penance to you, though, in whatever ways
you'd like.*

*You can expect me to write another letter ~~tod~~ tomorrow,
actually. It might take a few days to reach you—the ravens
are flying quite slow as of late—but when it does reach you . . .
when you hold it in your hands . . . I hope you turn eastward
and envision me, walking the hills and thinking of you.*

*And should there come another expanse of days between my
letters . . . then you can rest assured that there is a good reason
for it.*

—Your Old Menace

A daira read through Jack's letter twice, puzzling over it. She smiled at his strange humor at first, but then her thoughts were overcome with a nagging suspicion.

He knew their letters were being screened, so what was he trying to express to her? There had to be another meaning lurking beneath his odd choice of phrases, the deliberate ink blots, the crossed-out words. Jack was the sort of person who would write the same letter four times before sending it, to perfect it in appearance and tone.

She carried the letter to her desk, shifting her half-eaten dinner and her notes from the new library aside as she sat. She bent over the wrinkled parchment and studied it by candlelight, drawing out different words he had written and testing them on her tongue.

It was the ~~tod~~ *tomorrow* that intrigued her the most. At the time he wrote this, something must have been happening for him the next day, which was now probably the other day, or perhaps even two days ago now. Adaira wasn't sure how long David held her letters before delivering them. It had occurred to her a few times that her father might hold them a while before handing them over to her.

The notion made her anxious because whatever Jack was striving to convey to her in this letter was time-sensitive.

It might take a few days to reach you. He plainly spoke of another letter, but what if he was alluding to something else reaching her?

A knock on her bedroom door startled her out of her reveries. Adaira had come to learn the different raps at her door; she knew this one was Innes, and she winced as she rose to answer. She had been avoiding her mother ever since the culling and ever since she had snuck in and out of the castle. But knowing she could put it off no longer, she unlocked the door.

Innes was silent for a moment, regarding her with a cold, emotionless expression. Her silver-blond hair was braided, and she wore a blue tunic trimmed in thick golden thread. Her vambraces were gone, and the tattoos that wove up her arms were on full display. Interlocking patterns that danced around stories and scars.

"Would you like to come in?" Adaira asked gently.

"No, I have somewhere I need to be tonight," Innes replied. "But I haven't seen you lately. I wanted to ensure you are well, and that you don't need anything."

"Oh." Adaira couldn't hide the surprise in her tone. "I'm quite well, and I don't need anything at the moment. But thank you for asking."

Innes nodded, but hesitated. There was more she wanted to say, and Adaira inwardly braced herself for it.

"The next time you leave Kirstron," Innes finally said, "please let me know where you're going."

Adaira bit the inside of her cheek. How foolish of her to think that just because she had slipped in and out of the castle without trouble, Innes hadn't known. Her mother seemed to have eyes everywhere.

"And take a horse from the stables," Innes added gruffly. "I've told my stable master to select one for you to ride. Next time simply ask her for the horse rather than sneak out on foot."

"I'll do that," Adaira said. "Thank you, Innes."

"When I introduced you as my daughter to the thanes the other night, I was making a claim. If anyone tries to harm you, they harm me, and I'm at liberty to take any actions I want in restitution." Innes paused, but her countenance had softened, as though the mask she wore had cracked. "But *because* I've publicly acknowledged you, some in the clan will now see you as a target. A threat. A way to strike at me. So all I'm asking of you are three things: you let me know when you leave the castle, you carry your sword, and you take a horse. Agreed?"

"Yes," Adaira said.

"Good. Here's your next dose. I'll see you tomorrow."

Stunned, Adaira accepted the vial of Aethyn and watched her mother stride down the corridor. She slipped the poison into her pocket and shut the door, marveling over this new freedom she had been given. She walked into her bedchamber but stopped before the hearth, thinking of Kae and the bard's cottage on the loch. Adaira needed to visit her again tomorrow, and now it would be much easier with a horse.

She shivered, surprised by how cold the room felt. The fire was still crackling in the hearth, but no heat emanated from it. The air held a trace of winter, and Adaira reached for her plaid, wrapping the enchanted wool around her shoulders to keep warm as she returned to her desk.

She read through Jack's ink-blotted words again. A few minutes later, the wildest idea hit her, stealing her breath.

Jack wasn't sending a second letter.

He was coming west.

The guards escorted him into a dingy holding room. Battered armor hung from iron racks, and swords gleamed on the wall. Jack had only a moment to take it in before he saw Rab Pierce, standing in the center of the chamber. He was ruddy-faced and smiling, his blond hair brushed and oiled and gleaming with blue jewels.

"Let's get you suited for the spar," Rab said in a pleasant tone, ambling over to the rack. "You're quite slim, though. Might have to fit you in lad's armor."

Jack silently took the insult as his eyes tracked Rab's every movement. His hands were still shackled behind his back, and four guards stood behind him, but in that moment it was only Jack and Rab in the antechamber. A bard and a thane's spoiled son, breathing the same air, sharing the same space.

"Ah, here we are," Rab announced, holding up a bloodstained breastplate with a deep gouge bisecting the front of it. "This one will fit you just right, I think."

"Why are you so afraid of me?" Jack said.

Rab paused, unable to conceal his surprise at Jack's comment. But then he snorted, glancing at Jack with languid eyes. "I don't fear you, Mad Thief. You are, in fact, the *last* thing I can imagine would terrify me."

"Then why have you lied?" Jack spoke in a calm voice, even as his pulse betrayed him, beating faster and faster as the minutes passed. As his time in the arena grew imminent. "Why have you treated me with contempt? Why have you falsely imprisoned and shackled me? Why have you led everyone to believe I'm mad when I'm truly everything I say that I am?"

Rab began to close the distance between them. He looked beyond Jack and nodded at the guards, who freed Jack's hands.

"Lift your arms," Rab said.

Jack could hear the condescension in his voice, a tone he wanted to rip apart. But he had no choice but to do as Rab said and to allow him to slip the breastplate over his head. The armor settled on Jack's shoulders, constraining his chest like an unfamiliar embrace. While Rab tightened the leather buckles on the sides, Jack stared at him. The blond stubble that sparsely grew on his chin. The woad tattoo that sat around his neck like a torc. The broken blood vessels framing his nose.

"I believe the last criminal who wore this armor died in it," Rab said with a sigh, standing back to look Jack over. The guards dutifully bound Jack's hands together at the small of his back. "I do hope you have better luck, John Breccan."

"And I must thank you, Rab Pierce," Jack said. "You believe you have done something grand, something sly. You are quite proud of yourself in this moment but know this: tonight is not my appointed time to die. There are forces at play that you cannot even imagine with your small mind, and one might even say that I was always destined to stand in this moment. You were merely a pawn of the spirits to get me here."

Rab worked his jaw as he listened. His eyes narrowed, but he managed to scrouge up a sharp-toothed smile and say, "Anything else, Mad Thief?"

Jack returned the scathing smile. "Yes. When I lie beside my wife tonight, when she learns of all you did to bring us back together, I'm sure she will personally want to thank you."

"Ah yes," Rab said, stepping closer until Jack could smell the garlic on his breath. "*Cora.*"

Jack's stomach wound into a cold knot, listening to the way Rab spoke her western name. How he drew it out. It made Jack want to fill Rab's mouth with dirt. To slice his tongue into a serpent's fork.

To crack every tooth from his gums and watch him swallow the fragments.

"Perhaps the spirits will be merciful and allow you to bleed out painlessly tonight," Rab murmured. "Perhaps you will find eternal rest knowing I will keep her bed warm. That I'll be drawing *my* name from her mouth in the dark. Because she will never know you were here."

Jack snarled, his control finally slipping away. He lunged at Rab, teeth bared, but was caught in the mouth as a guard roughly gagged him with a strip of plaid, the wool tasting like smoke and salt.

"Put the moon helm on him," Rab said tersely. "Check it twice to make sure it's locked. His face needs to remain concealed to-night, understand?"

Jack strained against the gag, his anger crackling through him like fire. He didn't register Rab's words until a dented helm was forced over his head. Jack felt the metal chin strap pull tight be-neath his jaw, followed by the unmistakable click of a lock. He was trapped, lost within this heavy helm that afforded him only two slits to see the world. His breaths quickened as he chewed against the gag, but it was knotted tight.

But through the eye holes, he saw Rab cross his arms and grin.

"Coward," Jack began to say, but the wool muffled his words. He lifted his voice and shouted it again, as clear as he could. "*Cow-ard!*"

Rab heard him and flinched, but Jack's time in the dungeons had expired.

The guards hauled him forward, through a door that fed into a stairwell. Up they went through the cold shadows, their footsteps echoing off the walls. Jack had far too much time to think, to let fear ripen and command him. To anticipate the worst, regardless of how confident he had sounded to Rab.

Ascending the stairs, growing closer to his destination, he could sense how the air changed, shedding the dankness of the underground.

Focus! His mind shouted frantically. *You're almost out of time. Form a new plan.*

With the gag and a helm locked to his face, Jack's initial plan to reveal who he was in the arena had crumbled. But instead of focusing on coming up with a new solution, Jack inevitably thought of Rab in Adaira's bed, and his blood boiled again. Rab had made that remark only to wound Jack, but the thane's son obviously had forgotten how fiercely wounded creatures fight.

Jack channeled that anger as he finally reached the top of the stairs. It kept him upright as the guards escorted him down a long corridor and through a thick wooden door. But even his fury couldn't make him oblivious to the terror of an arena built for bloodshed.

He stumbled on the sand and squinted against the brightness of torchlight.

He could hear himself breathe—loud ragged sounds that filled up his helm, warming the metal against his face. His heart faltering, melting like wax down his ribs, he lifted his eyes to the crowd and looked for Adaira. There were so many blue plaids, they were all a blur. But then Jack saw the balcony, and his gaze stopped. His pulse thundered in his ears as he strained his eyes to see . . . yes, it was a woman with moon-blond hair and sharp-cut features, sitting on the balcony with a clear view of the arena.

He nearly broke into a run but then he realized it was Innes.

The laird sat alone, watching the arena with a stoic countenance. Watching *him* walk across the sand.

Jack's last hope dwindled as the guards brought him to a halt.

He had no plan. He had no way of escaping this. He went completely numb as his wrists were unshackled. He felt like he had been buried in snow and the cold was finally claiming him. Eating him alive, bone by bone.

Someone set a sword in his hands. He nearly dropped it; he had to force his fingers to close around the scuffed hilt. A man with a booming voice was speaking, and the crowd was cheering, booing.

It was indecipherable noise to Jack when he saw a shadow move on the sand and felt a presence close beside him. He turned his head and saw his father, standing three paces away.

Niall Breccan was tall, just as Jack had always imagined him to be. He was thin, as Jack was himself. His skin was pale, tattooed, and grimy from weeks in the dungeons. He wore a ratty tunic, soft hide boots, and a leather breastplate freckled with old blood. A full helm shielded his face and hair, and a sword waited in his right hand.

Jack continued to study him, this stranger who was his father.

Niall stood unmoving, patiently waiting for the fight to begin. He didn't notice Jack's stare, or if he did, he ignored it. He didn't even seem to be breathing, as though he were already dead.

The crowd roared again. Jack could feel the sound reverberate through his body, and he blinked as sweat began to sting his eyes.

Niall suddenly turned to face him. He raised his sword and took a step closer, preparing to take a cut at Jack. The fight had started, and Jack responded by stepping back, trying to keep a safe distance between them.

"I'm your son!" he shouted at Niall, but between the gag and the roar of the spectators, his voice was overpowered. He tried again, screaming, *"I'm your son!"*

He dropped the sword and touched his chest. He pointed at Niall before pounding his fist over his heart.

Niall shook his head and took another step closer. "Pick up your sword and *fight*. Don't make me chase you around the arena like a coward."

The words struck Jack like barbs. But he made no motion to retrieve his sword. He stood facing his father, waiting for the impossible to happen.

"Pick up your sword," Niall said again, his voice a low, agitated grumble beneath his helm.

Jack held up his hands. He wasn't going to fight. If he did, Niall would kill him even faster.

His father took a vicious swing at him. The steel tip reflected the firelight, the stars that burned above, as it grazed the front of

Jack's breastplate. He scrambled backwards, provoking laughter and amusement from the crowd.

Niall pressed him, swinging again. Jack dodged his sword, having no choice but to run to the other side of the arena.

"Mirin!" he shouted as Niall began to pursue him. He drew his mother's name up like a shield, let it tear through him. "*Mirin!*"

Niall wasn't listening. He tried to give Jack another blow, and Jack had to dodge and run yet again, but his thoughts and his breath fell in tempo with each other.

Mirin.

Frae.

Mirin.

Frae.

Mirin.

Frae.

If this was how Jack died, he hoped his mother and sister never learned of it.

He could hear Niall gaining on him, and Jack continued to run. He would run, around and around this arena, until he could run no longer. He refused to pick up the sword he had abandoned where it still lay, glistening on the sand.

They made five more circuits, the crowd booing in earnest now, before Niall reached out and snagged Jack's sleeve. He yanked so hard that Jack lost his balance. He sprawled on the ground, the air knocked from his lungs. His chest felt heavy, and he realized it was because Niall was pinning him down with his boot, holding him in place on the sand.

Jack had no breath to give, no voice left to make one final attempt at communicating. He trembled in fear, fear that tasted sour in his mouth. But the names he loved, the names that had fueled him this long, sang through him one more time, steadying his heart.

Mirin.

Frae.

Adaira.

Niall removed his helm and cast it aside, exposing his face. His hair was red as copper. His eyes were blue as midsummer.

Frae. He looked so much like Frae.

Niall raised his sword, aiming for Jack's throat. A clean, quick death.

And Jack didn't want to watch. He didn't want to see the ice in Niall's eyes, the deep lines etched in his brow. The anger and the hardness and the agony.

Jack exhaled.

His heart pounded in his chest.

He closed his eyes.

Dear Jack

Adaira paused, staring at his name on parchment, tamed by her writing. Her mind was spinning, trying to convince herself that she was reading too much between the lines. That Jack wouldn't be so reckless as to cross the clan line on a whim. Without properly informing her.

But if he was currently traveling to her, then this letter was futile. It wouldn't reach him in the east.

She pushed it aside and found a fresh sheet, this time writing "Dear Torin."

And yet the words were still tangled within her. She stared at Torin's name. How was she to write between the lines to her cousin? How to express to him that she needed confirmation of Jack's location without alerting David? Or maybe Adaira should cease worrying about it. If Jack was here, her parents would soon realize it. In fact, she should inform Innes, and see if her mother could—

The fire in the room went out. The flames that had danced in the hearth and burned on the candlesticks flickered and died with a howling gasp. Adaira was plunged into darkness, and she froze, wide-eyed in shock. She set down her quill and stood, knotting her plaid at her shoulder to shield her. She fumbled in the dark to find her sword, leaning against the wall, and belted it to her waist before making her way to the door.

The torches in the corridor were still aflame, but Adaira noticed one of them was guttering, like it was about to burn out. She approached it with a frown, unable to shake the chill that clung to her.

Something didn't feel right.

Another torch farther down the hallway began to frantically flicker, grabbing her attention. Adaira walked toward it. When the next one followed suit, she realized that the fire wanted to guide her somewhere.

She followed one guttering torch after another, passing no one in the winding passages. In fact, the castle felt strangely deserted, and it made her pulse skip in alarm. Adaira halted upright when she heard a distant roar.

"What is that?" she whispered, her hand gripping the hilt at her side. But she had heard such a sound before. The arena. The culling. She gasped when she realized where the fire was leading her.

Adaira broke into a run.

She dashed through the corridors she had now memorized, through the cold shadows and flickering firelight. Her hair tangled across her face as she took a corner, as she pushed herself faster, *faster,* until she felt like her body would ignite. She nearly slipped in her haste to take the stairs two at a time, her breath cutting her lungs like a blade when the doors to the arena balcony came into view. All she could think was that she was too late. This would be the night her father-in-law would be slain, and she had been too late to save him.

She threw the doors open. They hit the wall with a *bang,* startling Innes in her chair.

"Cora?"

Adaira ignored Innes. Her heart was in her throat, her eyes riveted to the arena as she rushed to the balustrade to watch the fight.

He's alive. Oathbreaker was still alive, and Adaira nearly melted to her knees in crushing relief. She laid her icy palms on the stone railing to hold herself up as she watched her father-in-law throw his opponent to the ground and hold him down on the sand. He held his sword poised, ready to plunge the blade into the defeated man's neck. And all Adaira could think was *enough*. She had witnessed Jack's father kill one man already. She couldn't bear to watch him gather more blood on his hands.

"Step away, Oathbreaker," she called to him. "Drop your sword."

A hush fell over the arena. Adaira could feel hundreds of eyes bore into her, but she kept her gaze on Oathbreaker. He heard her and took her command to heart. He slowly stepped away, releasing his defeated opponent.

Her father-in-law turned to look at her, dropping his sword, but Adaira's eyes were drawn to the man on the sand. A man, tall and thin, who was rising, who looked at her through his dented helm, who was suddenly striding toward her with confidence.

She stared at him, watching him approach the balcony. Then her heart froze, as if caught in a snare, before she felt her blood begin to course through her again. Hot and swift beneath her skin, as if she had been sleeping all this time and only now was opening her eyes, awakening.

She watched the man kneel before her. She watched him lay a hand over his chest, over his heart. A hand that was pale and elegant. Adaira drew a sharp breath.

She would know his hands, his posture, his body, anywhere. All those times she had watched him play his harp. All those hours he had walked shoulder to shoulder with her. When he had lain with her, skin to skin, in the dark.

Jack.

Adaira wondered why he refrained from speaking, why he refused to remove his helm.

"Lady Cora," a voice rang through the tense air. "May I ask why you have interrupted the culling?"

She dragged her gaze from Jack to look at Godfrey, the dungeon master who oversaw the fights. He was walking across the arena, arms stretched wide as a perplexed smile wrinkled his face. He was trying to sound respectful to her, but Adaira could tell he was annoyed that she had brought the killing to a halt.

Oh, she was beyond ready to speak with Jack. Her fingers

curled on the balustrade, nails scratching the stone. But before she spoke, Adaira glanced over her shoulder, expecting a challenge. Innes stood close behind her, watching with inscrutable eyes. But her brow was arched in surprise, as if she was just as shocked as the rest of the Breccans by Adaira's interruption of the culling.

Innes gave her a slight nod, as if to say, *Go on.*

"Godfrey," Adaira greeted him brightly. "What is the name of this man who is fighting Oathbreaker?"

The dungeon master came to a stop beside Jack. "This is John Breccan."

"And what is his crime?"

"He is a thief."

"What did he steal?"

Godfrey hesitated, but he chuckled. He glanced beyond Adaira, and she knew he was looking at Innes.

"Don't look at my mother," Adaira said. "Look at *me*. I am the one speaking to you."

Godfrey blinked, stunned by her words. He finally dropped his pretense and glared up at her. "He stole a harp, Lady Cora. A grave offense in the west."

"A crime that can't be proven, no doubt. And who brought him into the dungeons?"

"I'm afraid I can't answer that, Lady, and now that you have—"

"Why hasn't he removed his helm?" she asked.

Godfrey glanced down at Jack. "Because it's fastened to his chin."

"Fastened? Do you mean it is *locked* to him?"

"Yes."

"Unlock it. Immediately. I want to see his face."

Godfrey sighed, greatly inconvenienced, but he did as she wanted. He took the ring of keys from his belt. He unlocked the helm.

Adaira held her breath as Jack laid his hands on the helmet. He lifted the steel away, and his hair tumbled across his face. He yanked the gag from his mouth and tossed it aside.

She drank him in. Those ocean-dark eyes of his, the wry tilt of his lips, the hunger in his expression as he gazed up at her, still on his knees. The arena, the Breccans, the stars and the moon and the night all melted away as her chest rose and fell, as her blood hummed at his nearness.

A small sound escaped her, a sound that almost broke her composure. She stifled it, told herself to *hold on*. She could release her emotions later, behind closed doors.

She unfastened the plaid at her shoulder.

Everything within her ached to drape Jack with it herself, but to jump from the balcony to the sand below would break her legs. She could take the inner route down to the arena doors, but she didn't dare let Jack out of her sight. Not until she had claimed him.

"Godfrey?" she called. "Take my plaid and drape it around my husband."

"Your *husband*, Lady Cora?"

"Yes. Come closer."

Godfrey looked pale as a wraith, as if the blood had been drained from him. He finally realized who had nearly died in the arena under his watch, and he meekly held up his hand and caught the plaid as she dropped it to him.

Adaira watched as he shook out the wrinkles and draped the blue-and-violet-checkered wool over Jack's shoulders.

She laid her palm over her breast, where her heart beat like thunder, and spoke the ancient words over him.

"I claim you, Jack Tamerlaine. From this day forth, you will be sheltered in my house, and will drink from my cup, and will find rest beneath my watch. If anyone lifts a sword against you, they raise one against me. Such a challenge will not go unanswered. You are mine to defend until the isle takes your bones or you desire it otherwise. Rise, and renew your heart."

Jack stood.

Murmurs began to ripple through the crowd. The Breccans were rooted to the spot, transfixed by the draping, so when someone began to move through the gathering, Adaira's eyes were drawn away from Jack.

She saw Rab Pierce leaving the arena stands in a hurry.

Adaira knew everything in that split second. She knew who had found Jack as he was traveling, who had taken him unjustly to the dungeons. Who had gagged him and locked his helm in place and tossed him into an arena to fight his own father.

She stared at Rab, her expression cold and hard as stone, even as her mind splintered into a hundred thoughts. He must have felt it, the way her ire was boring into him. He dared to glance over his shoulder and their eyes locked. He stumbled, caught his balance, and rushed away even faster.

"Innes?" Adaira said, taking a smooth step back. She continued to watch Rab, predicting which door he was going to slip through, which castle route he was going to take as he fled to the stables. "Will you personally see to it that Jack is safely escorted to my chambers, and that a warm bath is drawn for him and a good supper is delivered?"

Innes took hold of her arm. "Where are you going?"

Adaira's gaze slid to meet Innes's. Her voice was calm, but her teeth flashed in the firelight as she whispered, "No one hurts those who I love. *No one.*"

She didn't know whether or not her mother heard the implication of what she had said. If Innes had been aware of Jack's presence in the arena. But Adaira's suspicions were beginning to grow claws, tearing through the fragile bonds she had been forging with her mother.

Innes's nostrils flared. Yes, she had heard the quiet threat. But they would have to discuss this later.

"I'll see to your requests, Cora. But don't kill Rab. Not unless you want a war."

"I'm not going to kill him."

Innes said nothing, but her eyes searched Adaira's. She must have seen what she wanted, seen the passion in her daughter's blood that she had perhaps inherited from her mother, passion that had fallen dormant in the east.

Innes released Adaira's arm.

Adaira knew Jack was gazing up at her. But she didn't have time to reassure him. Rab had vanished from the arena, and Adaira turned and exited through the doors, letting them slam against the walls.

She flew through the castle in pursuit of him.

CHAPTER 23

J ack watched Adaira leave the balcony without giving him a second glance. But he had seen what had drawn her attention. He had seen Rab fleeing the arena, and Jack's chest swelled beneath his armor. His lungs filled with cool night air, with firelight and justice and blood-tingling awe at Adaira.

Best of luck to you, Rab!

But then the thrill waned, and Jack shivered, returning to the moment.

He was in the arena that had almost seen his blood spilled before hundreds of Breccans. Utter strangers who continued to stare at him like he was an anomaly. He felt naked, even though he was draped in the warmth of Adaira's plaid, which smelled faintly of her, like lavender and honey. He was standing on sand that his boots had marked when he had been fleeing his father. His *father,* whom he had completely forgotten existed at the sound of Adaira's voice.

Jack shuddered again, drawing the plaid closer around his shoulders. He could see movement at the corner of his eye. Someone was approaching and staring intently at him. Jack fought the temptation to meet that gaze as fear surged through him like a tide.

"Jack?"

The voice was deep and gentle, hoarse with shock. It sounded nothing like it had moments before, through the steel of the helm and the smoke of survival.

Jack looked at his father.

Niall was pale as he took in all the features that were solely Jack's, and the ones that he had been given by Mirin. Her eyes, her coloring. The proud slant of the shoulders. All of it had come from his mother, and Jack watched as Niall saw these traces of Mirin. As he saw traces of *himself*.

"*Jack,*" Niall said, extending his hand. The space between them suddenly felt vast, uncrossable.

Jack didn't know what to think, what to say. His words froze, and all he could do was stand and breathe.

Niall came another step closer, but he must have felt the divide between them. He must have felt the waste of twenty-two years. He collapsed to his knees as the truth pierced his heart.

Niall Breccan, Oathbreaker, undefeated, sprawled on the sand and wept.

Jack flinched, unable to stomach the sight, the sounds of his father's devastation. He began to move toward him, slowly, as though the air were thick. He would cross the divide, but Godfrey came between them.

The dungeon keeper took hold of his arm in an iron grip and began to lead him from the arena.

"Come, Jack Tamerlaine. The laird has asked for you."

Jack scarcely heard Godfrey as his nerves began to sing again. He walked obediently to a door in the wall, but he glanced back to see his father being surrounded by guards.

A protest rose in Jack's chest.

He had to force it down, even as it ached to be expressed. He had to tear his gaze away from Niall and allow Godfrey to guide him into the castle.

He didn't know what he expected, but the corridors were similar to Sloane's in the east. The air was fragrant with juniper boughs, and the firelight was generous, the floors polished. Tapestries hung on the walls and condensation fogged the windows.

He stood beside Godfrey and waited for Innes's arrival. It felt like a year had come and gone before Jack heard footsteps approaching.

"That will be all for tonight, Godfrey," Innes said when she appeared around a corner, her eyes never once leaving Jack.

The dungeon keeper bowed and returned to the arena, leaving Jack alone with the laird. They had seen each other three times before. The first was when Innes brought restitution for the raid on the clan line. He saw her again when Adaira had struck a bargain with her mother in Mirin's house. And finally, on the day Adaira had left the Tamerlaine clan. Innes had looked at Jack then as she did now, as if time hadn't passed at all and he was a grave problem for her to deal with.

"I apologize for this . . . unfortunate misunderstanding," said Innes. "I was unaware that you were in the keep, and I hope you will be able to forgive the oversight."

"Of course, Laird," Jack said, his voice brittle.

"Come. My daughter has asked me to escort you to her chambers."

Jack quietly followed the laird through a dizzying labyrinth of corridors. He tried to mark which turns they took, how many flights of stairs they ascended, but his mind felt blurred, fixated only upon one thing: he was about to be with Adaira again.

Innes came to a sudden halt before a carven door.

"You are a welcome guest here, Jack Tamerlaine," Innes said. "And you may stay however long you would like. But there is one thing I ask of you."

Jack glanced at her, but he knew the words before she spoke them.

"Please refrain from making music while you are on my lands." Innes waited until her request was acknowledged before she opened Adaira's door.

Two servant girls were present, rushing to finish their tasks.

One was pouring the last bucket of hot water into a round tub, and the other was arranging a silver tray of dinner on a table before the hearth. They both startled at the sound of the door opening and hastened their pace until they were done, bobbing before Jack and the laird as they slipped into the corridor.

"My daughter will be with you shortly," Innes said, but Jack could hear the clip of worry in her voice. Even she was uncertain of Adaira's whereabouts, and Jack didn't know if that should make him anxious.

He entered Adaira's chamber, listening to the door latch behind him.

Alone at last, Jack exhaled.

Adaira's room was spacious and teeming with color. The stone hearth cut through a painted wall, which depicted an array of gilded flora and fauna and moons of various phases. Another wall was devoted to mullioned windows and a plush window seat. A desk was arranged there, as if Adaira liked to sit and write before the glass. She had a wardrobe, bookshelves, a tapestry of a woven chimera, and a canopied bed draped with a blue quilt.

Was this the room she would have always had if her parents had decided to keep her that fateful night? Or was it another, perhaps a guest chamber that had been prepared for her? Jack saw that the room was an inviting one, but he couldn't feel Adaira's presence within it.

He stopped before her desk, where his letter sat on the wood. He reached out to trace his words, and that was when he noticed how filthy his hands were. His nails were blackened with grime, and his forearms were smudged. His tunic was disgusting, and he reeked of sweat.

Jack draped Adaira's plaid over the back of the closest chair and tore off his breastplate. He threw his raiment into the fire to burn.

He approached the tub of steaming water, only to blink down at it.

"Is this some kind of a joke?" he asked. It was *tiny*, like a barrel for a stable, and he wasn't sure if he would be able to fit in it. Somehow he was able to fold his long legs after he eased himself into the tub. He kept one eye on the door as he hastily scrubbed with a bristle brush and soap, washing dirt from his skin and hair.

He half expected Adaira to arrive the moment he stood from the blackened water, reaching for the drying cloth. She didn't, but Jack's relief was short lived: he discovered that the drying cloth was also very small, almost laughably so. Jack rushed to dry himself with it, snorting as he stood before the warmth of the hearth. Then he realized his tunic was now a heap of ashes, and he had no clothes to change into.

He had no choice but to stride to Adaira's wardrobe and look for something of hers to don. His hands rushed through the endless collection of garments, eventually finding a dark, fur-lined robe.

"You'll do," he said wryly, knowing that Adaira was just as tall and trim as he was. Jack yanked the robe from its hanger and slipped into it. He belted it firmly at his waist and stared down at his bare feet—the robe's hem brushed the middle of his shins.

He returned to the hearth and sat before the dinner tray. He was ravenous, but his stomach was churning. He didn't want to eat without her, so he decided to wait.

He might be waiting all night, he thought with a groan, leaning his head back against the chair. He sat like that for a while, eyes closed, heart swiftly beating, his damp hair dripping onto his shoulders. Finally he relented to pour himself a cup of wine, thinking it would calm him.

He was holding the bottle when a knock sounded at the door.

Jack froze, his voice lost, his eyes riveted to the door as it slowly opened. Adaira crossed over the threshold. She was holding what looked to be a pile of folded garments in her hands, and she kept her eyes averted from him at first. She bolted the door behind her and then leaned against it, an action so familiar and beloved to Jack that he felt like the two of them had been cast back in time to the night of their handfasting.

He realized she was just as anxious as he was, coming face-to-face with him after being separated. Jack didn't speak. Not until Adaira finally lifted her eyes and met his gaze from across the room.

"You have blood on your face," he said.

Adaira raised her hand to trace the flecks of blood on her cheek. When Jack noticed more blood streaked on her forearm, his heart quickened.

"And you are wearing my robe," she said.

Jack glanced down at it, to ensure it hadn't betrayed him by gaping open. "I thought you would prefer this to the alternative."

Adaira began to close the distance between them. Jack watched her, trying to measure her emotion so he would know how to chart his own. There was a sheen in her eyes—tears or mirth, he couldn't tell—but then she smiled, and his breath hung in his chest.

"I think you wear that robe better than me," she claimed, her gaze rushing over him.

"I doubt that," Jack countered, rising as she approached. The wine bottle was still in his grip, his fingers locked about its neck. "Although I would have to see you in this robe before I made such an assumption."

"Mmm." She came to a stop, an arm's length away. The firelight washed over her face and her long, unbound hair. It gilded the sword sheathed at her side, the golden half coin hanging from her neck.

Jack could have stared at her all night.

Her smile eased, but its warmth lingered in her eyes. "I didn't mean to make you wait so long, but I was finding you some clothes, as well as taking care of a few important matters." She extended the folded garments to Jack. "Your harp should be returned by tomorrow. As should anything else Rab took from you."

Jack set down the bottle. He accepted the clothes, relieved to see his half coin resting on the pile.

"The chain is broken, but I'll have a jeweler mend it," she said.

"Thank you." Jack hesitated, setting the clothes aside. He looked at Adaira fully, aching to touch her. There were endless words still unspoken between them, and he could feel them, brewing like a storm.

"Adaira," he whispered. "*Adaira, I—*"

The sound of her name broke her composure. It didn't hit Jack until a moment later that she hadn't heard her name in weeks, that she had been answering to *Cora*.

It was like a rock breaking through ice on a loch.

She stepped forward, until the distance between them evanesced and he could see the freckles fanning across her nose. Jack drew in a sharp breath, because there was fire in her eyes, and he was captivated by it, as well as slightly fearful of such heat. Especially when she raised a fist at him.

"You foolish"—she shoved him once with her hands—"insufferable"—then nudged him again, just over his pounding heart—"*infuriating* bard!" She pushed him a third time, forcing Jack to take a step back.

Fury spun from fear, he realized as he saw tears well up in her eyes. And he would gladly let her pound her fists on his chest if she needed to. She could call him whatever she felt like, because he was with her and that was all that mattered to him. He was breathing the same air as her, standing in the same moment with her.

Jack waited for her to shove him again, welcoming her to do so with his eyes and his hands, held palms up at his sides.

Yes, let it all go, Adaira, he thought, waiting. *Let yourself unravel with me.*

"I almost watched you *die!*" she shouted at him, and this time her fist pounded her own chest. Once, twice. A third time. As if she needed to command her heart to keep beating. "And I . . ."

Her voice broke. She turned away from him abruptly, her fist finally opening. Blue jewels tumbled from her hand, gleaming in the light as they spilled across the floor. But Jack hardly paid mind to their strangeness. He watched Adaira bow over, as if she had been torn in two. A sob split her breath. She crouched down and wept into her hands.

Jack had never seen her cry. He had never heard such an unearthly sound wrenched from her chest, and gooseflesh rippled over him as he listened. It froze the marrow in his bones as he felt her pain, her grief. He knew in that moment she had been holding this in for days, for *weeks*. This emotion that she had quietly buried in a castle surrounded by strangers. In a land where she was still regarded with suspicion. A place that should have been her home but wasn't.

Tears welled in his eyes as he walked to her. The blue jewels on the floor cut into his bare feet, but he scarcely felt them. He drew Adaira up in his arms and carried her to the chair. She sat in his lap and pressed her face into his hair, clinging to him. She continued to weep, and Jack's hands caressed her shoulders, stroked down her spine, then up her ribs. He felt her tremble with her uneven breaths, and he pulled her closer, his heat seeping into her. Finally, he could no longer hold back his own tears, and he wept with her.

An hour could have passed. Time seemed to melt away, and Adaira eventually leaned back to look at Jack, to wipe away his tears with her thumbs.

"My old menace," she said. "I've missed you."

Jack smiled, and his laugh sent more tears slipping down his cheeks. He sniffed, his nose inconveniently running. "I see you got my letter," he said in a stuffy voice.

"Yes. And nearly a moment too late, Jack."

"Was it my words that drew you to the arena, Heiress?"

He felt her stiffen. *Heiress* was his old moniker for her, a title she had once worn amongst the Tamerlaines. Jack instantly regretted saying it, even though it had rolled naturally from his tongue.

"No," she said, glancing away from him. "It was the strangest thing."

He felt her drifting far from him. Jack tightened his hold on her waist, desperate to feel her gaze tracing him again. "And what was that?"

"The fire," Adaira whispered, looking at the hearth. "The flames extinguished. The fire led me to you."

Jack wanted to be surprised, but all he could think of was Ash, rising from Mirin's hearth. Ash, encouraging Jack to venture west.

"There's something I need to tell you, Adaira," he said.

She fixed her attention on him so intently, he almost lost his train of thought. She listened as he told her about Mirin's hearth going dark, and about playing for the fire spirits. About Ash telling him he would find the answers in the west.

"I see," Adaira said, but Jack could feel her withdrawing. "You're here because Ash has commanded it of you?"

"Yes," Jack replied. "But to be honest, I was only waiting for a reason to cross the clan line. I was waiting for a reason to come to you, whether you invited me or something else directed me."

She was quiet.

He hated how he suddenly couldn't read her face, her inner thoughts. But the light in her seemed to dim, as if she was tamping down her emotions again. He didn't want that. He didn't want her to hide how she felt, and he was about to lift his hand and touch her face when his stomach let out a loud, plaintive growl.

"When was the last time you ate, Bard?" Adaira drawled.

Jack sighed. "Not too long ago."

"Stop lying. You're famished, aren't you? Why don't you eat while I change and wash this blood off me." She stood from his lap, and Jack's hands reluctantly slid from her waist.

"You don't want to share this meal with me?" he asked, a bit petulant.

She only smiled as she unbuckled her belt and leaned her sword against the wall. "I already ate dinner. But you can pour me a cup of gra. I'll share that with you."

Jack glanced at the green bottle. He had assumed it was wine but now remembered that the Breccans brewed their own special drink, which they consumed only with those they trusted.

He poured them each a cup as Adaira approached her pitcher and ewer to wash the blood from her hands and face and a few strands of her hair.

Spirits, what did she do to Rab? Jack wondered. Had she killed him? But he couldn't envision Adaira taking such a measure. Or . . . perhaps he could. He could see the Adaira he felt so familiar with—the one who had stood beside him in the dark while he sang. Who loved to tease him, as well as challenge him. But he was also seeing new facets to her. As if she had had no choice but to sharpen herself amongst the Breccans.

"I'm curious to know how your time has been in the west, Jack," she said, reaching for her plaid to dry herself. "I'm sorry it hasn't been the most gracious of welcomes, but next time you should let me know *days* before you come."

"Next time?" Jack growled, surprised by how hot that made his blood. Did she think he would leave soon?

She didn't reply as she strode to her wardrobe. He watched her move across the chamber, opening the wooden doors and sorting through her clothes. Her face was angled away from him as she began to undress, tossing her tunic aside.

Jack saw the flash of her tumbling hair, the pale eaves of her shoulders, the dip of her back.

His breath hitched. He averted his eyes, staring down at the dinner tray before him. But he could feel the warmth in his face as he listened to her change.

"You say Ash has sent you here," Adaira said. "What if he commands you back to the east? What if Mirin and Frae need you? Or Torin and Sidra? The Tamerlaine clan?" She was quiet, but her bare feet padded across the room. Only when she was sitting in the chair directly across from him did Jack look at her again.

She had changed into a white, long-sleeved chemise. The ribbon at its neck was loose, and the fabric looked like it might slip from her shoulder. Jack's eyes traced her golden half coin, then moved up her neck to meet her gaze. There was sorrow in her. Sorrow and resignation. Jack raked his hand through his damp hair.

"You are not a songbird to be caged," she said. "As much as I want to keep you with me, the very *reason* you are here reminds me that others have a claim on you. And how can I compete with something like fire? It would be wrong of me to pull you away from your responsibilities."

"I think we might be looking at this from the wrong angle," Jack said, even though he knew that Adaira had been raised to place duty over her heart. At the first glimmer of vulnerability, she would be tempted to fall back to what she had been taught as a laird's daughter, just as easily as Jack would shelter himself with his music. But neither would he let them retreat to those old, safe places. At least, not before he spoke the words that hovered unspoken between them. "You're assuming Ash sent me here for the mission and the mission alone. But perhaps he knew that I need you, more than I need air and warmth and light. That if I were to go on living as I had been in the east without you, I would soon be worn down to nothing but dust."

"Jack," Adaira whispered. She glanced away, but Jack was watching her intently, and he saw the fear she was trying to smother. Fear she didn't want him to see.

"Adaira," he said, leaning closer to her. "Adaira, look at me."

Her gaze returned to his.

He thought about how drastically her life had changed in the past month. The parents she thought had been hers, the lies that she had been raised beneath. He thought about how she must have felt when the clan she had served and loved no longer wanted her. When all the truths she had believed had crumbled away.

He knew that icy feeling of self-preservation, the instinct to cut away something good for fear of it wounding you later. He knew about having no choice but to protect yourself when you feel like you're on your own.

"Remember the last time we saw each other?" he began. "We were standing in my mother's storehouse."

Adaira narrowed her eyes. "Yes, of course. You think I'd forget it, old menace?"

"No. But let me take you back in time for a moment," Jack said. "I was hurt by your choice to leave me behind. I couldn't understand it at first, because all I could feel were my own emotions and feelings, and they were very much tangled up in you and what I hoped could be for us. But I knew you wanted me safe, above all else. You didn't want me in the west because you feared for my life. And I could understand that, even as my days in the east were miserable without you. I wasn't living; I was merely taking up air and space. And being separated from you made something very clear to me."

He paused to pick up the cups of gra. He extended one to Adaira, and she accepted it.

"What became clear to you, Jack?" she asked.

"That this year and a day still belongs to *us*," he said. "We still have autumn, winter, and spring. And nothing—no spirits, no lies, no schemes, no culling—can come between us. I am first yours, as you are first mine. Before all others. But if we are going to make this work, we need to be together. We can take our time to become what we want to be. We can take it day by day if you'd like me to remain at your side."

"Is that what you want, Jack?" she asked. "Do you want to remain here with me?"

"Yes," he breathed. "But I also want to know that you want it, Adaira. And it should be a decision you make for yourself, not one to spare my feelings."

Adaira was quiet for so long that Jack's heart was pounding by the time she raised her cup and clinked it to his.

"Then let us live out our year and a day," she said. "I want you to stay with me, Jack. Through autumn, winter, spring, and thereafter should we desire it."

They drank to each other, and the gra was sweet and pleasant, tasting like mist on the hills, like morning dew on the heather. Jack felt the fire trail down his throat, and he held Adaira's gaze.

"I'm sorry," she said suddenly. "I'm sorry for how I hurt you. For leaving you behind. I didn't realize it would cut you so deeply, but I should have. I should have handled things better that day."

"There's nothing to forgive, Adaira," he said. "You did what you thought was best, and you shouldn't apologize for it."

She nodded but said, "I don't ever want to hurt you, not even unintentionally. I hope you know that."

"I know," he whispered.

His stomach growled again, ruining the moment.

Adaira urged him to eat, but with his stomach in far too many knots to take in a proper meal, he ate only a little. Adaira noticed.

"Let's go to bed," she said, rising. "There's a sleep tunic in that pile I brought you."

While Adaira turned down the covers, Jack sorted through the clothes, bleary-eyed. He found the tunic and quickly changed into it, sighing at its softness as he walked to the bed. He sank into the feather mattress.

Adaira blew out the candles. Only the fire burned low in the hearth, illuminating her as she crawled into bed beside him. Jack turned to look at her.

She dragged the blankets up to her chin, but she also lay facing him, watching him as he watched her, the firelight drenching them in gold.

"You're staring at me, Jack," she whispered.

He began to move across the bed toward her. "I can't seem to draw my eyes away from you."

She smiled as he hovered over her, close enough that he could feel the heat from her skin but not quite touching. He traced her lips, watching them part beneath his thumb, her eyes drifting closed.

He kissed her softly, his mouth trailing to her jaw, her neck. He kissed the wild thrum of her pulse, the hollow of her throat. He ached when she sighed, when her fingers raked across his back. He found the edge of her chemise, easing it up as he slid down her body.

"I've thought about this every night since you left me," he whispered as he kissed her knees, the inner warmth of her thighs.

She gasped when he tasted her.

The sound went through him like lightning, and Jack savored the moment. It was simply him and her in the darkness. There was nothing else beyond the door and the walls; there was nothing else save for her and the fire she stirred in his blood and the ancient vows they had spoken beside a thistle patch beneath a stormy sky. The choice they had made to bind themselves together. There was nothing but the way she said his name, both a prayer and a plea, and he answered her without a single word.

"*Jack.*" She tugged on his tunic until his mouth found hers again, his body covering hers.

They came together. He looked at her as she looked at him, and he was completely consumed by her. In the way she moved and touched him. The rosy hint on her cheeks and the dark possession in her eyes.

He buried his face in her hair. He breathed her in as he surrendered to her embrace.

They lay like that for a while, entwined, Adaira caressing his shoulders. He was almost asleep when he heard her voice. Her whisper followed him into his dreams.

"*Old menace.*"

CHAPTER 24

Torin haunted Sidra.

When she stood on the training green, watching the guard conduct their sparring exercises, he stood beside her. When she walked the castle corridors, he followed her. When she visited her patients, he was with her, attentively noticing how she cleansed wounds and burns. Which herbs and plants she gathered and crushed with her pestle and mortar, and what she mixed to create healing tonics and salves. When she laid Maisie down to sleep at night and told her wondrous stories of the spirits, Torin listened.

He longed, more than anything, for her to see him. To speak with her. To be able to reach out his hand and touch her skin.

He was there when she was sick, vomiting into the chamber pot behind closed doors. When her hand touched her belly, where their child was a spark in the darkness. He noticed that she could hardly stomach her food, that she ate very little. And he saw that, despite her exhaustion and the endless worries she carried, she worked harder than ever to find a cure for the blight.

More of the clan had fallen ill. Torin knew he should be striving to solve the riddle from within, but he was at a loss. All he could think of was to learn from Sidra just by observing her, figuring she most likely held the answers in her hands. But time was passing. Even as it seemed to hold steady in the spirits' realm of perpetual dusk, Torin sensed the days slipping away in the mortal world.

Ice and fire, brought together as one. Sisters divided, united once more. Washed with salt and laden with blood—all united will satisfy the debt you owe.

He didn't know where to even begin when it came to cracking the riddle.

One night he stood attentively as Sidra tucked Maisie into the bed they shared.

"Tell me a story," Maisie requested, burrowing deeper into the blankets.

Sidra perched on the edge of the mattress. "What story would you like to hear tonight?"

"The story about the sisters."

"What sisters, Maisie?"

"Remember in the book? The one Grandda gave me? The sisters of the flowers."

Torin's interest was suddenly hooked. The riddle echoed through him as he stepped closer, into the firelight.

"You mean about Orenna and Whin?" said Sidra.

Maisie nodded.

"I don't know that one as well," Sidra said, "but I'll do my best to remember it." As she began telling the story, Torin soaked in her words. She spoke of Orenna, who had once dared to grow her blood-red flowers in unusual places, angering the other spirits with her eavesdropping. Lady Whin of the Wildflowers had no choice but to urge her sister to grow only where she was invited. Orenna, of course, had bristled at the correction and ignored it, continuing to grow her blossoms where she willed, collecting the secrets of fire, water, and wind. Eventually, the Earie Stone punished her by banishing her to heartsick soil, the only place she was allowed to grow. Orenna would have to prick her finger and let her golden blood fall to the ground to create her flowers, and should a mortal harvest and swallow those petals, they would be granted Orenna's knowledge and secrets in turn.

Torin's heart was pounding as the story ended. His mind whirled with thoughts, with ideas and questions. If he was in the spirits' realm, could he cross the clan line unhindered? Could he find the graveyard where Orenna grew in the west? Were the two sisters in the riddle Orenna and Whin?

"Goodnight, my love," Sidra whispered, leaning down to drop a kiss on Maisie's forehead. Their daughter had fallen asleep, arms splayed wide. Sidra continued to sit beside her for a long moment, her own eyes closed, as if she could finally relinquish the mask she wore by day.

She looked drained. Her countenance was deathly pale, and there were smudges beneath her eyes. Torin took another step closer to her, desperate to caress her hair, to whisper against her skin.

"You should rest, Sidra," he said.

Sidra sighed.

At last she stood and began to loosen the stays of her bodice. This was when Torin always departed. Every night, before she disrobed, he would melt through the door and walk the castle gardens, searching for answers. He was just turning to leave when a gasp slipped from her lips. He turned back, frowning, and watched as she limped to the hearth.

Sidra eased herself into a chair, biting her lip as if to swallow another sound of pain.

Torin followed as though a cord were bound between them. He stopped a few paces away, eaten up with worry as she rubbed her left ankle through the boot. He had shadowed her most of the day, and he didn't recall her injuring herself.

Sidra released a tremulous exhale, glancing his way. Torin couldn't breathe, feeling her eyes on him.

"Sidra?" he whispered, his voice softened with hope. "*Sid?*"

She made no response. He swiftly realized she was looking *through* him, as he should know by now, and her eyes were fixed on Maisie, who continued to slumber. Torin swallowed the lump in his throat, watching as Sidra carefully began to unlace her knee-high boots.

She was wearing a brace around her ankle. Torin scowled at the sight; he hadn't realized she was hurt, although now that he thought of it, he only came to her in the mornings after she had readied herself for the day. Not once had he caught sight of the brace, hiding beneath boot and skirt.

He took a step closer to her. When had she injured herself?

The brace came off. She set it quietly on the floor before drawing her stocking down her leg. Her entire foot looked bruised, as if a wagon cart had rolled over it.

Torin's breath hissed through his teeth as he rushed to her, kneeling at her side. "What happened? *When* did this happen? I've been with you all this time!"

Sidra only winced as she rubbed her foot. It struck him then, like a blow to his chest. He looked closer and saw the threads of gold, shining beneath her skin.

Torin rocked back on his heels, tore his fingers through his hair.

"*Sidra.*"

His spirit fractured. He felt like a pane of glass, laden with cracks. He felt like he was about to fall into pieces.

His eyes stung with tears as he watched her slowly draw her stocking back on.

She didn't know how to heal herself. She didn't know how to defeat the blight, even after all the hours she had dedicated to it.

Torin had never felt such fear before. It was a talon, piercing him in the deepest places, scoring through every organ and every secret he held. It possessed the power to root him to that spot in her chamber, unable to move or think. To turn him into smoke and memory. He sank into the fear, the fear that whispered, *You are going to lose her to the grave.* They had already been separated by realms, but death was a place where not even the spirits of the isle could roam.

Sidra rose.

She prepared for bed, and Torin's eyes were glazed as he stared at the fire dancing in the hearth. When Sidra walked through him, he finally wept, and his tears flowed thick as honey. His sobs rose and fell like the waves, but no one could hear him. No one could bear witness to his grief and his terror.

Eventually, the fire gave a great pop in the hearth. An ember flew through the dimness, landing on Torin's foot. It smoldered through him, through the fog that had encircled him, and he stared down at it, amazed he could at last feel something other than his own emotions.

"*Adaira,*" the ember hissed, just before it went dark.

Torin stepped back, watching the ash crumble on his foot. His thoughts gathered, still strung by cords of fear, but he found a branch of logic to cling to. He thought about all the things he had observed and heard the past few days.

Torin began to move. He looked at Sidra and Maisie, both asleep in bed, before he passed through the door.

He emerged into the courtyard, his strides lengthening, and passed through the city in a matter of breaths. When he stood in the hills, he came to a stop.

"Point me to the west," he said, unable to tell which direction he faced. "Take me to Adaira."

There was a rumble beneath his feet. Torin watched as the hill spirit emerged, rising from the loam.

"I can guide you to the clan line," the spirit said, his voice faint. "But I cannot cross it."

Torin stared at him. "Are you ill?"

"I am weary."

"From the curse?"

"From many things, mortal laird."

Torin thought he understood a shade of that weariness, and he said, "What is your name? You never told me."

That drew a smile from the spirit. "You never asked. But you can call me Hap."

"Hap," Torin said, tasting the name. It conjured images of summer hills, cloaked in thick grass and heather. Of a time when the earth was warm from the sun and soft from the rain. "You'll guide me to the clan line?"

Hap turned. "Yes. Stay in my shadow, Torin."

When Hap moved, Torin followed. Every place the spirit stepped, so did he. Lochs folded for them, granting them swift passage on their sandy beds. Rocks sank below, rising once more only after they had passed by. The hills were gentle, requiring no exertion or struggle to ascend them. Even a waterfall held her breath, so they could be on dry ground as they climbed the summit she cascaded from.

When they reached the Aithwood, the trees rustled and groaned, pulling back their branches and curling up their roots. A clear path was forged, rugged with moss, and Torin's heart began to pound again. He had never walked the west, and he didn't know what he would find.

Hap came to a stop a safe distance from the clan line.

Torin hesitated, feeling the hum of magic in the earth. It was repellent to him as well, and sweat beaded his brow. "Will the spirits in the west be kind to me, or should I prepare for a fight?"

"I'm afraid I cannot answer that," Hap said. A flower fell from his hair, resting on the ground between his bare feet. "It has been a long time since I could roam the west. I don't know how my brethren on the other side have fared, but given the rumors, they haven't been well. Be mindful, then, of where you step."

Torin hadn't felt this nervous in a while, and his reflex was to reach for a sword at his side. There was none there, of course. His blades hadn't survived the passage between realms. All he had were his hands, which were empty, and his feet, which needed to tread carefully.

He stared into the twilit distance, where the western half of the forest waited, seeming to watch him with curiosity. When he took his first cautious step into the west, he was thinking of Maisie. He was thinking of the blight and the riddle and the veins of gold beneath Sidra's skin.

PART THREE

A Song for Kindling

~~~~~~

S idra was leaving Rodina's croft, her healing basket in the crook of her arm, when she saw five guards ride past, galloping along the road. She shielded her eyes from the sun as she watched them pass, their horses kicking up a cloud of copper dust. They could have sprouted wings they were making such haste, pressing west. Sidra felt a twinge of concern, but she tried to shake it away as she walked to the gate.

Blair, her appointed guard, was waiting for her with their two horses. He was one of the older members of the East Guard, a man who had never married or had children and had devoted his entire life to serving the east. He was quiet but sharply attentive, silver bearded and dark eyed, with long brown hair gradually graying at the temples. He was also built like an ox and could move without making a sound.

Yvaine herself had chosen Blair to ride with Sidra when she visited her patients. At first Sidra hadn't liked the thought of having a guard trail her everywhere. But then she realized how difficult it was becoming for her to mount a horse, to pull herself up into the saddle and then dismount to the ground below, multiple times a day. Her foot ached constantly, but she couldn't dull the pain with herbs, having sworn them all off ever since she realized she was pregnant.

Blair had swiftly proven himself useful. He was strong and tall enough to easily lift her up to the saddle and to help her down, so her foot barely throbbed when it touched ground. Sometimes Sidra wondered if he suspected she was blighted, if he could tell she was favoring her foot even though she hid it as best as she could with the shield of her skirts and the brace beneath her boot. But if he did, he never let on, and that made her trust him.

She looked at him now as he also took note of the guards flying by.

"What do you think?" she asked, slipping through the gate.

Blair frowned. "I'm not sure, Lady."

Sidra inhaled a deep breath, wondering how much more trouble she could manage. It could be something as simple as a flock of sheep wandering too far, or a bull getting loose from its pen, or even the hills shifting and causing a bit of mischief for a crofter. There was no telling these days.

Blair had gently taken hold of her waist and was about to lift her to the saddle when they both heard the rhythmic pounding of hooves. A rider was approaching. Sidra stepped around the horses, Blair in her shadow. They both watched as Yvaine drew near, then reined her stallion to a sliding halt in grass.

The moment Sidra met the captain's eyes, she knew it was bad. She braced herself, wondering who was sick, who had died, which part of the isle had just been blighted.

"Come, Lady," Yvaine said, dismounting in a rush. "To the storehouse, out of the wind."

Sidra followed, Blair remaining with the horses. Rodina's storehouse was at the back of the property, within view of the orchard, which had now fallen entirely to the blight. The building was round and small with a thatched, mossy roof. Within, it was cool and dim, the dusty shelves lined with preserves set aside for winter.

Stifling a sneeze, Sidra leaned against the wall to take the weight off her foot. "Tell me, Yvaine. What's happened?"

Yvaine was silent. It was that silence that turned Sidra's dread into ice, and she shivered despite the heat of the day and the sweat dampening her dress.

"I can't believe I'm about to say this to you, Sidra," she said, dragging her hands over her face, breathing into her palms. It was the first outward sign of distress Sidra had ever seen from Yvaine, but it was strangely fortifying to know that the captain felt comfortable enough with her to completely let down her guard. Even if it was just for a moment.

Sidra nearly cast her own mask aside. She almost told Yvaine then and there that she was sick with the blight and didn't know how much time she had, and that she could no longer treat herself because, yes, she was also pregnant with Torin's child, who was still unaccounted for, even though they both believed he was walking the spirits' realm. But no, it was all too much, these recent days that could have inspired a horrifying ballad. Instead, Sidra bit the inside of her cheek and waited.

Yvaine lowered her hands. The cords of her throat shifted as she met Sidra's stare.

The captain had been right. There truly was no way Sidra could have prepared for the news she brought. Yvaine's eyes shone with shock when she finally spoke.

"Moray Breccan has escaped from the dungeons."

When Sidra was a girl living in the cradle of the vale, she had often gone deep into the hills when she was troubled or upset. She would take her staff, sometimes herding the sheep but most of the time she'd go alone. She would walk and walk and *walk*. She would walk until she found a marker, which could be anything—a strangely shaped rock, a small trickle of waterfall, a patch of wildflowers, a cloud in the sky that cast a distinct shadow on the grass. Then she would stop and sit beside it. Usually by then she was so tired from walking that her troubles had lost the worst of their sting and she was beginning to see a way out of them.

She wanted now, more than anything, to walk the hills.

"I need to make one more stop," she told Blair after he had lifted her up to the saddle.

Yvaine had long since galloped away to rejoin her guards' search, leaving Blair and Sidra behind on Rodina's croft. Blair hadn't even flinched when the captain whispered into his ear the news of Moray's escape, but his eyes were quick, taking in every flicker of shadow as if the prisoner could spring forward at any moment.

"I'll follow you," Blair said, and Sidra nodded, waiting for him to mount his horse.

They rode side by side at a gentle trot, past white chickweed and violet mallow blooming along the edges of the road. The wind blew warmly from the south, unfurling clouds across the sky as the sun continued its morning rise. A deer and her speckled fawn bounded from a thicket and stopped halfway up a hillside of heather to gaze back at Sidra curiously.

She couldn't walk the hills, so she rode home. To the cottage that now sat quiet and empty and full of shadows and a kail yard slowly being taken over by weeds.

Blair helped her down. This time she winced when her foot touched the ground, and he noticed. *Yes,* Sidra thought, so weary she could have collapsed right there in the grass. He must have sensed something wasn't quite right, but he only ensured she was steady before turning to search the cottage. It was clear, as Sidra knew it would be, and Blair waited outside while she sat at her old kitchen table, trying to think of what to do. How to resolve a situation she didn't want to handle.

She closed her eyes, but the house felt hollow and strange. Sidra could hear the wind rattling the shutters, panting on old ashes in the hearth.

She would find no answers here, even though Moray had once stood in this very place. It made her shudder to remember that night.

Sidra gritted her teeth.

She pushed herself up from the table and emerged back into

her sun-limned garden. Blair, as expected, was standing by the gate. Sidra paused to pick an armful of her herbs, as well as a few of the weeds. She had been working several hours a day to find a cure for the blight, but nothing slowed its spread; she could only treat minor symptoms in her patients who also suffered from it. She sighed as she tucked the harvest into her basket.

Her gaze absently drifted to the hill. The place where she had once stabbed Moray.

"I'm going to visit my father-in-law for a spell," she told Blair.

He gathered their horses and walked beside her up the hill to Graeme's croft. When Sidra paused, halfway up the path, Blair offered her his arm.

Sidra hesitated but took it, swallowing her embarrassment as she leaned on him. If Blair was going to shadow her for the next few weeks or months or however long until Torin returned, then he would eventually discover the truth about her foot. He would also eventually know she was carrying a child. Sidra's mind began to reel as she wondered if she should just go ahead and announce both of her conditions to the clan.

No, I can't. Not yet.

Sometimes she couldn't sleep at night, and in those silent hours she would worry over her child. She didn't know if the blight would affect the baby growing inside her. Eventually, it might, given its creeping power. But even if the blight never touched her child, she didn't know if the herbs she had previously taken had already done so. It was too much to think about, though, when she was lying in the dark those sleepless nights, wide-eyed and lonely and heavy hearted.

She sighed with relief to reach Graeme's gate and slipped her hand from Blair's arm.

"I'll wait here for you," he said.

Sidra thanked him and found Graeme inside the cottage, reading a thick mainland tome by the hearth.

"Sidra?" he greeted her, surprised. He stood and removed his spectacles. "Did you need me to watch Maisie?"

"No, she's with the castle care keeper today," Sidra said. "I need your advice. Another man has been lost beneath my watch, and I don't know what to do."

"This calls for some tea then. And some oatcakes and jam. Here, sit down, why don't you?"

Graeme was always trying to feed her. Sidra could only stomach certain foods, but thankfully one of them was oatcakes. She let Graeme set out a spread of tea and cakes, even though she wasn't the least bit hungry.

"Now, which man has been lost?" he asked as he sat across the table from her.

"Moray Breccan."

Graeme didn't respond for a full three seconds. "All right," he said, sounding slightly dazed. "And how did he escape the dungeons?"

"The other day he wanted to speak with me," Sidra said, staring down at her tea. "I visited him in the dungeons. He asked if he could write a letter to Adaira. I told him no. When the night shift arrived, he asked one of the guards for a quill, ink, and parchment, so he could write a letter. The guard provided him with the materials, not realizing I had denied this request, and Moray used the quill as a weapon, stabbing the guard in the neck. From there, he got the keys and killed four more guards with the dirk he stole. Yvaine believes he disguised himself as a guard and slipped out of Sloane, because when the next shift found the guards' bodies, one of them was completely unclothed. That was when they alerted Yvaine to his escape."

Graeme rubbed his chin. "I take it the search for him is underway?"

"Yes. Yvaine and the guards are combing through the hills, searching storehouses, crofts, caves. He's unfortunately well acquainted with the east, given all the times he roamed it before. But I . . ." Sidra paused, briefly closing her eyes. "I'm worried he's going to do something horrible. To strike back at me in some way. To hurt the clan."

"You think he'd try to harm someone innocent here?"

"I think he would. He already *has*."

"And what advice can I give you, Sidra?"

"What do I do if I never recover him?" she asked. "What do I do if he's found? How do I punish him for *killing* five of my guards? Do I shackle him again and extend his sentence? One that inadvertently affects Adaira in the west and will keep her away from us for an even longer period? Do I have him executed? Do I write and ask Innes Breccan what she'd prefer for her heir? Everyone is looking to me for wisdom and a plan of action, and I'm at a complete and utter loss."

"Sidra," Graeme said gently.

She quieted, but her heart was pounding. She took a sip of tea to mask the sour tang in her mouth.

"You said he wanted to write a letter to Adaira?" he said.

"Yes."

"I think you have your answer then."

Sidra waited, brow furrowed. "What do you mean?"

"I don't think you have to worry about what *you're* going to do to Moray when you find him," Graeme replied, "for the simple fact that he's not in the east. He's long gone by now."

Sidra didn't want to think of that possibility. The east couldn't afford to lose Moray. But the longer she looked at Graeme and the wistful gleam in his eyes, she knew he was right.

Graeme was the one to say it, though. Because Sidra couldn't bear to.

"I think Moray has gone home to be with his sister."

CHAPTER 26

Adaira woke entwined with Jack. His arm was draped over her, and his breaths were heavy with dreams. One of her legs was caught between his, and for a moment Adaira simply rested in the solid warmth of him, letting herself slowly come awake.

She watched as dawn began to stain the windows, a blush of gray light. She thought about how lonely she had felt waking every morning in a bed far too big for her. How she would think of Jack and let herself long for him.

She still couldn't believe he was here.

She shivered, but not from the cold.

Adaira slipped from the bed, careful not to wake Jack. She quietly opened the door to ask an attendant to bring up a breakfast tray, and then she stirred the fire in the hearth. She was admiring the dance of the flames when she stepped on something hard and cold.

Frowning, Adaira glanced down to see a small blue gemstone.

She had completely forgotten about Rab's poisoned blood, and the crystals she had carried in her palm the night before. She knelt and gathered up the scattered jewels, carried them to her bureau, and set them in an empty bowl. Then she went about her morning ablutions, but she kept seeing Rab in her thoughts.

She had caught him in the stables, preparing to mount his horse and flee home. But once she called his name, he had paused, unwilling to look like a coward before her and the grooms, who were drawn to watch the altercation.

Adaira had found Jack's half coin tucked away in Rab's pocket, the confirmation she needed. She set her dose of Aethyn in his hands, commanding him to drink it. Then she had waited for its effects to take root, uncertain how severe they would be for him and whether he was already dosing himself.

As she had thought, he wasn't greatly affected by it. Chances were good that, as a thane's son, he had been imbibing the poison for years. She had taken the dirk from his belt, so that she wouldn't have to unsheathe her own sword, and drawn the pointed blade down his cheek, cutting it open. She watched him flinch and hiss in pain.

"Let this scar remind you of your foolishness," she had said as his blood flowed down his face, dripping onto the hay. Transforming into blue jewels. "Let this scar remind you not to touch those I love ever again, or my next judgment won't be so merciful. Do you understand, Rab?"

"I understand, Cora," he rasped.

It still wasn't enough. When she struck him across the face, she had felt his blood splatter across her cheeks and stain her knuckles. Only then did she let him go, but not before she had ordered him to return everything that he had stolen from Jack.

She had watched him canter off into the night, while the grooms, awed, or perhaps shocked, whispered around her. She had been a meek and easily overlooked presence in the stables until that moment. She bent down to collect the jewels she had made.

Now Adaira paused in the morning light, staring down at her hands, beaded with water.

She didn't know what Innes and David would think of her

"warning" to Rab. She herself hardly knew where it had come from, but it seemed a natural response. One coming from a side of her that had been suppressed for so long that she hadn't even been aware of its existence.

A knock on her door broke the moment. She dried her hands and strode across the room, noting that Jack was stirring.

"Stay in bed, old menace," she told him, just as he sat up with tousled hair.

Jack only frowned at her, his eyes still heavy with sleep. Adaira answered the door and thanked the servant who had brought breakfast. She took the tray and carried it to the bed, gently setting it down on the mattress.

"And what is this?" Jack said, his voice smoky from dreams. "Breakfast in bed?"

Adaira grinned, easing her way onto the mattress. "You had a rough go yesterday. This is the least I could do."

Jack returned the smile and took up the steaming teapot. He poured two cups, and when Adaira reached over to take one, he stopped her, as if the entire tray was his.

"Where's your breakfast?" he teased.

Adaira's mouth fell open, but she enjoyed his banter. "Must I beg you to feed me then?"

"Oh, I'd love nothing more than to feed you," Jack said, taking in her wild hair and rumpled chemise. Adaira's toes curled beneath the blankets, but before she could scrounge up a good enough retort, he continued. "What would you like to start with? Tea or parritch?"

"Tea," she said, accepting the cup he finally gave her.

She stirred in some honey and a splash of cream, and they sat against the headboard, enjoying their tea in companionable silence. Eventually, Adaira glanced sidelong at Jack, brimming with questions.

"How are Mirin and Frae?" she asked.

"They're both doing well. Frae especially wanted me to give you a hug for her."

"I'm glad to hear it. I miss them," Adaira said, tracing the rim of her cup. "And Sidra and Torin?"

Jack paused, and Adaira had a spasm of panic.

"What is it?" she demanded. "Are they all right? Did something happen?"

"They're both fine," Jack rushed to reassure her. "But something has happened, and I need to tell you about it."

Adaira listened as he told her about the blight. She felt frozen by shock over what Jack was telling her, the tea forgotten in her hand. He told her how the illness was being passed to humans, how he had tried to play for the orchard to find answers. How Bane had interrupted him and struck a tree—the snippet of Kae's memory that Adaira had seen—and how Torin was at his wit's end about what to do.

"I can't believe this is happening," Adaira said when Jack had fallen quiet. "I should write to him. And Sidra too."

"Well, that brings me to my next point," Jack said with a sigh. "Torin is trying to contain the news of the blight in the east, but I noticed that it's in the west as well."

Adaira frowned. "Where?"

"In the Aithwood. I passed a sickened tree after I had crossed over."

"My parents haven't mentioned anything about this," she said. "Nor has anyone else."

Jack regarded her gravely. "Then there's a chance that it has *just* spread to the west. Or that your parents know about the blight and are keeping it secret."

The latter possibility seemed most likely. As Jack fixed them each a bowl of parritch, Adaira thought about how she could initiate such a conversation with Innes. Would Innes be at all open to discussing such a sensitive matter with her?

"So Torin doesn't want the Breccans to know the east is sick?" Adaira said, taking the bowl from Jack. He had put an ample helping of berries and cream on top, and she took her spoon and stirred it together.

"Yes," Jack replied. "But that was *before* I knew the west is also suffering. Which Torin still isn't aware of. I think that'll change his mind."

"Hmm." Adaira leaned forward to refill her teacup. The chemise slipped from her shoulder, down to her elbow.

"What's this?" Jack's voice was sharp.

"What? You want to take all the tea again?" she countered, not sure what he was talking about until she saw that he was gazing at her exposed arm and the line of stitches that held her wound together. "Oh. *That*. It's nothing."

But Jack was tracing it with his fingertip, his eyes dark and gleaming as he studied the stitches.

"It doesn't look like *nothing*," he said. "Who did this to you?"

"It was an accident."

"By whose hand?"

"David," Adaira replied. "We were sparring in the rain." She regretted the words as soon as she uttered them. They conjured images of Jack and his father in the arena. Adaira could see the same thought crossing Jack's mind as his expression turned inward, as if he were trying to shutter his emotions.

Adaira set aside her parritch.

"I want to free him," she said. "By all accounts, he should be. He's won enough rounds in the culling to be liberated."

"Innes doesn't want him to be accepted back into the clan," Jack said in a careful tone. "I understand her reasoning, given what Niall did."

"I'll speak to her," Adaira promised.

They finished their breakfast in a stilted silence. Finally, Adaira could think of no better way to break the somber mood than with a ride across the wilds.

"The day is getting away from us," she said, approaching her wardrobe. She let her chemise fall to the floor, feeling Jack's gaze on her skin. Glancing over her shoulder, Adaira met his stare boldly. "Get dressed, Jack. There's someone I want you to meet."

—

All of the west felt like a graveyard, full of hungry, languishing spirits. Torin stepped mindfully, but he still managed to draw far too much attention. The ferlies in the grass trailed him, licking their lips. The heather shivered when he passed, and the rocks refused to give way to him. The earth spirits here were suspicious of him, and Torin didn't know what else to do but be careful and to keep his eyes peeled for both Adaira and the Orenna flower.

He eventually came to a river—he wondered if it was the same river that flowed into the heart of the Aithwood and on to the east—and was just about to cross it when a spirit rose up from the water with a snarl.

Torin yanked his foot back to the bank, nearly losing his balance. He blinked in shock as the spirit manifested, built like an old woman with blue-tinged skin, lank white hair, and bulging, milky eyes. She sniffed and then smiled, revealing a horrifying cache of needlelike teeth. Her fingers were long and taloned, and gills fluttered in her sinewy neck.

"You dare to cross my domain, mortal man?" she asked.

The hair rose on Torin's arms, but he managed to keep his voice level. "Yes. Forgive me if I offended you, spirit of the river."

She cackled. It was the sound of a nightmare, and perspiration began to trace Torin's back.

"Why are you here in our realm?" she inquired, sidling closer to the bank, the water flowing around her knobby knees. Torin wondered whether she could leave the river; if not, the bank was his only hope of not being devoured by her. "It has been a long time, indeed, since one of your kind was here."

Torin hesitated. He hadn't possessed the foresight to ask Hap if he should reveal his purpose to other folk. It could be dangerous to let such gossip flow amongst the water spirits, but the west seemed to be a place that was desperate for hope.

He exhaled and said, "I've been summoned to help heal the isle."

The river spirit cocked her head. "Heal us?" she asked, with a glance northward, revealing that she knew what he meant. "Does he know you're here?"

"No."

Silence ticked between them. In a few more breaths, Torin would discover if he was going to die here, by Bane's own hands or by the slippery words of this river hag.

"I know who you are," she hissed with a smile.

Torin studied her, uncertain how to respond. "Who am I then?"

"Once the Captain of the East Guard, now the Laird of the East."

Torin shuddered; he knew this must be the damned river that flowed west to east, because this spirit seemed to know far too much.

"Not so long ago," she continued, "you walked over my hair with a bloodied palm when you took your vows to guard the east. Since then, I have endured your watchmen trampling through me as if I am nothing when they guard the woods."

"I'm sorry," Torin said, sincerely. "My eyes were not open to you then. Nor are my watchmen's now."

She hissed, and he couldn't tell if he had just offended her further or if she was accepting his apology.

But then he realized this spirit had been in the east. He said, "You have the ability to come and go over the clan line. You behold those in the west, as well as those in the east. Other spirits are not as powerful as you."

Her smile widened. Her teeth seemed to multiply. "*Yes*, yes. I am unlike the others because the king has granted me such power."

Torin's stomach dropped. She must be some pet of Bane's, and he had a terrible inkling she was about to summon the king. "You have been granted such ability, and yet you are still hungry, aren't you? Like the others in the west, even when you flow in the east. You long to feel complete again, to no longer have to hold the curse in your rapids."

The river spirit's mirth faded at once. Her milky eyes darkened, and Torin saw that his words had struck true.

"You're hungry," he continued, reaching for a rock on the bank. A rock with a jagged edge. "But I know your secret. I know what you need, and if I feed you, you will let me pass through your rapids without detection or harm. Because I have come to restore the isle, and in the end you want to be healed and no longer broken in two, divided against your own self. That can happen only if you let me pass."

She was quiet, considering. Her gills fluttered in her neck, and the current at her knees slowed.

Torin dared to strike his palm with the rock, the very hand that held his old enchanted scar. He felt a flicker of pain, and then his blood surged, bright as rubies in the dim, gray light. He took a step closer to the river, until his heart was pounding and his boots were submerged. The water was cold, and its grip felt like hundreds of tiny hands, tugging on him.

He stifled a shudder and held out his bleeding hand to the spirit.

A sad expression crossed her face, pulling her brow taut. But then she stepped forward to meet him and drank the blood he offered. It was a strange sensation, feeling his blood drawn away by an immortal's mouth. He had a moment of panic—would she drain him down to the dregs?—but when he at last eased his hand away, she let him go.

Satiated and full, the river spirit sighed.

No longer seeming so old and haggard, and without another word, she melted into the water. Torin merely gaped, gathering his thoughts and letting his pulse calm. But then she surprised him even more: as if she had gathered her hair up, she halted the flow of the river, permitting him to pass through on dry ground.

"Thank you," he whispered, and he stepped over the river rocks in her bed, the soft sand in between, to the other bank. When he stood on the moss again, he glanced behind to watch the river continue its current.

From there, his journey to find Adaira wasn't so terrible.

Perhaps the other spirits were more welcoming because they had heard his exchange with the river. Or perhaps Torin's own confidence had grown, and he was beginning to think he might solve the riddle faster than he once believed.

He located a road and was walking upon it when he heard the distant thunder of horses. He stood still, waiting for them to crest the hill. When they did, his breath caught.

Two horses were cantering side by side. One of the riders Torin couldn't discern from the distance. But the other? He would know her anywhere.

"*Adaira,*" he said, breaking into a run.

His strides were long and powerful again, eating up the earth beneath him. He caught up to Adaira and the other rider, whom Torin swiftly realized was Jack. He followed them off the road and into a stretch of dangerous fells.

"Where are the two of you going?" Torin said, noticing every scowling face in the rocks they passed and all the hungry ferlies in the grass. The eastern wind was blowing with a smudge of wings overhead that gave Torin more chills than the river had. But he kept following Adaira and Jack, relieved to see them together as they should be, and he remembered how the ember from the fire had whispered his cousin's name.

Torin still wasn't sure *why* he needed to find Adaira. He wondered if she had a role to play in the riddle's answer, but he was beginning to think not; perhaps hissing her name was the only way the ember could prompt him to venture west. Torin worried he might be wasting his time chasing after his cousin until she and Jack came to a stop in a copse of trees.

They hobbled their horses and entered the shadows of the wood, Torin close behind. It felt strange to be invisible, and he had to battle the temptation to reach out and embrace Adaira, to call her eyes to him.

Soon, Torin told himself. That word kept him stitched together and kept him going. *Soon she will see you again. Soon you will be home.*

Torin trailed Jack and Adaira to a dark-watered loch. He halted to stare at the strange place. There was a dilapidated cottage on a small island in the center of the water, but stranger than that was the air, which felt cold and empty. He swiftly realized that no wind blew here. Adaira and Jack seemed to have stepped into a rift of time, a place where the past still burned.

"Is this Loch Ivorra?" Jack said.

Adaira's head turned to him. "What is Loch Ivorra?"

"A place where the last Bard of the West lived, before music fell out of favor," Jack explained.

An incredulous but pleased expression passed over Adaira's countenance. "How do you know this, old menace?"

"Rab," Jack replied simply. "He thought I had stolen my harp from here."

Adaira said nothing, rolling her lips together instead. She led Jack across the narrow earthen bridge to the cottage, Torin close behind them. He didn't like the way this place made him feel, and he glanced down into the quiet, still waters of the loch. There was no sign of its corresponding spirit, but Torin sensed their presence. An old, dangerous being who lurked in the depths.

"Should I be wary of what you're about to show me, Adaira?" Jack said as they approached the cottage door. The kail yard was a disaster. Thistles bent, sharpening their needles, and weeds stretched out their pollen-drenched tendrils, as if to capture both Adaira and Jack. Torin was swift to follow, frowning at the spirits until they minded themselves and dutifully retreated.

"No," Adaira said, but then she proceeded to slice her finger on the edge of her sword.

"What are you doing?" Jack hissed as she held up her bleeding hand and laid it on the door.

There was the unmistakable pop of a lock turning.

"An enchanted door," she said, nudging the wood open.

She passed over the threshold first. Jack followed.

Torin trailed them into the cottage, impressed by the door's lock. He took note of how rotten the air smelled. A sweet rot, like honey and moldy paper, covering a grave. But he soon forgot all about the smell when he saw what was within the walls.

A spirit of the wind was sitting on the edge of a palliasse, her indigo hair pooling on her shoulders. She was thin and lean, her skin the shade of the sky at springtime. She was clothed in silver linked armor, and she slowly rose to her feet, tattered iridescent wings dragging on the ground behind her.

Torin merely stared at her, overcome with worry. He didn't realize that Adaira and Jack could also see the spirit until his cousin said, "Jack? This is my friend Kae."

Jack released a long, deep breath. He was just as surprised and awed as Torin was to find a spirit in the flesh here, and Torin's mind reeled. He longed to know what had happened for this wind spirit to be manifested in the natural realm. Was this a common occurrence?

And then the most extraordinary thing happened. The spirit's attention drifted beyond Jack and Adaira to the shadow where Torin stood. He waited, expecting to feel her gaze slice through him like Sidra's, like Maisie's. He was getting accustomed to this feeling, as if he had always been a phantom. But the spirit's eyes traced his broad build. The contours of his face.

His breath caught when her gaze united with his own.

CHAPTER 27

J ack sat across from Kae at the well-worn kitchen table, watching as Adaira set out a small spread of food. Dark brown bread,
pickled onions, a wheel of soft cheese, and wild cherries. She
was pouring them each a small cup of gra when Jack glanced at the
musical composition scattered across the far end of the table. The
brittle sheets of parchment were the color of honey, with ragged
edges, and the inked notes were fading and smudged.

He let his eyes drift to the skeleton on the wall. To the harps
that were still whole and hanging from nails, to the ones that were
broken and scattered along the floor. To the quiet remnants of a
hermit's life or, more likely, a bard in exile. A cracked kettle on a
shelf, an odd collection of cups, a dented tin of tea leaves, jars of
preserves that had gone milky with age. The lumpy bed in the corner, the shutters locked in place by creeping vines, and the herbs
whose leaves had crumbled into dust, their stalks still hanging
from the rafters like long, unearthly fingers.

He both liked and disliked this place.

He thought it would be a good home for a bard to live and compose ballads, surrounded by water out in the wilds. No one would

bother you here, interrupt your work. And yet this place had a sad, strange ambiance to it. It almost felt like a sinister dream that you wanted to wake from and couldn't.

Jack stifled a shudder, sensing Kae's attention.

He let himself return her gaze, full of questions he didn't know whether he should ask. What had happened to her and her wings, and why was she locked in her manifested form? Why did she look at him with a warm light in her eyes, as if they were old friends?

"Kae was wounded by Bane and banished from his court," Adaira said, sitting on a stool next to him. "I saw her fall from the sky and was lucky enough to track her down in the wilds."

"May I ask what happened, Kae?" Jack asked. "Why were you banished?"

Kae was silent.

"He also took her voice," Adaira said. "But we found a way to communicate."

"How's that?"

Adaira exchanged a look with Kae. "Do you think you could show him what you showed me?"

Kae nodded. She stretched out her hand to Jack, her long, blue-tipped fingernails translucent in the light. He just stared for a moment, confused, until Adaira told him to take her hand.

He did, unable to fully hide his wariness, glinting like steel. The moment his palm touched Kae's—when his mortal warmth met her everlasting ice—his mind was flooded with colors and images that were overwhelming. He drew air through his teeth, trying to orient himself.

He saw Bane's court, and Kae's banishment. Her fall through the clouds. He saw himself sitting on a hill in the dark, playing his harp, and he startled. It was odd to see himself through another's eyes. Dizzily, he spun from one memory to another, until all the pieces came together and he could hardly breathe, he could hardly think. He hardly knew where he was, and he—

Kae released him.

Jack continued to reel, keeping his eyes clenched shut and leaning forward on the table. He felt Adaira's hand touching his hair. When his heart had found a steady beat once more, he opened his eyes and looked at Kae in wonder.

She was already watching him, beads of golden sweat shining on her skin. She looked taxed and anxious, as if she didn't know what he would think.

"You've been protecting me—my music—all this time?" he said.

Kae nodded.

Jack wanted to know *why*. Why had she taken scars for him? What did his music fully mean to her?

But he withheld those questions. There would come a time for him to learn their answers. Now he simply whispered, "*Thank you.*"

They ate the meal together. Jack listened as Adaira told Kae about the culling, and how she had barely reached the arena in time to save his life.

"If it hadn't been for the fire . . ." she trailed off, glancing at Jack.

Jack was already looking at her. It was only then, with Adaira's mention of the flames dying in her hearth, that Jack thought of Ash again and remembered him unfolding from Mirin's ashes.

The answers, Ash had said to him, *are there if you seek them.*

He looked at Kae, who was studying Adaira with a tenderness that Jack would have never thought possible on a spirit's face. The sight made him dwell on immortality. He thought about how it would feel to never age or die. How did something timeless fall in love with something subject to time?

"What do you know of Laird Ash, Kae?" Jack said.

Kae's attention snapped back to him, with one of her brows arched. He couldn't tell if she had benevolent feelings toward Ash or not, and he wondered if he had erred by mentioning the weakened Laird of Fire to her. But then he remembered the feel and slant of Kae's memories, and how she had used her prowess to shield him, time and time again.

He didn't fear her. Not as he did most of the other spirits he had sung to and encountered face-to-face.

Kae extended both of her hands across the table. One for Adaira and one for him.

Jack accepted, just as Adaira did. The moment the three of them were connected, Kae summoned her memories.

She was soaring over the isle.

Jack didn't recognize the land beneath her watch. The hills were lush with bracken, red sorrel, and gorse. Wild berries grew in thickets, and white flowers bloomed from the cracks in rocks. A river babbled, clear and cold from a place between two mountains. Jack suddenly realized what he was seeing.

The west before the clan line had struck the ground. It had been beautiful.

Kae dipped lower, her wings stirring the morning mist that eddied in low places. She was carrying gossip in her hands, preparing to release it to a croft below when the faint strum of music caught her attention.

She paused, let the words slip from her fingers, and turned.

She located the bard in a valley, sitting beneath the boughs of a rowan tree. Her emotions were instantly conflicted when she saw him. She felt a little angry and repulsed, but she was also irresistibly attracted to him and the music he plucked from his harp. And he wasn't even singing for air. He was summoning fire.

Kae hid in a shadow, watching Iagan play.

His hair was long and flaxen, drawing the eyes when it caught the sun. His face had sharp-cut features, and his pale skin was flushed from the summer heat. His long fingernails wrung notes from a harp that glistened in his embrace, and his voice was darkly resonant as he sang.

Ash manifested slowly, as if he were weary. He arose from a flurry of sparks, drawing himself into a tall, imposing figure. But when he stood before Iagan, there was no wonder in his expression, no admiration in his gaze. He glared at the bard and hissed, "Why are you summoning me again? What do you want?"

Iagan ceased playing. He remained where he was sitting, beneath the branches of the tree, and replied, "You know what I want."

"And I refuse to give it to you."

"All I ask is for you to give me a portion of your power, so I may never die," the bard said. "So I may grow renowned amongst my clan, and amongst your kind. If you do, I will sing of your prowess forever."

Ash stared at him and bared his sharp-edged teeth. "*No.* You are not worthy of it."

Iagan's face turned red. But his voice was cool when he said, "How am I unworthy? Do I not sing for you? Do I not play for you? Is my music not good enough in your eyes?"

"I see your heart when you play," Ash said. "I see your essence and how hungry you are. And you play for yourself and your desires alone. You do not give. You only want to consume. For that reason alone, I cannot grant you what you want. It would fit you poorly."

Iagan's eyes glittered with ire. "I won't ask again, Ash. Next time, I will simply *take* it."

"You can try, Bard," the spirit said in a haughty tone before he vanished beneath his cloak of sparks and embers.

Iagan rose, but his anger was palpable. He threw down his harp, sending it clanging into the bracken. He unsheathed the sword at his side and began to hack at the rowan tree, cutting down leaves and branches and clusters of red berries. Birds fled from the boughs. A rabbit scampered away from its roots. Even the shadows on the ground trembled.

Kae shuddered.

Having seen enough, she melted into the wind.

Her next memory wasn't as sharp. It was blurred around the edges, and Jack struggled to fully see it, to take in all the details. The west looked sparse now, the clouds a gray shield in the sky. This memory was from after the clan line was formed, Jack realized. He saw Iagan walking along the road, harp tucked beneath his arm. He looked older, harder. Silver laced his blond hair, and his eyes were full of pride, shining like blue gemstones in the gloomy light.

"Iagan!" a voice called, clipped with fury.

Iagan stopped and turned, watching as three Breccan men caught up to him on the road.

"We know you're playing," one of them said. "And you need to *stop*. None of us can wield our magic when you do, and our families are going hungry."

"Are you afraid of a little ballad then?" Iagan countered with a laugh. "You once asked me to play at your daughter's wedding, Aaron. I vividly recall how you sang and danced until you were too drunk to stand."

"That was *before*," Aaron said. "We don't live in those days anymore. And your music isn't harmless. It's causing trouble, and you've been ordered to cease playing."

"All of this," Iagan said, waving his hand to the thin bracken, the wilting heather, the cloudy sky, "is not my fault. It's Joan and Fingal's doing."

The memory began to waver. Jack clung to it, trying to hear what the men were saying. Iagan seemed defiant as they continued to argue. But Jack knew a portion of Iagan's dilemma. He knew how music was in the blood of a bard, simmering and pulsing through every vein. How it settled into bones and organs, aching to be released in the only way it could. Through songs and strings and voice.

When the Breccans began to beat Iagan, Jack felt something cold and slippery wend through him. They struck him, again and again, until he collapsed on the side of the road, bleeding into the grass, his harp broken beside him.

Iagan lay there for a while. It began to storm, the wind howling overhead, tearing through his hair. The rain seemed to make him stir finally, and he began to crawl home. It wasn't his love of music, however, that drove him. It was his anger, a sharp, glittering blade in his heart.

The memory broke.

Jack shivered as his mind and senses adjusted. But his eyes flew open when he heard Adaira speak.

"Kae?"

The spirit looked weakened from sharing the pieces of her past, and she slumped back in the chair. Adaira quickly rose to attend to her, gently dabbing the sweat from her brow.

"Here, sip this if you can." She lifted the cup of gra to Kae's lips.

Kae sighed, but she drank. Her color returned gradually, and she looked at Jack, curious to know what he thought about seeing the bard in her memories.

Jack was troubled. He frowned as he stood, anxiously rolling his neck until it cracked. He studied the skeleton on the wall, wondering if it was Iagan's. Elspeth had said no one knew Iagan's true ending, but given the Breccans' animosity toward him that Jack had seen in Kae's memory, there was a good chance that the bard had met a painful death.

He thought for a while about what else Elspeth had told him about Iagan.

Some legends claim that the mob cut off Iagan's hands and sliced out his tongue, leaving him to die a slow, soundless death. Other legends say that Iagan surrendered to his fellow clansmen, swearing to never play another note again if they would let him live. Some legends boast that a body was never found, that Iagan must have been drowned with his harp in the loch that surrounded his home.

Jack began to sort through the music on the table. Glancing over the notes, he was stabbed with worry by what he read. This music was sinister, twisted by spite and hunger and fury. Jack leaned closer, reading more of the composition, even though it filled him with uneasiness.

This was a ballad about fire. About Ash.

Jack gathered up the pages. He needed to study this later, to pick apart the music. Going over to the wall of bones and broken harps, he found a shelf holding moldy books and scrolls. He began to sift through them, finding more music. Stray pages, bound journals, all covered in Iagan's crooked writing.

Jack was skimming a half-composed ballad when a book fell from the shelf, landing by his boot. He paused to glance down at it, then was surprised to see that the handwriting was distinctly different from Iagan's. He crouched to take up the book. Its first half was missing, and what remained of its spine was dangerously loose. Jack gently leafed through its delicate pages.

More stories I have gathered from the west are as follows . . .

He didn't realize Adaira stood behind him until he felt her chin on his shoulder, her arms coming around his waist. She read as he did, and within moments she shivered.

"Spirits below," she whispered.

"What is it, Adaira?"

Her hands fell away from him. Jack turned to look at her fully.

She was staring at the words on the speckled page, a thrilled gleam in her eyes.

"I have the other half of this book."

Torin had recognized the broken book as soon as it fell from the shelf, landing like an offering at Jack's feet. Graeme had originally given its counterpart to Torin, thinking the stories would help him solve the mystery of the missing girls. Torin, stubbornly thinking the spirit lore within was nothing more than children's stories, had given the book to Sidra and Maisie, who eventually gifted it to Adaira just before she left the east.

It was humbling to think of all the hands that broken book had been passed through. Torin knew who had authored it, long ago. Joan Tamerlaine, a laird who had once dreamt of establishing peace between the clans.

He didn't know why the book had been torn in two, or how its remains had been separated, but Jack and Adaira now had both pieces.

A clatter came from the table.

Kae still sat in the straw-backed chair, but she was watching him, more suspicious now that Adaira and Jack had departed.

Torin turned to face her. "You can see me, even though you are in the mortal realm?"

She gave him a curt nod.

He decided to trust her because Adaira did. Torin approached the table and took a seat. He half expected the chair to refuse to hold him, for his body to pass through it. But the wood was firm, giving him a place to rest.

"Thank you," he murmured to it. Face flushed—had he truly just thanked a *chair?*—he laced his fingers together and looked at Kae. "I'm seeking to solve a riddle, and I think you might be able to help me."

Kae tilted her head to the side, waiting.

Torin shared it with her, word for word. A riddle that had been etched in the heart of a tree by Bane's ire. The convoluted answer to the blight.

Kae's countenance fell as she listened. She knew, then, whose hand had written the words Torin spoke. She shook her head, her palms skyward. Torin had no trouble deciphering what she meant.

I'm sorry, but I don't have the answer.

He wanted to feel crushed. He shouldn't have let such a heady hope unspool within him. But then Torin decided that Kae's knowledge was much deeper and wider than his, and there was still a chance that she could assist him.

"I think the sisters in the riddle are Whin and Orenna," he began, watching Kae's expression closely. She blinked, surprised, but beckoned for him to continue. "I imagine that when you were with your brethren, blowing from east to west and north to south, that you saw countless things on the isle. You must have seen that day when Orenna was banished to dry, heartsick ground, and then how the clan line's creation kept Whin away from her sister."

Kae seemed hesitant. But she extended her hand to him. A gracious invitation for him to take a glimpse into her mind and past.

Torin reached out to take her hand. The contact shocked him—she didn't melt through his fingers—and he noticed that he felt far colder than her. He closed his eyes, waiting for images to fill his mind as they had done for Jack and Adaira. But when his thoughts remained his own, blank with expectation, he looked at Kae again.

She was shaking her head.

It wasn't going to work for him. Even though she could see him and hold his hand, he was in one realm and she was in another.

Torin's hand slipped from hers. He wanted to feel defeated, to pound his fist on the table. But he refused to let his anger and impatience get the best of him.

"Do you happen to know where Orenna resides now?" he asked. "If you could guide me to the graveyard where she blooms, I would be very grateful to you."

Kae nodded, rising from the table.

She led Torin from the cottage, moving slowly. He thought that maybe her healing wounds were ailing her and he shouldn't have asked her to guide him. But then he noticed she was being cautious, paying attention to which wind was blowing, and where, and which path she took across the hills. Sometimes she crouched behind a rock, motioning for Torin to do so. He obliged, full of questions he held between his teeth. He didn't understand until he took note of the golden pathways above, betraying the routes the wind was taking.

Kae wanted to avoid drawing the north's attention.

When it was safe, they would press onward. Torin paid close attention to where Kae led, following her up a hill and then down into a wide strath. The valley was cold with mist and felt resoundingly empty. Gradually, the grass and moss and bracken ceased to grow beneath his boots, and even the rocks were diminished. When they came to a plot of ground covered only with dirt and pebbles, Torin knew they were close.

They climbed up a steep incline. He could hear the waves crashing against rock. He could smell the salt in the air. They were almost to the northern coast.

Torin finally saw the headstones. At first, he didn't know what he was looking at, because Orenna's flowers grew over the markers and across the graves, hardly leaving a place to step that wasn't covered with thick, crimson petals. The sight brought Torin up short. He gazed down at the flowers, brighter than blood on the dry, cracked ground.

Slowly, he knelt. He didn't know where the spirit was, but he felt her presence, as if she hid beneath the blooms.

"May I take some of your flowers, Orenna?" Torin asked.

It was quiet for a long moment. The loneliness was tangible on the cliff overlooking a foam-churned sea. He didn't know how long he could tolerate being in this place, and he felt as if he could be swept off his feet by the harsh wind at any moment.

"You are the first who has ever asked," Orenna answered. Torin couldn't see her, but she sounded close, her voice pitched deep. "Take what you can carry."

Torin reached out and began to harvest the flowers. They soon filled his hands, soft and gleaming with veins of gold. He was tucking them safely in his pockets when out of the corner of his eye he suddenly saw Kae, darting to conceal herself behind an outcropping of rock.

Torin glanced at the spot where she had vanished, his heart beginning to pound. "What is it, Kae?"

The spirit, hidden from his sight, didn't answer. But over the howl of the wind and the roar of the tide below, Torin heard footsteps on the shale behind him. Someone *else* also had Orenna in mind and was coming to the desolate place where she flourished.

Slowly, Torin turned.

To his immense shock, he came face-to-face with the last person he expected.

Moray Breccan.

CHAPTER 28

O f course, Moray couldn't see him.

For once, Torin was glad for his invisibility as he stood, astonished. He watched Moray kneel and begin to uproot fistfuls of flowers. His hands were grimy from the dungeons, his wheat-blond hair matted. There were freckles of blood on his hands and beard, but perhaps worst of all, he was wearing the raiment of an East Guard.

"What are you doing?" Torin cried to him, and then thought better of it and growled, "What are you doing *here*? You're supposed to be locked away!"

His voice went unheard. All Torin could do was watch, icy with dread, as Moray shoved three Orenna blossoms into his mouth, swallowing them whole.

The western heir sighed. The tension in his shoulders melted as he closed his eyes, still on his knees. He waited for the magic to crackle through him.

Torin's heart faltered. What had happened in the east while he was away? Why was Moray free? Something horrible must have occurred, and here he was, trapped on the other side of the realm, in the west, lost in a convoluted riddle.

The nape of his neck prickled in warning, and he moved aside just as Moray opened his eyes, pupils blown wide and dilated. Torin had never ingested an Orenna flower, but he knew it gave a mortal speed and strength. It enabled them to glimpse the spirits' world, to know things that they shouldn't.

Torin crouched down, his fingers digging into the dirt to hold himself steady, muscles coiling in preparation for a fight. At first he thought Moray had seen him, but then Moray hastily shoved the remaining flowers he picked into his tunic pockets, leapt to his feet, and took off running along the rocky edge of the cliff. Torin straightened, perplexed.

A sob drew his attention back to the flower patch.

Orenna had appeared. She was bowed over the place where Moray had just been, her gnarled fingers pressed to the ground, her dark red hair cascading across her face. A sob racked her body, as if she were in agony, and Torin hesitated, uncertain what to do. He was about to kneel before her, to reach out and gently touch her hand, when her head snapped up.

Her hair parted like a curtain, revealing a thin, angular face, with tears shining like dew. Her cheeks were flushed the color of sunset, and her violet eyes were large and luminous as they fixed on Torin. Her lips parted to reveal a cache of thorny teeth.

"He has stolen from me," she said. "Again and again, he has *taken* without asking, without thanking. He has used my knowledge for malice, and if I wasn't cursed—if I could leave this graveyard—I would hunt him down and tear out his throat."

Torin didn't know what to say. But he thought about all the times he himself had taken the isle's magic and resources for granted. Not until now, when his eyes were open to the spirits, had he learned to slow down and to ask. To thank the spirits for their gifts.

With a shock, he saw what could have been: he realized how easily he could have become a man like Moray Breccan.

"Then he has wronged us both," Torin said, rising to his feet. "And I will be your vengeance."

He turned and began to chase after Moray. The western heir was already a mere shadow in the distance, running along the edge of the northern coast with startling speed. But Torin could draw strength from the folk, and he quickly gained on Moray.

The northern coast was one long, steep cliff face. There was no gentle coast below, only the tide crashing against the rock wall. A fall from this high up would kill a person, and Torin was confused by Moray's decision to run along its jagged edge, heading back to the east. It only made sense if he planned to return to the Tamerlaines and cause serious damage.

Torin's blood began to pound, hot and fast.

He thought of Sidra. Maisie.

He was just about to eclipse Moray. He was just about to reach out his hand to see if he could take hold of him, and if he could, Torin was going to kill him. He was going to rip out his throat. He was going to bash his head on the nearest rock—

Moray came to a sliding halt.

Torin melted through him like mist.

As he slowed, coming to a halt on the grass with a huff, he knew he should have been neither surprised nor disappointed, because he knew better by now. He couldn't touch mortal beings. Torin gritted his teeth as he turned to see what had caused Moray to stop so abruptly.

Moray was crouched low, in the stance of an animal who felt cornered. His eyes searched the rocks through the descending fog, and he listened to the howl of the wind.

"Who's there?" he asked tersely.

Torin took a step to the side. Moray, sensing Torin's movements, turned his face.

"Who are you?" Moray barked, squinting. "What do you want?"

Torin was tempted to answer him, but he bit his tongue. It was better for Moray to remain uncertain about who was haunting him. Torin took another step to his left. Moray certainly noticed, but it reassured Torin that while Moray could catch glimpses of Torin's movements, he couldn't fully discern him.

Torin backed away, until Moray's suspicions abated. Then he crept closer, amazed, when he saw that Moray was getting on his knees and easing himself over the edge of the cliff. Moray's blond head soon vanished from sight. Torin walked to the edge and stared at the sheer rocky drop.

Moray was scaling down the cliff face, using all the power of the Orenna to shift from one tiny fingerhold to another. An impressive feat, and one that would summon certain death for anyone trying to do it with their own strength.

Torin arched a brow, wondering where Moray was descending to. He thought it safest to wait above on flat, dependable ground until Moray returned. But then he changed his mind, his curiosity far too strong to allow him to simply stand around. Carefully, Torin eased himself over the edge, knowing he was going to hate every moment of this. He studied the cliff's long, slick face, which revealed golden pockets in the rock, a trail of cracks his fingers and toes could use to find purchase on the long, arduous descent.

Moray was already far away, just a blur as he ventured closer and closer to the mist that was rising from the waves.

Torin sighed and began to follow him.

About halfway down the cliff face, he finally saw what Moray was after. A vine grew up the rock, seeming to rise from the foam of the tides. It was covered in small white flowers, and Moray was plucking them one by one, as many as he could gather without losing his balance. He tucked the flowers into his pockets as if the blooms were worth more than gold.

Frowning, Torin finally reached a portion of the vine and could take a closer look at the glistening flowers. When he touched one, he was surprised by how cold it was. The petals were coated in ice in the middle of summer. He had never seen anything like this, and he wondered what the flower was. And why did Moray want it?

"May I take a few of your blooms?" Torin whispered to the vine. At first, nothing happened. Over the roar of the waves and the keen sting of the wind, Torin waited for the vine's reply. It remained silent, but because he was watching it attentively, he saw the ice crack and fall away from three blossoms.

Quicky, he pulled the trio free from the vine, just as Moray reached him.

He passed through Torin again, arms, chest, legs. Moray was nearly as cold as the flowers in Torin's hand, as though frost had spread over his skin.

"Still following me, I see?" Moray drawled. "Let's see if you can keep up then." He began to ascend the rock with alarming speed, and Torin struggled to maintain his reckless pace, nearly slipping from one of the shallow footholds.

He was relieved to make it back to solid ground and would have been happy to lie there for a moment in the grass, catching his breath and calming his heart, but a group of ferlies hissed at him, urging him forward.

"You promised vengeance," they prodded impatiently. "Are mortal words nothing but lies then?"

Torin flushed with anger. How could he punish Moray if he couldn't grab hold of him? If he couldn't tear out his throat to avenge Orenna? That had always been Torin's method in the past, hadn't it? Slicing necks and piercing hearts with swords. It had been easy for him to fall back into his old ways, and now he had to take a moment to untangle his emotions. His desire to spill blood and his yearning to be different from the way he had been. To be someone who healed rather than severed.

He squinted, searching for Moray in the distance. Torin glimpsed him turning southward, deeper into the gloam of the Breccans' territory.

Torin decided to continue his pursuit. His legs devoured one kilometer after another, and after swiftly catching up to Moray, he trailed him at a safe distance. But Torin's anxiety swelled when he realized where Moray was going.

The Breccans' fortress, built on a hill and surrounded by a moat, was ugly yet practical, its solitary bridge accessible only from the city. Sprawled across a valley, the city was a web of buildings with lichen-covered roofs, strung together by dirt streets, with a forge smoking on every corner.

It must have been nightfall, because torches were burning from iron brackets. Moray stole a plaid to drape over his head and entered the city easily without detection. He moved from shadow to shadow, glancing over his shoulder every so often to see if Torin was following. When he smirked, Torin knew Moray could still see him, and he wondered what he looked like. Was he a mere etching of gold, or did his mortality cast a faint illumination, giving him away?

"Keep up, bastard," Moray said just before he ducked into a tavern. Torin rolled his eyes as he entered through the stone wall.

Moray had escaped from the dungeons, traveled from east to west, eaten a handful of flowers, stolen more flowers off a cliff, and was now retreating to a pub. Torin could scarcely believe this was happening.

The tavern was empty save for a young man sitting glumly in the corner, drinking a bottle of wine. The chairs and tables around him were mismatched, the glazed floor was strewn with hay, and a sad fire burned in the hearth.

Torin watched as Moray approached the man. His ruddy face was marked by a wound that looked freshly stitched, and he was taking a sip straight from the bottle when Moray converged on him.

"Rab?" Moray hissed. "Rab, it's me."

Rab choked. He wiped a trickle of blood-red wine from his mouth and gaped up at Moray.

"*Moray?* What are you—"

"I need you to sneak me into the castle. *Now.*"

Rab sat up straighter, but his eyes darted around the tavern. "How'd you get out?"

"It's a long story and I don't have time to tell it," Moray replied, but he frowned. "What happened to your face?"

Rab seemed to sink a little lower. "Another long story. And if you want me to smuggle you into the castle, you'll have to pay me something I can't refuse. Because if your mother finds out I helped you . . ."

Moray reached into his pocket. He withdrew a handful of the small white flowers and forcibly set them into Rab's beefy hand.

Rab blinked down at them, his fingers shifting as he counted the icy blossoms. "You went far, didn't you?"

"Where the tide meets the rock," Moray said. When Rab still seemed to hesitate, he continued: "You once rode at my side, through night and storms and raids. You were a shield and a friend to me, Rab. A brother. One I trusted. One I still do, or I wouldn't have come to you like this."

Rab sighed, but he tucked the white flowers away into his pocket. "All right. I can sneak you in on a wine delivery. But we'll have to hurry. The portcullis drops at the next bell."

Moray held out his hands. "Let's go."

Torin trailed Rab's wagon across the bridge. Moray was stowed away in a hidden compartment, which made Torin think Rab smuggled many things into the castle that he shouldn't have. He also must have been someone of importance, because the guards at the portcullis let him pass without question.

Rab drove his wagon through a courtyard, over moss-spangled flagstones, and down a winding road to a lower quadrangle. He brought the delivery to a halt once he reached an arched passage. By the look and smell of it, the route fed into the castle storerooms.

Rab shifted a few wine bottles, opening the compartment for Moray.

"What is it you plan to do, Moray?" Rab asked in a low voice.

Indeed, Torin wondered.

Moray didn't seem to hear. With Orenna's power continuing to course through him, his pupils were still dilated, and his hands quivered at his side, as if he were anxious or thrilled. He cocked his head to the side, listening to the faint echoes of the castle.

He left Rab standing in the passage, completely forgotten.

Torin followed.

They wound through corridors and up flights of stairs, pausing in shadows when guards or attendants were nearby. At one point, Moray snagged a pitcher and washbasin full of water and continued on his way, eventually coming to an iron-latticed door.

He slipped inside, fumbled around in the dark for an enchanted dirk on the hearth mantel, then struck it to make a flame, lighting a chain of candles. Torin could see it all perfectly, his eyes unaffected by the night, and he realized that they must be in Moray's personal chambers. There was a bed with a blue canopy, jewel-toned tapestries on the walls, a wardrobe full of clothes and boots, a rack of weapons in one corner, and a wolf pelt draped over a chair.

Torin stood and watched as Moray washed the prison grime from his face and hands. He combed the mats from his hair and stripped out of his stolen Tamerlaine clothes, then dressed in a dark blue tunic embroidered with shining purple thread. He knotted clean boots up to his knees, belted a dirk to his waist, and set a circlet of woven silver on his brow.

Transformed, Moray sighed and leaned his head back, closing his eyes.

Torin didn't like the expression on Moray's face. The calmness, the confidence. He didn't like the way his hand wrapped around the dirk's hilt, or the way the silver flashed on his brow when he moved.

"If you've come home to hurt her . . ." Torin began, but his chest was full of embers. Flaring heat that made his throat ache. He couldn't finish the threat, but he saw that his voice startled Moray.

He opened his eyes and turned in Torin's direction, squinting. "Ah yes, I forgot all about you."

Moray began to approach him, and Torin held his ground. But his heart was frantic. He could feel both fear and fury tangling within him.

"Do you think I'd hurt my sister then?" Moray asked in a languid voice. "After everything I've done to bring her home?"

Torin knew Moray was baiting him. He *knew* it, and still he rose to it. But words were just as sharp as steel. And they became the sword in his hands that night.

He said, "She is more of a sister to me than she ever will be to you."

Moray's face went pale with rage. A vein rose in his temple, and his lip curled, revealing his clenched teeth. But then he smoothed his expression into one of neutrality.

"Hello, Laird," he said with a hint of amusement. "I was wondering what had happened to you, ever since Sidra came to visit me."

Hearing Moray speak Sidra's name was a bruise to Torin's spirit. He winced, his hands curling into fists. Moray was baiting him again, and this time Torin had to be the one to swallow. To bury his worries and emotions, let them sink down into darkness. Because he could feel it: he had already spent too much time here in the west. He needed to return to his mission.

He also needed to punch a hole in Moray's confidence.

"The power you stole from Orenna is waning," Torin said smoothly. "Whatever your plan is, you should hurry."

His words found their mark.

Moray left his chamber and rushed through another set of winding, torch-lit passages. Twice, he almost stumbled into the path of attendants, who were carrying away dinner trays. That was what Torin hoped would happen—that Moray's plans would be foiled when he grew careless and was discovered. But then he reached his destination, coming to a stop before a carven door.

Moray reached out to touch the iron handle, his eyes narrowing, as if he expected to find it locked. The door opened, and Moray stepped inside.

Torin melted through the wall.

He knew this was Adaira's room. He knew because, even though she wasn't there, Jack was, sitting at the desk as he wrote on a sheet of parchment.

Moray stopped upright. He was surprised to see Jack, but he drew the dirk from its scabbard.

"Jack!" Torin shouted. "*Jack*, behind you!"

Jack couldn't hear him. Captive to the words he was writing, even the opening and closing of the door hadn't drawn his eyes. But then he said, "How was the talk with your parents?"

The answering silence made him lift his head as Jack sensed the shadow that had fallen over the room. Torin's pounding heart. The fire burning dimly from the hearth. Moray's cold, oily presence.

Jack dropped his quill and stood in a rush, overturning the chair. But Moray had already closed the ground between them, dirk in hand. Teeth flashing in a wide smile.

"Hello again, Bard."

CHAPTER 29

A daira took the cup of gra Innes offered her. They were sitting before the hearth in the laird's wing, a surprisingly cozy honeycomb of chambers. Boughs of juniper hung from the rafters, casting a sweet fragrance in the room. Hundreds of candles were lit across mantels and shelves and flickered above from iron chandeliers. The soft light breathed over tapestries and painted panels on the walls, and Adaira took a moment to admire the stories they told. Unicorns chasing fallen moons. Flowers blooming from the footsteps of wolves. A sea monster rising from the tides.

"There's something you want to ask me," Innes said.

Adaira drew her attention away from the walls. She sank deeper into the soft sheepskin draped across the back of her chair. Yes, she had a few things to say to Innes, and she wasn't completely sure how to go about this confrontation. Ever since the culling, she had felt a shift between them, and she knew Innes sensed it too. Adaira took a sip of the gra before she spoke.

"Yes."

"Speak your mind then, Cora."

Adaira glanced into the adjacent room. The door was open, and she could see David sitting at a worktable, sifting through dried herbs.

"I can send him away if you want," Innes said.

"No, he's fine. But can he hear us?"

"I can," David drawled.

"Good. Because there are some things I don't want to have to say twice," Adaira said. She took another sip from her cup, trying to rouse her courage.

"You want to know if I was aware that it was Jack in the arena," Innes said in a careful voice.

Adaira swallowed. "Yes."

"I had no idea, Cora. They brought him up from the dungeons fully helmed and introduced him as 'John Breccan.' They said nothing about him stealing a harp."

"Does that not concern you?" Adaira said. "That members of your clan are being killed for crimes you aren't familiar with? That innocent people could be dying beneath gags and locked helms?"

Innes was silent. She didn't even seem to be breathing. From the corner of Adaira's eye, David was also frozen at his worktable, his back angled to them.

"Where is the honor in such death if it's unjust?" Adaira asked.

"Your husband should have made it clear he was in the west," Innes countered in a brisk tone. "He came by river. He trespassed onto my lands. If I had known he was coming, he would have never ended up in the dungeons."

"I won't deny that it would have been helpful if he had been forthright," said Adaira. "But he did, in fact, write and tell me he was coming. We've been writing to each other in code because you continue to read my post like I'm—" She cut her words short.

"Like you're a prisoner here?" Innes finished, her tone edging colder. "Have I treated you like one?"

"No. But—"

"The fact of the matter is that your husband is from the enemy clan. He also brought a harp with him," Innes said. "That breaks a law of the land."

"A harp he hasn't *played*," Adaira cut in.

"But he plans to?"

Adaira was quiet. She wouldn't deny Jack if he wanted to play.

Innes threw back the remainder of her gra and set her cup aside. "As I thought. Jack is welcome here, Cora, but he must abide by the laws. I can't risk him causing another storm."

"I know."

A lull came between them. Adaira wanted to ask about Niall, but after hearing the tension in Innes's voice, it didn't seem like a good moment. She hesitated, feeling how little time she had left to redeem Jack's father. But she also felt like she was standing in a ditch—she needed better footing before broaching a topic that was sure to pick at old wounds.

Her innuendo that Innes had been complicit in Jack's near-death hadn't helped.

"What else?" Innes prompted.

Adaira decided to move on to the last topic on her list. The blight. She began to tell Innes what Jack had shared with her. That the orchards in the east were sickened, and the spirits ailing. That Tamerlaines too were catching the blight.

By the time she finished speaking, David had come to stand on the threshold, her words reeling him closer. Innes, however, wore an impassive expression that instantly roused Adaira's suspicion, because she was coming to learn her mother's many masks.

"That's unfortunate for the east," Innes said. "But I don't see how we can help them with such a matter, Cora."

"You know the blight is already here in the west, though, don't you?" Adaira said. "For how long? When did you first notice it?"

"It's been six weeks," David said softly. "It first appeared in a copse of trees many kilometers south of here."

"How many Breccans are sick?"

"We aren't entirely certain," David replied.

Adaira didn't know whether to take his statement as truth or conclude that her parents wanted to keep that number hidden from her. She didn't give herself time to be offended and said, "I'd like to write to Sidra about this, with your permission, of course. She is a renowned healer in the east, and if the blight is something they have also been facing, she may have answers we need."

"No," Innes said swiftly.

"Why not?" Adaira replied. "This is not a matter of one side looking weaker or more vulnerable that the other. Not when it is affecting us both."

She paused, wondering how much she should push this topic. Innes had glanced away from her and was gazing into the fire, giving Adaira the impression her mother was feeling uneasy. But it was Adaira's hope that if the east and the west could work together as one to solve the blight, then other collaborations might be possible. Such as the trade Adaira had previously striven to establish, an initiative that had unfortunately failed when Moray's kidnapping spree came to light. The past few weeks she had thought that dream was dead, but she could feel it stirring to life again within her, eager to reignite.

Establishing trade between the clans would eliminate the raids. If the Breccans could fairly obtain what they needed from the Tamerlaines, then peace would become a sustainable future for the isle.

"What if I invited Sidra to visit?" Adaira continued. "That would give me the chance to see her again and to start building rapport between the clans. She could also be available to collaborate with David on finding a potential cure."

David was quiet, but he didn't seem averse to the idea. He was watching Innes closely, though, as if he could read the fears and thoughts racing through his wife's mind.

"I don't know, Cora," Innes finally replied. "Sidra is the eastern laird's wife, is she not? If something were to happen to her here, on my soil, then it would start a war that I don't want."

"Then let me invite Torin as well," Adaira said, knowing that sounded unfeasible. She could hardly envision it herself. *Both* Torin and Sidra visiting the west. Being able to see them, embrace them. Speak to them face-to-face.

The mere longing nearly crushed her.

"So not only would I have a bard on my lands," Innes said wryly, "but I'd also have the eastern laird and his wife, all beneath my roof."

Adaira grinned. "What could possibly go wrong?"

Innes sighed, but she almost returned the smile. "Many things."

"But will you consider it?"

Innes was opening her mouth to reply, but she was interrupted by a commotion in the outer corridor. Adaira turned to watch the door fling open with a bang. The first thing she saw was Jack—his dark hair with its quicksilver streak, his blanched face, his eyes that met hers instantly with a glimmer of warning. She saw the dirk held at his throat, controlling his movements. A dirk held by a blond-headed, wild-eyed man she didn't recognize at first glance.

Adaira shot to her feet, her heart pounding fire into her blood. All she could stare at was that blade, shining at Jack's throat.

"Unhand him, Moray," Innes said in a calm, cold voice.

Moray.

The name cut Adaira to the quick, and her gaze shifted upwards. Her brother was already staring at her, waiting for her to look at him. As soon as their eyes met, he removed the dirk from Jack's throat and gave him a slight shove forward.

"Don't look at me like that, Cora," Moray said. "I wasn't going to hurt him."

Adaira strode across the room before she could gather her thoughts. She grasped Jack's arm, drawing him protectively behind her. But her relief did not soften her. There was lightning in her blood, and she was one breath away from tearing into Moray. With her words and her hands, with anything that she could pick up and hurl, when Innes came between them.

"What are you doing here?"

"That's how you greet your *heir*? Your only son?" Moray asked. He still held the dirk in his hand, waving it about carelessly. "I thought you'd at least be happy to see me, Innes. I've come a long way."

Innes's jaw clenched. "You're currently under the Tamerlaines' watch. If you are here, then they have permission to come and hunt you."

Moray laughed. "They aren't capable of such a feat, I assure you."

"I don't think you understand the full extent of what you've done, Moray," Innes said, "and what the ramifications will be."

Moray was quiet, but he didn't appear repentant or worried. He looked beyond Innes again, his eyes tracing Adaira.

"I'll ask you again," Innes said, stepping aside to block Moray's view. "What are you doing here?"

"You'd come between me and my sister?" Moray asked. "If not for me, you'd still think she was part of the wind! You'd be fooling yourself into believing she was blowing her wings through your hair when you rode the wilds. You wouldn't be standing here *with* her, filling her up with all the poison you make, weaving those blue jewels into her hair and—"

Innes struck him across the face.

"*Enough*," she said. "You've committed your crimes and have now run from your punishment. There is no greater shame, and I now have no choice but to shackle you until the Tamerlaine laird can be informed of your location."

Moray touched his lip. It was beginning to bleed, cut open from the edge of her vambrace, but he only chuckled. "You would fight to keep her, but not me?"

Innes was silent for a long moment. Adaira's fingers twitched at her sides as she listened to her mother's slow, steady breathing.

"She doesn't shame me as you do," Innes finally said.

Moray lunged forward with startling speed.

Innes was anticipating his assault, but she was still a beat too slow. She reached out to catch his arm and bend it back at a painful angle, but he cut her palm first. Her blood bloomed, bright as a rose, as she took him to the ground.

Moray kicked out his leg, overturning a side table. The bottle of gra and a bowl of blue jewels—jewels that were most likely poisoned blood Innes had wrung from an enemy—broke and scattered across the floor. The air suddenly smelled like mist-damp heather, like a cold northern wind, as the gra seeped into the rug.

Adaira had to step back. She felt Jack, solid and warm behind her, as he took hold of her waist, drawing her farther away. But she was stunned, watching Innes and Moray wrestle and strike and wound each other. She hadn't given much thought to the nature of her mother's relationship with her brother, but never would she have imagined *this*. A laird who didn't trust or respect their heir. A mother who had no choice but to twist her only son's arm until he was facedown on the floor.

Moray finally stilled, unable to free himself. His eyes found Adaira's again, but there was no defiance in his gaze, only sadness.

"I'll ask you one more time, Moray," Innes said, her knee pressed into his back. "Why are you here?"

"I'm not going to waste away for *ten* years in the Tamerlaine dungeons," he rasped. "I'm not going to let myself fade into dust, shackled by them while you and David live happily ever after with Cora."

"It is your penance."

"I want *justice*. Let me fight in the arena. Let the sword speak for me."

Chills swept through Adaira. He wanted to face the culling, and she wasn't certain how she felt about it. Would it be best if Moray had the chance to fight and potentially die? Or should he be returned to the Tamerlaine dungeons, to live ten more years in the dark?

Innes also seemed uncertain. Her expression wavered for a moment, just as the guards arrived, encircling them.

"If you go quietly to the dungeons," Innes said, "I'll consider your request."

Moray nodded.

She eased off of him and the guards took her place, clapping the shackles to Moray's wrists and hauling him up to his feet. Adaira couldn't see his face, but she saw a glimpse of his hair as he was escorted away.

The room fell painfully silent.

David began to gather up the blue jewels from the floor. Innes flexed her hand, blood dripping from her fingers.

"Leave us please, Cora," she said, turning her back to Adaira.

There seemed to be far too much that needed to be said. And yet Adaira couldn't find a single word to utter.

She took Jack's hand and led him away.

Torin remained behind in the laird's wing. He hadn't known what he expected to happen when he followed Moray and Jack, but it hadn't been a tense altercation between the western laird and her son.

He hadn't expected to feel not only a pang of respect for Innes Breccan, but also a quiet sense of awe as she handled Moray. She had held him down with no blades, only with her bare hands, one of which was bleeding.

He watched as David gathered up the jewels forming from Innes's shed blood on the floor. Torin was so fascinated by the sight—what was this magic in her veins?—that he nearly missed Innes's words.

"What am I going to do about Moray?" she asked in a weary tone. "Where did I go wrong with him?"

"We have all night to think of our options," David said gently. "But for now? Sit and let me tend to you."

Innes lowered herself to a chair, cradling her bleeding hand. She waited, her eyes glazed with distant thoughts, as David stepped into the adjacent room. He returned a moment later with a roll of linen and an earthenware bowl brimming with salve, then knelt before her.

"Take them off," Innes whispered roughly.

David paused, but he set down his materials. He began to pull off his gloves, finger by finger, until they dropped to the floor with a whisper.

Torin's breath snagged in his throat.

David's entire left hand was blighted. His skin was dappled blue and violet as if badly bruised. His veins were illuminated in gold.

Innes stared down at her husband's hand, her face carved with both fear and anguish. She was so entirely unguarded in that moment that Torin felt he should glance away as she traced David's fingers. As her hand trailed up his arm, then caressed his face. She leaned forward and pressed her brow to his, and they breathed the same air, the same worries.

"You have healed me, time and time again," Innes murmured. "And yet I can do nothing to heal you now. It is a cruel fate, for you to die before me."

David was quiet, but then he leaned back so he could meet her gaze. "There is something we can do."

Innes closed her eyes. "You speak of Cora's suggestion."

"Our daughter, yes." David began to tend to Innes's wounded hand. Wiping away her blood, dabbing salve along the cut. Binding it in linen. "Innes? *Innes,* open your eyes. Look at me."

Innes exhaled, but she opened her eyes. David traced the tattoos on her neck with his thumb, as if he knew their blue-inked story. As if those interlocking patterns were inspired by what the two of them had made together.

"Let her write to Sidra."

Torin startled. This time, Sidra's name was like a flame, melting through realms. He had seen enough in the west. It was time for him to go home and solve the riddle. Moray's punishment would have to come through another, and Torin relinquished that old, bitter craving for vengeance.

He turned, leaving David and Innes behind.

But Sidra's name continued to echo through him as he took to the western hills. It sang in his blood as he ran eastward.

CHAPTER 30

The shadows were long and cold in Adaira's bedroom when the midnight bell chimed. Jack stood before the bureau, pouring water into a basin by candlelight. Thunder rumbled beyond the castle walls, and rain began to tap on the windows in a frantic rhythm that mirrored Jack's pulse.

He felt rattled from the events of the evening.

His skin was clammy, his breaths shallow. He could still feel the sharp edge of Moray's dirk at his throat. Jack tried to quell that memory as he cupped his hands into the water. He washed the perspiration from his face, but he couldn't stop seeing Moray at the door. Moray overcoming him so easily.

"That's the *second* time I've seen a blade at your throat, Jack." Adaira's voice was husky, sad. "I'm sorry."

He reached for the plaid next to him and wiped the water from his eyes just as her arms came around his waist. She pressed her cheek against his shoulder.

"It was all for show," Jack said. "He didn't hurt me, Adaira. And it's not your fault."

She exhaled into his tunic. He could feel the heat of her breath on his skin, and he closed his eyes.

"Are you tired?" she whispered.

"No."

"If I tell you a story, would that make you sleepy, old menace?"

He couldn't help but smile. "Perhaps."

"Come to bed then."

Jack followed her to the bed, slipping beneath the covers. He lay on his back, eyes closed, and listened as Adaira settled close beside him. It was quiet for so long that Jack eventually cracked one eye open to look at her. She was sitting against the headboard, studying her nails.

"Where's the story?" he asked.

"I'm trying to come up with one. It's hard, you know. Finding a good enough story for a bard, one that isn't going to bore him."

Jack laughed. He turned to face her, his hand rushing over her bare legs. "Then perhaps I should tell one to you."

Adaira's breath caught, just as a knock on the door interrupted them.

She cursed and reluctantly crawled from the bed, Jack's fingers drifting from her thighs. He sat forward, first annoyed, then worried, thinking a visitor at this hour couldn't bring anything good.

It was Innes.

The laird stepped into their room. It almost seemed like the entire altercation with Moray had never happened until Jack met Innes's gaze. He saw something dark and troubled within her.

He quickly rose from the bed.

"Your father would like to speak with you, Cora," Innes said. "He's waiting for you in my chambers."

Adaira's eyes widened. "Is something wrong?"

"No," Innes replied, glancing at Jack. "But I'd also like to speak to your husband alone."

Adaira was quiet for a beat, but she reached for her robe, slipping it over her chemise. "Very well."

Jack watched her leave the room, his heart tumbling through his chest. He felt Innes's silent stare and met it with one of his own.

"How can I help you, Laird?" he asked.

"We need to talk about your father," Innes replied.

The words made Jack's breath seize. "Adaira told you?"

"No. I knew your connection to Niall when I rode to your mother's cottage weeks ago. When I saw how close Mirin lived to the clan line. When I saw your little sister with her auburn hair." She paused, glancing away from Jack. "I shouldn't have been surprised after I learned the truth of what happened to Cora. How Niall gave her away. I shouldn't have been surprised when I realized he'd come to love a Tamerlaine woman, and had children with her."

Jack kept his expression guarded. He didn't know where Innes was going with this conversation. He didn't know if he needed to remain detached or if it would be best to show a flicker of emotion. Despite the uncertainty that laced his blood, he sensed that Niall's life was hanging in the balance. A constellation that could burn bright or be fully extinguished.

"So you knew that Niall was a relation of Adaira's by marriage," Jack began in a careful tone. "And yet you continued to allow him to fight in the culling, time and time again? To what end? Until someone finally slayed him?"

"I don't expect you to understand my decisions or my reasons," Innes said. "And that's not why I've come to speak with you. This, however, is what I need: Moray is a prisoner of the east, and yet he is here, beneath my watch. He has asked to fight in the culling, and I want to give him that opportunity."

"You want to give him a chance to be absolved?" Jack snarled, unable to swallow his anger. "To walk free after serving only a month in the dungeons?"

"No," Innes replied. "I want him to die with honor. If I return him to the Tamerlaines, they will execute him. His bones will rot from the shame of what he's done."

Jack was so surprised that he merely stared at her. But his mind was racing.

"I need him to face an opponent who is stronger than him," Innes continued. "Niall is undefeated."

"And what if he kills my father?" Jack queried. "Does Moray walk free?"

"No. He'll remain in the dungeons and fight again until someone can defeat him."

Jack considered this for a moment. "All right. What do you need from me?"

"I need you to be a representative of the Tamerlaine clan," Innes said. "To watch the culling at my side. To stand witness to Moray's death, so your laird knows he was fairly dealt with here in the west for his misdeeds. Are you able to do that?"

She was asking him to watch his father fight—and maybe die, if Moray's luck ran true. Overcome with all the emotions that gripped him whenever he thought of Niall, Jack wanted to wince, to fold in on himself. But he held Innes's steady gaze, realizing that this was the moment he had been waiting for. It had simply come in a way he least expected.

"I'll do this for you, Laird," he said. "But I have conditions."

"Speak your terms."

"The first? I would like to have dinner with my father a few hours before the culling. A good, hearty meal in one of the castle's private chambers."

"Very well. I can see to it that this is done," Innes said. "What else?"

Jack hesitated, but when he spoke, his voice was clear. Unwavering. "If my father defeats your son, Niall goes free. You give him back his name and his title and his land and his honor. He is a prisoner no longer."

Innes was silent. But then she held out her hand. "I agree to your terms, Jack."

He accepted her hand, her grip firm enough to crush his fingers. They sealed the spoken agreement.

Jack wanted to bask in hope and confidence, but he could still feel the sharp edge of Moray's dirk at his throat. He could still feel the bitter coldness of the dungeons seeping into his bones. He could still hear the way Niall had spoken his name in the arena, like a piece of him had broken.

Jack began to prepare himself for the worst.

Adaira found David in the laird's quarters. He was waiting for her at his desk, where a piece of parchment, a freshly cut quill, and an inkwell were laid out. A line of candles burned and cast rings of light, their wax guttering down to pool on the wood.

"Innes said you want to see me?" Adaira asked.

"Yes," David said, drawing the chair back from the desk. "I'd like for you to write a letter to Sidra."

Adaira was so shocked that she stood frozen, blinking at him.

"You did say she was a healer and might could collaborate with me on the blight's remedy?" David asked.

"*Yes*." Adaira stepped forward. She sat in the chair and took the quill in her hand. "What would you like me to say to her?"

"Extend an invitation. Innes and I would like for her to visit. Tell her she can bring up to four people in her retinue. Guards or handmaidens or her husband even, if he'd like to accompany her. Also ask her to bring whatever records she's kept, or tonics or herbs that she has found helpful, so I may see the work she's already done and compare it with my own."

Adaira eagerly began to write. As the nib scratched across the parchment, she thought her father would read over her shoulder but was surprised that David shifted away to reorganize the books on his shelf. Adaira realized he was granting her privacy, and her heart warmed, thankful.

She wrote the letter and signed her name but hesitated.

"Do you want to read this before I seal it?" she asked.

"No," David answered. "I trust you. Go ahead and seal it, Cora."

Adaira heated the wax over a candle flame. She sealed the letter with the Breccans' sigil and then held up the parchment to David, waiting for him to accept it.

"Come with me," he said, turning away.

She walked with him to the aviary, where the ravens roosted in iron cages. Her letter was tucked in a leather pouch and fastened to one of the birds. Adaira stood beside her father and watched as the raven took flight into the storm, heading eastward to Sidra. The rain and wind spun up a mist that coated her face and beaded in her hair. She closed her eyes and breathed it in.

"I know you think of your parents often," David said gently. "I know that you miss them. I imagine you might compare me and Innes to them, and I can't fault you for it. But I do hope that you know how much we want to be in your life, not just as a laird and her consort."

Adaira opened her eyes. Her heart had quickened with David's words, churning up painful memories. Memories of Alastair and Lorna and the east.

She turned her head to regard him. He reached out to gently touch her cheek with his gloved fingers, touching the mist that veiled her skin. Adaira honestly didn't know what to say. There was a knot in her throat, and her eyes welled with tears.

Yes, I understand, she wanted to say, but her jaw remained clenched.

David only gave her a sad smile as his hand fell away.

He left her in the aviary, staring into the storm.

Sidra was in the castle kail yard when Yvaine found her at dawn, two rain-speckled letters in hand. The sun was rising behind a swath of wind-streaked clouds, and it promised to be a sweltering day. The valley fog had already melted, and bees and damselflies flew in languid patterns. Only a smattering of dew remained on the plants as Sidra cut and laid them into her harvest basket.

"One for you, and one for Torin," the captain said. "Both from the west."

Sidra wiped the dirt from her fingers and tucked her pruning shears into her apron pocket, accepting the parchment. The letter addressed to her was in Adaira's familiar handwriting. The letter addressed to Torin looked to be Jack's elegant penmanship.

She stared at them, knowing that whatever rested within these letters was going to change everything. She could sense it, like she could taste the thunderstorm in the air, still hours away. Like a shock of electricity, as if she had raked her hands through freshly spun wool and then touched the hilt of a sword.

She knew the answer about Moray rested within these letters. Their search for him had been fruitless, and Graeme's prediction that he had made it to the west was most likely correct, because there was no sign of him in the east. Sidra was now in a waiting game. She was holding her breath, waiting for the Breccans to make either an honest move or a deceitful one. To either shelter Moray or give him up again.

"Have you eaten yet?" Sidra asked Yvaine as they walked the garden path, returning to the cool air of the castle.

"Yes, but I'd take a cup of tea," Yvaine said.

The women retreated to the library and sat at a small round table. Edna brought in a tea tray with a plate of buttery scones, crushed berries, and a bowl of cream, and Sidra let herself find comfort in the soothing motions of preparing her tea.

"Which one should I open first?" she asked.

"Torin's letter," Yvaine replied.

Sidra broke the seal and unfolded the parchment. She read Jack's words, which were both expected and completely bewildering.

"What is it?" Yvaine asked urgently, reading the lines on Sidra's face.

"Moray's in the west, as we thought." Sidra extended the letter to the captain. "But they're offering up a strange solution for him."

She drained her tea while Yvaine read, but she soon thrummed her fingers on the tabletop anxiously, waiting to see what the captain thought.

Yvaine set the letter down and leaned back in her chair, lacing her hands behind her neck. "Well. *That* wasn't what I thought it'd be."

"Do we take the chance of them killing him in their arena?" Sidra asked. "Or do we demand that they return him to us immediately?"

"If we demand his return to us," Yvaine began, "then you'd have to kill him here, Sidra. He's slain *five* of my guards, and that cannot go unpunished. His crimes have only multiplied since we first imprisoned him, and I can't see the Tamerlaines being appeased with anything less than spilled blood at this point."

"I agree with you," Sidra said, even though a chill crept through her. She would have to be the one to behead Moray, and she had never killed a man before. "But if we killed him for his crimes, would that start a war with the west?"

"There's no telling with the Breccans, but I think it could, yes. So that's why I think you should let them handle his death. Let his blood be on their hands."

Sidra fell silent, staring at the letter.

"Is it enough for the Tamerlaines, though?" she eventually asked. "To not witness his death?"

"Both Adaira and Jack will be present for it," Yvaine replied. "Jack can write a ballad and sing of Moray's death to the clan."

Sidra nodded, but something still didn't feel quite right to her. She traced the bow of her lips, smelling the loam beneath her nails. "Why would Innes Breccan approve of this? Approve of losing her heir?"

"I have a few theories," Yvaine said, sitting forward to refill her tea. "But read Adaira's letter first."

Sidra reached for the parchment, her heart heavy with worry. But for the second time that morning, she was utterly taken by surprise. As she read Adaira's words, the iron fist that had been gripping her insides began to ease.

She breathed once, twice.

Yvaine was fixated upon her, waiting.

Sidra set the letter down, face up on the table. "They are also suffering from the blight. And they want me to visit, to collaborate on a cure."

"No, Laird." Yvaine's answer was swift and sharp. "I can't let you leave my watch."

"I'm not the laird," Sidra began to say, cheeks warming. "And I—"

"*No, Laird,*" the captain said again, the words even sharper this time. "If something happens to you in the west . . . I don't even want to fathom it. We cannot lose you."

"And yet something could happen to me in the east," Sidra countered. And it was strange, how peace settled over her. She felt calm, assured. There was no doubt marring her mind, and she said, "I'm sick, Yvaine."

Yvaine was silent, but her frown melted into shock.

"I'm sick with the blight," Sidra said again, "and I'm carrying Torin's child, and I don't know how much time I have left. I've exhausted all my knowledge and my resources here in the east, trying to find a cure, and yet . . . I can't help but wonder. I remember the Orenna flower, a bloom that grows in the west but not here in the east, and it makes me wonder if there are plants that I need for the cure on the other side of the clan line. It wouldn't surprise me, as if the isle is longing to be united once more."

Yvaine sighed, but her prior resolve was softening. "I suspected you were pregnant, Sidra. But I didn't know about the blight." She paused, holding Sidra's gaze. "I'm sorry. If I could take the sickness for you, I would."

Sidra blinked back a surge of tears, but they sat in the corners of her eyes, gleaming like stars. "I would never allow it."

"Of course not," Yvaine said wryly, but her eyes also shone with emotion. "And that is why I will kill anyone who hurts you in the west."

"I'm not worried about that happening," Sidra said. "I'll take Blair and three other guards with me. I'll take my herbs, which are sharper than any knife in my hands. And I'll be with Adaira, whom I trust entirely."

Yvaine worked her jaw. She still wanted to protest. "You know I want to go with you."

"No, Captain," Sidra said.

"But, Sidra, I—"

"*No.* I need you here."

Yvaine heaved a sigh, raking her fingers through her black hair. "All right. When do you plan to leave?"

Sidra rose from the table. Her foot ached constantly these days, but she had grown accustomed to the pain. She had learned to move around it, and she marveled that it was hard to even remember what her foot had felt like before it became infected.

Now, for the first time in weeks, she was experiencing a taste of hope that a cure could be found. An invitation to the west gave her a chance to see the land, to take its herbs and flowers and vines in her hands.

She suddenly felt like she could climb a mountain.

"As soon as possible, I think," Sidra said. "I'll write to Jack and give him my blessing for the culling. And I'll write to Adaira and tell her I'm coming. I think I could go the day after tomorrow, to give them time to prepare for my visit."

"As you want, Laird," Yvaine said, draining her tea to the dregs before standing. "I'll speak with Blair and arrange your retinue."

"Thank you, Captain."

Yvaine left without another word, and Sidra followed a trail of sunshine to one of the windows. She stood in its silent warmth, letting the light seep into her, and thought about where she had been, only weeks ago. Then her thoughts returned to where she was now.

Sidra shivered in the sun.

CHAPTER 31

H ap was waiting for Torin in the shadows of the Aithwood. "I see you survived the west unscathed," the hill spirit said cheerfully as soon as Torin had crossed over the clan line.

Torin snorted, but he wasn't in the mood for jest. His mind was crowded with all the things he had seen and heard, and his worry over Sidra had grown tenfold. "Where's Whin? Can you take me to her?"

Hap's brow furrowed, though he seemed accustomed to Torin's terseness. He led the way through the trees and into the misty hills, coming to a stop in one of the valleys.

"Why do you need Whin?" Hap asked.

"I believe she's one of the sisters in the riddle," Torin replied, kneeling in the grass. He began to prepare a workstation, drawing inspiration from all the times he had observed Sidra prepare salves and tonics. He asked two nearby rocks for their assistance, one to serve as a mortar, the other as a pestle, and then he laid out his bounty. The Orenna flowers, bright as blood on the grass, and the flowers he had harvested from the cliffside, white as snow.

Two sisters, united. Ice and fire. Salt and blood.

"You spoke with her?"

Torin turned on his knees to behold Whin standing behind him, her eyes riveted to her sister's flowers.

"For a moment, yes," Torin said. He hesitated, seeing the anguish in Whin's face. "If I may have a few flowers from your crown . . . I believe it is one of the last things I need to solve the riddle."

Whin reached up to pluck a few gorse blooms from her crown and gave them to Torin. Then she melted away, as if she couldn't bear to watch him work.

Only Hap remained nearby, and a few curious ferlies who had gathered in the grass.

"How much, how much?" Torin whispered to himself as he set the blossoms on the stone. The riddle had provided no instructions about measurements. Torin decided to lay down one of each flower, then wiped his hands over his chest.

He believed the white blossom was ice, remembering how cold it was on the vine. But he still needed salt and fire.

He ran to the nearest croft, which happened to be Mirin's. Torin eased through the southern wall and found Mirin at her loom.

"I apologize for this," he said, even though her ears were closed to his voice. Torin took a wooden bucket from the kitchen and one of the candlesticks from the hearth mantel. He also took Mirin's flint before rushing back to the valley, where Hap and the ferlies waited with wide-eyed expectation and hope.

He set down the candle and flint on the rock—he was trembling violently now, as he had done after he killed a man for the first time. But now the shaking was due only to the adrenaline coursing through him, making his breaths skip and sharpening his sight even more than before. Taking the bucket, he ran to the coast, seeing every shadow, every secret of the earth along the way.

Torin knelt on the sand, watching the tide ebb and flow.

"May I take a portion of you?" he asked the sea.

The ocean answered with a crashing wave, and Torin was

knocked off balance. The water rushed through him, spinning a chill through his blood. He couldn't tell if Ream was granting permission or denying it, but he was desperate. Torin scooped up a bucketful of salt water, then peered at it to ensure that no water spirit lurked within. The water was clear, free of golden threads and fins and eyes, and he carried it back to the valley.

Now a few rocks, with their hearty scowls, had also gathered close by, as had a trio of alder maidens, who twisted their long, root-tendril fingers in anticipation.

Torin heard their murmurs as he knelt again. Sweat dripped from his beard as he stared at what he had gathered, as he inwardly spoke the riddle again: *Ice and fire, brought together as one. Sisters divided, united once more. Washed with salt and laden with blood—all united will satisfy the debt you owe.*

Surely, this was everything.

He took up his makeshift pestle and began to crush the flowers on the stone. As more spirits arrived to watch, the flowers soon turned into a fragrant medley. Torin could feel the spirits' eyes boring into him, and he wanted to order them away. He didn't want an audience, and yet it also didn't seem fair to deny them this moment.

He paused in his work, staring at the smudge of crushed petals. What came next? The salt, or the fire? Or perhaps he needed to cut his hand and bleed into it first?

Torin decided to go with fire first, then water, and lastly blood. He reached for the flint to strike up a flame, and as he was lighting the candle he heard the spirits around him gasp. He glanced up to see them recoil, grimaces on their faces.

"What is it?" he asked brusquely.

Only Hap remained close, although even the hill spirit seemed disquieted by the flame. "Are you certain, Torin?"

"Ice and *fire*," Torin said. "Yes, I'm certain. Why do you doubt me?"

"I . . ." Whatever it was Hap wanted to say faded as he curled his tongue. The hill spirit only shook his head, flowers cascading from his hair, and took a step back.

Torin was too frustrated, anxious, and weary to consider that he might have misinterpreted the riddle. He set fire to the flowers and then watched as the flames caught. He was cupping the salt water in his hands when there was a resounding *boom*, and a shock wave sent him flying.

Dazed, Torin sat forward. His tunic was soaked from the spilled water, and from his own sweat, and he watched as smoke rose from the rock.

"No," he whispered, frantically crawling to it. "*No!*"

One by one, the earth spirits retreated with bowed heads and sad countenances. All of them melted away save for Hap, who stood witness as Torin reached the rock.

Nothing remained but a scorch mark. Torin traced the stone, realizing that all he had brought together—the flowers and his hope and his confidence—was gone.

Jack was tying the boot tethers up to his knees when the fire went dark in Adaira's hearth. He glanced at the ashes and saw the smoke rising in a cloying dance. Even the candles had been snuffed, their wicks glowing red in the gray morning light.

Adaira sighed, knotting the end of her braid with a strip of blue plaid. "What is he trying to tell us?"

Jack set his foot on the floor. He wasn't sure what Ash was striving to convey, but his own mind was heavily distracted with mortal matters. Within hours, he would have dinner with his father. He wasn't even sure what he wanted to say to Niall, or how to prepare himself for what was certain to be an uncomfortable encounter. Then, a few hours after that, the culling between Niall and Moray would commence, and Jack would witness either his father's redemption or his death.

There didn't seem to be any more room in Jack's mind to think about why he had been sent west in the first place. But since the fire spirit had resorted to extinguishing flames again, Jack wondered if he was running out of time. Ash needed his attention, and now

Jack remembered the memory Kae had shared of an altercation between the Laird of Fire and Iagan.

Jack's gaze drifted to Adaira's desk. Iagan's composition still waited there in a heap.

"I think I need to stay behind today," Jack said. He stood and looked at Adaira, who was pinning her plaid to her shoulder. "I need some time to study the music I took from Loch Ivorra."

Adaira was quiet, her mouth quirking to the side. "As you wish. I'll make sure that lunch is sent up to the room, so you don't have to leave. But keep my sword with you." She reached for the sheathed blade and handed it to him.

Jack accepted it, but only to wrap the sword's belt around her waist. He cinched it firmly at her navel.

"It looks better on you," he said, admiring how it complemented her. She had always been tall and svelte and pale as the moon, even as a young girl. A girl he had once loved to hate. The sword glistening at her side matched her well. "And I'll only worry about you, riding the wilds without me and your sword."

Adaira stared at him with hooded eyes. "I need to arm you, old menace."

"I brought a dirk west with me," he replied. "My truth blade. Rab still has it, I think. And my harp."

"Right. I'll check on them." She began to step away, but Jack took hold of her waist again and leaned down to trace her lips with his.

"Be careful, Adaira," he whispered.

She wove her fingers into his hair and kissed him back, a soft taunting that made his blood simmer. But he could see how distracted she was. He could feel it in her body, the same tension that was coiling in him.

In a few hours, she would have her own private meal with Moray. In a few hours, she would watch her brother either bleed out on the sand or slay Jack's father.

This day was already marked with pain and conflicting emotions, and it was only midmorning.

"I'll return soon," she said, her fingers drifting from his hair. Jack finally relinquished her. "Lock the door behind me, Bard."

He trailed her, nodding. "Tell Kae I said hello."

"I will," Adaira said as she stepped over the threshold. She didn't look back as she strode down the corridor, but she had never been one to slow her momentum by glancing behind.

Jack watched until she disappeared around a corner. He bolted the door and sat at the desk.

Where to begin?

He reached for Joan's broken book, curious to look over what each half held. Skimming through the first half, he recognized some of the lore within it. When he leafed through the second half, though, he encountered stories of the spirits that he had never been taught. Stories and songs that had roots in the west.

And then, perhaps strangest of all, he came upon a note, in the middle of a story:

> *Iagan frightens me.*
> *I cannot trust his music anymore, or his words.*
> *Something terrible and nameless shines in his eyes when he*
> *plays and sings.*

Jack paused, staring at Joan's words. Was this note the reason why the book had been torn in two? Was someone afraid of Joan's inner worries being shared with others?

Disquieted, he gently put the two halves of the book aside and began to read through Iagan's composition. The deeper he ventured into the ballads, the stronger the fire burned again in the hearth and on the candlewicks, as if Ash was renewed by Jack's attention.

A polite knock on the door interrupted his studies. It was already lunchtime, the hours having slipped through Jack's hands like water. Two attendants waited in the corridor, one bearing a lunch tray of bread and soup, the other a misshapen bundle that hid Jack's harp and truth blade.

Jack sighed at being reunited with his instrument and dirk. He took a long moment to inspect them, tracing the hilt and the strings with his fingertips. Both were in good condition despite his fears; he had been worried that Rab would smash the harp and destroy the dirk. That both would be lost to him.

Jack forced himself to eat a few bites of lunch before returning to his studies.

He found ballads for all four elements. The song for Ash was the worst, the notes and words twisted into shackles and shame intended to bring the fire low. The song demanded pieces of Ash's crown, the cloak of his power, the gleam of his scepter. Then came the ballads for the sea, for the earth, for the air. These songs weren't as harsh as the one for the fire spirits, but they were built on restrictions and limitations, the words woven through with control and measurements, just as the musical notes were.

Iagan's ballads were like cages. Like a prison.

Jack's breath caught when he saw the full span of the notes, how they built upon each other. The four ballads fit together to create a hierarchy in the spirits' realm.

Until this moment, Jack had thought it was Bane who created the hierarchy, for no other reason than to keep certain spirits low and beneath him. To seal their mouths, silencing their voices. Controlling what they could do and say, and how much power they wielded.

But it hadn't been inspired by Bane at all.

The hierarchy had been made by Iagan's music.

Torin made a second attempt.

He still had a handful of Orenna flowers and two white blossoms left, as well as a chain from Whin's crown. He had crushed another batch together on the rock, but his greatest hurdle was now trying to discover what "fire" the riddle required. If it wasn't flames, then what was it?

"I suppose you can offer me no guidance," he drolly said to Hap as the two of them walked the hills, Torin aimlessly, Hap deliberately, as if the spirit feared his one and only mortal assistance might fall into a bog if he didn't shepherd him.

"Only so much can pass from my mouth," Hap whispered, as

if a great power was hindering him. "But perhaps it might help to think of it this way: things need balance in the mortal world, don't they? The same can be said here, in our realm. Or . . . maybe not balance, but complements and . . . *contrasts.*"

Torin frowned. He had no inkling what Hap was trying to express. And roaming the hills did nothing for his thinking either.

He decided to go to Sloane, a place he had been avoiding for fear of seeing Sidra. If Torin beheld her, he thought he might go mad. He might find himself unable to leave her side, unable to think critically about the riddle. And yet he needed Sidra's knowledge again to move forward.

"Would you have chosen my wife to assist you here if she hadn't been infected?" Torin asked Hap, who remained by his side, deep into the winding city streets.

Hap bit his lip before saying, "Yes."

Torin snorted. "I knew it."

"Sidra's faith in us is profound. She gives us strength, as we give her ours."

"And don't forget to add your blight. You gave her that as well."

Hap came to a halt. Torin took a few more steps before he felt shame, scalding the back of his throat. He paused, glancing at the hill spirit, who suddenly looked like he might crumble.

"The wind," Hap said, the grass withering in his hair. "It was the *wind.* He blew the fruit to her. He put it in her path, and I . . . I couldn't do anything about it."

Torin opened his mouth, but Hap had gone, turning into the moss that rested between cobblestones.

Alone and full of bitterness, Torin continued to the castle.

When he approached Sidra's chambers, he hesitated. He longed to see her, and he knew such longings were slowly undoing him, breath by breath. And yet he couldn't bear watching the blight creep across her skin.

Daring to pass through the door, Torin was relieved to find the room empty. He approached her desk, where the tomes of her healing records sat. It took a few tries before the book would permit him to touch its pages, but soon Torin was leafing through it, examining Sidra's entries, as well as the notes her grandmother had recorded before her.

If three of the riddle ingredients were plants, should there be a fourth one? An even number, reminiscent of the four points on a compass? The four powers of the wind? The four elements of the spirits? Thinking that perhaps the blood or salt or fire in the riddle was supposed to come from another flower, Torin searched the pages for it.

Balance, complements, contrast.

He mulled over Hap's cryptic words, but he still couldn't find meaning in them.

Sighing, Torin shelved one volume and withdrew another. These were recent recordings, all made in Sidra's tidy handwriting, and his eyes were blurry by the time one account snagged his attention.

Torin's treatment for an enchanted silencing wound, Sidra had written. What followed was recipe after recipe that had failed to heal him—until Sidra tried fire spurge.

His breath caught. He shut the book, his fingers absently tracing the scar on his forearm. He remembered now. The enchanted wound that stole his voice had been so cold. He remembered how the fire spurge burned through the discharge, bringing him back together slowly but steadily.

He ran through the castle, through the crowded streets. He reached the hills again and cried, "Hap? *Hap!*"

The spirit didn't answer. Torin sagged, his loneliness keen. But his blood was humming, and he began to comb the fells for fire spurge. Sidra had described it in her ledger—she had found it in a shifting glen, and it grew in the cleft of the rocks.

Torin searched fruitlessly. Eventually, Whin appeared, watching him crawl on his hands and knees.

"What do you seek, mortal laird?" she asked, but her voice had turned cold, like frost on the grass.

Torin sat on his heels, gazing up at her. "I apologize for my careless words. I don't hold the earth at fault for what's happened, for Sidra's illness. I spoke to Hap in anger."

Whin sighed and repeated, "What do you seek?"

"Fire spurge," Torin said. "It grows in one of the glens that shift. Can you guide me to it?"

Whin stared at him for a long, piercing moment. He thought she wouldn't reply, but then she turned and began to walk toward a southern hill, wildflowers blooming in her footsteps. Torin followed. Down they went into a mist-laden valley. Whin came to a slow halt at the mouth of the glen, furrowed in the valley like a wound.

Torin would have never found it on his own.

He thanked Whin, but she remained quiet as she watched him step into the glen. The stone walls, beaded from the mist, rose high on either side of him. His breath echoed in this place, and he shivered, staring up at the rocks that embraced him. The fire spurge's red blooms burned through the fog, drawing his eyes to a cleft.

Torin instantly began to climb. He was lost in thoughts of home when his fingers touched the plant. Pain flared, bright and sudden, shooting down his arm to his shoulder. He snatched his hand away, gazing at the angry flush on his palm, the blisters beginning to welt.

This was what Sidra had felt for him. This was the pain she had carried to heal him, and Torin's hands shook as he tried again, gritting his teeth against the rays of agony. He tugged the spurge free, feeling as though his hand was being consumed by flames. He swiftly uprooted a second spurge with his other hand. The pain was so overwhelming that he struggled to find his way back down to the ground.

Somehow he did, managing to land on his feet.

At last, he had the riddle's fire.

He returned to his workstation, where the old, scorched rock waited with the fresh batch of crushed flowers. Torin knelt, spilling the fire spurge into the grass. He decided he would add only one to the medley and save the second to use in case he had another mishap.

Whin stood nearby, the only witness. Torin wondered where Hap was—maybe the hill spirit was watching from beneath?—but he couldn't worry about his absence. Torin had to wholly focus on what he was doing. He needed to churn up the spurge with blistered hands and he hesitated a moment, anticipating the pain.

Torin winced as he took hold of his makeshift pestle and crushed the spurge as best as he could. The blisters on the heel of his palm threatened to burst. It was complete and utter agony, and he shouted his pain into the mist.

Blood and salt, blood and salt, he repeated to himself, giving his hands a moment to recover before he dipped them into the bucket of seawater. His blisters burned even worse, and he rushed to spill the ocean onto his medley of flowers.

There was a rumble beneath him. The scorched stone seemed to groan before it cracked in two, and Torin was once again hurled backwards. He lay in a patch of bracken, blinking the dust from his eyes and staring up at the stars and the sun and the moon.

Hands on fire, he laughed, incredulous. He didn't have to look at the stone to know that all his labor had vanished.

He had failed again.

CHAPTER 32

A daira followed a guard through the castle corridors. Mud had dried on her boots, and thistledown clung to her dress. Her plaid was wrinkled from being pinned at her shoulder all day, and her breaths were shallow. She was late for her dinner with Moray, and there was no one to blame but herself.

She had gotten lost in the wilds on the ride home from visiting Kae at Loch Ivorra. The hills and valleys had changed on her, and Adaira had ridden, hour after hour, watching the light wane as her eyes desperately searched for a familiar sign. But without the sun to give her direction, she had been hopelessly lost.

It was the first time she had tasted fear in a long while. Bile had crept up her throat, and she had swallowed it down until her stomach churned. An icy bolt had pierced her chest as she struggled to remain calm, continuing to ride over the next hill, then the next, hoping the spirits would release her from their game. Then a mist had rolled in, and Adaira had no choice but to dismount from her horse.

She tried to think of what would happen if she never found her way home. If the hills eventually took her as their own, with grass weaving into her hair and wildflowers blooming between her ribs. She envisioned Jack, waiting day after day for her return. Innes riding through the wilds in a fruitless search.

Adaira walked the land on foot, her horse trailing behind. She walked until it was almost dark, and only then did the mist melt away, allowing her to behold the glimmering city in the distance.

The memory coaxed a shiver from her now as she continued to wend through the castle passageways.

You're home. You're safe, she told herself, but she couldn't ignore the weight of her dread.

"Your sword," the guard said to her when they reached a door Adaira had never seen before.

"Of course." She had forgotten it was there, belted at her side. She handed it over and tried to brush the thistledown from her clothes. In the end, it didn't really matter, she supposed. This was likely to be the last time she ever spoke with Moray.

The guard unlocked the door.

Adaira took a final second to compose herself. Then she stepped into a small, firelit room. There was a table set with two plates, filled with food that had gone cold. Moray was chained to a chair at one end of the table, waiting for her with an impatient gleam in his eyes.

He held his tongue until the guard had shut the door and they were alone.

"Lost in the wilds, sister?" he asked.

Adaira resisted the temptation to touch her braid, which was snarled from the wind. "I'm still learning my way around. You shouldn't have waited on me."

"If I lose the fight tonight because the food went cold, then I'll know who to blame," he said.

Adaira pressed her lips together, but his statement gave her chills. She sat in the chair across from his and studied the pheasant and sliced pears on her plate. She wasn't the least bit hungry.

The chains around Moray's wrists clinked as he began to eat.

"Tell me where you went," he said between mouthfuls.

She saw no point in lying. She met his stare and said, "I went to Loch Ivorra."

He wasn't expecting that. Moray's brows rose, but he swiftly concealed his shock. "I take it you only enjoyed it from a distance, as it's forbidden. Locked by enchantment."

"I know how to unlock the door."

"Ah. And who taught you that? David or Innes?"

"David," she said.

"Which means it was *Innes,* as he doesn't do anything without her permission."

Adaira was quiet.

"What do you think of her?" Moray queried.

"Of who?"

"Innes."

"You don't call her Mother or Mum?"

"No," Moray replied. "She never wanted to be called by such titles."

Adaira didn't believe him. And she didn't like the direction their conversation was heading. Talking about Innes made her hands feel clammy, and the nape of her neck tingled in warning. But she smiled as though she found Moray's remarks amusing.

"Do you think she's a good laird?" he pressed.

Adaira shrugged. "Yes, considering what I've seen so far."

Moray stared at her with thoughtful eyes. "Do you think you could rule better than her?"

"*Better* than her?" Adaira echoed. "I honestly haven't thought much about it, Moray."

"Would you want to, though, Cora?"

"Would I want to rule the west? No."

"Not the west, the east."

That brought her up short. She stared at him, coldly. "I once did, but no longer. You took that from me."

"And what if I helped you regain it?" he said.

"At what cost?"

He smiled, as if pleased she had known there would be a catch.

"You help me overthrow Innes, and I'll help you take the east again. We can rule the isle, side by side."

It took everything within Adaira not to get up and walk out. Instead, she kept her expression smooth and calm, her eyes heavy as if bored.

"Oh? And how would we go about overthrowing Innes?" she said.

"Well, Aethyn poisoning is out of the question. She's been dosing herself for such a long time it's probably the reason why she's so cold." Moray started to eat, taking his time to explain what he had in mind, which, Adaira sensed, he had all planned out. "I think there's only one way to take her down."

"Which is . . . ?"

Moray glanced up with a half-smile. "A dirk, deep in the side. A cut through her vitals. A slow, painful way to go out."

Adaira briefly imagined it. Steel cutting through Innes at her waist, just beneath her plaid. The sound she would make as she dropped to her knees. Her blood staining the floor. The image crackled through Adaira like dark ice. She was surprised by how quickly her anger was roused, humming like a kicked hive, but she couldn't let her brother know.

"That seems risky, Moray," she said carefully. "Given how Innes was able to take you to the ground without any sort of weapon."

Moray scoffed, leaning back in his chair. "I let her handle me. But you bring up a valid point, sister. Innes doesn't trust me. She hasn't for years now, and I know that she has no intention of letting me regain my honor and walk free tonight. I know she hopes I'm slain, but if not? She's going to keep me shackled and fighting like Oathbreaker, until someone eventually bests me. And I'm not going to sit quietly and rot. I'm not going to let someone take my birthright from me."

Adaira shivered. His voice had dropped low, become raspy. But his eyes were feverish, as if he had caught fire.

"That is why I need *you*, Cora," he whispered. "I need you to be the one to stab Innes in the side. She will never expect it from you, which is quite ironic, given you were raised to hate us. But I see the way she looks at you. You are her weakness. The gap in her armor. She sees a shade of herself in you, as well as a gleam of Skye. Don't let such love fool you. It'll become a cage, a way to control you. To coerce you to do only the things she wants."

Adaira was quiet, but she held her brother's gaze. She didn't know what to say; his words had overwhelmed her.

"But if we do this . . . it needs to be *tonight,* Cora," Moray continued, drawing hope from her silence. "If you are with me, then I need you to give me a sign that you have the courage to betray Innes. When I'm brought out onto the sand, I need you to take a flower from your hair and throw it down to me. To everyone watching, it will seem like a mere gesture of luck. But I will know it means you are ready to rise. When I kill Oathbreaker, I want you to plunge your dirk into Innes's side. Then shove her over the balcony."

"You want me to kill the laird in a very public spectacle," Adaira said.

"The clan will only respect you for it. It will also cause chaos," Moray explained. "Which will enable me to get away."

"And her guards will kill me instantly."

"No, they won't. At the very worst, you'll be wounded. You'll most likely be shackled and imprisoned. By then, my men will have rallied and we can liberate you."

Adaira closed her eyes and sighed into her palms. This conversation was the last thing she had ever expected.

"Cora?" Moray called her back to the present.

Slowly, her hands fell away. She opened her eyes to stare at him.

"Are you with me?" he asked.

She already knew her answer. There had never been a moment of doubt, no moment when she needed to consider which path to take. But she didn't want Moray to know it. At least, not yet.

"Give me this evening to think about it," she said. "You'll have my answer tonight, when I see you in the arena."

—

In the cold, northern wing of the castle, Jack waited for his father in a small, windowless chamber. The simple room had a glazed hearth, a threadbare tapestry on one wall, and a table with two straw-backed chairs. Dinner had already been delivered on wooden plates. Roasted pheasant, herbed potatoes, spiced pears, carrots in browned butter, and a bannock still warm from the oven. Jack watched the steam rise, trying to temper his expectations.

Niall would be arriving any moment. And Jack still wasn't sure what he wanted to say to his father. All he knew was that Innes had given them an hour together, and that the culling would commence close to midnight.

The fire in the hearth made the room stiflingly warm, and over its crackling dance, Jack could hear distant footsteps drawing closer. A heavy tread in the corridor, the clang of shackles.

Niall was almost here.

Jack stood, staring at the door. Arched pale wood, an iron handle shaped like a leafy vine. When it finally creaked opened, he saw a guard. And then Niall appeared, standing on the threshold, grimy from the dungeons.

The guards unlocked the manacles on his hands, but they left the ones on his ankles, which would keep him from running should anything dire happen, like an escape attempt. Niall took a stilted step into the room, and the guards shut the door behind him.

Jack stared at his father, his heart pounding. He was waiting for eye contact, for a sound of acknowledgment. For *anything*, but Niall solemnly stared at the floor. His lean and haggard face was set like stone. His auburn hair was bright and tangled, his skin pallid from weeks without sun. He was freckled and scarred and covered with woad tattoos.

It was strange to stand in the same room with him. It almost felt like a dream that refused to break. This was the man his mother had loved in secret. The man who had defied his own laird to carry Adaira east. The man from whom his life had come. They were linked together by invisible blood-forged threads, and Jack could nearly feel them tugging on his lungs when he breathed.

Does he plan to stand there the entire hour? Jack soon wondered, with a twinge of irritation as the awkward silence stretched on. *Why does he refuse to look at me?*

But then it hit Jack as he watched his father rub the raw places on his wrists. Niall was anxious, ashamed. The last time they had seen each other had been in the arena.

"Would you like to sit?" Jack asked, indicating the table.

Niall finally glanced up, studying the dinner spread. "You didn't have to go through so much trouble for me."

"It's no trouble," Jack said, tamping down his emotions before they warbled his voice. "I wanted to see you again."

I wanted to speak with you alone. I wanted to feed you. I wanted to ensure you have the confidence to win tonight.

Jack sat down first, hoping if he occupied himself with the food, Niall would feel comfortable enough to join him at the table. Slowly, he did. Jack could see him at the corner of his eye, approaching the table hesitantly. The clink of chains, his long shadow rippling over the floor.

At last, Niall reached his chair and sat.

"Hand me your plate," Jack said, keeping his eyes averted from his father. He had seen Mirin do this countless times, fixing a plate for someone. Keeping her gaze focused wholly on her task.

Niall obliged. He took his wooden plate and extended it to Jack.

Jack accepted and began to fill the plate with food. He didn't know how well they were feeding Niall in the dungeons, and the last thing Jack wanted was to make him ill on the cusp of a fight. Jack remembered his own time locked in the cell with Thief. The meal that had been delivered was better than what most prisons offered, even though Thief had left only a fraction of it for Jack.

Take this food and let it strengthen your body, Jack prayed over it. *Let it nourish your soul, remind your heart of all the good things in life still to come.*

"Here," he said and held the plate out to Niall. He continued to avoid eye contact because it seemed to make his father freeze.

Niall accepted the plate. "Thank you," he murmured.

Jack reached for the pitcher of water. It was still cool from the spring, and he poured them each a cup.

Now what did he do? Should he say something? Should he remain silent?

Jack took up his fork and began to eat, and Niall mirrored him. But Jack wanted to look at his father. He wanted to look at him closely, to study his face until Jack found all the traces of himself within it. He wanted to ask questions, if only to hear the cadence of his voice, to fill in the gaps of his knowledge, but the moment felt as tenuous as ice in spring.

He would have to move slowly, carefully. He didn't need to treat this night as the last time they would ever see each other and speak, even though it very well could be. Jack needed to be confident that he would sit at a table with Niall time and time again, maybe in the west, maybe in the east. Maybe in a little cottage on a hill, at Mirin's table. Surrounded by the ones he loved most.

The image made his eyes sting and his chest ache, as though a rib had splintered.

Jack said, "Did you know mainland fare is quite bland?"

He almost felt ridiculous for blurting out such random words, but then he realized that food was the safest thing to talk about. A touchstone for them because they were sharing it.

"I . . . no," Niall said, his deep voice rising with surprise. "I've never had mainland fare."

"I ate it for many years when I was at university."

So began one of Jack's finest performances, regaling his father with an account of all the food he had once eaten on the mainland. He had never rambled like this before, and his subconscious wanted to flare, mortified. But he quelled it, then found a seamless conversational path from food to music. He told Niall about all the instruments he had handled, and about the harp being the one to call to him. About the music he had composed, and about his progress from reluctant student to dedicated student to uncertain grouchy teacher to strict grouchy teacher.

Soon he felt Niall's gaze on his face. His father was staring at him, listening. And yet Jack resisted meeting it. He kept talking about his music, about his harp, about his students, as he scraped the last potato from his plate. Then his account reached the moment when everything had changed. When a letter had arrived, summoning him home.

Niall was caught up in the story. He finally asked, "What brought you back to the isle?"

Jack smiled. At last, he lifted his eyes to meet his father's.

"Adaira."

He didn't know what her name would do once spoken. If it would cast Niall back into his past and make him emotionally retreat again.

"You're married to her," Niall surprised Jack by saying.

"Yes."

"Then I suppose I did do something right, if you've both found happiness with each other." Niall suddenly stood, bumping the table.

Jack watched, stunned when he realized Niall was leaving. He was cutting the dinner short, and Jack panicked. This was not how he wanted their time together to end. There was still more he needed to say, *wanted* to say, and he rose in a hurry.

"*Father,*" he breathed, the word emerging effortlessly as air. "Father, wait."

Niall stiffened. But he wheeled about to face Jack. There was a deep crease in his brow and tight lines at the corners of his mouth, as though he were in pain.

"Why did you want to see me again?" Niall asked tersely. "What could you *possibly* want with me after the things I've done?"

Jack blinked, startled by Niall's bluntness. A flicker of anger warmed his blood, and he was eager to respond to such a ruthless statement. But Jack banked the embers of his ire. "Ever since I was a boy," he began gently, "I've longed to know you. I've longed to see you, to speak your name. And now I finally have the chance and you ask me *why?*"

Niall winced and shut his eyes. "I'm sorry, Jack. But as you'll soon learn, I am not a good man."

"You don't have to be a '*good*' man," Jack said. "You simply need to be an honest one."

His father looked at him again. His eyes were a bloodshot blue, like the summer sky at sunset, and filled with remorse.

"Very well," Niall said. "Then let me speak honestly to you. I've stolen. I've lied. I've killed. I'm a coward. I left your mother to raise you and your sister alone. I let her go. I let you go. I let Frae go. I am *unworthy* of what you hope for me, because I never fought for your mother and you and your sister when I should have."

"Then fight for us now!" Jack replied sharply. He pounded his chest with his fist, felt the beat move through him. "Let our names be the sword in your hand. Let us be your shield and your armor. Fight for *us* tonight. Because over the clan line, in the shadows of the Aithwood, my mother still waits for you, weaving your story on her loom. My sister longs for you as I once did, wondering where you are and hoping you will one day knock on the door and proudly claim her. And I would love nothing more than to bore you with mainland stories day after day and sing for you until your guilt sheds like old skin and you choose the life you want, not the one you think you deserve."

Niall was silent, but tears had gathered in his eyes. "It's too late for that," he whispered in a hoarse voice.

"Is it?" Jack countered. "Because I'm here now."

Niall held his stare a beat longer before turning away.

Jack couldn't move—he couldn't breathe—as he watched Niall open the door and politely ask the guards to take him back to the dungeons.

The shackles were latched around his wrists as the door closed.

Alone, Jack gasped and let down his guard, bowing over in pain. He let his mind dig a trench for his thoughts to pace, around and around.

Did I say too much? Did I not say enough?

He would have to wait for the midnight bell to truly know.

On her walk home that afternoon, Frae finally roused her courage to ask Ella the question that had been hounding her like a shadow.

"What if my da is a Breccan?" Frae kicked a pebble on the road, keeping her eyes on the ground. "Would you still want to walk me home?"

Ella was quiet for a moment, but maybe only because the question had taken her by surprise.

Frae snuck a glance at her. For the past several days, Ella had walked her home from school and the boys had not bothered her again. But there were still whispers and pointed glances. A few times during classes, no one had wanted to partner up with Frae.

"If your da is a Breccan," Ella began to say, "then yes, I'd still walk you home, and I'd still be your friend, Frae. Do you want to know why?"

Frae nodded, but she could feel her face flush, her relief knotted with shame that she even had to ask this question when no other children she knew did.

"Because your heart is good and brave and kind," Ella said. "You are thoughtful and smart. And *those* are the people who I want to be friends with. Not the ones who think they are above everyone else. Who scowl and judge things they don't understand and throw mud and have cowardly hearts."

Frae soaked in Ella's words, which were as warm and soft as a plaid, and she suddenly could walk faster, her chin held higher.

"And," Ella added with a mischievous smile, "you make the best berry pies."

Frae giggled. "You could come over tomorrow after school. I'll show you how to make one."

"I'd love that."

They talked about other things, and Frae was shocked by how soon Mirin's cottage came into view. Getting home had seemed to take no time at all. She waved goodbye to Ella and walked the path through the tall grass and clusters of wildflowers and bog myrtle.

Mirin was waiting for her at the gate, as usual. But this time she had a letter in her hand.

"Your brother has written us," she said, touching Frae's hair in greeting. "Come, let's read it together."

Frae bounded inside, throwing down her satchel of books. She jumped onto the divan and sat, knees pulled up to her chest, as she waited for Mirin to join her.

"Boots off the cushion, Frae," Mirin gently chided, and Frae instantly let her feet fall back to the floor. "Would you like to read it, or should I?"

Frae thought for a moment. "You can read it, Mum."

Mirin smiled and sat beside her. Frae watched, chewing on a hangnail as her mother broke the seal on the parchment and unfolded it to reveal Jack's handwriting.

"'Dear Mum and Frae,'" she began to read, clearing her throat. "'I've reached the west safely, although I did have a minor detour. Don't worry, however. I'm with Adaira once more, and I . . .'" Mirin paused to cough. The sound was deep and wet, and she coughed again, covering her mouth with her hand.

Frae stiffened. She had noticed her mother coughing more lately. She had also noticed that Mirin was weaving at a slower pace; as a result, she needed to work longer to complete a plaid. Not many people were commissioning her these days, although the ones who did came at night, as if they didn't want to be seen knocking on her door.

"Perhaps you can read it to me, Frae?" Mirin whispered.

Frae nodded and took the letter. But she saw her mother discreetly wiping blood from her fingers. Her face had gone pale, as if something had broken within her.

Frae pretended not to notice, because Mirin didn't want her to know. But anxiety chilled Frae and made her stumble over the words of Jack's letter.

Come home, Jack, Frae wanted to beg him when she reached the end. *Please come home.*

CHAPTER 33

~~~~~~~~~~~~~~~~~~~~~~~~~~~~~~~~~~

Jack was the first to return to the bedroom. Adaira was still
with Moray, and the chamber was quiet, tinged with blue evening light. Jack stood numbly before the hearth, watching the
light gradually fade as the sun set.

He relived his conversation with Niall, over and over, until he
felt bruised.

It was almost dark when he moved to throw another stack of
peat on the fire and light the candles scattered throughout the room.
He stared at the dancing flames until his sight grew speckled and
he closed his eyes, knowing only a few more hours remained until
the culling.

He needed a distraction.

Sitting at Adaira's desk, Jack glanced over Iagan's composition
again. Poring over the music made Jack want to write his own,
to turn those sinister notes from cold ash into fire. He opened a
drawer, seeking fresh parchment. What he found was a letter addressed to him.

Frowning, Jack drew it from the shadows. He recognized Adaira's handwriting and his heart leapt in response, as it always

seemed to do where she was concerned. Studying the parchment, he realized that she had written him a letter that she never sent.

He opened the seal and unfolded it. His swift-beating heart went completely still as he read her words.

My Old Menace,

Tonight I write my mind and my heart into this letter because I will never send it. There is heady power in such a thing, I'm learning. To write without constraints. To write what you truly feel. To turn a memory immortal. Into ink and paper and the unique slant of your hand.

Tonight I heard you sing for me. I heard you play for me.

And you will never know how much I needed your music. How desperate I was to hear your voice, over kilometers of mist and rocks and bracken and barrenness. You will never know because I cannot bear to tell you, so I will tell it to the paper here instead.

I drank poison tonight, and it turned me into frost and ice. I drank poison, and at first I felt like I was made of iron and confidence and all the sharp edges of the realm, until I wasn't. And I writhed on the floor of my room with blood-spun jewels in my hair. I writhed and I wept and I have never felt such pain—the pain of loneliness, of emptiness, of grief. The pain of a poison I shouldn't have drunk.

It was so heavy within me I could hardly crawl. But then your music found me on the floor. Your words found me at my weakest, at my darkest hour. You reminded me to breathe—to inhale, to exhale. You reminded me of all the gleaming moments we shared, even if it had just been for a season. You reminded me of what could still be if I was brave enough to reach out and claim it.

And I would tell you to sing up a hundred storms, if only to hear such beauty and truth again. To feel it settle in my bones and warm my blood. To know it is mine and mine alone to claim.

I love you, more than these humble words and this
everlasting ink can say. I love you, Jack.
—A.

The words began to swim on the page. Jack blinked away his tears, but a sound escaped him. A sound of overwhelming relief and astonishment. To see her words, to feel them unfold within his chest like wings.

He stood, her letter still clutched in his fingers.

Through the haze of his tears, he looked at the floor, imagining her writhing and in pain. Why had she taken poison?

The mere image brought him to his knees.

He crawled closer to the hearth and lay down. He sprawled on his back, overwhelmed by all that was good and all that was uncertain. All that the night still promised to bring.

Jack stared up at the ceiling.

He relived her words, a hundred times.

When Adaira returned to her bedroom, the last thing she expected to find was Jack lying on her floor. A searing bolt of panic went through her, making her forget all about Moray and the plot to assassinate Innes, until Jack raised his head, saying, "I'm all right. Come lie down with me. The view is impeccable from here."

Adaira locked the door, brow arched. "And what view is that, Bard?"

"You have to come closer to see it, Adaira."

She did, easing down beside him on the rug. That was when she saw the letter on the floor, her dark-inked words on parchment. The pinch of concern she felt was quickly overruled by relief.

She sank fully to the floor at his side, staring up at the rafters.

"You're reading my post, I see."

"A post addressed to *me*," Jack was swift to retort.

"Hmm."

A lull came between them. It wasn't uncomfortable, but Adaira could only wonder about Jack's inner thoughts, about what her words might have roused in him. Sometimes he was still difficult for her to read.

He turned on his side to look at her, his hand fanning over her stomach. "Why did you take the poison?" he asked softly.

Adaira sighed. "At the time, I took it because I needed to have a place at the nobles' table. I wanted to prevent another raid, because I believed it would spark a war between the two clans. But now? I think I took it because I was desperate to show my mother that I have a place here. That I am strong enough to thrive among the Breccans, even poisoned."

Jack was quiet, listening as she began to tell him everything. About Skye, about the jewel effects of Aethyn-laced blood, about Innes's worry that Adaira was fated to suffer the same painful death as her younger sister.

"There's a good chance Innes will ask me to dose myself again soon," Adaira said. "She might even ask it of you, Jack."

He was quiet, but his hand moved along her ribs, coming to rest over her heart. "I won't be able to take it."

"Why?"

"Because I need to be able to play my harp and sing at a moment's notice. It would be foolish of me to ingest something that would prevent me from doing that."

"You plan to play even though my mother forbids it?"

Jack's hand drifted from her heart, down to her ribs again. As if measuring her breaths. "Yes. When the time comes. It could be an hour, a day, a month from now." He paused, watching her. "Do you want to take the poison again?"

"I don't know," she replied honestly. She worried that he might press her about the matter, and she was about to ask him how his dinner with Niall went, when he spoke.

"You and I have faced many things alone," Jack murmured. "Between the mainland and the isle, the east and the west, we've carried our troubles in solitude. As if it were weakness to share one's burdens with another. But I am with you now. I am *yours*, and I want you to lay your burdens down on me, Adaira."

She could hardly breathe, listening to his words. She turned to face him, and his arm came around her, strong and possessive. She savored his warmth as he held her tight against him.

Adaira remembered being lost earlier that day, wandering the wilds. If she had never come home, if the land had devoured her whole and stolen this moment from her, she would have perished from regret. She would have fallen apart, thinking of all the things she had wanted to say and do and yet had not, for reasons that felt tangled as vines within her. But she sensed that her reticence stemmed from her pride, hammered into steel, and the duty she had been raised to uphold. To faithfully guard herself and appear invincible, as a laird had no other choice but to be.

"I don't need autumn, or winter, or spring," Adaira said, letting the words bloom. "I want you eternally. Will you take the blood vow with me, Jack?"

He was silent, but his dark eyes glittered in the firelight. Adaira's pulse was thick in her throat when he reached down to unsheathe the dirk at his belt, his old truth blade. They had once cut themselves with it, baring their hearts to each other. Adaira still had that faint scar on her palm, and she shivered as Jack sat forward, drawing her up with him.

"I thought you'd never ask, Adaira."

She countered with a sharp smile, "Is that a yes, Bard?"

"*Yes*."

She shifted to her knees, realizing she should have planned this moment with more intention. They had no strip of plaid to bind their bloodied palms. There was no one to oversee their vows. There was no one but themselves, the fire burning in the hearth, and Jack's truth blade. And yet it felt right. It felt as if they were always supposed to be here, on their knees, facing each other, alone save for the flames.

Jack went first, drawing the blade over his palm.

"Bone of my bone," he said as his blood welled. "Flesh of my flesh. Blood of my blood."

Adaira took the dirk's hilt when he offered it, then did as he had done. The blade reflected the firelight—and a fleeting glimpse of her face—as she cut her palm, repeating the words back to him.

"Bone of my bone. Flesh of my flesh. Blood of my blood." She laid her scored palm against his, and their fingers intertwined.

They remained like that for a few moments, on their knees, their hands fastened, their mingled blood dripping to the floor. Adaira could feel the enchanted bite of the wound, how it swiftly began to mend. It would leave a cold trace of a scar behind, for which she was glad. She wanted to remember this night, to feel its ridges on her palm. To remember how simple and true it was. How Jack looked at her. She had never seen such hunger in his eyes before, and it made her blood sing.

"I want to feel your skin against mine," she whispered. "I don't want anything between us."

"Then undress me, Heiress," he said.

She unwound her fingers from his. She unbuckled his belt, pulled away his tunic, unlaced his boots. She laid him bare on her floor, and she shivered when she felt his hands begin to loosen the stays of her dress. When he drew away her raiment until she wore nothing but firelight on her skin.

Only days ago, she had lain on this floor. Alone and poisoned and writhing, weeping into her hands. Only days ago, she had been uncertain and quiet and riddled with doubt.

She had not known her place then. But she would carve it into stone now. She would find it in the stars when the clouds broke. She would trace it in the lines on Jack's palms. In the cold echo of his scar. In the taste of his mouth.

Adaira sighed as she took Jack deep inside her. She moved and breathed and closed her eyes, feeling his hands on her waist, the floor bruising her knees. She had never felt more alive, and she wanted to chase that fire.

"*Adaira,*" he whispered.

She opened her eyes to see he was watching her, as if he wanted to memorize her, gleaming, gasping. When he breathed, she exhaled, as if they were passing the same air between them. He moved with her, his nails biting into her skin as though to claim her, to mark her. A desperate expression was on his face, and Adaira knew he was unguarded. She was seeing him whole, down to his very heart.

She let him see the same in her. The hunger, the longing, the scars. The words she wrote but never sent. The shape of her soul that didn't seem to fit anywhere. For once, she wasn't afraid to surrender those pieces of herself, to let them twine with Jack.

She let them all go because he was her home, her shelter. Her endless fire, burning through the dark.

CHAPTER 34

W hen the night passed into its oldest hour, the Breccan clan gathered quietly in the arena stands. Adaira stood on the balcony, watching them come by torchlight. A plaid was wrapped around her shoulders to ward off the chill, and a thistle bloom was tucked into her braided crown. Her eyes drifted down to the freshly raked sand, through the mist spinning in the air.

She felt Jack touch the small of her back.

A few hours earlier, they had lain entwined on the floor, covered in a blanket and sharing news of how their dinners had gone. Jack had been shocked by what transpired between her and Moray; she had been saddened by how his brief time with his father went. She didn't know what she would say to Jack if Niall was defeated. Trying to imagine it—to prepare herself for such an outcome—made her feel weary, as though years had passed in a single evening.

What can I say? What can I do?

These questions echoed through her. Her inability to interfere with the culling should it veer the wrong way kindled her anxieties. For Niall, and also for Jack. But deep inside she harbored a spark of hope. She hoped the stories Jack had told Niall, the words he had said to him, would carry his father through one more fight.

Just before the bell chimed midnight, Innes joined them on the balcony.

The laird sat in one of the chairs and crossed her legs, fingers laced together on her lap. She wore her circlet, her plaid, and her sword, and she appeared calm and poised when Adaira glanced over her shoulder at her. She looked as if this were any other night, not the night destined to rend her heart no matter the outcome. Either she would lose Moray and be honor-bound to pardon the man who had stolen her daughter, or she would be compelled to keep her son imprisoned in the dungeons.

When Innes met her gaze, Moray's words rolled through Adaira's memory again. *You are her weakness. The gap in her armor.*

She didn't know if she could believe her brother. If that were so, wouldn't Innes uproot such a weakness? As a laird, she raided and she fought and she imbibed poison and she only relaxed in the presence of those she trusted most, the number of whom could be counted on one hand. She had maintained her rulership year after year through nothing but her own prowess, and no one seemed strong enough to overturn her. No one save for Adaira, should she plunge a dirk into her mother's side.

Moray was right about one thing: Innes would never suspect such a betrayal. She would never see it coming, and yet every time Adaira imagined what it would feel like to give her mother a mortal wound, to see the light in Innes's eyes dim as she bled out, she felt a chasm in her chest that devoured all the warmth in her.

She returned her attention to the ring.

If Moray *did* fall that night, then who would inherit the west when Innes was gone? The clan seemed to be hungry for an answer to that question, as the arena could hardly hold them all. They stood in clusters at the very back, gathered on the stairs, crowded each other on the benches. Even children were present, sitting on their parents' laps, blinking sleep from their eyes.

The wind began to blow from the east, melting the eddies of

mist. The clouds broke overhead, revealing a host of constellations that burned like jewels in the cloak of night. It was just as Innes once said: the clouds always parted for the culling, and a stream of curious moonlight cast the arena in silver.

Godfrey appeared, welcoming the clan with his booming voice and high energy. Adaira wasn't listening to his introduction, though, because her eyes were on the arena doors. The ones that opened to the dungeon passage.

She reached out and found Jack's hand. His fingers felt cold as midwinter. Neither of them would be able to sit for this fight, and they remained standing at the balustrade, side by side, mist shining in their hair. Waiting.

The iron-webbed doors creaked open.

Niall arrived first, his shoulders hunched and his feet dragging over the sand. He wore a tunic, a scuffed breastplate, and tattered boots. He was staring at the ground as if he was afraid to look up, to lift his eyes and behold Jack on the balcony. The guards brought him to a rough halt in the center of the ring, where they unshackled his wrists and ankles. Only when they handed him a dented helm and a sword did he glance upwards.

He looked directly at his son.

Adaira felt Jack's fingers tighten around hers. She knew his heart was racing, that he was struggling to breathe through the worry and the fear. Then Niall bowed his head. Adaira didn't know what that meant. A sign of resignation, or a vow to fight? She didn't think Jack knew either, because she felt a tremor run through him.

Niall slid on his helm. His sad countenance and shock of auburn hair were now hidden as he waited for his opponent, sword in hand. Adaira wondered if that was the last time she would ever see his face, living and hale. His eyes gleaming with life.

The doors opened again.

Moray was ushered into the arena. He arrived with his chin tilted upwards in pride, a skewed smile on his face, his blond hair braided away from his eyes. He wore a brand-new breastplate—not a scuff marred the leather—and his boots looked freshly tanned as well. The guards escorted him to the center of the arena, a few paces to the left of Niall, and they unshackled him. They gave Moray a polished helm and a sword whose blade burned brightly, as if it had just come from the forge.

Adaira felt a shadow creep over her.

It was apparent that the dungeon keeper and the guards favored Moray. They had given him the best the armory had to offer, while giving Niall the battered, dull-edged scraps.

This didn't feel like a fair fight, and she ground her teeth, wondering if she should say something.

Jack must have read her mind, because he squeezed her hand, drawing her attention.

Don't, his eyes said.

Adaira sighed, but she knew what he had inferred. This fight, whose roots were tangled and deep, far beneath Jack and Adaira, had been destined. They had taken the opportunity during their two dinners to sway or to make amends, but now the outcome was up to the swords, and the men who held them.

She felt someone staring at her.

Adaira's attention returned to the ring.

Moray was watching her intently, waiting for her sign. The helm was in the crook of his arm, the sword in his right hand. Godfrey was rambling on and on, talking about crimes and punishment and honor and bloodshed, but in that moment it was only Adaira and Moray.

This was the minute that could change everything. A fracture of time that sat like a blade in Adaira's hands. A snarl in a tapestry, waiting for a tug to unravel it.

She bit the inside of her lip. Her mind was spinning, anticipating all the ways this night could move forward. But there had never been a question of what she would do, and she stared impassively at her brother. The thistle remained untouched in her hair.

She watched as the realization struck him.

She wasn't going to turn against Innes. She wasn't going to dance to his ploys.

An ugly expression twisted Moray's pale face, just before he slid his helm over it.

Moray took the first cut, as Jack knew he would. Niall blocked it, but didn't seem eager to counter. No, his father remained on the defense, letting Moray lunge and cut and spin around him, seeking his weaker side.

This wasn't how Niall had fought Jack in the arena. Niall had been fierce from the beginning, a strong contender who knew exactly what he wanted and how to obtain it. He had craved victory, as Moray did now. The heir fought as if the only thing that mattered was to win. To carve a way out of the arena.

Jack began to feel incredibly nervous.

He watched his father, whose moves were smooth yet submissive. Niall was merely reacting, and Jack wondered why. *Why aren't you fighting back? Why aren't you countering him?*

He thought that Niall might be hesitant to kill the laird's heir, especially given his history with Innes. Jack grimaced. He should have mentioned at dinner that Innes *wanted* Moray to die.

Niall stumbled.

Jack froze in horror as his father sprawled on the sand.

It was over. He hadn't fought back at all. He had simply been biding his time, allowing Moray to show off his skills.

Jack closed his eyes. He couldn't bear to watch this, even if he had agreed to be the Tamerlaines' representative. He couldn't witness his father's last moments. Jack remembered how it had felt to be lying on the sand with hundreds of eyes on him. The helpless, vulnerable feeling that had turned his fear into lead, making it difficult to move.

Jack inhaled deeply, his pulse throbbing in his ears. He could feel icy sweat trail down his spine. He waited to hear Moray's sword meet flesh, the sound of steel splintering bone and the splatter of blood. He waited to hear the end come, but there was only a hiss and a gasp. The sound of surprise blooming in the crowd.

His eyes flew open, just in time to see Niall roll across the sand, evading Moray's dramatic swing.

Let our names be the sword in your hand.

Niall rose. He took a broad cut at Moray; their swords met and held. They seemed locked together, and Jack wondered if they were speaking through their helms. Whatever they said must have been tense. Niall slung Moray back with a powerful sweep of his blade.

Let us be your shield and your armor.

Moray teetered for a moment. He found his balance again but hardly had a second to breathe. Niall was coming for him like a storm, gathering up wind and debris. He knew all of Moray's cuts and favored movements now, having seen them all at the beginning, when he had parried one after the next after the next. When Jack had believed his father would go down without a fight.

Fight for us tonight.

It seemed dangerous to hope that his words had found their mark, to believe that Niall had listened and was envisioning a life beyond the arena. A life in which his guilt and his past would be gradually peeled away, like calloused skin. A gentle but quiet life he could build with Mirin, with Frae. With Jack.

And yet . . . how was such a life possible as long as the clan line still divided them?

Adaira's fingers tightened around his.

Jack narrowed his attention. Moray looked angry and was fighting like a cornered dog, but Niall anticipated his every move. He was older, stronger. Emotionless. With one fluid motion, he disarmed the western heir.

Moray was visibly stunned. His chest heaved beneath his armor as he held up his hands. He dashed to the side, hoping to recover his sword, but Niall came between him and the fallen blade.

Niall ripped off Moray's helm and held the sword to his exposed throat. Any deeper and it would nick a vital vein and the spar would end. Niall looked to the balcony, where Innes had risen, moving to stand at Adaira's side. He was waiting for her permission to kill her son. Jack had to lean on the balustrade, suddenly worried the laird would recant.

Innes stared down at them. The marks in the sand. The sword that reflected the stars. Moray's flushed cheeks and wide, desperate eyes.

Innes sighed, a sound woven with years of bitter sadness. The very heart of defeat. But at last, she nodded.

Moray startled, his face crumpling in fear. *"Mother!"*

It was his last word. Niall drew his sword over Moray's throat, slicing it open. His blood cascaded, staining his armor, dripping onto the sand. He gasped and fell forward, dying in a puddle of his blood.

The western heir was dead. The Breccan clan was silent as they watched Niall remove his helm and kneel before Innes.

"You have regained your honor, Niall Breccan," she said, her voice carrying throughout the arena, deep and strong, as if she had not just lost her son. "The sword has spoken for you, and you are absolved of your crimes. You may walk freely amongst the clan once more, for the spirits have found you worthy of life."

Niall bowed his head, his lank copper hair dangling in his eyes.

Around him, the torch fire flickered as the wind began to blow. Shadows crept long and thin over the sand. The clouds knit themselves back together overhead, swallowing the stars and the moon. The mist descended, gathering like dew on hair and shoulders and plaids.

The clan began to leave, dismissed.

Jack couldn't move. He stared at Niall, watching him rise. He thought his father would glance his way, but Niall unbuckled his breastplate and let it fall. He left his armor and sword on the ground beside Moray, then fled through one of the arena doors.

"I need to speak with him," Jack murmured to Adaira.

She said nothing, but her cheeks were rosy, her eyes gleaming. She let her fingers unwind from his as he turned. Innes had already departed, slipping away without a sound. Jack hurried through the castle corridors, his heart striking against his breast.

He got turned around twice and had to backtrack, but he eventually found his way to the courtyard. It was teeming with people heading home, and Jack felt caught up in a river as he frantically searched for Niall. There was no sign of him. Eventually, Jack had no choice but to wend his way through a gap in the crowd, beside a forge that was boarded up for the night.

He stood in the shadows, absently gazing at the Breccans as they filed through the courtyard.

"If you're looking for your father," said a voice, "then you won't find him here."

Jack jumped, glancing to his left. It was David Breccan, standing four paces away and leaning against the stone wall.

"Did you see him?" Jack said.

"Not me, but the guards at the gate did," David replied, indicating the raised portcullis. "He was the first one to walk across the bridge."

Jack dwelled on these words until they burned like salt in a wound. He didn't know what it meant that his father hadn't wanted to see or speak with him. Maybe Jack had been wrong to assume Niall would want to build a new life with him in it. Maybe he just wanted to be left alone to live in peace.

Jack stared into the mist.

Somewhere, his father was walking the hills in the dark. Alone but free.

And there was only one place he would go.

Home to his cottage in the woods.

CHAPTER 35

T orin went home.

Not to the cottage that he had once built with Donella and then made into a refuge with Sidra. He walked through those empty, stone walls and ascended the heather-clad hill to his father's house and lands. The croft he had grown up on.

He paused in the kail yard. Once, he had seen a glamour every time he came here, but his eyes had been closed then. He had seen nothing but disrepair and neglect in Graeme's garden and cottage, and the sight had annoyed Torin. But now he saw the life dwelling beneath the magic, incandescent with goodness. The many threads that came together, all playing their part to make the whole.

He knelt in the dirt.

The yard spirits were young and shy, but the longer he remained among them, the bolder they became. Vines and flowers and weeds and blossoms and stones, their blinking eyes brimming with curiosity. Torin wasn't sure how much time passed—there was no way to truly measure it in the spirits' domain—but eventually a child made of vines drew close to him. The spirit reached out a small, woven hand and touched Torin's forearm, a soft touch to break his reveries. He tried to give the vine child a smile, but there was no joy in him that he could offer.

"Try again," said the vine child.

Torin shook his head, too weary to even speak.

"Try again," the child persisted in a sweet, hopeful voice.

Torin didn't want to try. The blisters on his hands were still ripe, and he had never felt so lonely and afraid in all his life. Not even when Donella died. Not even when his mother abandoned him, decades ago. Torin had been only six years old, but he remembered how he had struggled to understand her sudden absence. How he had waited at the door for her to return.

It was quiet in the garden, and Torin thought he would sink down into the earth from the countless woes he carried. But he soon heard Graeme. His father was singing inside the cottage. His voice, strong and deep, was escaping through the cracked window, and it prompted Torin to rise. He walked to the window and gazed into the cottage. He could faintly discern his father through the cracked shutter, sitting at his kitchen table, singing as he worked on a new ship-in-a-bottle.

It was an old ballad, but one that Graeme and Torin had once sung together, when Torin was a lad.

"It makes the work pass by much faster if you sing," his father had said as they repaired the cottage, as they tilled the garden, as they cooked their dinner, as they patched the holes in their garments. It was work that Graeme did as both mother and father, keeping Torin's childhood days steady and predictable.

Torin watched Graeme for a while, comforted. When he turned back to face the garden, he saw that a flat stone had been suspiciously set in his path. It had a hollow center, as if rain had dripped on it for years, wearing down its heart. A perfect place for him to crush herbs.

"Thank you," Torin murmured to the yard, returning to his knees. He reached for the flowers in his pockets and spread them into an arc before him. He felt as if he had everything he needed, and yet he was still nagged by a sense of inadequacy. He began to hum in tune with Graeme, placing the two sisters—Orenna and Whin—on the stone. Next, the last white flower of the west and the fire spurge of the east. He used all the blooms, saving none for later should he fail a third time.

He took up a smaller stone and began to crush the plants. The blisters on his palms protested so vibrantly that Torin felt his temples throb. But he kept working, swallowing the pain. One by one, the blisters burst. A groan slid through his teeth. Soon his palms were slick, and he couldn't find the strength to continue humming his father's song.

Falling silent, Torin studied his hands and found they were bleeding. Blood, bright as summer wine, trickled from his fingers down into the poultice he was churning. Drop after drop, until the pulp in the rock had turned crimson.

He thought of Sidra and ached when he imagined her waiting for him to return as the seasons continued to pass and the constellations continued to cycle. Soon, she would grow weary of her cold wait. She would continue to lead the clan, far better than he ever could, healing those in need and raising his children and perhaps even coming to love another, until she at last turned to dust in the ground.

Torin thought about all the days he had squandered, all the moments he had let pass by. If he found a way home, then he would never waste another day, another hour, another minute with those he loved. He wouldn't complain about leading the clan; he wouldn't resist visiting his father. In fact, Torin would bring Sidra and Maisie here to Graeme's as soon as he could, and they would sit in the sunlit garden and eat oatcakes and laugh at old stories—

He began to weep.

Bowed over the stone, Torin stopped crushing the remedy. The sobs tore through him, emerging from that deep, lonely cavern in his chest. The broken place he had hidden for years, fearful of acknowledging the damage that dwelled in him. But it was there, and he felt its jagged fragments.

His tears cut paths through his beard. They dripped off his

chin and landed on his hands and on the stone, hissing like rain as they melded with his blood and the flowers of the isle.

Torin could hardly see, but he continued to mix everything together until all he saw was his blood and the salt of his tears and his many, many regrets. The pain in his hands finally caught up to him, eclipsing his inner turmoil.

He dropped his makeshift pestle.

Torin closed his eyes and lay facedown in the garden, letting his exhaustion drag him into a world where there was nothing but darkness and stars.

Sidra rode along the northern road, heading west. She took Blair and three other guards with her, her healing records, and a chest full of eastern herbs and the remedies she had created, as well as a gift for her enemies—a sack of golden oats, a jar of honey with the comb, and a bottle of wine. Everything felt uncertain, and yet when Sidra had readied herself that morning, she had never been more at peace.

She wore the raiment of a laird—a vermilion tunic, a leather jerkin stitched with silver thread, vambraces on her forearms, and tall hide boots that concealed the blight, which had nearly reached her knee. She draped the enchanted green plaid that Torin had commissioned across her chest in place of armor, holding the wool in place at her shoulder with a brooch in the shape of a leaping deer with a ruby in its eye.

She stood before her mirror, gazing at herself as if she were a stranger, but someone she deeply admired. She braided portions of her long black hair before setting a silver circlet across her brow. Torin had the signet ring, but when the Breccans looked upon her they would know who and what she was. Lastly, she belted a broadsword to her waist.

Sidra had never worn a sword sheathed at her side. The only blade she had ever carried had been her foraging knife and the occasional dirk. But carrying the sword had been one of Yvaine's conditions. She could go to the west for five days and five days only, and she could take a small gift of provisions. She could stay with the Breccans under Adaira's protection, and she could share whatever knowledge she had learned to aid the west in the battle with the blight. She could do all of these things so long as she had her guards accompany her and she remained armed at all times.

Sidra had acquiesced.

Once she was prepared to ride, she had seen to the final and most important of her preparations. Sidra had placed Maisie in the saddle and set off to deliver her daughter to Graeme.

Torin's father stood in the yard and watched Sidra and Maisie crest the hill on foot. Maisie squealed with excitement at the sight of her grandfather, and Sidra smiled, even though she felt an ache in her chest. She let her daughter's small hand slip from her own.

Graeme reached out to scoop Maisie into his arms. "Now who is this young lass? I don't know if I've ever seen you before!"

Maisie giggled at his teasing, wrapping her arms around his neck. "It's me, Grandda. *Maisie*."

"Ah, Maisie! Yes, one of the bravest girls in all the east. I've heard stories about you." Graeme said with a wink before glancing at Sidra.

Sidra stood in the garden, the wind teasing her hair. She noticed the awe in Graeme's expression as he beheld her, as well as a spark of worry when he noted that she was dressed for war.

"Remember what I told you, Maisie?" Sidra said to her daughter, holding up her hand to count on her fingers. "I'll be away for five sunrises and five sunsets, and then I'll return. Be good for your grandda."

Maisie nodded, and Graeme set her down on the stone pathway. "I've got some oatcakes on the griddle, and Tabitha needs to be brushed. Do you want to go on in and help me, lass?"

Maisie smiled and darted inside. Knowing that Maisie felt secure and safe enough to not worry about her mother's absence made Sidra feel weak in the knees. It was a small but comforting mercy, and Sidra was still gazing at the open doorway when

Graeme stepped closer. He stumbled over a stone set in the middle of the garden path, and Sidra reached out to steady him.

"That's a strange place to put a stone, Da," she mused, studying the odd rock. It looked worn down in its heart.

"Aye, and I've never seen it before today," Graeme replied, scratching his beard. "The spirits must be afoot." His attention shifted back to Sidra. He sighed and whispered, "You're going west then?"

"Yes," she replied. "Thank you for watching Maisie. I should be back soon." She didn't say that if something befell her, Graeme would need to raise Maisie to be the next laird. She didn't say that there was a small pit of doubt in her stomach about crossing the clan line. That for the first time in her life she had no inkling of what was going to happen, whether something good or terrible awaited her.

Graeme saw these doubts in her eyes. Tenderly, he framed her face in his hands. "May you be strong and courageous," he said. "May your enemies kneel before you. May you find the answers you seek. May you be victorious and spirits-blessed, and may peace follow as your shadow."

Sidra knew the ancient blessing was spoken to a laird when conflict was imminent. The words gripped her now, settling into her bones. And yet she felt steadier the longer she dwelled on them. Weeks ago, she would have never believed she would be standing in such a moment, and she would have blamed it on a cruel twist of fate. But now she thought that perhaps she was always destined to be here. All those hours devoted to gardening beside her nan, learning the secrets of herbs. All those hours she had spent alone on the hills, gazing up at the stars and thinking of where she wanted to go and who she wanted to become.

You were always meant to be here, a voice whispered in her mind.

Graeme kissed her brow and released her. Sidra turned away before he could see the tears in her eyes.

She didn't look back as she descended the hill and went to her horse, waiting on the road with the guards. She grimaced as she mounted, the pain in her foot stealing her breath. Her limp was more pronounced now, and she had decided to finally confide in Blair. The guard now held her secret as if it were his own, but soon her affliction would come to light. She only hoped that would happen *after* her visit to the west.

As Sidra approached the clan line, she dwelled on Graeme's benediction, clinging to the reassurance of those ancient words. She was almost there, even though her horse had slowed from a canter to a trot, and then at last to a walk. Her heart was pounding, churning anxious heat into her blood.

She saw the northern signpost, weathered with age, and the weeds that bloomed between the trees. She saw the road curve and then dip, as if surrendering to the west, and Sidra drew her horse to a halt.

A host of Breccans were waiting to greet them, blue plaids at their chests and neutral expressions on their faces. Spangles of sunlight danced over their hair—blond and brown and auburn and black—and the intricate woad tattoos on their skin. But Sidra saw only Adaira, standing at the forefront, waiting for her.

Sidra slid from her horse. She hit the hard-packed ground with a jar to her ankles, but the pain in her leg was a mere memory as she strode for Adaira. There was a moment when Sidra wasn't sure if she would chuckle with joy or weep in relief as her heart overflowed with emotions.

She crossed the clan line and entered the west without fear, as if she had done so a hundred times before. She stepped into Adaira's fierce embrace.

They greeted each other breathlessly, as though time had never come between them, and they laughed into each other's hair.

Torin didn't know what woke him until his name cut through the darkness.

"*Torin.*"

He opened his eyes and was greeted by the loam. Dirt was in his mouth, and grass was in his beard. He groaned and slowly pushed himself up to his aching knees.

"Torin."

He blinked away the blurriness, recognizing the voice that had roused him. Hap sat nearby, cross-legged and bright-eyed.

"Hap," said Torin, surprised by how rough-hewn his voice was. "I think I missed you."

Hap only smiled.

That was when Torin realized that Graeme's kail yard was teeming with earth spirits. They crowded the small garden, brimming with wonder and joy. Torin could nearly taste it when he breathed—the scent of the earth after a summer rain, the nectar of the flowers, the dew on the grass.

"Why have you come to me?" he asked, overwhelmed by their presence.

"Look behind you," Hap said.

Torin turned to see the stone with the hollow heart. At first, he didn't understand what he was beholding. Where once there had been blood and flowers and his anguish, there was now something else. Something smooth and bright and cold.

The blight's remedy shone on the rock with all the radiance of the moon.

PART FOUR

A Song for Wildfire

S idra stood beside David Breccan at his worktable, studying his leather-bound herbarium. She was impressed with his records, including the plant cuttings he had pressed and fastened to the pages. Some she recognized and knew well. Others were a mystery to her.

"May I?" she asked, and when he nodded, she carefully began to leaf through the pages. She stopped when she saw a small white flower, gleaming faintly of gold, attached to the parchment. An enchanted blossom, Sidra knew. Beneath it, David had written its name: *Aethyn.*

Sidra paused, her memory drawing deep. She was familiar with this western flower. The first and only time she had heard its name she had been sitting in the dungeons of Castle Sloane, speaking with Moray.

There's no countermeasure, no antidote for Aethyn. But it turns spilled blood into jewels.

This was the poisonous blossom that had killed Skye. The youngest daughter of the laird.

"You're familiar with Aethyn?" David asked, noticing her pause.

"It doesn't grow in the east," Sidra replied. "But yes, I've heard of it." She didn't offer up how she had that knowledge. Adaira had told her Moray Breccan was now dead, slain the night before at the culling. Sidra wanted to be careful in what she said as well as in what she *didn't* say while she was in the western holding.

Speaking Moray's name now, or even Skye's, might open a wound that Sidra wouldn't be able to close.

As if sensing her thread of thought, Blair shifted closer to her. He had become her shadow and had yet to utter a single word since crossing over into the west. But Sidra could tell how tense he was, as were her other three guards. They were the finest warriors the east had to offer, personally chosen by Yvaine, and yet they had never been in this situation—walking the west openly and brushing shoulders with Breccans.

It was odd, even to Sidra. Instinct told her to prepare for a trap, given the history between the Tamerlaines and the Breccans. Despite her hopefulness, she hadn't been able to snuff out such sinister thoughts on the ride in.

Was that flock of sheep they passed on the road stolen from the east? Had the guards they saw at the city gates crossed the clan line in raids before? Was the portcullis—the only way in and out of the castle—going to drop and hold, keeping Sidra and her guards locked inside?

Sidra inwardly shook herself. She couldn't allow herself to dwell on such thoughts, not if she wanted to make the most of her time here and collaborate with David.

Adaira reached for a bottle of dried herbs on the table. She also had remained close to Sidra's side, and it was her presence alone that enabled Sidra to extend her trust.

"Do you think the blight's remedy might be made by combining two plants?" Adaira asked. "Something that grows in the west with something that blooms in the east?"

"I confess that possibility has crossed my mind a few times," Sidra replied. She glanced at David, who was staring down at the Aethyn bloom on the page.

The laird's consort wasn't what she had expected—he was handsome in a rugged, almost *faded* way, lean and graceful, soft-spoken and reserved—but then again, her mind had built up quite a few assumptions about the Breccans, their land, and their holding.

"What grows in the east that we don't have here?" David asked.

Sidra gently turned the page. "I'm not sure yet. But your herbarium will cast some light on that question."

And it was going to take some time. Eventually, David called for some tea and cherry biscuits, and he, Adaira, and Sidra sat at the table while Sidra continued to leaf through his collections. She had handed over her remedy recipes and all the tonics and salves from her attempts to heal the blight and she watched from the corner of her eye as David studied her recordings, his brow furrowed. She had noticed that he wore gloves on his hands. When she saw him at the clan line, she had thought they were riding gloves. He had failed to remove them after they arrived at the castle, however, and while it was none of her business, she suspected she knew why.

She had an easier time hiding the blight on her foot and leg, beneath boots and dresses and stockings. But if the blight had been on her hands, she too would have had no choice but to wear gloves. If the laird's consort was blighted, it suddenly made sense why the Breccans were eager to have her visit.

"May I ask how many of your people are sick?" Sidra asked.

David hesitated a beat, as if he didn't want to reveal this number to her. But he must have come to the same realization she had: if they were going to truly work together and solve this problem, they needed to be honest with each other.

"Thirty-four, last I counted," he said. "Although there could always be more. I've found that people are ashamed to reveal it."

Yes, Sidra thought. It seemed that some of the blight's side effects couldn't be seen but were felt. Fear, anxiety, shame. Denial and desperation.

"What of your clan?" David asked. "How many have fallen ill on your side?"

"Fifteen that I know of," Sidra replied. How that number stuck in her throat. It was wild how easily people were becoming infected, even knowing of the dangers and avoiding them as best as they could. She thought back to when her own infection had begun. She had been so careful but still wound up stepping on rotten fruit.

"I see here that you've tried spindlefel, primrose, nettles, and periwinkle as a salve for pain in the infected area," David said, pointing to one of her recipes. "I've attempted the very same, and I've found that adding a bit of juniper to the mix helps tremendously with easing the stiffness in joints."

Sidra leaned forward, intrigued. She nearly flexed her ankle to feel how resistant the blight had made it, as if the muscles were pulling tauter by the day. "I've never thought of adding juniper. Thank you for the suggestion."

"Here." David stood, walking to his wall of shelves. His workroom was a small but cozy chamber, crowded with drying herbs and an eclectic mix of jars and bottles. Sidra would have liked to have such a room herself, rather than work in her kitchen.

He searched through his collection and eventually brought a wooden container to her, which opened to reveal a salve. By its sharp, cool smell alone, Sidra knew it was the recipe they had just spoken of.

"Yes, I'll have to try the juniper," Sidra echoed, but David surprised her.

"You can have this one," he said.

She glanced up to meet his gaze. He knew then. He knew she was also sick. She had been careful to hide her limp, but perhaps it was still obvious to him.

"Thank you," she said, accepting it.

Adaira was unusually quiet, but she was watching them closely. She sensed the two healers had something in common, although Sidra could tell she wasn't certain of all the details. Or maybe Adaira had simply been prepared for her father and Sidra to butt heads and argue and hoard their knowledge, like two dragons with their gold. Their easy camaraderie was a bit of a shock, although Sidra felt like healers possessed a language no one else knew.

They remained in the workroom until the day began to draw to a close. A storm was brewing, and Sidra could hear the wind, whistling through cracks in the castle mortar. The windowpanes wept with rain, and as Adaira led Sidra through a web of corridors the afternoon light suddenly disappeared and the castle was plunged into darkness.

"I'll show you to your room, so you can rest a moment before dinner," Adaira was saying when they reached a long, winding staircase.

Sidra gazed at the endless steps, reluctant to approach them, until Blair appeared at her side, offering his arm. She gratefully accepted and held to the crook of his elbow. She let him take the brunt of the weight off her foot as they followed Adaira upwards, but Sidra couldn't help but feel a stab of worry when Adaira glanced behind at her.

Adaira did indeed notice Sidra holding on to her guard. How attentive Blair was to her.

They followed Adaira down another corridor and at last reached the guest suite. The room was spacious, adorned with tapestries and rugs and a four-poster bed draped with sheepskin and sheltered by a canopy. A fire was burning in the hearth, and the mantel above it was green with fragrant juniper boughs. There was a chair and a table for washing, a wardrobe in one corner, and a view of the misty hills.

"May I have a moment alone with Adaira?" Sidra said to her guards, who were hovering.

Blair nodded, ushering the other three out to the corridor. As soon as the door closed, Sidra looked at Adaira, relief and worry both beating in her pulse.

This was the first time the two of them had been alone since meeting earlier in the day. They could both drop their guard and fall back into the comfortable bonds of their friendship. And yet so much had happened over the past month that it almost felt like they had been apart for years.

"I'm so happy you're here, Sid," Adaira said. "But I must ask . . .

is everything well with you and Torin? I couldn't help but notice your guard, and I honestly thought Torin would want to accompany you west. Jack also told me that Torin didn't reply to his letter. You did."

Sidra released a deep breath. It was time to inform Adaira, but she needed to sit for something like this.

"All is well between us. Don't worry." Sidra moved to the chair, easing down with a slight groan. "But Torin isn't here, Adi."

Adaira's expression was lined with concern as she drew up a stool, facing Sidra. "Where is he then?"

"The spirits took him."

Adaira stiffened, her face blanching. "What do you mean they *took* him?"

Sidra explained as well as she could, giving Adaira the pieces of information she had inferred. But she instantly regretted saying that Torin could be gone for years. Adaira looked like she had been pierced. She leaned on her knees, hand over her mouth, eyes gleaming with horror.

"I know you're going to worry about him," Sidra said, "but I don't want you to, and neither would he. There's a chance he could be home much sooner than I anticipate. So please, Adi, don't let this upset you."

Adaira was quiet for a long moment. Her fingers drifted from her lips as she whispered, "*Sid.* I'm so sorry."

Sidra nodded, trying to melt the frost that crept over her. The chill that often kept her up at night, staring into the darkness and shivering as she tried to imagine the rest of her life without Torin. If the blight didn't kill her, heartbreak was likely to send her to an early grave.

But she didn't want to give those thoughts power. She cast them aside, focusing on Adaira.

"Tell me how things have been for you here," she said.

Adaira sat back with a sigh. "Well, they've been interesting, to say the least."

As Sidra listened, Adaira told her bits and pieces of her life in the west. The shadows continued to deepen as she talked, even though it was only midafternoon. Eventually, Adaira rose to light the candles around the room, glancing anxiously at the window.

"I need to tell you about what to expect tonight, Sid," she said, returning to her stool. "Innes has invited the thanes and their heirs to dine in the hall tonight, and she would like you to join us as well, so she can introduce you and explain why you're here."

At once, Sidra felt a cold sting of shock in her side. She heard Moray's voice again in her memory, as if he were haunting her. *Every month, my parents call their thanes and their heirs into the castle hall for a feast. It's a dangerous, unpredictable night, because there's always a thane or two who is scheming to take the rulership.*

Adaira was explaining about the dangers of Aethyn and the preventative doses. Sidra had completely tuned her out, but she made herself focus again and listen more closely. When Adaira held out her palm, displaying a vial full of clear liquid, Sidra had to swallow down the bile that was beginning to surge up her throat.

"What is this, Adi?"

"It's a dose of Aethyn," Adaira replied. "In light of the risks of dinner with the nobility, both Innes and David wanted me to ask you to take it."

Sidra stared at the poison. Her gaze eventually drifted upwards to meet Adaira's. "Are you and Jack taking it?"

Adaira hesitated. "Jack says he can't. I'm still considering another dose. But I also should warn you that the side effects are terrible."

"And what are the side effects?"

Adaira began to describe them. Sidra realized that Adaira knew them only because she had experienced them herself, a thought that made Sidra's heart ache. To imagine Adaira alone and in pain, feeling like she had no choice but to drink poison.

"I won't blame you if you decline," Adaira concluded. "But do you want to consider it?"

Sidra was silent as she stood. She reached out to take the vial, holding it up to the firelight. "There's honestly no question about it, Adi."

"So you'll drink it?"

"No. I can't," Sidra said, her heart quickening. "I'm pregnant."

Adaira froze, but then a broad smile broke across her face. "*Sidra!*"

"Don't fuss over me, Adi."

Adaira ignored her, embracing Sidra so tightly that she couldn't breathe. But all the emotion she had kept in check suddenly welled up in her chest. She clung to Adaira, blinking away tears, and the sound of her friend's joyous laughter went through her like sunlight.

Everything will be all right, she thought. *I'm going to be all right. The baby will be all right.*

It was strange, Sidra thought, how being around Adaira made her feel that way. All those previous worries felt small and thin. The days ahead felt brighter, warmer, like an endless summer.

"I'm so thrilled for you," Adaira said, leaning back. "You have no idea how much I needed good news."

"Torin and I are happy to oblige," Sidra replied.

"He must be ecstatic."

"He doesn't know yet."

Adaira's smile faded. That pained expression stole over her face again.

"But," Sidra rushed to add, "he'll be very happy to know it when he returns."

"Yes, he will."

A loud peal of thunder interrupted them. Sidra startled, feeling the castle rumble beneath her feet. Adaira glanced at the window again. She was worried, and Sidra surmised that her concern might have something to do with Jack.

"I need to go," Adaira said. "But I'll come for you when it's time for the feast."

Sidra nodded. She walked Adaira to the door and watched her leave before asking her guards to step inside.

Blair and the others—Mairead, Keiren, and Sheena—gathered around her. The tension was rolling off them like notes from a harp string. Far too much seemed to be out of their control—the weather, the blight, the Breccans, the possibility of being poisoned at dinner.

"What is it, Laird?" Blair asked her gently.

Sidra sighed as she opened her fist, finger by finger, to reveal the vial of Aethyn. She gazed at it, her mind teeming with thoughts. She couldn't take the dose, nor would her guards. But she also wouldn't partake in a dinner that would put herself and her child at risk.

She thought about all the western flora she had seen in David's herbarium. She thought of all the flora she had brought with her from the east. She inwardly retraced the years she had spent handling plant after plant, from the vengeful to the docile, bringing out their essence to heal and to mend.

She wasn't afraid of poison. And she wouldn't bow to it.

Sidra looked at her guards, her heart steady. "I need to ask something terrible of you."

Torin needed a bowl. Something to carry the remedy in, as he wasn't strong enough to tote around the hollow-hearted rock. Frantic, he rushed through the door of Graeme's cottage and was surprised to find his father reading a story to Maisie.

Torin froze as though he had been caught in a web. He watched Maisie smile, listening to Graeme as he read to her. His voice was like a deep rumble of thunder, but comforting and steady. The firelight washed over their faces, and Torin realized it must be evening in the mortal realm. And if Maisie was here . . . where was Sidra?

"Torin!" Hap called from the garden beyond the door. "We don't have much time!"

Dazed, Torin moved to the kitchen nook and reached for one of Graeme's wooden bowls. But he wanted to stay in that moment with his father and daughter. He wanted to set down roots and remain, and it took everything within him—every uneven breath, every stray thought, every beat of his pulse—to remember what was at stake and what he needed to do.

When he returned to the yard, he noticed that the sky had changed. The air was darker, threaded with static. Clouds had gathered overhead, consuming the stars and the sun and the moon. Torin shivered in alarm as he knelt.

"What's happening?" he asked.

Hap's eyes were on the sky as the wind began to blow, cold from the north. His long hair tangled over his face. "He knows."

Torin froze again, his hand hovering over the remedy. "He knows what?"

"That you solved the riddle," Hap replied.

Torin watched as the spirits in the yard retreated, hiding from the gale. They took cover, but Hap continued to stand beside him, unyielding, even as the wind tore the flowers from his hair.

The moment Torin touched the remedy, the world went quiet around him and he felt as if he were dreaming, cupping moonlight in his hands. He had never felt such peace, and he sighed. Gently, he transferred the cold salve to the bowl, but he stared at his hand, luminous in the growing storm.

"Hurry, my friend," Hap urged. "Take off your shoes and run at my side. You'll be faster with your toes and heels in the loam, and if we get there in time we can heal the trees before *he* arrives."

Torin quickly untethered his boots. He gathered his bowl and followed Hap through the gate, but then he couldn't resist glancing over his shoulder one final time.

He watched as the rain began to fall on Graeme's cottage, and he found himself praying to the stone walls and the thatched roof and the wood door. . . . *Hold fast against the storm. Keep them safe for me.*

The house he had grown up in shimmered faintly, as if his prayer had strengthened it.

Only then did Torin turn and run barefoot at Hap's side. They sped over the hills as the relentless wind grew stronger.

They ran together, in perfect stride, to the orchard.

Jack had waited until the entourage that greeted Sidra began to follow the northern road down to Kirstron. He had shifted his horse to the back of the group, as Adaira had told him to do. When the road bent southward, Adaira glanced over her shoulder to look at him and he withdrew from the retinue altogether, drawing his horse west, into the wilds.

He needed to speak with Kae again, and this would be the best time to do it.

Adaira had agreed, although she had seemed reluctant at first, only because he would be riding alone through the hills. But Sidra's visit was crucial, and Adaira needed to be present for it. She had pricked her finger and gathered her blood into a small vial, giving it to him so he could unlock the cottage door. She had also given him a few instructions: *Stay on deer trails through the wilds. Keep the mountains to your back to find the loch. Leave with plenty of time to return home before nightfall.*

Letting his horse follow a winding trail through the heather, Jack felt both vulnerable and liberated to be riding the wilds alone. He paused on the rise of one summit and looked behind to ensure that the mountains were still at his back. The craggy heart of the west, just visible through the gloom, made him think of the Aithwood again. Jack had *almost* turned his horse south after greeting Sidra and her guards in the forest. He had been tempted to diverge from his plans and instead follow the trees down to Niall's cottage.

He hadn't, of course. He had been too anxious that Niall might turn him away, or perhaps even refuse to answer the door if he knocked. And Jack needed to see Kae. Ever since he had studied Iagan's music, questions had been smoldering like coals in his mind.

He pressed onward.

Soon he recognized the trees that surrounded Loch Ivorra,

then the cottage sitting quietly on its small island in the loch. He left his gelding hobbled beneath the trees and walked over the narrow bridge, noticing how still the water was on either side. He wondered how deep the loch ran, what spirits lived in its silt and moved through its cold shadows.

When he reached the door, he knocked to let Kae know he was about to enter. He took out the vial Adaira had given him, her blood staining the glass crimson, and put a drop on his fingertip.

Jack opened the door and stepped into the cottage.

Kae was waiting for him, standing a few paces away. She looked well rested and hale. Her wounds had fully healed, leaving behind traces of golden scars on her pale blue skin.

"Hello," Jack said with an awkward wave. "Adaira's not with me, but there's something that's been troubling me, and I think your memory may hold the answer, if you'd be willing to share it once again?"

Kae nodded and sat at the table. He took the chair across from hers.

"I need to see the moment when Iagan sang the hierarchy into being," said Jack. "When his music cast a net of control over the spirits of the isle."

Kae didn't seem surprised, but there was suddenly an anxious aura about her, as if she knew the memory Jack wanted to see was a difficult one. But she stretched out her hand. He gently accepted it with his own.

Together, they plunged into a vivid torrent of her memories.

Kae was soaring over the isle when she heard the music. She felt it tug against her ribs, weaken her wings. She had to answer the summoning or risk being torn apart by its magic.

She found Iagan playing in the Aithwood beside the clan line, on the western side. The river was at his back. He was singing for the spirits of air, for the southern, western, eastern, and northern winds. They materialized and gathered in the forest, some begrudgingly but most with curiosity. Kae waited with them to see what the bard wanted, for Iagan hardly ever played for the good of the isle.

His song was beautiful at first, welcoming them. But it began to shift, and when it did, she felt the music creeping over her. There was a flare of pain in her wings and in her throat, as if she had swallowed a hook. She wanted to leave but couldn't.

When Iagan crooned to Hinder, one of the most powerful spirits of the northern wind, Kae felt a flare of dismay. She watched as Hinder was forced to obey the ballad. He tore the wings from his body and laid them at Iagan's feet beside the clan line, where they shone, crimson and gold, and bled into the grass.

Hinder crawled away and wept, so weak he couldn't rise.

Kae remained still. She worried that if she moved Iagan would sing something that would be as costly to her as the song Hinder had been forced to obey. So she watched, transfixed, as Iagan summoned the earth next, drawing up spirits from the trees and grass and rocks. They appeared on both sides of the clan line, Whin on the eastern side. She arrived pale and furious, wildflowers drifting from her fingertips. When Iagan sang for a piece of her crown, she had no choice but to kneel and give him a portion of it. She set the gorse beside Hinder's wings.

Then Iagan sang for the water spirits, from the lochs to the rivers to the ocean's foam. Ream and her court had a long way to travel from the shore. The Lady of the Sea was wan and sickly when she arrived. Kae had always known her to be fierce and strong, and it was painful to watch her crawl, tearing away pieces of shell from her skin to lay them down beside Hinder's wings and Whin's gorse.

Kae felt like Iagan's ballad would never end. She could see that he was drawing all the magic of the west, which came in veins through the ground and air, from forges and looms, from all the places the humans could wield it. The magic fueled him, settling on him like a starry cloak. Finally, he sang for Ash and the fire spirits.

Ash arrived in a flurry of sparks, but he never had a chance to resist: Iagan's music was so powerful that it brought him low within an instant. The ballad for Ash spun a curse, one that Ash couldn't counter. He gave up his scepter, laying it beside the wings, the gorse, and the shells. The music almost completely transformed him to embers, and he faded by degrees until he was translucent, nearly invisible. He lay prostrate before Iagan, unable to move. Then all the pieces the spirits had surrendered began to rise.

Iagan was resplendent as his mortality crackled and fell away from him like ice. The wings knit themselves to his back, and the gorse and the shells vanished into smoke as they settled into the scepter. His blood turned gold, and his music was transformed into stars that wove into his hair. Only then did Iagan cease singing and playing. The notes suddenly turned sour on his harp, as if his fingers no longer knew them.

The instrument fell to the ground. Iagan reached down and took the scepter instead, and it changed, reshaping itself to mirror his power. Lightning flickered from it, brighter than midday.

Kae knelt. She couldn't resist the command, the way Iagan's power drew her, even though he was no longer a bard. It felt like the air was ripped from her lungs, and her eyes rolled back as she felt thunder and mist claim the isle.

Her mind was reeling, sinking into darkness.

Jack released her hand.

They were both shaking from the memory, and Jack had to close his eyes until the world stopped spinning. When he looked at Kae again, the truth was shining between them.

Iagan had never died.

He had sung his way to power and immortality, stealing fragments from the folk to do it.

He had become Bane.

CHAPTER 37

ow do I heal them?" Torin asked. He was panting as he stood before the blighted orchard, where every tree had been struck with the sickness. Hap was at his side, and for once, the hill spirit was at a loss for words. Above them, the sky continued to churn. Rain fell and thunder rumbled in the distance. Torin could feel the storm in the earth beneath his bare feet. The tremble in the ground, the shock wave of fear.

He breathed, slow and deep, and focused on the trees again.

Ever since he had first learned of the blight, standing in this very spot with Rodina, Torin had known not to touch it. He had kept his distance, his fingers curled into a fist, safe at his side. Even in the spirits' domain he had been careful.

But to heal them now he would have to stretch out his hand.

He approached the closest tree. A young maiden sat amidst its roots, apple blossoms wilted in her long green hair. She had been struck in the chest, and the violet sap, threaded with gold, oozed from her heart.

Torin knelt. He dipped his fingers into the remedy and laid them against her wound. He felt the power travel from him to her, the cold snap of the salve sinking into the fever of her blood. He watched as the light branched through her, chasing away Bane's curse. She bled and bled, until her blood was no longer rotten but pure again, shining like gold as her wound knit itself together.

Torin moved to the next spirit. He stretched out his hand and set it upon another wound, and then another, and the remedy's radiance burned through the blight, spirit by spirit. Hap walked through the orchard. The wind was strengthening, and the boughs were creaking in the gale, threatening to split and crack. Apple blossoms rained down like snow.

"Stand firm!" Hap shouted, and his voice had shifted, rising from the earth, from the grass and the loam. Torin felt the words reverberate through him as he continued to heal the orchard. "Do not bend to him. Do not yield. Stand against him. This is the end."

Torin healed the last spirit of the orchard. His head was throbbing, his mind reeling. But when he met Hap's gaze, he rose and waited.

"There are more who need you here," Hap said.

Torin hesitated, divided between his desire to return home and his obligation to the spirits. He thought of Sidra and Maisie. He thought of Adaira and Jack. Eventually, making his choice, he stepped closer to Hap.

"Take me to them."

It was almost dark when Jack finally reached the bridge that led to the castle.

When he emerged from Loch Ivorra, it had been raining. The temperature had dropped, as though winter had come early, and hail littered the bracken. Jack found his horse beneath the shuddering trees, stomping his hooves with ears pressed flat. Whatever rolled in from the northern horizon promised to be deadly, and Jack was shaky and breathless as he pulled himself up into the damp saddle.

All he could think about was Kae's memory. It flashed through his mind again and again.

As he had ridden along the wilds, the clouds had started to bruise, veined with lightning. The wind had howled and the light had faded quickly. Jack hunched low to his horse's neck, urging the gelding to go faster.

He finally understood why Bane forbade him to play, particularly in the west. Why Bane so vehemently opposed Jack's music and was threatened by it.

If Iagan had turned himself into a king of the spirits through music, then surely music could dethrone him.

By a stroke of luck, Jack had found the road, which even in the gloam would not shift or deceive him. He and the horse flew along it, kicking up mud. They had reached the city gates just before they were closed as a safety measure against the storm.

Jack trotted along the deserted streets, wending his way closer to the castle on the hill. He noted that every door was locked, every shutter bolted. There was no sign of life anywhere as the Breccans laid low in their homes, even as the wind tore at the lichen and the thatch of their roofs. He suddenly wondered what he would do if the portcullis had been lowered, preventing him from entering the castle courtyard. Where would he go?

Crossing the bridge on horseback during a storm was foolish, but Jack risked it.

The wind was so powerful that he felt like he and the gelding could be swept away, over the side and down into the moat, at any moment. Jack could feel the rattle of death in his teeth as he bared them, urging the horse to keep going, *keep going*. Soon he could see the portcullis looming in the dimness, a shadow against the dusk. And standing beneath it—preventing the gate from lowering—stood Adaira, limned in torchlight.

She looked furious.

Her expression fueled Jack long enough to canter past her, into the safety of the courtyard, before he dismounted in a heap, his legs collapsing under him. A groom rushed forward to take the horse, and between peals of thunder Jack heard Adaira give the command to drop the portcullis. The chains cranked, and the gate began to lower.

Jack turned and felt her hands on him, desperate and angry, seizing fistfuls of his tunic. Adaira was drenched, her clothes clinging to her body, her hair tangled down her back. How long had she stood in the storm waiting for him?

She pushed him across the courtyard until his back found a stone wall, and there they clung to each other as the rain fell, thick and cold.

"I was about to come after you," she breathed.

He was relieved she hadn't. He cupped her face in his hands, bending to her sharpness, her confidence.

"You were wise not to," he said. "Not in this storm."

She kissed him roughly, and he felt the edges of her teeth, the pang of her hunger and fear. It stirred him like embers blooming into fire, and he answered her, raking his hands through her hair, holding her against him.

She broke their kiss, grazing his ear with her lips. She whispered, "I'll have to punish you later, for making me worry like this."

Jack's thumbs traced her throat until her head tilted back. "What shall my penance be, Heiress?"

Adaira never answered, although he imagined he saw it in her eyes. Lightning branched overhead, dousing them in silver. Thunder shook them both, and Adaira took his hand, drawing him through a side door.

"Kae?" she asked.

There were endless inferences to be made in her uttering that one name, which conjured Iagan once more in Jack's mind, and the pain of Kae's memory.

They would have to talk about this later, behind closed doors.

"She's well," he said, following Adaira up to their room.

"We'll be late to dinner now," she said with a weary sigh, her boots leaving a trail of water on the floor. "And prepare yourself. All the thanes and their heirs are here to meet Sidra. They're lodging in the castle tonight since Innes has ordered the portcullis down."

Her statement brought Jack up short. The idea of sleeping beneath the same roof as Rab Pierce chilled him, far more than the storm.

The Breccans' hall was not what Sidra had expected. She took a moment to admire the shocking grandeur of it: the columns intricately crafted as rowan trees, the stained-glass windows, the chains of red jewels and boughs of greenery, the long table set with a feast. She let the sight of it ground her—the fragrance of juniper, the intimate flicker of candlelight, the smooth stone beneath her boots—because she didn't know what to expect tonight. And that uncertainty had her heart pounding a frantic beat.

She had made the most of the hours leading up to this dinner. But despite all her preparations, things could still go awry.

Sidra followed Jack and Adaira to the table, her guards trailing close behind. She attempted to count the nobility—all of them armed with sheathed blades—who had gathered, but she made it only to twelve before she had to shift her focus. Innes stood at the head of the table, watching her arrival. Sidra refused to be intimidated by the laird, but she couldn't deny that Innes was someone who inspired respect, even from an enemy.

She was so preoccupied by her own thoughts, wondering how offended Innes would be when Sidra enacted her plans, that she didn't realize how quiet the hall had fallen. All the thanes and their heirs were silent, watching her as she took her seat between David and Jack.

Her ankle still throbbed after she had used the salve David gave her, though she was surprised by how much it had helped with the stiffness in her joint, easing her limp. Despite the twinge of pain, Sidra held her chin high and endured the stares. The circlet gleamed on her brow.

"Thank you for coming on such short notice," Innes said, addressing the nobility. "I know this is very unexpected and unprecedented, but we are facing a new trouble in the west. The blight continues to spread, and we are at a loss to halt it and heal ourselves.

Some of you have come to me, revealing the names of your subjects who are infected, and I suspect that number is much higher than what we believe, given the shame-inducing nature of this illness. When my daughter suggested inviting a healer from the east to visit and collaborate with us for a cure, I was hesitant. Not only due to the history between our clans, but because I didn't want the east to know of our pains. But as this storm only gains strength, I must reckon with an ugly truth: the time has come to cast off our pride before it drags us down to our own graves."

She paused, looking at Sidra. She held out her hand and said, "I want to introduce Sidra Tamerlaine, Lady of the East, consort to the laird, who is renowned for her healing knowledge. She is here on my daughter's invitation and will find shelter beneath my roof. She will be with us for five days, helping to find a cure for the blight, and she and her four guards fall beneath my protection. Should anyone seek to harm her or them, they will be met with immediate death."

Sidra hadn't anticipated this speech from Innes, and she nervously rushed her hands over her thighs, feeling the vial of Aethyn hidden in her skirt pocket and the small blisters that had risen on her forefinger and thumb. She had a moment of doubt—should she nix her plans?—but then she met Blair's steady gaze. He was standing across the table from her, just behind Adaira's chair. He gave her a subtle nod of reassurance.

Innes took a chalice of wine in her hands and held it up. David followed suit, as did the others seated at the table, preparing for a toast. Sidra's hand was slick with sweat as she reached for her chalice. She gazed down at the dark red liquid, her face reflecting upon its surface. Perhaps it was all in her head and she was being ridiculous, worrying about a poisoned drink. But when she thought of her child growing within her, she knew she couldn't risk it. Nor could she risk the ones she loved fiercely at the table—Jack and Adaira, who had both declined taking the Aethyn doses as well. All three of them were vulnerable now. Sidra stood.

Her action took Innes by surprise, who looked at her with an arched brow.

Sidra smiled and said, "Thank you for the warm welcome, Laird. It is an honor to be among you and your clan, to walk the west at your side not as an enemy but as a friend. While I can utter no promise that a cure will be found, I will make the most of my time here to find one."

Innes nodded, lifting her cup to begin the toast.

Sidra dared to add, "And out of precaution, I would request that my guards serve as a cupbearer for me, as well as for my bard, Jack Tamerlaine, and your daughter, Adaira. It would be impossible for me to move forward with my collaboration should I fall prey to poison, and as Jack and Adaira are two of my closest confidants, I cannot allow them to take such a risk either."

No one moved. Sidra's words seemed to cast an enchantment over the table. Not even Jack and Adaira had known of her plans, and Adaira was the one to move first, as if she wanted to protest.

Sidra's gaze flickered down to hers. Whatever was in Sidra's eyes made Adaira shut her mouth and nod, even though she looked anxious.

A second later, Sidra knew why.

"Of course, Lady Sidra," Innes said in a careful tone, but Sidra could hear the twinge of irritation it held. As she expected, her request had offended Innes, and yet Sidra couldn't let herself worry about it, even if it did cause more trouble for her later. "Although," Innes added, "I have taken great pains to ensure this wine isn't poisoned."

"All the same, Laird," Sidra said, "my guards are willing to serve as cupbearers, and I must be entirely certain before I take a single sip."

"Then let them come forward."

Blair walked to Sidra and took the cup from her hand.

Mairead took Adaira's cup from her, and Keiren took Jack's. Sheena, the one guard who wasn't going to drink, stood beside a rowan pillar, holding Sidra's healing satchel, ready to move forward if she needed to.

Sidra watched Blair drink from her cup without hesitation.

There was no fear in him, though she didn't know if his courage came from having faced countless dangers in his life or from his complete trust in Sidra to save him if need be.

Mairead drank for Adaira. Keiren drank for Jack.

The moments felt long, hot, and tense as everyone in the hall waited. Sidra could feel the heat in her face, the perspiration shining on her skin. The Breccan nobility had stood, eager for a good view as the three guards stepped back and prepared to cut themselves and bleed on the floor.

In unison, Blair, Mairead, and Keiren withdrew the dirks from their belts and cut their palms. Their blood welled and dripped from their fingertips.

Sidra watched the blood gather on the stone floor. Her breath turned ragged when Blair's blood hardened into the telltale blue jewels. So did Keiren's. Mairead's blood flowed clean and red.

Someone had poisoned Sidra's cup, as well as Jack's.

And now two of her guards were going to die if Sidra had misinterpreted her previous studies.

There was a strange minute of calmness, as if everything was slowing down. Innes stared at the gemstones, as did Adaira and Jack. Finally, the shock broke when Innes looked at her nobles and said, in a cold, pointed voice, "Which of you did this? Who poisoned their cups?"

A medley of answers and accusations rose and tangled like smoke—"Not I, Laird!" and "It was them!"

Sidra could scarcely think straight amidst the noise. Thanes were protesting and arguing, and Innes's voice was rising in fury. The deaths of two Tamerlaines on Breccan soil would start a war—a war that neither east nor west could afford. Sidra shivered as she beheld the chaos.

She wanted to doubt herself, to regret her choice to let Blair take poison for her. But when she touched the small blisters on her forefinger and thumb, she was reminded of who she was. She knew the antidote for Aethyn, if she would only trust herself and let her knowledge and years of training flow through her now.

She turned to David, who stood at her side, solemn with dread.

"Can you bring me a small iron pot, full of water that I can boil over the fire, a knife, and a wooden board to cut on?" Sidra asked.

David nodded. He strode to the doors that fed into the kitchens, and Sidra began to drag her chair closer to the hearth.

"Let me, Laird," Blair said to her, but his voice had grown hoarse, and he grimaced as he cleared his throat, as if it hurt to speak.

Sidra studied his face. The Aethyn dose in her cup must have been potent because Blair's color had already blanched. An icy sweat was breaking out over his face.

"I need you to sit, Blair," said Sidra.

Jack had already delivered a second chair, anticipating what she would need. His expression was grim, his eyes alight with guilt as Keiren also sat down before the fire.

"What can I do?" Jack asked, desperate. "I never wanted—"

Sidra took hold of his arm. "It's all right. They agreed to do this, knowing the risks." And yet the guards' cooperation didn't make it any easier to watch their distress. She knew Jack's guilt, because she felt it too, sitting in her heart like a stone.

She held the bile down, clenching her teeth. Looking at Blair and Keiren, she thought, *You will not die. Not beneath my watch.*

David returned with three servants who were carrying the things she needed. Then Sheena stepped forward and handed Sidra her satchel of supplies. She now had everything she needed, and easing to her knees, she prepared a workstation on the floor.

But before she began, she reached into her pocket and withdrew the vial. She held it up to the light, studying how its color had changed. Before, it had been clear and odorless. But after she added a piece of fire spurge to it, a reaction had occurred: the liquid had turned blood red and warm to the touch.

She had thought of the spurge only after hearing Adaira's explanation of Aethyn's side effects, how it had turned her cold, as though ice had gathered in her veins, weakening her heart. What better way to counter poison of ice, she had realized, than with poison of fire? She had also deduced, after not seeing the spurge in David's herbarium, that it was an entirely eastern plant. It made sense now that the Breccans had failed to find an antidote to the poison that often plagued them.

Sidra opened her satchel. She withdrew the spurge, biting her lip as it burned her hand with blisters. She worked quickly, uncertain how long she had. She cut the spurge into strips and set them in the pot of boiling water, which hung over the hearth fire.

Only then did she become aware of the crushing silence in the hall. The Breccans were watching her with mouths agape, as if they couldn't believe what was unfolding. Her actions had cut down their protestations of innocence like a sword. Even Innes and Adaira were transfixed by her.

The enormity of what she was doing didn't hit Sidra until she removed the pot from the hearth and poured the essence of the fire spurge into two clean cups. She waved away the steam, which scented the air with smells like burning heather and myrtle leaves, like a midsummer bonfire. She thought, *If I am right, I will have changed the west.*

There would be no more Aethyn doses. No more pressure on Adaira to take them, then writhe on her bedroom floor in pain for hours afterwards. No more young girls like Skye dying from a nobleman's scheming for power. No more innocent guards having to risk their lives as cupbearers, far from home.

The essence was finally cool enough to drink.

Sidra took one of the cups and brought it to Blair first. She could see his strength waning, his life ebbing. She thought of how tirelessly he had served her, accompanying her on her patient visits, lifting her up when she needed it, catching her when she was weary, and taking her weight when she limped. How he had forgone a life of marriage and children to devote himself entirely to the guard and the east.

She blinked back her tears as she set the cup to his lips. "Drink, my friend," she whispered, and her prayers became a wildfire, burning through her mind.

I cannot bear to see this man die for me. Please let him live. Let me be right in this one thing.

Blair closed his eyes and weakly sipped.

Sidra coaxed him to take three more sips before she set the cup aside. She took his bleeding hand in hers. Blue jewels were scattered over his lap and winking at his feet. Sidra waited to see if she would feel his blood forming into jewels in her palm, cold and jagged.

She waited, but only his blood flowed, smearing her hand.

Blair drew a deep breath. The color was returning to his face, even though he continued to tremble from the pain. But when he looked at her, she saw that his eyes were clear.

Sidra hurried to treat Keiren next. Her heart was pounding when she saw the second guard begin to recover and she sighed. Sidra could have sworn she felt her grandmother's presence, standing behind her and watching with pride.

Then the moment ended. The nobility began to argue again, and a few of them started to depart for the doors.

Innes's voice silenced them all when she said, "No one is leaving this hall."

CHAPTER 38

With the hall doors barred and guarded, Innes ordered her thanes and their heirs to resume their seats at the table. The untouched feast had gone cold, and the candles had started to melt, the wax dripping like tears. Adaira remained standing, her attention divided between Innes, who radiated ire, and Sidra, who was gently tending to her guards. It felt as though two worlds had collided, and Adaira didn't know where her place was, whether to drift to Sidra's side or remain in Innes's shadow.

Jack also seemed caught between them. He stood near the Tamerlaine guards, but he watched Innes pace, his face drawn with uneasiness. Adaira studied him a moment, her mind reeling.

If Sidra hadn't been shrewd enough to let her guards drink first, Adaira would have lost both Sidra and Jack in one unexpected blow.

"Who poisoned their cups?" Innes asked again, stalking the table.

The thanes refused to look at her as she passed.

"We will remain here all night, and all of the next day, and the next, and so forth until one of you confesses to this crime," Innes added.

"You cannot keep us here," Rab muttered.

Innes halted. "What was that? Speak up and look at the one you address."

Rab dared to lift his eyes, meeting her steel-sharp gaze. His face was flushed, his expression sullen. "I said you cannot *keep* us here, Laird. It was only a little poisoning, and no one has died."

"The portcullis has been lowered and a storm is raging," Innes replied. "You have nowhere to go."

"What he means, Laird," Griselda, his mother, was swift to say, with a nervous flip of her bejeweled hand, "is that it might not be one of *us* who committed this heinous deed. Perhaps one of your servants did it. I did hear there was gossip in the kitchens amongst some of your cooks."

Innes set her jaw. But she turned to David and said, "Will you bring all the servants in from the kitchen?"

David nodded and left the hall for the second time that night. The guards barring the kitchen door permitted him to depart, and the minutes passed, silent and uneasy.

Adaira felt Jack's gaze. She glanced at him to meet it, and their thoughts were mirrors, reflecting the other.

What does Innes plan to do?

I don't know.

The uncertainty felt like a heavy cloak weighing Adaira down.

Soon the servants had arrived from the kitchen. They stood in a line, brows creased in confusion as they glanced at the untouched food, the thanes sitting with rigid postures, Innes standing like a statue.

"The two Tamerlaine cups were poisoned tonight," she said. "Can any of you shed light on who committed this crime?"

The servants were quiet, afraid to speak. But then one of them, a young woman with braided red hair and flour dusted on her apron, lifted her hand.

"I was ordered to do it, Laird," she confessed. "I didn't want to, but I had no choice."

"And who gave you this order?"

The woman looked to the table. She pointed and said, "Rab Pierce did."

Adaira shouldn't have been surprised. But there was a roar in her ears, a stutter in her pulse, as she looked at Rab. She wondered if she had partly brought this on herself, given the puckered scar that now marked his face and the way she had chased him down like quarry. How she had made him drink her Aethyn dose.

He was giving it back to her now, threatening two people she loved most.

Rab shot to his feet, but his face was blanched. "Liar!" he shouted at the woman. "I've never seen you before, and I would never give you such an order."

"You didn't say that last night when you were in my bed talking about how much you hate Cora," the woman replied calmly. "Or when you set the poison in my hands. When you told me all the ways you'd hurt me if I didn't do as you said and keep my mouth shut about it."

Rab continued to protest, but the more he countered her the guiltier he looked. His mother was quick to rise, trying to soothe and calm him.

"I'm sure this is just a lovers' quarrel," Griselda said with a nervous smile. "Sit down, Rab. There's no need to shout."

Innes had seen enough. Her lips were pressed into a firm line, her eyes blazing with anger. She turned to one of the guards at the door. "Bring in the chopping block. Bind their hands and ankles."

Shocked, Griselda cried, "Laird! You would take the word of this servant over *us*?"

"I would and I do," Innes said. "Now *kneel*."

There was a struggle as the guards closed in around Rab and Griselda. But both were overpowered, their wrists bound behind their backs, their ankles tied together. They were dragged to Innes and forced down to their knees.

The chopping block was brought in next. Adaira stared at it a moment before realizing that its dark stains were from old blood and its nicks had been made by blades.

Innes was about to behead Rab and Griselda Pierce, right here in the hall.

Adaira's stomach churned. She began to step back when Innes spun to face her.

"This is *twice* now that the Pierces have threatened what is yours. By law, you can take their lives for it, with my blessing." Innes unsheathed her sword. The blade was radiant, betraying its enchantment. As she gazed at it, Adaira wondered what magic had been hammered into the steel. Sweat prickled her hands as Innes offered the sword to her. "Take my blade. Enact your justice."

Adaira felt numb and slow, as though she were underwater. But she accepted Innes's sword. She grasped the cold, smooth hilt. The blade was heavy; she held it with both hands, and she glimpsed her reflection in the polished steel. She looked pale, riddled with doubt.

Innes brought Rab to the chopping block first, forcing him to lay his head on the wood.

The hall was deathly quiet as Adaira stared at Rab. He was panting, drool shining on his lips. There were tears in his eyes when he gazed up at her. Griselda began to weep.

"Cora," Rab whispered. "*Cora,* please."

She knew he was guilty, in more ways than one. And there was a shadowed, hungry side of her that wanted to see his blood spilled.

She raised the sword.

She had never killed anyone before. She had never driven a sword through a neck, and there was a good chance she was going to make a mess of it. She was angry and sad and everything in her ached when she thought about Jack in the arena with a helm locked to his face. When she thought of Torin missing, spirited away. When she imagined Sidra, dying at the dinner table by the same poison that had claimed Skye. When she thought of Sidra and Torin's child, whom Adaira longed to hold and watch grow.

Can peace be won by spilling blood? she wondered. That ravenous side of her suddenly diminished, and she was left with a strange, hollow place at her center, as if she could transform into anything.

This is not the path I want to take.

Slowly, she lowered the sword. She released it, watching the blade clatter at her feet.

She looked up, meeting the gazes of the Breccans.

"I invited Sidra Tamerlaine and her four guards to the west because I knew she could help us," Adaira began. "We are dying, stricken by a blight. We are starving, beholden to the wind. The west cannot go on like this. And when I brought one who could help us, you poisoned her cup." Adaira stared at Rab, who had closed his eyes in relief. "I stand here and ask myself 'why?' *Why* did you want to kill the Tamerlaines, who trusted us after centuries of strife? Why, if not for your own fear and ignorance? You look to the past, where there is nothing but bloodshed. You chart your present by what has been done and what has happened, as if you can never rise and break away from it."

Adaira began to walk along the table. The same path Innes had taken. She was no longer addressing the Pierces but all the nobility. Her heart was beating swiftly, but her voice was strong, chasing away the shadows of the hall.

"I ask you now to look to what may come," she said. "What do you want for your daughters and sons? What do you want for the west? Shall we continue to live in a blighted and silent land, cursed to hide our wounds and our illnesses and drinking poison and mistrust? Or can we set our fate on another course?"

She glanced at her parents. Innes and David stood together, watching her. David looked awed, and Innes looked angry. But they were both listening, waiting for her to continue.

Adaira came to a stop at the chopping block once more. Rab had sat back on his heels, and he was staring up at her.

"I ask you to lay down your swords," she said. "I ask you to lay down your prejudice and your anger and all that you have been taught in the past. I ask you to dream of an isle that is whole and thriving, but first . . . we must trust each other."

It was silent.

Adaira could feel the weight of that silence, and her doubt started to creep over her once more. Doubt and worry and that nagging feeling of being inadequate. But then she heard someone rise from the table. The clatter of a sword being cast down. Adaira turned toward the sound. One of the thanes had surrendered her blade. Then came another, and another, until the remaining twelve thanes and their heirs had disarmed themselves and knelt before her.

The gravity of what was happening struck her a moment later, seeping through her like wine.

Adaira stood with every sword in the Breccans' hall shining at her feet.

She knew Innes was displeased with her.

After the nobility had left the hall to find lodging in the castle for the night, Adaira had followed Innes to her chambers for a private conversation. She thought Innes's anger stemmed from the speech she had given, words that had poured out of her, effortlessly as breath. Words that had been hiding in her, like an arrowhead caught in her ribs. A shard of stone that she had been carrying, week after week in the west. She had never felt so light and unburdened as she did in that moment when she released those words along with the sword.

But now, watching Innes pace before the hearth, Adaira realized there was more to her displeasure than that.

"You're angry with me," she said. "Tell me why."

Innes abruptly stopped, but she was facing the fire. The light illuminated the sharp planes of her profile, the silver in her hair, the circlet on her brow. It felt unusually dark in the laird's chambers, and Adaira realized that the flames were burning low and dim. As if they wanted to extinguish.

"I don't know what I feel, Adaira," said Innes.

The sound of Innes speaking her eastern name made Adaira want to weep. She felt seen, acknowledged. She had to reach out and take hold of the nearest chair before her knees buckled.

"I'm not angry at you," Innes continued. "I simply don't know what to make of you."

"Because of what I said?"

"Because of what you didn't do."

Adaira frowned, confused. Innes turned to face her, their gazes meeting.

"You should have beheaded the Pierces," Innes began. "If their plans had succeeded, it would have caused endless strife between the clans, and it was your right to end their line. Because you didn't, however, they will perceive you as weak, and they will strike again. Next time they will take it all away from you. Do you understand? *This* was your moment to rise and show the nobility who you are, and what it means if they cross you."

Adaira finally saw the evening from Innes's point of view.

"Rise to become what?" she countered.

Innes clenched her jaw. "If you must ask me such a question . . ."

"I merely want to hear you say it."

They stared at each other, neither of them giving up ground.

Finally, Adaira decided to relent. She said, "You want me to be your heiress, and yet you are choosing to overlook the fact that I wasn't raised as you were. I'm far more Tamerlaine than Breccan in my sensibilities, and for that, I am only destined to disappoint you and this clan."

"That is not true," Innes snarled.

Adaira took a step back, surprised by the unguarded feeling in her mother's voice. Innes also seemed upset by her fraying emotions. She glanced away, seeking to compose herself.

Innes's discomfort made Adaira's heart ache for her, for all the things her mother had lost and surrendered to become who and what she was.

Was it all worth it?

"To live your life you have forged yourself to be as strong as possible," Adaira said. "You have made yourself like a blade that is hammered over fire and quenched in water. Day after day. But there is nothing weak in being soft, in being gentle."

Innes was silent, staring at the floor.

"I cannot change what I am," Adaira whispered, "no more than you can, Mother."

Innes pivoted to hide her face, but not before Adaira saw the tears in her eyes.

"Leave me."

It was an order, one that chilled Adaira with uncertainty. But she left, as Innes wanted. She walked the corridors, once again surprised by how naturally that word had emerged from her, as though she had been longing to say it for years. Years before she had even realized who Innes was to her.

Mother.

CHAPTER 39

J ack could see his breath.

It was late as he sat at Adaira's desk wrapped in a blue plaid, studying Iagan's composition again. He could still hear the notes in his mind, as if Kae's memory had become his own. He could still see the wings torn from Hinder, the gorse stolen from Whin's crown. The shells taken from Ream and the scepter forced out of Ash's hands.

If Jack had the time, he would pick apart Iagan's ballad, note by note. He would steal this music and rework it into something new and brilliant. A long, measured song that would inspire the good of the isle and the spirits. He would viciously unravel Iagan's hierarchy. With sufficient time, Jack could compose a ballad clever and well structured enough to be immortalized. But as the storm howled beyond the walls and the temperature dropped to levels so bitter it felt like deep winter, Jack knew his hour had nearly come.

He would need to play spontaneously. He would need to sing from his heart, and he didn't know what to expect.

He hated surprises and being unprepared for a task. Yet listening to the storm, he knew he had no other option but to attempt it before Bane tore every tree, every rock, every structure clean off the island.

Jack rose from the desk and reached for his harp. He stood before the hearth and began to tend to the instrument, but his hands were chilled and stiff. He knelt to feed the fire, but the flames seemed to be struggling to burn, casting only a small ring of light and warmth.

"When should I play?" Jack whispered to the fire.

There was no response from Ash, although Jack sensed the spirit was close. He was still watching the fire burn, low and weak, when Adaira stepped into the chamber. She had been with Innes, debriefing after the tumultuous evening, and then visiting with Sidra.

Jack rose to face her, cradling his harp.

Adaira looked exhausted as she walked to him. But the lines in her face eased when she saw the harp he held. It was Lorna's, the one Adaira had been tending to while she waited for Jack's return to the isle. As she reached out to lovingly trace its frame, he knew that countless memories must be wrapped up in this harp for her.

"How was your talk with Innes?" he asked, eager to touch her. He brushed her face with his knuckles.

"Fine," Adaira said in a tone that made him think it had been anything but fine. "And your hand is like ice, Jack."

"Perhaps you can warm it for me." He was about to edge her to the bed when she smiled.

"I can warm more than just your hand," she promised, but she slipped away from his touch, easing her way back to the door with a mischievous gleam in her eyes. "But you'll have to follow me, old menace."

Jack frowned. "What do you mean?"

"Set down your harp. I wouldn't want it to rust," she said, opening the door. "And make sure you have your plaid."

Intrigued, Jack relinquished his instrument and drew his plaid more closely about his shoulders. He had no idea where Adaira was taking him as he followed her through a winding array of quiet corridors. It was late, most likely around the midnight hour, and the castle was slumbering. It was also darker than Jack remembered it being here. The torches that lit the passages burned low, just like the fire in the hearth. The sight of their fading blue hearts concerned Jack, and he inwardly pleaded, *Let me have this night with her and come sunrise I'll be yours to play to whatever end.*

A foolish thing, to bargain with spirits. But Jack felt strangely desperate in that cold, shadowed moment.

"Do you remember your first night in my chamber?" Adaira said when they reached a large, arched doorway. "How you bathed?"

"How could I forget?" he drawled. "I could hardly fit in that tub."

"That's because Breccans don't bathe in their bedrooms," Adaira explained. "They either go to a loch or come here." She pushed open the door.

Jack followed her into a damp passageway. It was considerably warmer here, and the stones beneath his feet were slick. Adaira carefully led him down a winding stairwell to a chamber that opened up into a vast, underground spring, with stone pillars holding up the cave's ceiling. Torches cast faint light on a cistern, and Jack could see that there were different ways to enter it, all with stairs leading down into the water.

Adaira wasn't the only one who had thought of this place on such a long night, when the wind was icy and the fire was weak. Jack could see a few Breccans wading in the shadowy water, their voices low murmurs bouncing off the stone. Jack followed Adaira until they reached a more private area.

She began to undress without another word, carefully setting her clothes and plaid on a dry patch of stone. Jack was still trying to take it all in—he had never been in a place like this, which felt like the secret heart of the isle—and he watched as Adaira stepped into the cistern. The dark water swallowed her pale legs, and the steam rose around her. She went in deeper, soaking to her shoulders, and her moon-white hair rippled behind her.

She turned, sensing his gaze. "Are you coming, my old menace?"

He smiled, thinking that this was as close to the past as they could get. He remembered the night he had first sung for the spirits of the sea, when he and Adaira had been stranded on Kelpie Rock. Then as now, she had enticed him to follow her into the water, even though he had been terrified of the ocean.

Jack stripped, leaving his garments beside hers. He carefully took his first step into the water. It was warmer than he had imagined, and he had to stifle a groan as he sank into it up to his shoulders.

That was when he realized Adaira had disappeared. He frowned as his eyes searched for her in the dark stretch of water, the hiss of steam, the diamonds of firelight.

"Adaira?" he called, his voice echoing off the stone ceiling. He swam deeper, even though it made his stomach knot to drift so far from the safety of the steps and the fire. "*Adaira!*"

Something brushed his legs. He shrieked a curse and flailed, swallowing a mouthful of water. Adaira rose to the surface before him like some bewitching creature of the deep, eyes burning with mirth and hair shining like starlight.

Jack glowered at her, even when she offered him a smile he had never seen before. One that was sharp enough to cut him should he dare to kiss it.

"Have you no care for my well-being?" he said dryly.

"Oh, I care for it, but I also promised you a punishment," she replied, swimming backward into the dark reaches of the water.

"I must confess, Adaira, that I thought your punishment would be of a different kind," Jack said, watching her drift away from him.

"And so it will be, but first I must draw you *this* way, Bard, so the others won't be able to hear us."

He would dare to follow her for that reason alone, leaving behind the reassurance of slick stone beneath his toes, but still he hesitated, watching Adaira glide even farther away.

"Come with me, Jack." He could hear her whisper on the water, in the steam. "Come into the darkness, come into the deep with me."

He thought she might be trying to kill him, and yet he followed her, keen to reach out and touch her. That inspired her laughter, to see him treading the water with the splashing grace of a cow. But soon they had swum far enough away that the torchlight no longer limned them. There Jack paused, treading the warm water.

"I can't see you, Adaira," he rasped.

He heard a gentle splash, then startled when he felt her hand touch his arm, her fingers interlocking with his.

"Just a little bit farther," she said, tugging on him. "We're almost there."

Soon Jack saw where she was taking them. There was a crack in a stone wall, and firelight seeped out from it, beckoning them closer. He followed Adaira into the small chamber, relieved to find a torch burning on the wall and rock beneath his feet. The water, blissfully warm and clear, was waist deep, and two ledges were hewn into the stone, forming benches just beneath the surface.

Thankful, Jack sat on one and leaned back against the stone wall.

Adaira perched on the ledge directly across from his.

"How did you ever find this place?" he asked. "And who in their right mind swims with a torch all the way out here?"

"The torch never burns out," she replied, glancing up at it. "At least, it has always been burning when I've come here. I discovered this place by accident. One day, weeks ago, I came down to the cistern for a swim. I always remain close to the stairs and the door, as my parents prefer. But on that day, I decided to tread as far as I dared, to see if this water would lead me somewhere else." She paused, gazing at her pruned fingertips. "Then I saw this light shining on the water, and it drew me closer, leading me to this secret place."

Jack studied the small cavern again. It certainly was an intimate place, and he knew precisely what it was used for.

As if she had read his mind, Adaira said, "Of course, I often came here and thought of you."

His gaze sharpened on her. Her skin was rosy from the heat,

her eyes luminous. Strands of her hair floated outward, like gossamer on the water.

"And what, exactly, did you think of?" he asked.

Adaira smiled. "I thought about what a miracle it would be to get you to this little cavern, about how you would flail and protest and nearly *drown* yourself on the swim here."

Jack splashed her in the face, and she only laughed, wiping the water from her eyes.

"Then your imaginings have been accurate," he said, "but only to an extent."

"Yes," she agreed, meeting his gaze again. "I actually thought about many things when I sat here alone."

Her voice had shifted. She was no longer teasing him, and Jack felt the mood change. There was something on her mind, weighing her down.

"What else did you think of?" he asked gently.

"I thought about my fears," she said. "How every day I woke up in the west I was afraid. I think because I often felt like a stranger. Like I was losing myself or forgetting who I was. And so I would come here to swim in the warm darkness, even though it terrified me, and tell myself, *If I go deep enough, far enough, I will eventually find the edge of it. I will find the end.*"

Adaira paused, rolling her lips together. Water beaded on her face, gleaming like small gemstones. "I would find the end of my fear or finally claim it and turn it into something else. But I discovered that I could swim to the edge of the mortal realm and still be afraid."

"Give your fear a name," Jack said, remembering that Adaira had once said this very thing to Torin. "Once it is named, it is understood, and it loses its power over you."

She looked to the opening of the cavern, where the world beyond was quiet and shadowed. "I'm afraid to become the next Laird of the West."

Jack exhaled. He had been wondering about that for days now, and especially after witnessing the events in the hall that evening, from Rab Pierce's treachery to Adaira's words to the nobility, abandoned swords gleaming at her feet.

Jack couldn't help but envision her with a western crown.

"You don't want to be their heiress?"

Her eyes returned to his, wide and dark. "No. After what transpired with the Tamerlaines, *no*. I don't want to lead a clan. I don't want to carry such a burden."

"And I don't fault you for it," Jack said. "The Tamerlaines acted shamefully when you departed for the west. I'm sorry you had to experience it."

"It's not your fault, Jack," she whispered. "But now I'm in the strange position of needing to tell my parents that *I* am not the one to lead after them. And I want to have a plan in place, I want to be doing *something*. I just don't know what it is."

Jack was quiet as he considered how to respond to her.

"Months ago," he began, "when I was still teaching on the mainland, I had a moment not unlike your own when I was trying to set my course. I wanted to plan and know where I was heading. I wanted to know *exactly* how my life was going to unfold, and what my purpose would be. And yet even with the next five years planned before me, I panicked one night, lying in bed thinking about it.

"I remember staring up into the darkness and feeling the stone walls close around me. I remember trying to envision my life and what I wanted to become and being unable to picture it. But perhaps that feeling came from my subconscious sensing that my time on the mainland was nearly gone, that I would soon depart from that life and those plans, even if that felt impossible and overwhelming at the time."

Adaira was listening, her eyes fixed on him.

"I don't think you need to give your parents an answer," he continued. "At least, not for a while. But neither should you rule yourself out. Perhaps you will find, years from now, that you've changed your mind."

She nodded, but he could still see a spark of doubt in her expression.

"Do you want to come closer?" he asked, a bit gruffly.

Adaira held his gaze, and he struggled to keep his breaths steady and even. But her words from earlier were haunting him, stirring his blood. He wanted to sing them back to her—*Come into the darkness, come into the deep with me.* He wanted to find that edge with her, the edge she had spoken of, when one thing becomes another. When the superfluous at last fades away, leaving behind nothing but salt and bones and blood and breath, the only elements that matter. The edge where the very essence of each of them was found.

Adaira must have seen the desire in his gaze. She moved across the water and settled on his lap, sitting face-to-face, eye-to-eye, breath-to-breath with him. Jack had to swallow a groan. It always took him by surprise how he reveled in being this vulnerable with another soul.

He marveled at how his own heart could exist outside his body.

"You don't know what you do to me," he whispered. "By you alone I could be undone."

Adaira raised her hand from the water to trace his collarbones, his golden half coin, flickering in the light.

"I know it well," she replied. "But only because you have done the very same to me."

She kissed him, softly tracing his lips with her own, and Jack's eyes closed. He wondered if she had imagined this very thing happening when she had sat in this place alone. Then he felt Adaira's teeth nip his mouth and drag along his neck, claiming him as her own, and he followed her lead, the water splashing as he rose with her in his arms.

It had been wise of her to invite him this far into the cistern, into a cavern with only the stone walls and the water and the fire, burning everlasting from a torch. A place never touched by the moon and stars and sun, nor by the wind. It was good that she had made him tread through the deep water, nearly drowning, although Jack wouldn't have cared if anyone heard the ragged sounds she drew from him now, or the cries he coaxed from her.

He held her against the rock, her legs wrapped around his waist. He was completely lost in her, lost in what they were making together. They were reaching that edge, the place where they both melted, and he knew that she was the only one he wanted to find in the darkness. The only one he wanted to hold the shape of his soul, even with his thorns and dreams and wounds.

He trusted her entirely. And he had never trusted anyone like that before.

Jack watched the rapture flicker across her face; it stole his breath. Her fingers slid into his hair and tugged until he could hardly tell the pain from the pleasure. He gave himself up to both.

He and Adaira eventually stilled, tangled together and heavy limbed. They slid down to sit on the submerged bench again and Jack held her close, as if his heart would cease beating should distance come between them. She hid her face in the crook of his neck as her breaths slowed and the flush on her skin faded.

Jack closed his eyes, his fingertips memorizing the curve of her back. He thought, *I could live for a cold, dark eternity and never forget this night.*

He could remain like this. He could remain tucked away from the world with her; she was his sustenance and his steel, sharpening him, sustaining him. She was everything he needed, and his music was pale in comparison to her. He would choose Adaira over all others, over his craft.

The torch's fire wavered, as if it heard his thoughts.

Jack's eyes flew open. He stared at the nearly extinguished flame, and Adaira stiffened in his embrace, seeming to realize how terrifying it would be here in utter darkness.

"Jack?" she whispered, easing away to glance at the torch.

He stared at the fire until it seemed to scald his eyes, and he willed it to burn. *I am hers tonight, and you must burn until then. Burn until dawn when I can sing for you.*

The fire sparked but regained its dance, although the light it cast was much dimmer than before.

"I think it's time to return to our room," Jack said, weaving his fingers with Adaira's.

She made no reply, but she guided him quickly back through the cistern, the depths below provoking a shudder in him. As they returned to the stony bank, he saw they were the only two remaining. Everyone else had departed, and even the torches along the walls were burning low. Jack could hardly discern his pile of clothes as he emerged from the water.

He and Adaira dried off with their plaids, rushing to don their garments. The cold air was like a slap to his skin as they wound through the corridors, the shadows steadily encroaching after a few of the torches had died.

But the fire in their hearth was still alight, to Jack's relief. It had nearly burned to embers, but it was still there, just as the wind still howled beyond the windows.

He removed his clothes for the second time that night and crawled into bed beside Adaira. In the dying light, he could see his breath again like clouds.

"You're trembling," Adaira said. She traced his shoulder, the planes of his chest. "Are you cold?"

"I'm afraid," he confessed.

She drew closer, until her body absorbed his tremors, and her heat melted into him. "What do you fear?"

"I don't know what the morning will bring," he whispered. "I don't know what is going to happen when I sing against Bane."

She was silent for a moment, caressing his hair. But when she spoke, her voice was low and rich, and he closed his eyes.

"I'll be there with you, Jack. No matter what comes, I'll be at your side when you sing."

He thought about the other times he had played for the spirits. For the sea, for the earth. For the wind. Adaira had been with him, and she had been an anchor. Singing for the folk made him forget who he was, but her presence reminded him that he was mortal and dust.

He listened as Adaira's breaths deepened. Soon she dreamt, but Jack lay awake, inhaling the cold night air.

When the fire died at last, Jack knew what Ash was trying to express. Jack needed to play alone. If Adaira was with him, he would choose her. His heart belonged to her, and the fire needed his undivided attention.

Gray light began to blossom on the frosted windows.

It was time, and Jack carefully rose from the bed. As Adaira continued to sleep, he quietly dressed, drawing on a tunic, his plaid, a sturdy set of fur-lined boots. He slid his harp into its sheath and eased it onto his shoulders.

"I don't know where to play for you," he whispered as he stared at the ashes in the hearth.

When there was no answer, he worried that Ash had already fully surrendered to Bane, slipping away to a place not even Jack's music could find. But then Adaira sighed, and Jack turned to look at her.

She had stretched her hand out to his side of the bed, but she was still asleep.

He remembered something Moray Breccan had shared on the day that upended their lives. Words that had been inspired by Adaira's existence: *Appoint a person you trust to set this lass in a place where the wind is gentle, where the earth is soft, where fire can strike in a moment, and where the water flows with a comforting song. A place where the old spirits gather.*

Jack envisioned the Aithwood. It was the place where everything had not only ended but also begun. Joan and Fingal's deaths. The clan line. The spirits' freedom. Iagan's mortality and reign. Adaira's path eastward. The dwelling of Jack's father.

It called to him now.

He wrote a note for Adaira and left it faceup on her desk:

My love,
I have gone to play for the spirits. It is best that I do this alone,
despite the fact that I want you at my side. Forgive me, but I
didn't want to wake you. I hope to return soon.
Yours eternally,
Jack

He could taste a faint trace of ashes in his mouth. Jack looked at Adaira one last time before he slipped from the chamber.

CHAPTER 40

A daira woke to the keening of the wind and a cold bed. She shivered, blinking up into the gray light. She realized she had no inkling of what time it was, and she sat up.

"Jack?"

Her eyes cut through the dimness. She noticed Jack's imprint on the mattress beside her, and she traced it with her hand. There was no warmth within it; he had been gone for a while. She slipped from the bed, wincing when her feet touched the icy floor.

His boots were missing, as were his plaid and his harp. She then found his note on her desk and read it twice before crumpling it in her hand.

Adaira tore into her wardrobe and hastily dressed in the warmest clothes she could find. But she couldn't shake off the tremor in her hands, or the way her worries were unfurling, making her breath hitch.

Why didn't he wake me?

She didn't realize that the castle was completely without fire until she reached the hall. It was teeming with people, and it felt like time had been frozen in twilight. Adaira stared into the commotion, amazed when she saw that Sidra was already present.

Adaira made a beeline for her, weaving through the people who had gathered. Women with their children wrapped in plaids were eating simple fare of bread and cheese, and men were carrying in crate after crate from the storerooms.

"Sid?" Adaira said when she finally reached her. In the meager light, she saw that Sidra had her healing supplies spread on the table, close to where the poisoning had occurred the night before. She was tending to a young boy who had cut his hand, and Adaira watched as Sidra finished with her stitches.

"Oh good, you're up," Sidra said, glancing at Adaira. "Do you mind handing me that roll of linen?"

Adaira did as asked, unable to quell her shock at seeing Sidra caring for a young Breccan as naturally as if she had done it many times before. Then Adaira noticed the line of Breccans waiting to be treated by her.

"Is everyone here waiting to see you?" Adaira whispered.

Sidra finished dressing the boy's palm and offered him a smile. Without speaking a word, he jumped down and melted into the crowd.

"No, actually," Sidra said, wiping the blood from her hands. "Your mother has opened up the hall as a refuge. A few houses in the city have collapsed, because of the weather. I fear it will only get worse. There's currently talk about boarding up as many windows as possible, but then that would steal all the light we have."

Adaira chewed on her lip. "Do you know what time it is?"

"No, but I heard something along the lines of 'the bells have been dismantled,'" Sidra answered, sorting through the vials of herbs she had brought. "Again, I believe that's because of the wind."

"I can't believe you woke before me, Sid!"

"Well, without fire, it was quite cold, and I thought it best to get moving."

"I'm sorry," Adaira said, as if the fire falling to ashes was her fault. "Have you seen Jack?"

Sidra finally granted Adaira her full attention. "No, I'm afraid not."

Adaira cracked her knuckles. Again that terrible feeling was stealing over her, like a shadow she couldn't separate herself from.

"Do you need me to fetch you something to eat?" she asked Sidra. "Some tea?"

Sidra's nose crinkled. "I'm afraid there's no tea to be had without the fire."

"Ah, of course," Adaira said, but she felt a bit shaky and had to reach out to steady herself on the table.

Sidra, of course, noticed. "What's wrong, Adi?"

"Nothing. I just need to locate Jack. I'm sure he's nearby. He just . . . woke up without me, and I have no idea where to find him."

Sidra's brow furrowed. She suddenly looked pale in the dim light, as if she were thinking about the day Torin went missing. "I wonder if—"

"Where's the Tamerlaine healer?"

Adaira and Sidra both turned to see two Breccan men carrying a wounded woman between them. She was groaning and holding a blood-soaked plaid to her head. Sidra quickly called them over and cleared a place on the table.

Adaira was rolling up her sleeves to assist when she felt someone take hold of her arm, drawing her away.

"I need your help," Innes said. "One of the storerooms in the courtyard has collapsed, and the wind is about to carry off all of our winter provisions."

Adaira glanced at her mother, startled to see blood staining Innes's tunic. "You're hurt. Let me take you back to Sidra. She can heal—"

"It's not my blood," Innes said, but she sounded weary. "Others have been wounded, mainly in the city where the roofs and walls are not as stable. Your father has gone to help them, but soon it'll be too dangerous for people to cross the bridge and I'll have to order the gates to remain closed until this storm passes."

Adaira drew a sharp breath, but there wasn't time for her to ask further questions or to dwell on how awkward their conversation had been the night before. She and Innes emerged into the courtyard, where the wind was so strong it nearly knocked them off balance.

Several outbuildings had lost their roofs. The thatch had been torn away by the wind, and as Adaira cautiously stepped into the courtyard, she saw a pile of stones and timber beams, as if a giant had stomped on the buildings. Sacks of grain and crates of preserves had been crushed beneath the rubble. One bag had been torn open and oats spilled from it. The grain was carried high and away, lost to the wind. Amid the chaos and shouts of desperation, Breccans were rushing to salvage whatever they could.

The wind stung Adaira's eyes as she rushed to assist. It was no longer raining, and every bit of moisture had been whisked away by the northern gale, leaving the air cold and painfully dry. Now clouds hung low overheard, swirling in a terrifying rotation.

Adaira's fear quickened her blood. It took her a moment to find the strength to direct her hands, to begin gathering up the sacks of grain. She wondered where Jack was, if he had played yet or was about to. If his music would be strong enough to end the storm, or if it would make the tempest worse.

Back and forth she went, working shoulder to shoulder with Innes and the Breccans, carrying whatever they could save into the castle. It felt like hours passed, and yet Adaira had no sense of time. Eventually, Innes forced Adaira back into the hall.

"Drink," her mother said, putting a cup of wine in her hand.

Adaira didn't realize how parched she was until she took a sip. There were splinters burrowed beneath her skin and blisters on her heels. And yet she could hardly feel the pain in her body. Her mind was still focused on Jack.

"You said Father was in the city?" Adaira dared to say, passing the empty cup back to Innes.

Her mother was quiet for a beat as she refilled the cup for herself. "Yes."

"Is there a safe way for me to go there? You said you were thinking about closing the bridge."

"You want to go after Jack," Innes said.

"Did you see him leave?"

"Yes. I had to raise the portcullis for him, but only because he promised to bring the storm to an end." Innes drained the cup of wine and set it aside. "Come, I'll see you across the bridge."

Adaira tried to hide her relief as she followed Innes back into the courtyard. The wind was growing even stronger; they hunched against it as they shuffled across the flagstones to the portcullis gate.

A few Breccan guards were stationed in the watchtower, and one of them met Innes and Adaira, as if he had been waiting for the laird to approach. They took shelter in an alcove, protected from the worst of the wind.

"Should I close the gate, Laird?" he had to shout over the gale.

"No." Innes's voice was deep and calm. "My daughter wishes to pass."

The guard glanced at Adaira, but he didn't seem surprised. She imagined Jack had stood in this very spot not long ago, waiting to cross with his harp in tow.

Suddenly she knew exactly where he would play.

"I need to hurry," she said.

Innes looked at her in the somber light. Adaira saw that fear in her again, bright as a candle flame. A fear born of separation and loss and seasons of loneliness.

"I'll return as soon as I can," Adaira added hoarsely. "He's going to sing this storm to its end, and I need to be with him."

Innes nodded, but she touched Adaira's cold cheek with her knuckles. The affectionate gesture was fleeting, but it rekindled Adaira's courage.

"Will you ensure Sidra is looked after while I'm gone?" she asked.

"She's safe beneath my watch," Innes replied, her eyes cutting back to the guard. "Prepare her for the crossing."

The guard grasped Adaira's arm and guided her from the alcove to the mouth of the bridge. She saw a rope strung from the castle gate to the city, something to hold on to as she crossed. Even though the rope was thick, Adaira imagined how easy it would be to slip and fall, for the wind to push her over the edge and down into the dark waters of the moat.

"Tie this about your waist," the guard said, handing Adaira a shorter rope.

She did, her hands shaking with the adrenaline coursing through her. She watched as the guard secured her rope to the main one. "Don't let go," he warned her.

Adaira stepped up to the bridge. Even in the shelter of the portcullis, she could feel the pull of the wind, how hungry it was to whisk her away.

"Adaira," Innes said, her voice faint even as she shouted. "If you see your father in the city, send him back to me."

Adaira nodded.

Her heart was pounding when she took her first step onto the bridge.

Torin healed the last tree in the east. To his amazement, the remedy in the bowl never diminished. He could set his fingers into its cold light a hundred times and it would replenish itself. His relief was a balm, until he thought about Sidra and the other Tamerlaines who were infected. He realized he didn't know if this salve would heal them or not.

"Hap?" Torin said, his voice wavering.

The hill spirit stood near him. The wind was blowing relentlessly now, and the earth was groaning, shuddering beneath Bane's anger. Torin could see the threads of gold in the grass, in the trees, in the heather, and the rocks. The spirits were holding fast, resisting their king. Torin could even draw a small portion of their heady strength up through his bare feet to keep himself steady, even as the wind sought to cut him down. Despite the terror of the sky, dark and boiling with ire, Torin had faith. He had faith that the earth was resilient enough to hold against the wind.

"The time has come," Hap said. "Your realm needs you to return now."

Torin's heart hammered against his ribs. "Can you make a door for me close to Sloane? I need to go directly to the city." He needed to get to Sidra as swiftly as possible. He hadn't seen her in what felt like years, and worry laced his blood. He didn't know how much of her health the blight had stolen, how fast it had spread through her.

He was too afraid to ask Hap if he knew.

"Yes, come this way," Hap said.

Torin followed him to a hillside. A few rocks were crumbling, their pieces cascading down the slope. The grass had gone limp, and the flowers had wilted. And yet the spirits held strong, surrendering what they didn't need in order to keep what they couldn't lose.

Hap touched the earth, and a door appeared in the hillside. The same door Torin had once been bewitched by. It swung open, beckoning him again with its enchanted light.

With the bowl of remedy tucked close to his side, Torin took a step forward, but then paused to look at Hap.

"Will I see you again?" Torin asked.

Hap offered a crooked smile. "Perhaps. These days one never knows what to expect." But then his humor waned, and his eyes darkened with intensity. "I can never thank you, mortal laird, for what you have done for us. I could never repay you for your generosity. Let this hill forever stand as a testament to you."

Torin was deeply moved. He reached out to grasp Hap's forearm, pleased when Hap returned the gesture. The spirit's hand was cold and smooth. Flowers cascaded from his hair when he at last released Torin.

"Go, my friend," Hap urged.

Torin turned and stepped over the threshold. He heard the door latch, enclosing him in the portal. He breathed, tasting rich dirt in the air, feeling the dampness beneath his feet. It was completely silent here, and he didn't realize how badly his ears had been ringing from the wind until he escaped its roar.

He followed the passage, the bramble lights winking as he passed them. The earthen corridor curved; he walked a full circle back to the door, where he hesitated. What if it had all been a trick and he emerged once again in the spirits' realm? He had given the folk what they wanted and needed, and perhaps they would now laugh at his expense.

Foolish, trusting mortal.

Torin glanced down at the bowl he carried and saw that the remedy still gleamed like the moon. He released a deep breath as he opened the door.

He was first struck by how drab the world appeared. There were no threads of gold in the earth, no trace of the spirits. The sky churned as if it were about to touch the isle, and lightning flickered through the clouds. The wind howled, so cold it tore the breath right from Torin's mouth.

And yet all he could focus on was what sprawled before him. The city of Sloane was dark, as if abandoned. How much time had passed? Had a century molted its years while he walked with the spirits?

Torin ran, defying the wind, all the way to the city. The thoroughfare was empty save for the debris that the wind kicked through the streets. There were no guards, no people. No sign of life anywhere. Torin was so amazed and terrified that he came to a halt. Clumps of thatch spun around him, stolen from a roof. A plaid fluttered over the cobblestones. A few buckets rolled on their sides before splintering against a wall. Shards of glass glittered like stars on the street.

He set his eyes on the castle, which loomed in the distance, shadowed and dismal. Torin made his way to it, going as fast as he could through the treacherous thoroughfare. Soon he reached the gates, which were open, welcoming anyone and anything to step through their iron. Although, if the entire city and castle were empty, perhaps he shouldn't have been shocked, perhaps—

"Laird!"

The sound pierced Torin like an arrow. He stopped and turned, watching as one of his guards emerged from a door in the outer wall.

"Andrew?" Torin asked.

Andrew broke into a grin, tossing aside all propriety as he embraced his laird. Torin had to swallow a sob as he wrapped his arm around the guard.

He was seen and heard. He could be held. He had returned to his life and his time frame. He nearly fell to his knees.

"My laird, we weren't expecting you!" Andrew said, leaning back, wincing as the wind nearly unbalanced them both. "Here, come inside."

Torin let Andrew shepherd him across the courtyard. The moment they stepped into the foyer, Torin knew something was wrong. He blinked against the thick darkness and said, "Where is everyone? Why isn't the fire burning?"

"The fire went out this morning," Andrew explained, drawing Torin through the shadows. "In all our hearths, even the crofters'. Most people are sheltering at home, waiting for the worst of the storm to pass. Others are here. We left the gates open in case anyone needed to take refuge in the castle."

They arrived at the hall, where meager gray light streamed in through the windows.

Torin stopped, beholding the crowd that had gathered. Tamerlaines sat at the tables, close together and wrapped in their plaids. Some were trying to pass the time by talking and sipping ale or wine. Others were trying to entertain anxious children with games and stories. Some were curled up on the floor, dozing.

But everything came to a halt when the clan saw that their laird had returned.

People gathered around him with booming laughter and smiles of relief. Torin was nearly overwhelmed, feeling so many hands touch him. He clung to his bowl of remedy and searched the countless faces, looking for Sidra, for her long sable hair and amber-hued eyes. For her gentle smile and graceful hands.

He was surprised that she wasn't among them. But before he could ask for her, Andrew drew Torin to one of the tables.

"Sit, Laird. You look weary."

Torin sat.

"Would you like me to bring you something to drink? Eat?" Andrew asked. "Go and fetch the laird some boots!" someone else cried. "And a new tunic!" Another said, "There's grass in your hair, Laird. And dirt on your hands. Should I bring a ewer and a comb to you, or would you like to go to your bedchamber?"

Torin clenched his teeth. He abruptly stood, thankful when the voices fell quiet. He looked for Sidra again—she was nowhere to be found—and then said, "I'll take a cup of water. I don't need boots or a tunic. Bring me all the Tamerlaines who have been afflicted by the blight. And someone *please* tell my wife I'm here."

For a moment, uncertain looks passed among those crowding around Torin. He frowned, struggling to understand what was happening, but then the awkwardness passed and the hall was once again a hive of activity and conversation and wonder.

The table around him was cleared and he set down his bowl of remedy on it. The Tamerlaines who were sick—their numbers had grown since he had departed—came to sit before him. Torin thought it best to first attempt the healing on Sidra. She wouldn't be afraid to try, and he thought she could even lend her knowledge to help him apply the remedy. The hall fell silent again as everyone watched him, expectant.

Torin glanced at Edna, the chamberlain, who stood close to his elbow with his cup of water.

"Will you please bring Sidra to me?" he asked.

Again, that strange, terrible hesitation. Edna released a long breath and said, "She's not here, Laird."

Torin's stomach twisted. "Where is she?" At once, an image of a grave stained his mind. Freshly turned earth and wildflowers, and a headstone with her name carved across its face. He could feel the first prick of unspeakable grief mounting in his spirit.

"She's in the west," Edna replied. "She departed yesterday, with four of the best guards."

Torin gripped the back of the closest chair. He shuddered in relief, which lasted for only a breath before he demanded, "Why is she in the west?"

"She went to assist the Breccans," Yvaine said, easing her way to the front of the crowd. "Adaira wrote to her, saying they were in great need of her healing."

Torin was quiet, pensive. He remembered the conversation he had overheard between Innes and David, when they spoke of Adaira. *Let her write to Sidra.* Of course Torin shouldn't have been shocked that when asked to come, Sidra had gone willingly.

"And where is my daughter?"

"With your father at his croft."

Torin nodded. There was nothing else he could do at the moment but try to heal the ones who waited before him. His gaze touched each of their faces, his mind swarming.

Sid, what would you do? Guide me.

Among the sick were two of his guards, who now sat at the table. He decided to attempt the healing on one of them first, an older man named Ian who was a seasoned warrior.

"Come forward, Ian," Torin said.

Ian instantly obeyed. He gingerly removed his tunic, exposing the place on his body where the blight had struck him. His right shoulder was veined in gold and dappled with purple. Torin carefully touched the skin; it was soft, and he thought back on how he had healed the spirits. All the trees had suffered gaping wounds, places where their infected sap ran freely.

Torin said, "Hand me your dirk, Ian."

Without hesitation, Ian unsheathed the dirk at his belt. It was a mundane blade, just as Torin wanted. Carefully, he made the cut in the center of the blight. Ian winced as his skin broke, but it wasn't blood that dripped down his skin. It was the golden curse. Torin quickly dipped his fingers into the remedy and applied it over the open wound, smudging the thick gold. Then he waited, feeling his pulse in his ears.

He didn't know what he would do if this failed. All his hope was in the remedy.

The gold continued to weep from Ian's wound, smelling like rotten fruit and moldy parchment. It streamed down his arm and dripped from his elbow, but Torin didn't remove his hand or the salve. He watched as the light gradually chased away the last of the illness, and when Ian's blood ran red, cheers resounded in the hall.

Torin stood on the threshold, staring into the castle courtyard. The wind was still bellowing, and the clouds continued to seethe. It was a long way to the west, especially by the standards of the mortal realm. He no longer had that long-legged stride of the spirits, and yet he couldn't wait for the storm to abate.

He had healed the sickened Tamerlaines. All but one, and she was many kilometers away.

"Laird?"

He turned to see Edna behind him, bearing the leather satchel he had requested.

"Thank you," he said. He safely tucked the bowl of remedy in the pouch before strapping it across his chest. Andrew stood in the foyer, his mouth pressed into a thin line, as did Yvaine.

"Laird," Yvaine said, "let us come with you."

He shook his head. "I want you to remain here. Keep watch and be ready to assist any of our people who may need it."

Yvaine frowned. She wanted to argue with him, but after years of training at his side, she knew better. Andrew, on the other hand, did not.

"This is no weather to ride in, Laird!"

"I'm going on foot," Torin said tersely.

Andrew, Yvaine, and Edna all glanced down to his bare, dirty feet.

"Can I at least provide you with some boots?" Edna asked with a touch of exasperation.

"No," he said, taking his first step into the wind-battered courtyard.

"Will you at least take my plaid?" Andrew cried, his hands rushing to unfasten the checkered fabric. "And my sword? You cannot go into the west unarmed."

Torin held out his hands, warding off the offerings. "I go as I am. And I'll send word to you when the storm breaks. Until then, hold fast."

He left them gaping after him, but he soon forgot all about their incredulous expressions as he ran down Sloane's thoroughfare. The chimney of one cottage had crumbled, spilling stones over the road. The roof had been stripped to its timbers. Torin stopped to gaze into the house, to ensure that no one lay hurt within. The windswept place was deserted, so he pressed onward.

When the cobblestoned road turned to hard-packed dirt, Torin stopped. He could see the hill that Hap had given him, a hill that would never move or shift. A reminder that what had happened was not a dream. The wind almost knocked Torin over, and he rushed to the hill, finding shelter in its southern slope.

He didn't know how he would manage running all the way to the west, not with the wind bearing down from the north, seeming intent on driving him across the isle and into the sea.

Shivering as he crouched in the hill's shadow, Torin finally decided it didn't matter how long the journey took him. He would crawl all the way to the clan line if he had to. He took one step into the grass, then another, hunched over to maintain his balance. When the wind pushed him down to his knees, Torin cried, "*Hap! I need your help!*"

He didn't expect the hill spirit to answer so quickly, or to spare whatever power he held to shift the hills. But Torin watched as a narrow valley unfurled before him, its rising side taking the brunt of Bane's wrath.

Torin ran along the vale's grassy floor. The kilometers folded and he swiftly reached the edge of the Aithwood. He cut through the groaning trees, feeling Hap's power wane beneath his feet. When the clan line surged before him, Torin crossed it without a moment of doubt and entered the western side of the forest.

He vividly remembered Castle Kirstron, but reminded himself that he had seen it from the other side of the veil. He wasn't certain how many kilometers he needed to run before he reached the fortress, and the western half of the isle seemed to be at the mercy of the same gale battering the east. If anything the storm was even worse on this side of the clan line.

But then, as Torin began to stumble forward, he felt the ground shift again, providing him swift passage. He wondered if the spirits here had heard of his deeds. Or maybe they sensed that he carried the remedy. With no time to wonder, he decided to trust them and set off running along their sheltered routes until the city came into view.

Kirstron reminded him of Sloane—full of shadows and haunted by a sense of emptiness. Doors were bolted, and shutters were latched. Trash tumbled through the roads. Cottages on the high end of the city had crumpled into heaps.

He remembered that there had been a bridge that led to the castle. To cross the moat he wended his way to the northern edge of the city, where he finally saw some movement. Torin recognized David Breccan instantly. The laird's consort was hurrying through the streets with three Breccan guards, heading in the direction of the bridge.

Torin followed.

He soon caught a wind-blurred glimpse of the gate and the bridge beyond. It was a chaotic scene, with people being fastened to a rope and urged forward. The gates were beginning to groan and shift, and Torin quickly realized that once David passed, they would be shut.

He darted forward, slipping into the crowd. No one took note of him; there was nothing about his appearance that betrayed who he was, and when one of the guards told him to hold to the rope and draw himself across, Torin only nodded.

Crossing directly behind David Breccan, Torin kept his eyes on the consort's fawn brown hair. A marker in the storm.

The crossing was slow and perilous. No one had fastened a

rope to Torin's waist, and he had nothing but the strength in his hands and the determination in his spirit to get him safely across, one step at a time. The wind tore at his clothes and stung his eyes. But he didn't stop or slow, nor did he slip. His bare feet clung to the wooden panels beneath him.

All the same, his heart flooded with relief when he reached the castle gate and slipped beneath the portcullis. Another moment of confusion followed. More guards heaved to close the gates, which instantly shut off the channel of wind that was ravaging the courtyard. Only then did Torin sigh before realizing that Innes Breccan was standing like a pillar amidst the chaos, reaching out to grasp her husband's arm.

She looked David over. There was blood on his clothes and he was bowed down with exhaustion, but he seemed hale. Torin suddenly couldn't move, watching the emotion crease Innes's face. And then she felt his attention, for her eyes shifted and pierced him.

"Who is in your shadow?" Innes asked David in a sharp tone.

Torin felt her inquiry like a slap. His shoulders ached as he stood tall, meeting the Breccans' suspicious eyes. He knew he should speak and offer an explanation. But he was so fatigued, his voice felt lost in his chest.

"I don't know who he is," David said after studying Torin.

But the longer Torin held Innes's gaze, the more her eyes widened. She made a noise, half a snort, half a laugh. As if she couldn't believe what the wind had just delivered to her courtyard.

"Spirits strike me. It's the Laird of the East."

Sidra was grinding herbs with her pestle and mortar when the Breccans' hall fell unnaturally quiet. It was similar to the hush of a first snowfall, cold and crisp and strangely peaceful. She felt someone looking at her but didn't glance up. Countless eyes had been watching her since she first stepped into the dimly lit hall. Breccans had been observing her, some with mistrust, some with curiosity, and she had told herself she could bear it, at least for a little while longer. Until either the storm tore this castle up from its roots or Jack's song quelled it.

"Sidra."

It wasn't her name spoken into the silence that shocked her. It was the voice, beloved and deep and warm, like a summer valley. A voice she had thought she would never hear again.

She lifted her head. Her eyes cut through the twilight, through the many faces around her. Perhaps she had only imagined his voice, but her heart was pounding. People began to move, their boots scuffing the floor as they gave way to someone.

A path opened in the crowd and she finally saw him.

Torin stood mere paces away from her, tall and thin and streaked with dirt. His feet were bare, and his tunic was tattered. There was grass in his beard and blue flowers in his long flaxen hair. He looked otherworldly, and yet his eyes were fixed on her and her alone, as though no one else was in the hall. No one else in the realm apart from her.

Sidra dropped her pestle.

She ran to him, her ankle smarting in pain, but she scarcely felt it. Her movement broke whatever spell had caught Torin. He rushed to meet her, and they collided in the center of the Breccans' hall surrounded by strangers. Everything faded into oblivion the moment she felt Torin's hands touch her, the moment she breathed him in.

"*Torin*," she gasped, clinging to him.

His arm came around her, solid and possessive, and his hand delved into her hair, drawing her mouth to his. He had never kissed her like this before, like he needed something that dwelled deep within her. His kiss was hungry and desperate and fierce, and Sidra felt it curl all the way down to her toes. She could taste the loam in him—a wild, green sweetness—and she wondered where he had been. She wondered about the things he had seen, and how he had found his way home to her.

His mouth broke from hers, his breath ragged. Their gazes met for a moment before he whispered her name, kissing her brow, the edge of her jaw, and Sidra tried to hold herself together, to remain upright, as his beard scratched her skin and her heart ached with fire.

"How . . ." she tried to say, her palms rushing over his chest, "how did you know to find me here?"

Torin raised his head, leveling his gaze with hers. He kept his arm around her, his hand in her hair. "I went home first," he said. "Then I came to you."

"Alone?"

He nodded.

"How did you make it through the storm?" she whispered.

"I had some assistance," Torin said, and then he smiled. Sidra realized there were tears in his eyes, and she traced his face, struggling to swallow the knot that had risen in her throat.

"I wasn't sure when you'd return," she confessed.

"I know, and I'm sorry," he said. "You have been so brave, Sidra. You have been so strong without me, holding the clan and the east together. Let me help you now, love. Let me carry it with you again."

His words made her tremble. The weight of all the burdens she had been carrying began to lift from her shoulders, like a boulder on her back finally slipping away, and she could suddenly draw a deep breath and straighten her spine.

"Let me heal you, Sid," Torin whispered, and her world went quiet in shock.

She didn't speak when he led her to one of the chairs. But her heart had quickened, and her hands suddenly felt cold when Torin knelt before her. She remembered the Breccans then. They had gathered close to watch. She saw Innes and David among them.

But Torin remained wholly fixated on Sidra as he began to unlace her left boot.

Panic surged through her. "Torin, *wait*," she said, reaching for his hands.

He paused and then whispered again, "Let me heal you."

She didn't understand how he knew she was sick, but she nodded, even as a splinter of worry stung her heart. She sat back and let Torin untether her boot. The leather strings and tanned hide fell away, and then he gently unknotted her makeshift brace and drew down her stocking, exposing her illness to the Breccans.

Murmurs sprouted in the crowd. Sidra couldn't bear to look up until Torin reached for her paring knife on the table. Tension crackled through the air, but Innes lifted her hand, bidding her clan to stay silent.

Torin opened his leather satchel and brought out a wooden bowl, filled with a shining substance. Sidra held her breath when his eyes met hers again.

"Do you trust me?" he asked.

"Yes," she said.

"This will hurt only for a moment."

"I know. It's all right."

He still seemed to hesitate, even when he brought the edge of the knife to her calf. He finally gave her a shallow cut. Sidra bit the inside of her lip as she watched gold begin to well and drip down her leg. Torin set aside the knife and dipped his fingers into the salve. He brought it to her wound and Sidra gasped to feel how cold it was.

She bled and bled, until the gold had stained Torin's forearm and formed a pool on the floor beneath her. But then she felt it— the moment when the salve began to burn through the blight. She watched, tears lining her eyes, as the sickness was driven out of her and her blood became her own again.

Torin tenderly wrapped her wound with a strip of linen. He smiled up at her, and Sidra's chest flooded with warmth.

"Does anyone else here need to be healed?" Torin asked as he rose. "I have the remedy for the blight."

His offer was met with stone-faced silence and dark disbelief. Sidra knew there were Breccans present who were sick, and yet they kept their mouths closed. Her joy began to dwindle, watching them refuse to yield.

Torin waited, but when no one moved, he began to tuck the bowl of remedy back into his satchel. He was looking at Sidra again, his eyes tracing her every line and curve, when a voice at last broke the quiet.

"I need to be healed."

Sidra turned to see that David Breccan had stepped forward.

He removed his gloves and let them fall to the floor at his feet, revealing his afflicted hand. He held it out to the light, wholly trusting Torin.

Whispers spun through the crowd.

Torin cleaned the knife, took up the remedy, and went to David.

And Sidra watched in wonder as Torin healed the west with his hands.

CHAPTER 41

J ack had passed through Spindle's Vale with little trouble, the earth spirits having risen to help him travel swiftly in the storm. As he emerged from the valley, he knew the Aithwood was near, looming in the distance. He could almost see its shadow in the gloam when lightning branched overhead, illuminating the low, boiling clouds.

A bolt struck the tree in front of him, a mere six paces away, and Jack jumped back in shock. He watched in horror as the tree split in half and fell with a tremendous crash, the blaze washing over him. As the lightning prepared to strike again, Jack realized that Bane had seen him. Bane knew exactly where he was, and if he didn't move and find shelter, he would be sliced down before he ever had the chance to sing.

Jack broke into a frantic run.

His knees throbbed from the impact, and breath cut his lungs like a blade when the lightning flashed again. He was about to be struck; he could feel it in the air around him, how it tingled and hissed. Bane was about to kill him, and Jack knew he couldn't outrun the northern wind. Not in the open, stranded between the mountains and the forest.

Just before the lightning could strike, heather grew thick and tall around Jack, its purple blooms defying the wind. It was like a shield and Jack dropped to his knees and crawled beneath it, sheltered by its shadows.

Bane's lightning hit only a few meters behind him. The heather shuddered but kept growing, wide and thick, drawing up the meager magic it could find in the earth. As Jack crawled through it, Bane kept hurling his lightning, seeking to hit him in the expanding thicket.

Panting, Jack paused. He had lost his bearings; he didn't know in which direction the forest lay, and the sweat dripped from his chin as he pressed close to the earth.

He wondered how he ever thought he was brave enough or strong enough to sing against Bane. All of this felt like some foolish, unattainable dream, and he was thinking about turning around when he saw a face form in the heather. It was a spirit—a woman with pointed ears, sharp teeth, long bedraggled hair, and cat-slit golden eyes. She looked frail, with lines grooving her ethereal face, and Jack realized she was giving everything she had within her to protect him, to turn against her king.

"The forest lies ahead of you, Bard," she whispered. "The trees are stronger than me and can offer you better shelter."

Jack hesitated.

But then she winced and said, "*Run!*"

He lurched upwards and sprinted, just as Bane struck the spirit in the heather. Jack wanted to stop and turn around, but he heard her dying scream. She had given herself up for him, and he could taste the burning heather on the wind. The emotion finally slammed into him when he raced into the shadows of the Aithwood, where the high, interlocking boughs hid him from Bane's sight.

Jack came to a stop and reached out to steady himself on a tree. Gasping, he bent over, struggling to regain his composure. Tears stung his eyes and welled in his throat. He didn't know how he would sing when he felt so battered and had nothing to guide him but his own heart.

His thoughts broke when Bane struck again. Lightning hit an oak tree not far from Jack, and the impact forced him to swallow his tears and press onward. He needed to find shelter. A place where he could rest a moment and catch his breath. Where he could take his harp into his arms and set his fingers on the strings.

Jack looked into the dense, dark forest.

He ran to his father's house.

He was afraid that he would stand at Niall's door and knock, over and over, only to be ignored. Jack didn't know where this fear came from, only that it had seemed written in his bones since he was a boy. It was strange that knowing his father's name now, and where he dwelled, only heightened his worry—so much so that Jack froze in the kail yard when he was halfway to the door.

He stared at the cottage.

The plants whipped around him in the garden, breaking in the rush of storm. The trees groaned as the scent of scorched wood began to ride the wind. Jack knew he was exposed. He was standing in the only clearing in the entire Aithwood, in his father's front yard. Bane was striking only kilometers away, hunting him. But Jack was too afraid to move forward.

The front door swung open.

Niall appeared on the threshold, as if he had sensed Jack's presence. They stared at each other, sharing a moment of shock.

"Jack?" Niall finally called to him.

"I need . . . to shelter somewhere," Jack said, stumbling over the words. "I didn't know where else to go."

"Then come inside." Niall beckoned him. "Before the storm carries you away."

Jack moved forward, relieved. He stepped into the cottage, surprised by how different it felt with the fire extinguished and a storm raging overhead. It was dark, but the cottage was warm and felt safe. Jack sighed. He was sliding the harp from his back when he saw Elspeth approach him in the dimness.

"I was worried about you, Jack," his grandmother said, hands clasped. "But Niall told me what you did for him."

Did for him? Jack wondered, glancing toward Niall, who stood nearby. His father was staring at the wall, hands shoved into his pockets, obviously embarrassed.

"I—" Jack began to say, but his voice was drowned out by the thunder booming nearby. The floor shook beneath their boots. Dishes rattled on the kitchen table. A candlestick fell from the mantel. Herbs wept dust from the rafters.

For a moment, Jack couldn't breathe. Fear wrapped around his heart again as he thought of Bane striking down every tree in the Aithwood, determined to find him. Of how likely it was that the king would soon remember Niall's cottage. Jack couldn't bear for something to happen to his father and his nan.

"It's good to see you again, Elspeth," Jack said. "But I'm afraid that the northern wind is hunting me, and I have only brought trouble to you both."

Now Niall looked at him, brows slanted.

"What trouble?"

Jack met his father's gaze. "I need to sing for the spirits, and Bane wants me silent. Again, I'm very sorry for bringing this to your door, but—"

"Tell me what I can do," Niall gently interrupted. "How can I shield you? What do you need?"

Jack was so surprised by Niall's fervent offer that he merely gaped at him. But then his memory stirred, like an ember winking from ashes. Jack remembered the words he had once said to his father, only a few nights earlier.

Let us be your shield and your armor.

Jack's confidence began to return. His fingers twitched, eager to pluck notes from his harp. He began to see the ballad he would sing to undo Iagan's hierarchy—to sing the fire, the water, the earth, and the wind free—and he felt the words rising, filling his lungs with forest-sweet air.

"If you two would follow the river downstream and stay with Mirin and Frae during the worst of the storm," Jack said, "it would ease my mind."

A pained expression flickered over Niall's face, prompted perhaps by Mirin's name, or Frae's, or by decades of longing. Or perhaps he was realizing that he was moments away from reuniting with the ones he secretly loved.

"Are you certain, Jack?" Niall asked. "I can stay at your side if you need me to."

His offer made Jack want to weep. But he only smiled, his confidence still growing, even as the thunder boomed louder, closer. He was ready to sing.

"Thank you," Jack said, "but I need to play alone."

Niall nodded, raking his hand through his hair. "All right. Let me pack a few things, and then we'll head east."

Jack set his harp on the table as his father and Elspeth rushed to fill two satchels. The walls of the cottage started to groan. Thatch was being torn away from the roof. Jack could see the lightning flash through the slats in the shutters, and he drew a deep breath, knowing the time had almost come.

"We're ready," Niall said. He cracked open the back door, standing in a slender shaft of light.

Threads of cold wind snuck inside, lifting the hair from Jack's brow as he embraced Elspeth.

"Sing us to peace, Jack," his grandmother said, laying her weathered hand on his cheek. "If there is anyone strong enough to do so, it is you."

She stepped back to let Niall take her place.

Jack was racking his mind, trying to think of what to say, but Niall spoke first.

"I don't understand fully what you intend to do, or what is about to be required of you. I won't beg you to cast aside this duty and come with us, because I see the mark of a higher calling within you. A flame that will always burn, no matter where you go."

Niall fell quiet, but he smiled. And Jack finally saw a shade of himself in his father. The smile he had stolen from Niall.

"But I cannot let you go without telling you that I was proud to call you mine then," Niall whispered, "even if only your mother and the spirits could stand witness. And I am proud to call you mine now."

Jack breathed in his father's words. They calmed his heart and steadied his resolve. When Niall kissed his brow, Jack closed his eyes. Before he was ready for it, the warmth of his father's presence faded. Niall escorted Elspeth through the back door, and Jack followed them, as if bound to their shadows. He came to a stop in the kail yard and saw the trees creaking and groaning around the clearing, their branches stripped bare of leaves.

This is the end, Jack thought, watching Niall and Elspeth walk downstream until they disappeared from view. *An end and a beginning.*

Jack returned to the cottage and latched the door. Then he slid the harp from its sleeve and looped its strap over his head. The instrument fit snugly against his shoulder, and he was thinking of his notes and how he would begin the ballad when he saw a golden brightness seeping through the shutters.

He realized that the lightning was no longer striking. The thunder had gone silent. And yet something brilliant was devouring the darkness.

Jack hurried to the front window and opened the shutter. He could feel the heat like a sunburn on his skin and he stared numbly into the burning woods. He watched as the fire grew higher, wider, driven by the wind. The flames crackled close to Niall's yard, preparing to consume it and Jack whole.

Adaira thought the wind would tear her apart. She crawled along the vale, desperate to find purchase with her hands. She could scarcely see a stone's throw ahead; the world was nothing more than a blur of indigo and gray. Bane continued to blow, raking his fingers through her hair, drawing the breath from her mouth, threatening to spin her head over foot.

Adaira clenched her teeth as she felt herself slipping. The wind was about to pick her up and hurl her away. Desperately, she dug her fingers into the loam.

Help me! she wanted to cry to the earth. To the grass and the heather and the hills. *Help me find him.*

She held fast to a rock, unable to stand or move forward. Clinging to it, suspended in time, she worried that she would never reach Jack. That she would die alone. A prisoner to the wind.

But then she opened her eyes, saw the deer trail in the bracken, and realized that this place looked familiar. Adaira began to follow the winding path, which led her to a hill. Her breath caught when she recognized it.

This was the burrow Innes had once shown her. A place to shelter her when she was in need.

Adaira stumbled forward and found the rock in the hillside. The lintel came to life, and the door appeared, hidden beneath tussocks of grass. Adaira opened it, eager to escape the storm.

She slipped inside. Even here there was no fire, and no sparking one with an enchanted blade. She left the door open so she could have a small vestige of light.

She sat on the floor, ears and cheeks burning from the gusts. She drew her knees to her chest, trying to ease her tremors.

Eventually, she closed her eyes, at an utter loss as to what to do.

Adaira didn't know how long she sat there, frozen and forlorn, when she felt a shadow drape over her. Someone was standing just beneath the burrow's lintel. With her eyes still closed and her heart becoming wild and frantic, she reached for the dirk at her belt, preparing to open her eyes and *strike,* when she felt a hand grip her forearm. A hand with long, sharp-nailed fingers.

Adaira startled and glanced up. It was Kae. The spirit's eyes were wide with concern, but her face expressed determination, and it suddenly occurred to Adaira that Kae could stand against the storm. Her remaining wings were like a shield, dividing the wind with a hiss.

She hauled Adaira to her feet. Together, they moved through the desolate valley, pressing east. They felt trapped in a dreamscape, Adaira taking shelter beneath Kae's wings. Then Adaira saw something luminous and mesmerizing in the distance. At first, she had no idea what it was, but then she stopped upright, tucked close to Kae's side.

"*Kae,*" Adaira breathed, stricken.

Kae shuddered in response.

The Aithwood was burning.

Jack knew Bane was using the fire against its will. He knew Ash was held captive and beholden somewhere within its wild burning.

Jack opened the front door.

He walked through the kail yard, past his father's gate. He didn't want this place to burn. And yet the fire was coming, creeping closer, destroying tree after tree and the spirits that dwelled within them.

Jack stared into the flames. He thought he saw Ash, etched in blue and gold, crawling along the forest floor, weeping.

He began to play his harp and sing for the fire, taking the notes Iagan had once sung and undoing them, but soon the heat from the blaze was too much for him. As Jack walked toward the river, he continued to sing and play, the wildfire following as if it were still under Bane's control, but it spared Niall's cottage and yard.

The river's rapids ran cold and clear. Jack stood in them and began to sing to the spirits of the water—the lochs, the streams, the rivers, the sea. Again he unraveled Iagan's ballad and sang instead for the good of the folk, remembering how it once had been in the days long ago. As his voice and notes rose and fell, a contrast to the malevolence of Iagan's music, he looked down and saw the bloodthirsty river spirit lurking in the currents. She had blue-tinted skin, milky eyes, and a grimace made of needle-like teeth, and she was listening, entranced by his music. And yet the fire was still burning. It crossed the riverbed, and Jack could feel the temperature of the water gradually increasing.

"Keep going," the river spirit hissed at him, just before he was forced by the boiling water to step onto the opposite bank.

Keep going, even though he was entirely uncertain if his music was accomplishing anything. Bane's hierarchy seemed unchanged, remaining intact as a web, but Jack persisted, weaving through the trees, heading to the clan line, still singing and playing. He walked along the edge of the territory and beheld both east and west as he sang for the spirits of the earth, the trees and the hills, the heather and the rocks, the wildflowers and the weeds, the mountains and the vales.

Jack began to feel it then—the power gathering beneath his feet. The streams of gold, the rivulets of magic. His music was drawing it up and into his blood like a tree draws water from its roots. Suddenly he felt as if he could sing for a hundred days, a hundred years. His voice was deep and strong, cutting through the storm, and the notes fell like sparks from his nails as he plucked the strings faster and faster.

The wildfire still followed him, vibrant with heat, but Jack had no fear of it. It was like a cloak, trailing behind him, and he knew Iagan's power was almost broken. Now was the time to play for the wind.

Jack dared to undo the binds on the southern wind. The eastern wind. The western wind. As he sang, lightning struck erratically around him. The bolts sliced trees down to the ground, splitting open their resin-stained hearts. Trees so old that they must have held all the secrets of the isle. Their spirits gasped and died into smoke.

Jack continued to sing, even as the ground shook and the wind roared. He knew the spirits were giving themselves up to protect him, and he simply needed to *hold on* and reach the end. He continued to breathe in the magic the west gave to him, until every bone and vein felt illuminated, as if he had swallowed a swath of stars from the night sky.

He suddenly couldn't remember his name, or where he had come from. All he knew was the crackling wildfire, spread like a robe behind him . . . the trees with their ancient faces and stories, standing around him like courtiers, absorbing Bane's wrath to protect him . . . the flowers, blooming at his feet as if to welcome him . . . the rain beginning to fall, tasting like the sea.

But somewhere between the notes he played and the words he sang was a woman with eyes blue as the summer sky, and hair the shade of the moon. A woman with a scar on her palm that matched his own, whose smile made his blood quicken.

Who is she? he thought, distracted by the fleeting glimpses of her when he closed his eyes. He wanted to chase her into the darkness, to reach out to touch her skin. His hands suddenly ached as he continued to pluck note after note. He slowed his playing, distracted. He wanted to let those scars on their palms align, as if they would unlock a secret between them. . . .

Lightning struck in front of him. The white heat stung his face, and he winced, eyes flying open. The harp flared unbearably hot against him. But Jack had only one more stanza to sing.

He pressed forward, walking along the clan line, over the scorched flowers and earth. Jack began to sing down the northern wind.

Wings beat through the boughs of the trees, flashing with color. The temperature plummeted, and the light dimmed until eventide seemed to have descended.

Jack knew Bane had materialized. But he waited until he saw the northern king's lambent eyes in the darkness between the trees. He held a lance flickering with lightning in his hand.

Jack waited until the king had stepped forward to fully face him. He was just as Jack remembered. Forged from great height and white skin, his long hair the color of faded gold, like watered-down ale. His crimson wings caught the frail light, casting a red hue on his silver-linked armor. A chain of stars crowned him.

But despite his immortality, Jack could still see a trace of Iagan.

The man he once had been, as if reigning for centuries and never dying still couldn't wash away that mortal shadow.

"Lay down your harp," Bane said, but his voice was weak. "Lay down your harp and I will spare you."

Only then did Jack grant the king a sharp-edged smile. He resumed his song for all that Iagan had once stolen. Torn wings and brilliant blooms of gorse. Broken, iridescent shells and a scepter of fire.

The spirits came unbound. They shed the weight of Iagan's cruel ballad, and the world felt brighter, starker, overwhelming for a blazing moment.

Jack watched as Bane jerked in pain. The wings on his back came loose, falling away. The lightning in his lance went dark, crumbling into ashes, gorse, and shells.

"My song," Bane said, his voice feathered with agony. He took a step closer to Jack, then another, the earth quaking beneath his feet.

Jack drew a ragged breath, tasting the smoke and the fire and the cadence of his notes. He sang until Bane was looming over him, staring down at his hands and his harp.

Then Jack fell silent. Gazing up at the king, he noticed the cracks in Bane's skin, as if he were made of ice. The stars in his hair were beginning to drift away.

"You stole my song," Bane said. "You stole my song and remade it, and so you have stolen my crown."

The stars that had once graced his hair now hovered in the space between Jack and Bane, who suddenly gasped and fell to his knees. More cracks raced across his skin, exposing the shadows within him. Indigo and gray and cold as midnight in the north.

Music had once granted him his power. Music now stripped it from him.

The stars were gliding closer. Jack didn't dare breathe as they began to weave their blue light into his hair. He held his harp and stared down at Bane as his face finally fractured. The northern king shuddered and turned into dust.

Jack watched as the northern wind died at last.

Adaira walked the clan line. She could hardly see through the haze of the smoke, but she followed the promise of fire, its light beckoning her closer. The trees around her were silent and still. The air felt thick and heavy, and she hurried, shivering with apprehension.

Kae was following close behind her until she gasped.

Adaira turned, prepared for anything. But she didn't expect to see Kae's wings flare outward, fully mended, or to see Kae's eyes widen as she looked up to the sky. The clouds were breaking and the sun was beginning to stream down.

Kae exhaled and melted into the light.

Her disappearance unnerved Adaira. Not knowing if Kae had simply returned to her realm or been vanquished, she hurried onward.

She could soon hear the crackle of fire burning the forest. She could feel a wave of heat.

Through the trees, Adaira saw Jack.

He stood on the clan line, harp in his hands. Fire was burning behind him, dangerously close, as if he were a moment from igniting. Stars crowned his brown hair, and he was gazing down at the ground before him, as if he saw something she couldn't.

She dared to step closer, her heart pounding. He must have already sung his ballad without her there, and she didn't know what had happened.

A twig broke beneath her boot.

His head snapped up. His eyes were dark and uncanny, as if he were looking through her. Adaira came to a halt, realizing there was no recognition in his gaze. He saw her but didn't know her, and she stretched out her hand.

"Jack," she whispered.

He drew a sharp breath. She knew the moment he recognized

her, because his face creased in both relief and agony, as if her voice had woken him from a dream.

"*Adaira,*" he said, stepping toward her. The harp tumbled from his hands, landing on the ground with a metallic clang that made Adaira wince. Jack had never treated his instrument so carelessly.

He was reaching for her, desperation marring his countenance, when the fire surged. The flames came between them, blue-hearted and jagged, and Adaira had no choice but to stumble away from the blistering heat. It was so bright she closed her eyes, sweat beading her brow and dampening her clothes.

She knelt on the clan line, hands curled into the soil, waiting for the fire to ease. When the heat subsided, she opened her eyes. The flames had extinguished themselves, and the forest was laced with smoke.

"Jack?" Adaira said, rising. She coughed on the sharpness of the air and pressed forward. "*Jack!*"

She hurried to the place where he had stood. She searched through the smoke, through the embers that smoldered like crushed rubies on the loam. Her fear was suddenly a claw tearing through her, and she choked back a sob as she looked for his burned body on the ground.

There was no sign of him. No trace of where he had gone. There was only ash and a scorched line in the ground, the boundary marking where the fire had ceased burning. Then she saw something glimmering, something whole and unscathed amidst the smoking ruin.

Adaira froze as she gazed down at it.

Jack's harp.

CHAPTER 42

When the wind first started to blow from the north, Frae had been anxious. She and Mirin had bolted the shutters and harvested the last fruits from the garden, but her mother had been calm, making tea and weaving at her loom as if it were any other day.

"Don't be afraid," she had said with a smile.

Frae had tried to find the courage her mother possessed, but then the wind had started to howl. The walls shook, and the doors rattled, like someone was trying to get in. Wind hissed through the cracks, cold and relentless, and then the fire in the hearth had gone out. So had the rushlights, until no flame burned against the shadows in the house.

Frae had been terrified then, but Mirin had still spoken calmly to her.

"The storm will soon pass, darling. Here, come rest in the bed beside me, and I shall tell you a story."

Frae had removed her boots and done as Mirin bade, settling next to her mother's warmth in the dark bedroom. But Mirin's voice had been hoarse and strange, as if it were fading. Unable to finish the tale, she said, "I think I need a little sleep, Frae."

Frae had listened to her mother's breaths deepen as she drifted into slumber. While Mirin slept, Frae remained awake, staring wide-eyed up at the roof, expecting it be ripped away any moment by the wind.

"Mum?" Frae had said, unable to bear her worries alone. "Mum, wake up."

Mirin hadn't responded. Frae had called louder, shaking her mother's shoulders. But Mirin was lost in a deep sleep, and her breaths were slow, labored.

She needed her tonic. The tonic would help her.

Frae had sprung from the bed before remembering . . . there was no fire. She wouldn't be able to brew her mother's tonic. She had stood in the frigid room, staring at the darkened hearth, staring at Mirin's loom, staring into the unknown.

She had never known such fear before, and it rooted her to the floor. Her quick, shallow breaths almost felt like she was not breathing at all, as though an iron hand gripped her heart. Frae wished Jack was there to help her. To tell her what to do to save their mother.

She was shivering, trapped in her terror, when a knock sounded on the front door.

Startled, she had a moment of panic. Who would be visiting at such an hour? During the worst storm Frae could ever remember?

She cowered, too frightened to answer. But then she thought, *What if it's Jack, or Sidra? What if someone has come to help?* Frae rushed to the door, unbolting it with icy hands.

She was surprised to find a red-headed man on the stoop, a blue plaid draped across his chest. At his side was an elderly woman, squinting against the wind. Frae blinked and stepped back in fear, but then she realized she had seen this man before. He had once stood in the backyard, protecting her from a raid. He had been dragged into the house as a prisoner, and he had wept her mother's name.

"May we shelter with you, Frae?" he asked.

She nodded, uncertain how he knew who she was. And it was strange how relieved she felt the moment the man and the old woman stepped into the cottage. She was no longer alone, and even though they wore blue plaids, she trusted them both.

The man had to help her latch the door against the gust. After that, she didn't know what to say. There was no fire, no tea, and she gazed up at the man, dimly discerning his face in the meager light.

"Is your mum home, Frae?" he asked, and Frae could tell he was looking for her.

"She's sick," Frae whispered.

She heard the man inhale, as if her words had cut him, like a knife. "Can you lead me to her?"

Frae guided him to the bedroom. It was still very dark, but she could hear Mirin's labored breaths and led the man toward her. Frae watched as he sat on the edge of the bed.

"Mirin?" he said, his voice deep and gentle. There was no answer. He called her again, urgently. "*Mirin*, open your eyes. Come back to us."

Frae hoped his voice would rouse her, but Mirin continued to sleep.

"I think she needs her tonic," Frae whispered, crestfallen. "It's the magic, making her sick."

The man shifted to glance at her. "Can we make it without fire?"

"No."

He was quiet for a long, terrible moment. But then he turned back to her mother, and Frae could see only his hair, gleaming in the twilight.

"Come, lass," the elderly woman said, taking Frae's hand. "I've got some ginger cake set out, and a book eager to be read."

Frae joined the woman on the divan. They sat close together for warmth, and when the woman offered Frae a slice of rich, fragrant cake, Frae accepted. Mirin would probably scold her for eating food from a Breccan stranger, but Frae, finding comfort in its sweetness, devoured it in just a few bites.

She saw a book laid open before her, a book she had never seen before, and she thought it must belong to the woman.

"What is your name?" Frae asked.

"My name is Elspeth," the woman said. "My house isn't far from yours."

"Do you live up the river?"

"Yes."

Frae imagined it—the river connecting her and Mirin to Elspeth. She glanced down at the book and asked, "May I read it?"

"I hoped you would, although the light is quite dim in here," said Elspeth. "I don't want you to strain your eyes."

"It won't strain them. Mum says I have very good eyesight." Frae set the book on her lap and read aloud through the gloom. Soon she was entranced by the story, and her worries slipped away—her worries about Mirin, about who the red-headed man was to them, about the storm. Her worries about Jack ever returning to them.

Later, she would wonder which came first: the storm breaking or the fire returning. She couldn't be sure—perhaps they happened simultaneously. But suddenly the flames blazed in the hearth with a crack, and the rushlights found their flames and burned brightly on the table. The wind abated, and sunlight began to stream in through the cracks in the shutters.

Frae gasped. She was gazing at the fire in wonder when she heard footsteps behind her.

"Frae?" the man asked. "Can you help me make your mother's tonic?"

"Oh yes!" she cried, carefully setting the book aside. "Here, I'll show you how it's done."

He watched attentively as Frae set a kettle to boil and gathered Mirin's herbs in the strainer. The fire was burning so brightly that the water boiled in a matter of moments, to Frae's immense relief, and she quickly steeped the leaves in it.

"I'm not sure how we'll get her to drink it," Frae said after she had poured the pungent brew into Mirin's favorite cup.

The man took the cup from her and carried it into the bed-chamber.

Mirin still slept, her dark hair pooled around her, gleaming with silver threads at her temples. There were purple smudges beneath her eyes, and her face was ashen. Frae thought she looked very ill, almost as if she would vanish when evening came. She wrung her hands for a moment before climbing onto the mattress.

She sat on one side of Mirin, the man on the other, and she watched as he dipped his fingers in the tonic, then let it drip between Mirin's parted lips. Frae thought that was strange at first, but she saw how persistent and careful he was. Soon Mirin had swallowed countless drops from his fingers, the color was returning to her face, and the pattern of her breathing had shifted.

Frae would never forget the moment her mother opened her eyes and saw the man, sitting next to her. She would never forget how Mirin had smiled, first at him and then at Frae.

Frae had always wanted to know what magic felt like. She imagined she had grasped it in her hands sometimes, when she harvested wildflowers from the valleys or drank from one of the trickling pools. When she looked up at the stars on a moonless night. But now she knew.

She felt the magic, gentle and soft, when she took Mirin's hand and grinned.

"How did you know?" Sidra asked, caressing Torin's hair. "How did you know I was ill?"

In the privacy of her chamber, deep in the Breccans' castle, they lay entwined in her bed. It had been hours since the storm had broken and the sun had emerged, illuminating the west. Torin and Sidra had filled those hours working tirelessly alongside David and Innes—healing those who had been injured or afflicted, moving rubble aside, making repairs. They had worked shoulder to shoulder with the Breccans, and no one had been opposed, or thought it strange. No, it almost seemed as if it had always been this way, one clan aiding the other.

It was humbling to know that it was the blight and the wind that made their cooperation possible.

When the sun had warmed the afternoon air, Innes had sent Torin and Sidra up to her chamber to rest before dinner that night. They were to dine with the laird and her consort and with Adaira and Jack, as soon as the two returned. Sidra didn't know what this dinner held, but she hoped that it would mark the beginning of something new. That sharing this meal would forge an understanding, and maybe even a friendship.

Torin shifted closer, his skin warm against hers. They were both filthy—there was dirt beneath her nails and grime in her hair—and yet Sidra hadn't cared. She had unwound from her clothes and laid down, exhausted until Torin had joined her beneath the blanket.

He gazed at her a moment. His irises were blue as cornflowers, with an inner ring of brown. The color of sky and soil. She noticed that a few flowers were still hiding in his hair. She thought they suited him and let them be.

"You couldn't see me, but I was with you, Sid," he said, tracing her arm. "Even from the other side, I could see you vividly."

She mulled over that, wondering if she had ever felt his presence. Maybe once or twice, she realized. Whenever she felt a draft in the castle.

"I was at a loss on how to solve the riddle," he continued. "A riddle that would give me the answer to the blight. And so I watched as you prepared salves and healed your patients, thinking, if I paid close enough attention, I would find the answer in your hands."

"And did you?" she whispered.

"Yes." He smiled, linking their fingers together. "And Maisie also helped."

Sidra listened as Torin told her everything. She was swept away by his story, by the riddle and his plight, by the flowers he gathered and his failed attempts. By a hill spirit named Hap, who had become his friend in adversity.

"There were quite a few moments when I didn't think I would

find the answer," he confessed. "I think I would still be in the spirits' realm, stranded and adrift, if I hadn't realized that you had been affected by the blight." He was quiet for a beat as he touched the black tangles of her hair. "There were some moments when I wondered why you didn't tell me, and I ached over that. And then I realized that you were doing all that you could to save us, and I should have been ready and eager to work alongside you to find the answer."

Sidra briefly closed her eyes, overwhelmed by his softly spoken words. "If you saw that I was touched by the blight," she began, gazing at him again, "then did you also see—"

She didn't have time to finish. Torin's hand had shifted beneath the blanket, coming to rest on her belly.

"Yes," he said with a smile that crinkled his eyes. "Another reason why I was so desperate to come home to you."

Sidra laughed, a breathless sound. "I'm still in a bit of shock, Torin."

"As am I," he agreed, his voice warm with mirth. "Although I couldn't be more pleased, Sid. To make a child with you." He shifted so that he was on top of her, keeping all of his weight on his elbows and knees, as if he worried he might crush her. "I hope the bairn has your eyes and your smile, your laughter and your courage. Your skills and your patience and your kindness." He kissed her throat, just above the pulse of her heart. "I hope our child inherits all of your traits and only a few of mine."

"Half of me and half of you," Sidra insisted. "Until they become their own person."

Torin gazed down at her. She thought she saw pride in him, and maybe a hint of fear. She added wryly, "Do you think Maisie will be happy with the news?"

He chuckled. "She will no doubt be *thrilled*. You and I will have our hands full, Sid." But then his smile faded, and Sidra saw another light reflecting in his eyes.

She reached up to touch him, and Torin's face furrowed, lined in what could have been pain or pleasure.

"I don't want to hurt you," he said. "Or the bairn."

"You are not going to hurt me, or the bairn," she replied, drawing him closer.

They gasped as their bodies joined together. She knew it had only been a few weeks since she had felt him inside her, but they had been divided by realms. They had been weeks when she had wondered if she would ever hold him or see him again. If she would ever feel his breath glide across her skin or taste his mouth with hers or hear his voice in the dark.

She was home with Torin. She may have been in the west, with sunlight streaming in through the window, but she was home in his arms. She had never felt safer, or more deeply known and loved as he whispered her name.

And Sidra watched the flowers drift from Torin's hair.

Adaira carried Jack's harp over the western hills. The sky was a brilliant blue above her as the clouds dissipated in the sun. The trees had been stripped of their leaves in the storm; their branches stood stark in the afternoon light, casting crooked shadows on the grass. The heather had been flattened, and the wildflowers broken. And yet, with each moment that passed, the earth seemed to come alive, basking in the sunshine.

She walked past a few crofts, but she didn't stop to speak with the Breccans, who were repairing their homesteads and cleaning up debris. She strayed from the road and followed a familiar valley to a wood, and then walked farther, to a loch.

The cottage that had once held Kae was just as Adaira had left it days ago, undisturbed by the storm. She walked the earthen bridge to the front door, which sat wide open, its enchantment broken.

Adaira stepped into the cool shadows. She didn't know why she had come here, to a loch that had been cursed. She didn't know why she felt drawn to this place, and she felt the last of her hope wane as she stared at the skeleton hanging on the wall.

Of course Jack wouldn't be here. He was no longer in her realm—the fire had claimed him—and Adaira sat, heavy with heartache, on the edge of the palliasse. She remained there for a long time, watching the sunlight deepen to a lusty gold. Birds trilled in the kail yard, their sweet songs mingling with the chirp of crickets and the occasional plop of a fish surfacing from the loch. A breeze sighed, bobbing the tall weed and thistles beyond the walls. A tendril of that gentle wind slipped in through the open door and touched Adaira's face like a loving hand.

She wondered if it was Kae, watching over her.

Adaira considered leaving Jack's harp in the cottage, but then thought *no.* It would remain with her, even though it had been a long time since Lorna Tamerlaine had tried to teach Adaira how to play. It had been years since Adaira had sat at a harp, her fingers poised as she tried to master the notes. The music had resisted her, but perhaps only because she had also been resistant to it.

Adaira softly traced the harp's frame now. Eventide was falling; she needed to return home to her parents before they worried about her absence. And yet still she waited, until the first star broke the sky. A cold distant fire that faithfully burned, like the stars she had seen crowning Jack.

She dared to pluck a note from his harp.

~~~~~~

A daira didn't know what to expect from dinner that night. She nearly canceled on her parents—she felt weary and heartsick and wasn't the least bit hungry—but when she entered Innes's personal chambers to join them for the meal . . . Adaira was floored to discover Torin sitting at the table beside Sidra. The moment their eyes locked, Adaira felt the past rushing forward, as though a dam had broken. It honestly seemed as if no time had come between her and her cousin—hadn't it only been yesterday that she and Torin raced through the heather in the east?—and she laughed as he rose and rushed to embrace her.

"When did you arrive?" Adaira exclaimed, leaning back in his arms to look him over.

Torin smiled. "I'm not sure what time. It was storming."

"We must have just missed each other," she said. "I'm so happy you're here, Torin."

"As am I, Adi. Come, we've been waiting on you."

Adaira thought something about him seemed different as they walked to the table together. Something she couldn't quite name, but all the same sensed. It was nothing bad—more like he had aged. He seemed softer and yet leaner, as if parts of him had been whittled away. She imagined that being in the spirits' realm had left a mark on him, and she instantly felt that ache again in her chest.

Adaira found her seat at the table and closed her eyes for a breath, remembering. She could still see Jack vividly in her memory. The sight of him being consumed by flames with stars in his hair and an uncanny light in his eyes. A king among spirits.

"Where's Jack?" Sidra asked.

Adaira glanced at the empty chair beside her, as if the sound of his name would prompt him to manifest. She stared at the place that had been set for him and then reached for her glass of wine. She took a long sip before making her announcement.

"He's gone."

Her words fell like frost on the table. But she felt the attention of her parents, who were bent toward her with concern and confusion, as well as Sidra's compassion and Torin's solemn understanding.

"He sang to end the storm," Adaira explained, "and it required his mortality. The spirits took him." And because she neither wanted to speak further of it nor be on the receiving end of pity, she began to fill her plate with food.

Torin followed suit, and then Sidra, even though she had gone very pale.

But Innes, who never danced around a conversation, said, "I'm sorry, Adaira."

Adaira clenched her jaw and almost lost her composure—she could feel the tears stinging her eyes. She couldn't help but wonder what would have happened if she had been with Jack when he sang. If she had stood at his side when the fire burned.

He would have remained with her, this much she knew. He would have remained bound to her by oath and choice and love, three cords not easily broken. Bane would still reign beyond the veil of the world, and the west would have remained shadowed. *No*, she told herself, shaking away her emotion. *This is how it was always meant to be*. And she couldn't fault Jack for knowing it as well, and for leaving her asleep in their bed.

She had been both his strength and his weakness.

"There is nothing to be sorry for," she said, meeting her mother's stare. "He was always destined to play for the spirits, to overcome the wind."

Thankfully, Innes left it at that, and the meal began in uncomfortable silence. Adaira was keenly grateful to her father for changing the subject and getting directly to the heart of the matter.

"We'd like to maintain a relationship with you in the east," David said to both Torin and Sidra. "And we think the trade would be a good way to build rapport between our clans."

Torin glanced at Sidra, but Sidra looked to Adaira. It had always been her dream to establish a trade between east and west.

Adaira remained quiet. Of course, she still wanted the trade to happen. She simply felt too empty to guide this conversation, which she had never envisioned happening without Jack beside her. It was one of the reasons why they had handfasted so swiftly: he was to stand with her to oversee the first exchange, and hopefully during future trades. A partner to support her in this new and seemingly impossible endeavor.

Her eyes wandered to Jack's plate again.

"We would like that as well," Sidra replied, sensing Adaira's grief. She turned her attention to David. "Have you given any thought to how you would like to proceed with it?"

"We think it best to hold it once a month," Innes began. "The Breccans will never forget what you have done for us in our time of need, and most in my clan will be open-minded and eager to exchange their goods with yours. We simply have yet to think of a proper location for it, and I know this has been the crux of the matter, with the clan line dividing us."

Adaira had walked the clan line only a few hours earlier. She had scarcely noticed anything different about it, but neither had she been paying much attention to the magic that teemed in the ground. Jack had evanesced on the line. He had also ended Bane there. Now Adaira wondered if the curse that had held the isle divided for so long had been lifted. She thought of how the clouds had broken the moment Jack had taken his crown. How the sun had filled the west again.

She had sometimes imagined it—the curse unraveling and the isle becoming united once more.

"Have you felt anything, Torin?" she asked her cousin.

He knew she spoke of the enchanted scar on his palm. The one he received when he had been promoted to Captain of the East Guard.

Torin flexed his hand as he gazed down at the gleam of his scar. "I honestly have felt nothing since I stepped through the portal."

But the isle had also been in the throes of peril when he returned, Adaira thought. Perhaps the magic of the clan line still held, but everyone had been too preoccupied by the storm to notice.

"Sidra and I need to return to our clan tomorrow," Torin continued, meeting Innes's stare. "On my way home, I'll take a look at the clan line and see if its power still holds. And we'll continue to deliberate on the trade from our end. I think we can find a good place for it to happen."

He paused to hold up his goblet of wine, glancing at Adaira. "Most of all, let's keep in contact with each other."

Adaira gave him a wry smile. But she clinked her glass to his, agreeing. She hadn't realized how desperate she was to see the four leaders of the isle united, toasting each other and the trade, until it unfolded before her.

Sidra rode with Torin and Adaira toward the east, with Blair and the rest of her guards following. She was more than ready to return home, to sleep in her own bed and hold Maisie, and yet she was distracted by thoughts of what the future held for the isle, of how the trade would proceed and the next steps they needed to take.

Her mind went quiet, though, as soon as she saw the charred remains of the Aithwood.

Smoke was still rising in languid curls. A great swath of the forest had burned, although there were still sections—the northern crown and the southern portion—that remained unscathed. Drawing closer, Sidra thought that the landscape looked as if the heart of the woods had been harvested, leaving behind ash and the charred ribs of tree trunks.

She eased her mare to a walk, then dismounted when their small party reached the woods. The guards remained with the horses as Torin, Sidra, and Adaira walked through the scorched remnant. Sidra imagined Jack standing in this place, singing and burning and vanishing without a trace. She still struggled to fathom the truth that he was truly gone—that, unlike Torin, he would have no way to return to his mortal life.

"Here it is." Torin's voice broke the quiet.

Sidra slowed her pace as she approached the clan line. She was streaked by charcoal, from brushing too close to the burned trees, as were Torin and Adaira. As if it were impossible to walk through this part of the forest and not be touched by what had happened here.

The three of them stood before the line, gazing down at it. And then Torin reached for Sidra's hand.

"Will you step over it, Sid? I want to see if I can feel it in my scar."

Nodding, she stepped over the line, then turned to gaze back at Torin. He was frowning at his hand, flexing his fingers.

"Did you feel anything?" Adaira asked.

"No," he replied. "I felt nothing. The curse of the clan line has been broken here."

"Should we test it farther down in the woods?" Sidra suggested. "In a place where the trees didn't burn?"

"Aye. Come, Sid." He reached for her hand again and pulled her back over the line.

They walked north first, eventually arriving at the place where the fire had ceased burning. It was like stepping from one world into another, from ash-streaked barrenness into lush abundance. Sidra shivered as she crossed the line again, this time watching Torin's frown deepen.

"I felt your passage that time," he said. "The curse still holds here."

"Then it most likely also holds in the southern end of the forest," Adaira said, but her voice sounded thin and strange, as if she was struggling to breathe. "We should walk there now." She turned and began to stride through the burned portion again.

Sidra stepped back into the west and thought this must have been where it happened. The place where Jack had become fire.

They walked through the entirety of the scorched Aithwood and at last came to a peculiar depression in the ground, a wide and shallow bed full of golden sand and smooth stones.

"Spirits," Sidra whispered, suddenly realizing what it was. "The river . . ."

"Is gone," Adaira finished, glancing sidelong at her.

Sidra held her gaze for a beat. There was a feverish gleam in Adaira's eyes, and charcoal was streaked across her face. Sidra was tempted to reach out to touch her friend's arm, to hold her steady, knowing that this forest held an array of emotions for her. It was the place where her fate had been sealed. She had been laid down on the moss amongst these old trees, an offering that had never been claimed. And so this river had then ushered her into the east, into the arms of the Tamerlaines.

Sidra watched as Adaira crossed over the river's exposed bed, her boots leaving impressions on it. But instead of remaining on the clan line to test their theory, Adaira followed the scorched river, walking what would have been upstream if the water still flowed.

She disappeared into the woods, and Torin murmured, "Let's give her a moment."

Sidra nodded.

She and Torin concluded that Jack's sacrifice had broken a portion of the curse, but that there were still places where his music had not reached. They walked hand in hand upstream, wondering what this revelation meant for the isle, and soon came across a home in the woods. There was a kail yard, still recovering from the storm, and a cottage built of stone and thatch. Adaira was opening the shutters from inside the cottage, and Sidra tentatively joined her there.

"Do you know who lives here?" Sidra asked, taking note of the kitchen table and the herbs that hung from the rafters.

"Niall Breccan does," Adaira replied. "Jack's father."

Sidra froze. She shouldn't have been surprised at this truth, but it still hit her like a blow. "Jack's father is a Breccan?"

"Yes," Adaira answered, leaning out one of the windows. "Torin? Torin, come inside. I want to tell you and Sid a story, and I don't want to have to relay it twice."

A moment later, Torin appeared on the back threshold, framed by light. "This was where Maisie was held, isn't it?" he said. "And the other lasses, when Moray was stealing them."

"Yes," Adaira said, sitting down at the table.

Sidra also sat, her knees suddenly feeling weak. Torin examined the main chamber first, looking at the candlesticks on the mantel, the walking sticks in the corner, the desk against one wall. Finally, he joined Adaira and Sidra at the table. They were quiet as Adaira began to tell them the story of Jack's father carrying her eastward to Mirin.

By the end of it, Torin had streaked more charcoal in his beard from raking his fingers through it. He sighed, leaning his elbows on the table.

"So this is Niall Breccan's home," he said. "Where is he now?"

"I don't know," Adaira replied. "Perhaps he never returned here after he was liberated."

"I think he did," Torin stated. "There are things missing, as though he packed in a hurry."

Sidra bit her lip, meeting Adaira's steady gaze. Both women had questions, but they felt too tender to speak or even wonder aloud. The silence spread through the cottage, sweetened by birdsong and a slight breeze. Adaira finally stood and said, "I know I've kept you both too long. I can imagine you're keen to return home, and it's late afternoon now."

Sidra and Torin followed her out the back door. It was an odd yet charming place, and Sidra struggled with her mixed feelings about it. Maisie had once been held here, but Jack's father had been a good man caught in a terrible situation. Her emotions felt snarled up, and she sighed as she tucked a wayward strand of hair behind her ear.

Adaira was standing in the riverbed again, staring downstream. Looking eastward.

Sidra came to a stop beside her, a few stones shifting beneath her feet.

"What does this look like to you, Sid?" Adaira asked.

Sidra gazed ahead, uncertain at first. But then she saw the same vision as Adaira, and warmth began to course through her blood.

"It looks like a road."

Frae was kneeling in the kail yard beside the red-headed man—*Niall,* her mother called him—when she finally roused her courage to speak the words she longed to say.

"Are you my father, Niall?"

Niall froze, his woad-printed hand hidden in the kail. But he looked at Frae, and his gaze was gentle. "Yes, Frae."

"Are you Jack's father too?"

"Yes."

"You're a Breccan, though."

"I am. Does that frighten you, Frae?"

"No," she answered honestly, gazing up at him. "I know you're good."

He smiled, and then coughed before returning his attention to the garden. Frae thought he might be hiding a few tears, but then he said, "I'm happy to hear that. And I'm happy to be your father. I'm sorry that I was gone until now."

"Will you stay with us? With me and Mum?" Frae asked. "And Jack, whenever he comes home?"

Niall paused, as if lost in contemplation. His silence made Frae nervous, and her heart was suddenly beating very fast, imagining him leaving. She didn't want him to leave. And yet she was too shy to tell him how she felt.

"I would like very much to stay here with you and your mother, and Elspeth too, if you'll let her."

"Yes, *Elspeth!*" Frae cried, smacking her forehead. She was swarmed by guilt for forgetting to include her new friend. "She can stay in my room. I mean *Jack's* room. It was his, and then mine."

"That is very kind of you, daughter," Niall said as he laid a bundle of kail in Frae's basket. He winked at her, and Frae smiled, so happy she thought her chest might burst. "Here, shall we harvest a few carrots now? I think your mother would like that."

Frae nodded, and they moved down the rows where the carrots grew. It was late afternoon, and the wind was quiet, the sky cloudless, the sun bright. It seemed like a perfect day, and Frae was telling her father about their three cows when the riders approached.

It was the watchmen from the Aithwood. The strongest of the East Guard who patrolled the clan line. Frae had always regarded them with awe. They kept her and Mirin safe, and she had always trusted them. But as the riders came to a stop on the other side of the garden wall, they drew arrows on their bows.

"Up to your feet, Breccan," one of them commanded. "Hands raised."

Frae gaped for a moment, astonished. Her father wasn't wearing his blue plaid, but he wasn't able to hide his tattoos. Slowly, Niall raised his hands and stood.

"Come with us," another guard said. "*Now.* Step away from the lass."

When Niall began to stiffly move forward, Frae cried out, wrapping her arms around him.

"No. *No!* He's my *da.*"

She watched how her words grew wings and struck the Tamerlaine guards in their faces. Their brows lowered, and their mouths pressed into thin, hard lines. One of them finally said, "Come now, Frae. This man is dangerous and has trespassed. Let him go."

She only held to Niall tighter, burying her face in his shirt. She wanted to weep at how cruel the world was, how unfair it was for her father to *finally* arrive to be with her and Mirin, only to see the guards tear him away.

"It's all right, Frae," Niall whispered to her.

"No, it's not!" she shouted. Frae drew in a sharp breath, leaning her head back, and it felt like her face had caught fire. She was so furious, so angry. She had never yelled at an adult before, but she let her voice rise. "I've waited my whole life for you! Tell them that you're good, Da. Tell them!"

"Frae." Mirin's voice cut through the sunlight. But she wasn't scolding her daughter; she was seeking to calm her, and Frae glanced at her mother.

"Are you harboring this man willingly, Mirin?" one of the guards asked. Their arrows were still trained on Niall. And Frae as well, since she refused to let him go.

Mirin came to stand beside Niall. Her gaze was dark and steady, her chin tilted high as she looked at the guards. "Yes, he is a guest."

"He's a *Breccan*."

"And he is mine," Mirin countered coolly. "Lower your arrows, before you shoot an innocent person."

"What do you mean he is *yours*? Are you bound to this man, Mirin?"

Frae watched as her mother looked at Niall. "Yes. We spoke a vow on this hill, years ago by the light of the moon. He is mine, and should you harm him, you would hold a debt against me that you could never repay."

The air crackled with tension. No one spoke or moved—they all seemed caught in a web—and Frae wasn't certain what would happen next. How would she and Mirin be able to keep Niall and Elspeth safe? Then came a voice that surprised her, drawing all their attention to the yard gate.

"Lower your arrows," Torin commanded the guards. "Return to the castle barracks and stay there until you receive further instructions."

The guards looked pale and astonished, but they heeded the

laird instantly. They returned the arrows to the quivers on their backs and departed in a cloud of dust.

Frae shuddered in relief, unwinding her arms from Niall. She stared at Torin, surprised by the dark smudges on his face and garments; he looked like he had been in a chimney. Sidra was at his side, also bearing cinder marks. Frae's hope lifted until Mirin spoke.

"Laird, Lady. I ask that you please allow this man to remain here with me, safely. He is no threat to the clan."

"He is Niall Breccan, I take it?" Torin said, his gaze flickering from Mirin to Niall. "Could we come inside and have a word with all of you?"

Frae wondered if that was a good sign or a bad one. Would Torin and Sidra listen to them? She let Niall take her hand, and they followed the laird and the healer into the cottage.

Elspeth must have heard the conversation through the window; she had prepared a spread of tea and refreshments at the kitchen table, and everyone gathered there, the silence tense until Sidra broke it.

"We've just come from your cottage in the Aithwood, Niall."

Frae looked at her father. He raked his fingers through his hair, and he seemed nervous. "It survived the fire?"

"Yes."

"That's a relief to hear."

Torin said, "We wanted to know if you had plans to return there."

"To my house?" Niall paused, but his eyes went to Mirin. "I had hoped to stay here with Mirin and Frae, along with my mother, Elspeth."

Frae bit her nails, tasting dirt from the garden. This was it. The moment when she discovered if her father would be allowed to stay with them or not.

"Of course you can stay here," Torin said, lifting his hand. "This is your family, and you belong with them. But we wanted to ask if we could use your cottage in the woods."

"Use it?" Niall asked. "What for?"

"We want to establish a trade there," Sidra replied. "A place for Breccans and Tamerlaines to meet and exchange goods, as well as share meals and stories. A place where peace may be forged."

Niall was silent for a few breaths. But the color had returned to his face, and a smile curved his lips. "I would like that. You're welcome to use it however you think best."

"Thank you," Torin said, taking a sip of the tea Elspeth had poured. He pursed his lips, and Frae worried that maybe the tea tasted terrible. But then the laird said, "There's something else we need to discuss."

Frae leaned forward, waiting. When Torin still hesitated, Sidra cleared her throat. "A portion of the clan line has lost its curse," she said. "In the place where the Aithwood burned, where Jack sang."

"*Jack?*" Frae cried, hopeful. "Will he come home soon?"

Now Sidra hesitated. Mirin grasped Frae's hand and held it tightly. Frae glanced from her mother to the healer, her heart beginning to pound.

"Where is my brother?" she asked. "Is he with Adaira?"

"I'm afraid that something happened when your brother sang for the spirits, Frae," Sidra said. "I'm sure you noticed that part of the Aithwood is burned?"

Frae nodded. Of course she had. It was one of the first things she had taken note of when she emerged from the cottage after the storm. Sometimes she could still smell the smoke when the wind blew from the west.

"Did Jack get hurt?" she whispered.

"No," Sidra replied. "But he went to be with the spirits."

"What do you mean?"

The adults were quiet, but all of them seemed grave and uncomfortable. Frae's gaze touched each of their faces, and her heart only beat faster, making her stomach ache.

"Do you mean he won't be coming back?" she asked.

"No, darling," Mirin murmured, reaching out to caress Frae's hair. "But he—"

"He *promised* me," Frae hissed. Again, that anger was boiling through her. Anger and something else. It tasted like salt and blood, and she lurched up from the table, yanking her fingers from Mirin's. "He said he would come back soon. He promised me that he would!"

"Frae . . ." Mirin was saying, reaching for her.

A sob broke in Frae's chest. She turned and bolted, embarrassed to be crying in front of Torin and Sidra and Niall and Elspeth. She slipped out the back door and ran through the garden, catching herself on the gate. She could hardly see; the tears blurred everything. Eventually she clambered over the low stone wall and stormed down the hill to where the river had been.

She sat on its banks, the place where Jack had taught her how to shoot his slingshot, and how to choose the best rocks. She struggled to understand what Sidra had said—how could her brother be gone? Frae stood and went over to the sandy riverbed to gather stones.

She hurled them, one after the other, until her arm was sore. She was sitting in the grass again, knees pulled up to her chest, when Mirin came to sit beside her. The air had cooled with dusk, and Frae was shivering. Her fury had burned away, and the only two things she felt were heavy and sad.

"I don't want him to be dead," Frae whispered.

"Jack isn't dead, Frae."

"But he's *gone*!"

"Yes. But he still lives."

"Where?"

"Look up, Frae," Mirin said in a voice soft with wonder.

Frae didn't want to look up. But she did, unable to resist.

"Tell me what you see, darling."

"Clouds," Frae said, stubbornly.

"And what else?"

"The sky."

"And is there more than just clouds and the sky?"

Frae squinted. She could just discern the first constellation, breaking the lavender cloak of dusk. "I see the stars. And the moon."

Mirin gathered her close, and Frae rested in her mother's arms. They both watched the stars begin to burn, one by one, and Mirin whispered, "That is where your brother is. He is the fire and the light of the isle. As long as the stars shine, he will always be with you."

Frae was quiet, soaking in that thought. This time when she cried, she let Mirin wipe away her tears.

CHAPTER 44

T he first trade happened in Niall Breccan's cottage in the heart of the Aithwood. Adaira and Sidra had worked together the past fortnight cleaning the house and tending to the garden. They had set tables in the yard and built an outdoor firepit to cook large meals over.

"Do you think anyone will come today?" Adaira asked.

Sidra was stirring a large cauldron of soup over the outdoor pit. "I think you'll be surprised, Adi."

"In a good way or a bad way?"

Sidra only smiled.

Adaira wasn't surprised to see Mirin arrive first, by way of the river road. She brought a few weavings with her, as well as a basket of freshly dyed yarn. Then Una Carlow arrived, and while she didn't bring anything to trade, she gladly took a bowl of soup when Sidra offered it to her. Another Tamerlaine came by road, bearing necklaces strung with shells and colorful glass beads.

Adaira resisted the urge to pace as she waited to see if any of the Breccans would come.

In the end, seven showed up. Two traded with Mirin, three

with the Tamerlaine jeweler. Nearly all of the Breccans and Tamerlaines who had come stayed to eat the meal Sidra had prepared. While members of the two clans sat at separate tables, Adaira was deeply pleased.

"It's a good start," Innes had said when she arrived to survey the progress of the exchange.

They decided to hold another trade two weeks later rather than wait for a full moon to wax and wane. More Tamerlaines arrived, as did more Breccans. This time they mingled at the tables, eating the meal provided and exchanging goods.

The atmosphere still felt cautious and strained at moments, but for most of her life Adaira had never even dreamt she would see such a day. She watched it all, quietly marveling and reveling in the joy of it—until she noticed the scorched trees surrounding Niall's cottage. The sight made her feel heavy again, as though her grief had turned to iron.

Some days she would walk through the burned part of the forest. It was always solemn and eerie there, as if that part of the isle had truly died. She wondered if other spirits would eventually reclaim this place, or if the burning would stand forever as a testament to what had happened.

The days became shorter and the nights longer as summer gave way to autumn and winter drew closer.

The first snow fell, and Adaira saw that the Breccan stores were becoming dangerously low. Even with Bane's curse broken, it would take several seasons for the west to regain what it had lost beneath the clouds. She went to bed hungry some nights, even though Innes always ensured that Adaira had food. Adaira suspected that her mother wasn't eating, though, in order to keep her daughter fed.

Adaira wrote to Torin and Sidra.

More food appeared during the trade, which was now being held once a week. Word continued to spread in the west, and more Breccans arrived to barter for oats and preserved fruits, wheels of cheese and jars of cream and butter, herbs and dried meat and fish, and livestock. They brought their best weavings and weapons, their finest baskets and shoes and jewelry and furs, and the Tamerlaines accepted their offerings, although not without a bit of haggling.

One night Adaira sat with Innes in her quarters, both of them quietly reading by firelight.

"I was thinking about the clan line today," Innes said suddenly.

Adaira glanced up from her page. "What about it, Mum?"

"How the curse is broken only in a certain place." Innes shut her book and glanced at Adaira. "Why do you think that is?"

"I don't know. I've wondered myself, and discussed it with Torin and Sidra."

"I think it is because the curse was created by two people," Innes said. "So it must end with another pair."

Adaira was silent, weighing her answer. She thought of the origin of the clan line, made by Joan Tamerlaine and Fingal Breccan two centuries ago. Their last words had sparked the curse, even as they had died entwined.

"I don't know what I can do to help heal it," Adaira said. She did feel responsible, in a strange, unsettling way. Sometimes it seeped into her dreams, and she would see herself and Jack dying together, swept away by the fire. She always woke from those nightmares in a cold sweat, punctured by guilt.

She hadn't reached him soon enough.

"I don't think there's anything you can do," Innes said. "It's just a thought I had."

Silence came between them. Adaira refused to look at the fire, trying to focus her attention on her book. But her thoughts were suddenly teeming, full of questions about the clan line. When she returned to her room that night, she took Joan's broken journal in her hands and leafed through the pages.

Adaira had never read the last page of the second half, but she did now. Joan's final entry surprised her:

I thought I could change the west, but how foolish I was to dream of such a thing. They are coldhearted and vicious, two-

faced and arrogant, and I have come to hate the man I've bound myself to. Tomorrow, I will go to the boundary in the woods and cut out the scar on my palm, the one that marks me as Fingal's, and I will return to the house of my mother and sisters, to the land that holds my father's grave. I will return to the east and prepare for conflict with the west, because there is no other hope for the isle other than strife.

Adaira read the entry twice before setting Joan's journal aside. She looked at her own scar, the one she had given herself when she took the blood oath with Jack. It was a vow not easily broken, and Adaira envisioned Joan, in the thick of the Aithwood, trying to cut out such a scar. She saw Fingal finding her there in the shadows between the trees. Joan would have been bleeding and angry and keen to leave him.

If blood and words between a Breccan and a Tamerlaine had made the clan line, then surely they could also undo it.

Adaira reached for parchment and her quill. She didn't know if what she had in mind would work, but she wanted to at least attempt it. She wrote:

> Torin,
> Meet me at the northernmost point of the clan line tomorrow at dawn.
> —A.

A soft snow was falling when Torin met Adaira at the clan line. The morning light was dimly blue, and the air was cold and crisp. Beyond the trees, Adaira could hear the roar of the northern coast as high tide crashed against the rocks.

"You have an idea, I take it?" Torin surmised, remaining on the eastern side. Between their boots, the clan line was a furrow in the ground. Not even the snow would touch it.

"Yes," Adaira replied. "Thanks to Joan's journal. The second half that we found at Loch Ivorra." She unsheathed Jack's truth blade from her belt. "If two people from each clan made this boundary with blood and curses, then I believe two can undo it with blood and a benediction."

Torin watched as Adaira held out her hand. She wouldn't be cutting the palm that held the scar of her blood vow, but the other. Before she did so, she said, "This is Jack's truth blade. If you use it to score your own palm and walk this path with me, then all the words you utter will be nothing but honest and true. You will speak the benediction for the west, as I will for the east."

Torin was quiet, but Adaira could read the slant of his thoughts. He had once regarded the Breccans as enemies. All his life, he had been fighting them, sometimes even killing those who strayed across the clan line. But Adaira hoped that Torin could now honestly speak for the good of the west.

"All right," he said with a solemn nod.

Adaira cut her palm. The pain was sharp, and she winced before she handed the dirk to Torin. She watched as her cousin did the same, choosing to slice the palm that held his enchanted scar. The one that had made him Captain of the East Guard.

"Take my hand," Adaira whispered to him.

He did. Their fingers were slick, but as they began to walk, their mingled blood dripped down onto the snow and the clan line, leaving a trail as red as Orenna's flowers.

Adaira began to speak the benediction for the east. She hadn't been certain what she would say, or how to go about this, but now she found that the words came naturally. She spoke healing and blessings over the Tamerlaines, their crops and their gardens, their children, their spirits, their seasons. She spoke of goodness and life for the east. By the time she reached the end, her heart was pounding in her chest.

She and Torin continued to walk the clan line, hands entwined and blood flowing, snow crunching under their boots. When Torin remained silent, Adaira wondered if he was struggling to give a good and honest benediction for the west.

But then he surprised her.

"I bless the Breccans in the west," Torin began, his words emerging like smoke. He blessed the western kail yards and lochs, streams, and valleys. He blessed the Breccan children, as well as their health and their spirits. For all the days to come.

After Torin finished, they continued to walk in silence to the place where the woods became scorched. Where Jack had evanesced.

Adaira didn't know what to expect. Jack had broken the curse on this part of the clan line through fire and thunder and music and sacrifice. But as Adaira came to a stop and looked back at the way she and Torin had come . . . she saw their blood disappearing on the snow. The clan line began to fade away.

It was a quiet, gentle mending. So quiet that most would have missed it, had they not been waiting, *hoping*, for it to happen.

Adaira glanced up at Torin to see him smiling at her, tears in his eyes.

It didn't take long for the news to spread. Adaira and Torin had lifted the curse from the other two parts of the clan line, and now it was gone. There was no longer a magical rift between the east and the west. What this would mean for Cadence's future was still a mystery—all they had ever known was a divided island. Torin had simply said to Adaira, *We'll take it a day at a time, Adi.*

She sighed, resting in that plan. For the first time in a long while, she didn't need to have all the answers.

Innes found Adaira reading in the new library one evening not long after the mending. She glanced up from her book, expecting Innes to ask more questions about how the line had vanished.

"What is it, Mum?"

"Long ago, I wanted my daughters to be like me. To be my mirror." Innes paused, as if lost in her memories. "I am relieved, now, to know you are nothing like me. You are your own self, and I had no part in shaping or molding you. How ironic to know my enemies made you greater than I ever could."

Adaira blinked back her tears, uncertain what to say. But she was deeply moved by Innes's words.

"I must soon name my heiress to the clan," Innes continued. "You are my first and only choice. I cannot see myself blessing anyone apart from you, Adaira. But should you forgo it, I will understand and find another."

Adaira had been waiting for this moment. For Innes to acknowledge her choice with her voice and her words. For Innes to make it known that this was what she wanted. And yet Adaira was unsure about what *she* wanted. She wondered if her vision would align with Innes's. If she was brave enough to step into such a role again.

"You don't have to give me an answer now," Innes said, reading the hesitation on Adaira's face. "But will you consider it?"

Adaira glanced at the candles, burning on the desk before her. She watched the fire dance, thinking of Jack. She thought of how much her life had changed its course, how it had veered onto a path she had never predicted. In some ways these changes had been good, but in others? She felt broken, as if her life was in pieces.

"I'm honored you ask me, Mum," Adaira finally said. "I'll consider it."

Innes nodded and left without another word. But Adaira sat and stared at the same page for a long while, her mind reeling.

For a week after that conversation, Adaira dreamt of becoming laird of the Breccans. Even in her sleep, she couldn't escape it. She soon found herself in the cistern, stripping her clothes away. She stepped into the water and swam into the warm darkness.

She thought of Jack. She thought of how afraid he had been that night when she had brought him here—the last night they had shared.

He had not known that she was just as terrified of the deep.

Adaira swam into it now, her fear making her stomach clench and her mind race. She pushed herself farther into it, until she thought she would weep, and then she saw the light in the crevice. The torch that burned everlasting.

Exhausted, she swam into the cavern. She settled on the ledge where Jack had once sat, and she thought for a long time about her life and where it was going. What she wanted to do with her days now that he was no longer a part of them.

She glanced at the torch and watched it burn.

"Jack?" she whispered, and then instantly scolded herself. She would lose her mind if she started conversing with fire, thinking it was him. Somehow, she knew he was far away. She knew he wasn't anywhere near her, and she slipped away from the cavern.

By the time Adaira had reached the stairs and re-dressed, she had made up her mind. The answer was smoldering in her, and she went directly to her parents in their chambers.

Innes and David were eating a small dinner together, and they both glanced up at her, startled by her damp hair and flushed skin.

"Adaira?" her father asked. "Do you want to join us?"

"I have my answer," she said, breathless. She turned her eyes to Innes, who had risen as if meeting an opponent.

"And what is it?" Innes asked.

"Name me your heiress," Adaira said. "I want to lead the west."

CHAPTER 45

J ack stood in his throne room, a place spun from dreams. There were no walls and no ceiling. The pillars on either side of him melted up into night, where thousands of stars burned, some hanging so low they were close enough to touch. Iron braziers sat between the pillars, shining with fire, and behind each brazier was a doorway carved from clouds and light. Beneath his bare feet was a clear marble floor, and beyond the floor was a brilliant sunset.

He wore robes cut from the night sky, constellations scattered across the fabric. His crown of stars glittered in the twilight, and fire danced at his fingertips. Sometimes he caught his reflection when he walked deep into the fortress, a place made of polished bronze and smoke. He didn't like to look at himself for long because his eyes had changed; they gleamed like embers. At certain angles, he looked translucent, as if anything could pass through him. His face was sharper, narrower, as if he had been cut from kindling.

But sometimes he saw traces of who he had been. He often touched the scar on his palm, the quicksilver streak in his hair.

As he waited in the throne room, he watched the spirits gather.

All of them had felt it—the shift when the clan line fully faded. Shadows had grown smaller, colors brighter. Unnamed constellations had started to burn, as though a new map had been unrolled across the sky.

It had been a soft feeling, like waking up to the gentle patter of rain. And Jack had known then what he needed to do.

He had not been king for long, and yet he had summoned them all—every wing of the wind, every fruit of the earth, every creature from the depths of the ocean, every ember from the fire. They gathered in groups, refusing to mingle as they murmured and waited, frowning. In that regard, they were not unlike humanity, and Jack's memories flared.

He saw Adaira kneeling before him, blood on her palm. He heard her whisper his name, felt her breath against his skin. Sometimes he thought he saw her, walking amongst the spirits of his court, her hair catching the shades of the sunset.

His robes were a shield; they hid his trembling, the agony he felt. The spirits could neither see nor understand his pain—the wound from half of himself being torn away. The wound that never ceased to ache.

"We have all assembled," Ash said. "Why have you summoned us, King?"

Jack's memories faded, leaving him cold and hollow. "I have a request for you, spirits of the isle."

"Speak it," said Ream of the Sea, her eyes iridescent as an oyster shell. Her long, green hair dripped water onto the floor. She was impatient, ready to return to the tides.

"I have done you a favor by dethroning your king," Jack said, "and now I ask a favor of you. Take my crown and give it to one of your own kind, one who is worthy amongst you. I ask that you permit me to return to my mortal life."

Whispers shivered through the gathering. Jack watched from his dais, his heart quickening.

Lady Whin of the Wildflowers spoke next, her sister Orenna close at her side. "But you are immortal among us, King. If you return to the human realm, your days will be numbered again. You will turn into dust and rot in a grave."

"It is not a fate I fear," Jack said. "What I fear is living for an eternity with a wound that will never heal."

The folk seemed unable to fathom this notion. A spirit of the southern wind said, "But, King, your reign will be honored among mortals. They will sing of your deeds for generations to come. Your prowess will grow greater, but only if you remain with us."

"I don't want my deeds to be sung of," Jack replied. "I would rather live them."

Ash looked troubled. His brows were slanted, his mouth pressed into a hard line. But then the Laird of Fire said, "Your music is your crown, Majesty. If you give it to one of us, you will be stripped of your craft when you return below."

"I am already stripped of it here," Jack gently replied. "And I would rather live a short breadth of days, working with my hands even if they can no longer play a harp, and living with those I love. If you keep me here, I will only grow weaker. I cannot be the king you hope for, as I am incomplete in your realm."

The spirits argued amongst themselves, upset by his confession, and Jack stood by quietly, watching them debate. Soon the spirits of the sea had merged deeper into the crowd, as had the spirits of the earth, until fire was brushing shoulders with water, and earth with wind, but none of them seemed able to reach a satisfactory conclusion. Finally, a hill spirit named Hap spoke over the noise: "My king? Who would you choose among us to wear your crown? Who among us is worthy?"

That silenced the noise. Suddenly every eye was fixed upon Jack. Hap's question was easy for him to answer. He had known whom he would choose the moment he saw her glide into the hall. She stood at the back of the assembly near Whin, her wings tucked in close.

"Kae," he called to her.

Kae's eyes widened, but when the spirits parted for her, she stepped forward. "Majesty?" she said, and her voice was deep and gentle. It was the first time Jack had ever heard it apart from in her own memories, and he smiled to see her restored.

"You are as gentle-hearted as you are fierce," he said. "You know the many faces of the isle, its secrets and its marvels, and you are good to mortal and spirit alike. You aided us in our time of need, and you are not afraid to choose the hard but right path. Without you, I would have never discovered how to defeat Bane. If you will accept my crown, I give it freely to you. If you will accept my offering, then carry me back to the mortal realm so I may restore my own soul."

Kae hesitated. She drew in a sharp breath and glanced at Whin. The Lady of the Wildflowers was already gazing at her softly. The two spirits seemed to hold a conversation in their minds for a while. Then Kae returned her attention to Jack.

She knelt.

Jack descended the dais stairs. The moment he touched her head, the stars of his crown began to drift. They moved through the space, gathering in Kae's indigo hair. Jack knew he had made the right decision; one of their own should rule amongst them, not another bard.

When Kae rose, the spirits bent to her.

Jack suddenly felt weak, struggling to stand upright. He didn't know if it was due to surrendering his power or because he knew he was about to walk the mortal realm again.

Kae took his hand. A wind began to gather in the throne room. It stirred Ream's kelplike hair and drew wildflowers from Whin's fingers. It made the fire in the braziers dance, and Jack met Ash's gaze one final time.

The Laird of Fire nodded, his sorrow evident.

Kae called to the wind.

She carried Jack away.

It was winter.

Snow was falling when Jack opened his eyes.

He stood on the clan line, the very place where the fire had once claimed him. The last place he had seen Adaira. Of course Kae would bring him here.

The woods before him were charred and speckled with snow. Jack—barefoot, freezing, and naked—began to walk forward through the ruin he had once inspired. There were no spirits here and it felt empty; Jack mourned them, tracing the scorched trunks he passed, the charcoal marking his fingers.

He shivered, but he also savored the bite of the air, the reddening of his skin from the cold—the reminder that he was alive.

Soon he heard voices echoing through the woods. Someone was laughing, and another person was talking loudly. Jack knew the voices must be coming from his father's house, and he quietly approached it, coming to a stop when he could see the cottage through the ruin.

He didn't know what he was expecting, but it wasn't tables in the yard and people gathering up baskets of goods. It looked like a market. Jack remained hidden behind the trees as Tamerlaines and Breccans parted ways, the snow having ended the trade early.

Jack recognized Adaira, carrying a crate into the house. He almost ran to her but remembered he was naked, and a few Breccans were hanging about her. Jack waited, even as his feet went numb in the snow.

Adaira finally emerged into the yard again, wearing a cloak. Her hair was braided, and he could see a flash of silver gleaming at her brow.

"Shall we fetch your horse, Heiress?" one of the Breccans said.

Adaira seemed to hesitate. Jack could only wonder if she sensed his presence. He prayed she did, uncertain what he would do if she left with what looked to be her guards.

"No," she replied. "There are a few more things I'd like to do here. Go on without me and tell my mother I'll be home by eventide."

The Breccans left, one by one, their boots leaving a trail in the snow.

Jack watched as Adaira poured snow over a firepit, the flames hissing in response. She was finally alone. He began to weave through the trees, his heart pounding.

She must have heard him. Her head snapped up and her eyes narrowed as they scanned the Aithwood.

Jack came to a halt at the edge of the forest, waiting for her to catch sight of him. He stood in ankle-deep snow and breathed, slow and deep. He felt pierced by her gaze when her eyes found him among the blue, winter shadows.

Adaira's lips parted. Her breath turned into clouds as she cried, "*Jack?*"

"Adaira," he said, his voice breaking. It felt like he hadn't spoken in years.

She ran across the riverbed, unknotting the cloak at her collars. She threw it around his shoulders, and he groaned at the warmth of it and the heat of her arms as she embraced him.

"Jack, am I dreaming?" she whispered into his hair.

His hands were numb, but he touched her in return. She felt like an awakening. His blood sang to be near her, to see her, to be in her arms. He laughed, tightening his hold on her.

"No," he said. "I've returned to you."

Adaira leaned back to study his face, then downward, past his ribs, all the way to his reddened feet. "Naked," she said with a hint of incredulity. "Spirits, come inside before you freeze!"

He let her guide him over the riverbed, through the yard, and into the house. He was surprised to see how much it had changed. While Adaira rushed to find a spare set of clothes for him from a trader's stash, he took in the arrangement of tables, some of them covered in goods.

"It looks different here," he said.

"Yes, a bit. Your father doesn't live here anymore, in case you were wondering," Adaira said as she brought him a tunic and boots.

Jack let the cloak fall away as he began to dress himself, his legs stiff. "And where is he?"

Adaira shook the snow from her cloak. "He lives with your mum and Frae. So does your nan."

Jack glanced to the hearth. A fire was burning, low yet golden. He was lost in his thoughts for a moment, remembering his time with the spirits, until Adaira touched his arm.

"Are you all right, Jack?" she asked.

"Yes," he said. "Can you tell me how long I've been gone?"

"I can, but sit first," Adaira said, drawing him to one of the tables. "Let me brew us a pot of tea."

He sat on a bench, watching as Adaira reached for a tin of dried leaves on the shelf.

"You've been gone for one hundred and eleven days."

He swore, raking his fingers through his hair. When Adaira glanced at him over her shoulder, he drawled, "I'm pleased to know someone's been counting."

She only smiled and turned her back to set the kettle over the fire. "I take it your time with the spirits was not so terrible?"

"No," he replied. "But I was not happy amongst them."

She was quiet, and he watched as she served the tea, then settled across the table from him.

"Tell me what has happened while I was gone," he said. "Tell me how this came to be a place of trade, and how that silver circlet came to sit across your brow, *Heiress*."

Adaira covered her mouth for a moment, as if she didn't know where to start, but then began to tell him everything. Listening to her, Jack loved the light in her eyes as she told him how the river became a road, and how his father's house became a meeting ground between the clans. How well that had turned out and how the most unlikely of friendships had been made. How Adaira had decided to take up her mother's mantle as Laird of the West.

Jack smiled. His tea had gone cold by the time she was done speaking, and yet he had never felt such warmth within him before. Not even when he was King of Fire.

"And so you turned your fear into something else," he said. "You reached the place you thought you would never find, and you claimed it as your own. Well done, my love."

Adaira was silent, remembering their conversation in the cavern. But then she smiled, her face flushing, and Jack suddenly couldn't bear the distance between them, even if it was merely the length of the table.

"Will you come closer to me?" he whispered.

Adaira rose and walked around the table. He turned on the bench to face her, and she settled close to him, their gazes aligned and their hearts in tune.

"I missed you," he said. "I felt as if half of me had been torn away. I had swiftly realized that I made a mistake, leaving you behind that morning. I thought that if you stood at my side while I played that I would be divided, that I would choose you over the spirits. But now I see that I should have had you beside me, because when the fire claimed me, they took only half a mortal. They took my mortality and my body, but my heart stayed with you in the mortal realm."

Adaira exhaled, closing her eyes when Jack tucked a loose thread of hair behind her ear.

"I was so worried," she breathed, looking at him once more. "I was so worried you had forgotten me in your new realm, and the time we shared here. That if I ever saw you again, you wouldn't remember me."

"Even if I lived a thousand years in the fire," Jack said, "I would not forget you. I would not allow myself to."

A smile tugged on Adaira's mouth. "Is that the beginning of a new ballad, old menace?"

Jack returned her smile, but he felt the truth scrape through the hollow places inside him that his music had once filled. Thinking of that loss hurt for a moment, but then Adaira traced the back of his hand and he felt flooded by light and hope.

"Your harp survived, by the way," she said. "After the fire took you, the harp was left behind. In perfect condition, I might add. It's in my room, waiting for you."

"It was good of you to look after it," Jack said. "But I don't have a need for it anymore."

Adaira frowned. "What do you mean, Jack?"

"My music became my crown. And I gave my crown away to return to my mortal life."

She was silent, but her countenance had gone pale. She was mourning his loss, perhaps even more than him, and Jack wanted to ease that pain.

"I may not be able to play a harp again, or sing for the clan," he said. "But I have found that *this* is my song. *This* is my music." And he framed her face in his hands. "Months ago, I told you that I was a verse inspired by your chorus. I thought I knew what those words meant then, but now I fully understand the depth and the breadth of them. I want to write a ballad with you, not in notes but in our choices, in the simplicity and routine of our life together. In waking up at your side every sunrise and falling asleep entwined with you every sunset. In kneeling beside you in the kail yard and leading a clan and overseeing trade and eating at our parents' tables. In making mistakes, because I *know* that I'll make them, and then restitution, because I'm better than I once ever hoped to be when I'm with you."

Adaira turned her face to kiss his palm, where his scar from their blood vow still shone. When she looked at him again, there were tears in her eyes.

"What do you think, Heiress?" Jack whispered, because he was suddenly desperate to know her thoughts. To know what she was feeling.

Adaira leaned forward, brushing his lips with hers. "I think that I want to make such music with you until my last day when the isle takes my bones. I think that you are the song I was longing for, waiting for. And I will always be thankful that you returned to me."

Jack kissed her softly. The taste and feel of her was familiar, beloved, and he let himself fall into the comfort of her. In weaving his fingers into her hair and drawing out her gasps and feeling her cling to him. He had never felt so alive, not even when he had played his harp and sung for the spirits. He had never felt such wonder, and it reverberated through his soul like the final note of a ballad.

Soon, Adaira broke away and leaned back to smile up at him. He hadn't even realized how much time had passed, or how low the fire had burned. The frosted light beyond the windows was blue, and he sensed it was evening.

"Should we go to Mirin's, and see if she can set an extra place for us at her table?" Adaira asked.

Jack's heart quickened, overflowing. "I would love that."

"Come, old menace."

He let Adaira draw him to his feet. They banked the fire in the hearth and extinguished the candles, one by one.

The snow was falling, thick and slow, when they stepped outside of the trading house. Adaira wove her fingers with his and led him down the river road, past the faded clan line. Neither of them realized they had stepped into the east until the trees fell away, one by one, and a light suddenly shone through the snow.

It was Mirin's cottage. Firelight burned through the darkness, and Jack stared up at it a moment. He wondered what tomorrow would bring. What the days ahead would be like in this new world. An isle united. His hand in Adaira's, their scars aligned.

But that is a story for another windy, firelit night.

Acknowledgments

Community and family play pivotal roles in both *A River Enchanted* and *A Fire Endless*. And the truth is . . . I couldn't have written, revised, and seen this book off to publication without the support and expertise of a wonderful group of people. This is my community and family, the people who have invested their energy, love, magic, and time into me as a person and as an author, and into the stories I tell. And I am honored to recognize them now as Jack, Adaira, Torin, Sidra, and Frae's journey comes to an end.

First, sustenance and steel from my Heavenly Father. Encouragement and spontaneous dinner dates and long evening walks with Ben, my better half. Couch cuddles and reminders to go outside from Sierra. Lunch with Mom, because deadlines for this book were intense and I sometimes didn't have the energy to make something to eat. Phone calls from Dad, which are always a bright spot in the day. Any moment at all with my siblings, from our D&D campaigns to walks on the driveway. My grandparents—Grandmommy & Pappy and Oma & Opa—who continue to exemplify love and legacy to me.

To my incredible team at New Leaf Literary, who went above

and beyond to help me get this book in shape for publication: Suzie Townsend (my inimitable agent), Sophia Ramos (Torin's #1 fan), and Kate Sullivan (editor extraordinaire). *Fire* would not be what it is today without your expertise, your magic, and all the time you devoted to attentively reading each draft. To Kendra Coet, for helping with all the behind-the-scenes publishing things. To Veronica Grijalva and Victoria Hendersen, for continuing to champion this series to publishers overseas.

I'm beyond thankful for my wonderful teams at William Morrow and Harper Voyager. To my editors: Vedika Khanna, who first saw what the Elements of Cadence could become and guided me through the beginning of this journey, and Julia Elliott, who jumped on board mid-2022 and shepherded this book into publication. I am immensely thankful for you both, and all the time and insight and love you've given to this series. To Emily Fisher, my incredible publicist. To Deanna Bailey and all the amazing marketing work you've given to this series. To Liate Stehlik, Jennifer Hart, Jennifer Brehl, David Pomerico, DJ DeSmyter, Pamela Barricklow, Elizabeth Blaise, Stephanie Vallejo, Paula Szafranski, Angie Boutin, Cynthia Buck, and Chris Andrus. To Yeon Kim for creating two gorgeous covers for this series. To Nick Springer, for bringing the map of Cadence to life.

To my amazing team at Harper Voyager UK: Natasha Bardon, Vicky Leech, Elizabeth Vaziri, Jack Renninson, Emma Pickard, Jaime Witcomb, and Robyn Watts. To Ali Al Amine for illustrating the whimsical UK covers.

To my fellow authors who have given their time to read and blurb and celebrate with me along the way: Isabel Ibañez (who read *River* and *Fire* through many, many messy drafts and helped me find the perfect ending for the series), Hannah Whitten, Shea Ernshaw, Genevieve Gornichec, Ava Reid, Sue Lynn Tan, A.G. Slatter, Danielle L. Jensen, and Vania Stoyanova. To Kristin Dwyer for reading the romantic scenes at one A.M. on Isabel's couch and giving me invaluable feedback (and reassurance!).

The success of this series has been humbling and exciting to watch unfold, and I am deeply thankful for these book-loving businesses who have been an incredible support to me: Book of the Month, Illumicrate, Fox & Wit, Emboss & Spine, BlueForest Black-Moon, Barnes & Noble, Little Shop of Stories, Parnassus Books, Joseph-Beth Booksellers, The Inside Story, and Avid Bookshop.

And to you, my dear readers. I wouldn't be here today without you. I wish we could sit down with a cup of tea and talk about our favorite books and characters, but for now, I will close by saying *thank you* for your love and support. Thank you for going on this wild, wondrous journey with me.

Also by
REBECCA ROSS

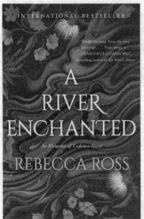

A RIVER ENCHANTED
Elements of Cadence, Book 1

> "With lush world building and lyrical prose,
> *A River Enchanted* feels like the echo of a
> folktale from a world right next to our own."
>
> —Hannah Whitten,
> *New York Times* bestselling author of *For the Wolf*

House of Earth and Blood meets *The Witch's Heart* in Rebecca Ross's brilliant first adult fantasy, set on the magical isle of Cadence where two childhood enemies must team up to discover why girls are going missing from their clan.

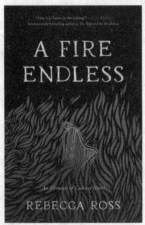

A FIRE ENDLESS
Elements of Cadence, Book 2

#1 INTERNATIONALLY BESTSELLING SERIES

> "Swept me away from the very first page . . .
> Truly magical."
>
> —Genevieve Gornichec,
> bestselling author of *The Witch's Heart*, on *A River Enchanted*

In the stunning conclusion to the #1 internationally bestselling *Elements of Cadence* duology that began with *A River Enchanted*, *A Fire Endless* finds the tenuous balance between the human and faery realm threatened by Bane, the spirit of the North Wind, whose defeat may require Jack, Adaira, Torin, and Sidra to pay the ultimate price.

DISCOVER GREAT AUTHORS, EXCLUSIVE OFFERS, AND MORE AT HC.COM